KENDRELL
PUBLISHING

SOME TIMES

it's the

FORK

MICAH HOUSE

Sometimes It's The Fork

First published 2026

Copyright © 2026 by Micah House

Published by Kendrell Publishing, Birmingham, Alabama

Edited by Sara Kamalsky

Cover design by Paul Palmer-Edwards

ISBN: 979-8-9922157-3-1

Library of Congress Control Number: 2025918153

Also by Micah House

The Blanchard Witches of Daihmler County

Prodigal Daughters

Stitches in Time

The House of Duquesne

Half Sick of Shadows

Becoming Olympia

My Soul To Keep

Red Blue

CONTENTS

RECIPES

This book is dedicated to my two grandmothers,
Lettie Mae Robertson and Bessie Louise House,
my Great-Aunt Virgie Hogue,
and all their many friends which I grew up around.
They are all reflected, in part, in this novel's characters.

CHAPTER ONE

Home is Where You've Never Been

Scanning the highway for the elusive road sign was now becoming a ridiculous game. The GPS insisted she'd missed the turn again, but Laurel had seen no road. The two-lane highway running through Scroggins, Alabama, was practically deserted. Since turning off the interstate a few miles back, she'd only seen a couple of pickup trucks, two cars, and one Amazon van. For what the drive lacked in vehicles, it made up for in little country churches and rundown houses. As for businesses, she'd only seen one antiquated gas station, which she couldn't tell if it was still in use or a relic from a bygone era.

Again, the GPS marked the same spot on the highway where her turn should have been. Laurel pulled over and stepped out of the car to investigate. It was now a test of technology over common sense. The GPS may believe there was a road there, but Laurel wasn't buying it. However, once she stood outside of the car, she caught sight of something she wasn't able to see behind the wheel. A patch of strewn gravel sloped downward from the main highway, revealing a thin dirt road winding behind an overgrowth of brambles and kudzu-choked trees. The GPS had been right all along, only the road was invisible to anyone unaware of its location. The realization did not improve her mood. Laurel didn't like it when technology won. It had already derailed her life. Like the vines strangling the trees in this rural hole of a place, technology had choked her out of relevance.

To the right of the road, a faded green sign with rusted edges was nearly swallowed by a honeysuckle vine. It read: **Hogg Road**. *Well, you can't get more rural than that,* she laughed to herself. Laurel Holden stood still for a moment, stunned she was even here. She had spent the better part of her adult life traveling the country, authoring articles on regional cuisine, highlighting local interests, and suggesting to readers how best to enjoy a city. Now, at 33 years old, she looked out over this foreign landscape and realized though she'd seen the country, she had never seen *the country*. And yet, somehow, this was home. Sort of. Though she had never been here, this was where her people came from, at least her father's people. Who knew what gutters her mother's people crawled out from? But this briar patch of a town in backwoods Alabama belonged to a branch of her family she had never known.

She returned to the car and drove down the pitted gravel road as swirls of red dust rose from beneath the tires. It was a bumpy ride and the sporadic flecks of gravel popping up to hit the sides of her car let her know she was driving it too fast. Slowing her pace, the dust thinned, and ricocheting rocks stopped. Woods lined either side of the road. Not the picturesque kind she would have imagined when thinking of country life. These were brushy and dense. Vines swallowed trees which had probably once been beautiful. A few houses went by as she crept slowly down the antagonistic road. Simple homes, but clearly lived in. A few had well-manicured yards and freshly painted shutters. Cheery plants hung on porches, counterbalancing the gloomy gray window screens. In one yard, a woman beat a broom against a floor rug strung across a clothesline. For some inexplicable reason, Laurel waved at her. The woman waved back. The exchange made Laurel smile. It was an uncharacteristic gesture on her part. Laurel Holden was not the *wave to a stranger* type, but oddly enough, it felt natural here.

A small meadow opened two houses down, revealing the house depicted in the photograph lying on the passenger seat. It accompanied the documents of ownership and title transfer sent by the lawyer a few weeks earlier.

Her grandmother Hogue's house was a dingy white, with a long gray front porch and steps. The house was covered in large shaker-style siding, with uneven edges. It wasn't the shiny vinyl kind often seen on lower-end homes. These shingles appeared wooden. She confirmed it once she got out of the car, rubbing her hand across the side of the house. A chalky powder residue dusted her hand. *Is this what they used to call whitewash?* She noticed the porch needed painting as she stepped up. Beneath the flecks of peeling gray lay an older shade of green she'd never seen before. Long dead plants in the hanging baskets along the porch swung slightly in the breeze. There were two front doors. She spent a moment wondering why, especially since they were only about five feet apart.

Inside the manila folder holding the deed was an envelope containing the house key. Laurel opened it to find something she considered a relic from another century, a skeleton key. At first, she thought the attorney made a mistake, but the lock on the door was shaped to match. A gust of wind rushed over the porch, swaying the hanging baskets again and causing a gentle squeak to the swing. In a world of keypads and swipe cards, turning a lock with a skeleton key felt foreign. Less like opening a door and more like opening a past she had never wanted to know.

Inside, the house was much like she expected. Nothing fancy. Just a country woman's home. The walls weren't sheet-rocked or plastered but constructed of wide plank boards painted white. She remembered reading in the lawyer's notes that the house had been hand-built by her grandfather back in the 1940s. And it certainly looked hand-built, down to the slightly uneven floors, which may have always been uneven or become that way with time and settling. Slanted slightly

11

or not, they felt sturdy under her feet. As she explored the first room, she wondered what her grandfather had been like. Had most men of their time in this desolate region built their own houses? She couldn't begin to fathom the skills that feat might entail.

The floor was covered with a kind of padded linoleum, unlike any she had seen before. It was a rather beautiful maroon with gold trimmings at the edge, like a picture frame. Centered within it was a scrollwork of roses and vines—like stepping into a story. A maroon vinyl sofa sat against the front window. The cushions looked wrong, shrunk somehow. Years of summer humidity must have warped them. Already, sweat beaded on Laurel's brow. The house felt like a sauna. Looking again at the plank walls, it occurred to her the only insulation this house had were those chalky shingles on the exterior.

An oversized chair, upholstered in some kind of dark navy-blue velvet, sat at an angle in front of the side window, but no light passed through the glass. Pulling back the dusty sheers, Laurel saw an air conditioner filling the space. Relieved to find it still worked, she clicked it on HIGH. A low hum filled the room, which she found oddly comforting, ending the dramatic silence of the house. Leaning her face toward the slatted vents, warm air blew into her eyes. It would take a few minutes to wake up before it could start cooling things off.

She continued through the house, each room revealing something about the stranger who had lived there. Discolored lace doilies, yellowed by time, lay over the backs of chairs and on tabletops. A few knick-knacks and porcelain figures sat around, and one coffee table featured a large, illustrated Bible with a picture of Jesus on the cover. A few neatly stacked magazines sat on end tables and nightstands throughout the house. Most were old issues of *Guidepost* magazine. Though unfamiliar with the Christian periodical, Laurel had once written an article covering the best places to travel for older adults, which *Guidepost* had purchased and printed. Though she didn't see that specific issue among the pile here, the sheer number of magazines made her think it was probably somewhere.

Laurel stared at a small, padded rocker and stool, with the table of magazines beside it, and imagined her grandmother sitting there, reading her work. It was doubtful the woman would have even known the piece she would have read was Laurel's. After all, Laurel Holden wouldn't have been a name Bessie Hogue would have recognized. Even the name of the deed referred to her as Laura Hogue. And since there were no issues of other magazines Laurel had written for represented in the stacks, *Guideposts* was more a reflection on her grandmother's devout religious beliefs than any interest in Laurel's now-defunct career.

The house had no hallway, just one room flowing from another. While each had its own gas heater, most rooms didn't even have a door—only a strange vinyl partition mounted in the doorframes. It was Laurel's first experience with an accordion door. Gripping the brown plastic handle, she slid it to the left, applying a bit of pressure to detach the magnet sealing it shut. The glossy brown vinyl folded back on itself offering her passage to the adjoining room.

She was confused by the haphazard layout of the rooms. For example, the living room didn't lead to a kitchen, but a bedroom, which opened to two other bedrooms. But soon Laurel discovered the kitchen lay at the far back of the house, but only after passing through another living room. By the time Laurel reached the second living room, she was drenched with sweat. The house was sweltering.

Busy green and yellow linoleum, straight out of the 1970s, covered the floor. Another vinyl couch sat against a bank of windows which suffered the same fate as the other misshapen cushions in the front room. A matching brown chair sat a few feet away, beside a large metal object venting to the ceiling. Laurel had never seen one before, but she could tell it was a larger gas furnace. "We get it," she said aloud. "Winter gets cold. But Jesus, what did you do in summer?"

From the kitchen archway, a voice answered with a laugh, "There is an air unit."

Startled, Laurel turned around to see the woman coming from the kitchen. "God! You scared me!"

"I'm sorry," the woman smiled. "I saw you driving in and thought I'd walk down to say hello. Welcome. My name is Janice. I live in the house past the field."

"Field?"

"Yeah," Janice grinned, pointing to the meadow outside the window. "I'm on the other side."

Reaching out to shake, Laurel replied. "You're the woman I waved to. I'm Laurel Holden."

"Oh, I know who you are. Your granny and I were close friends." Janice shook her hand, then moved toward the couch. She kneeled on the cushions, fumbling behind the curtain sheer. With the flip of a switch another air conditioner roared to life. The breeze ruffled the white sheers, which she swept aside, draping over the armrest. "There is another one in the front room, and a third in the kitchen."

"I found the first one," Laurel replied, watching Janice move with casual familiarity to the kitchen where she switched on the other window unit. She definitely knew her way around this house, proving she must have been very close to Laurel's grandmother. Janice opened a drawer under the kitchen counter and pulled out a hand towel before rejoining Laurel in the living room.

"Here," Janice winked, handing it to Laurel.

"Thanks," Laurel replied as she wiped her sweaty face and neck with the cloth. "I haven't even made it to the kitchen yet, but this towel is already saving my life." She gestured to the couch, inviting her guest to sit down.

"The den air conditioner is stronger so it can cool the three rooms connecting to it," Janice said, taking a seat. "But I warn you, the kitchen is the hottest room in the house if that air isn't on. Those windows get direct light most of the day."

Laurel glanced back through the arch and saw that the long bank of windows over the counter and sink flooded the kitchen with light. It made the little living room seem rather dark in comparison. She moved to the light switch on the wall.

"Oh, not that one!" Janice cautioned.

Laurel froze.

"I really should have taped over that before you arrived," Janice added, apologetically.

"It doesn't operate the overhead light?"

A quick shake of the head and a narrowing of Janice's eyes alerted Laurel that the answer was definitely NO. "Never touch that switch," her new neighbor warned. "Unless you're in trouble. It's an alarm of sorts. Very loud. If your neighbors hear it, they will all come running."

"Glad you told me," Laurel said, blushing as she sat down beside Janice. "You know this house backwards and forwards."

Janice explained again how she and Laurel's grandmother had been very close friends, besides being neighbors. "Of course, anyone in town can tell you anything about this house or any other. Bessie had many friends and knew everyone."

"I am afraid I never knew my grandmother," Laurel admitted. "Couldn't tell you anything about her. I don't even know why she left me this place."

Janice smiled sympathetically, patting Laurel's knee. "I am sorry the two of you never knew each other. Bessie was a special lady."

Laurel could tell Janice held her grandmother in higher regard than she or her mother ever had. It felt surreal to even be there. Sitting on her grandmother's couch, chatting with a total stranger who had known the grandmother Laurel had never even spoken to. It was a little overwhelming, but everything lately in Laurel's life had been so. And though Laurel was not normally the kind of person to like someone right away, she liked Janice. There was something disarming about her. She made Laurel feel at ease in this strange new place she would never have come to if she'd had other options.

"As for why she left you this place and her savings," Janice continued, as if sensing Laurel needed to hear it. "You are her granddaughter, after all. I assume it is Bessie's way of letting you know she considered you family."

Looking around at her modest, but well-appreciated surroundings, Laurel admitted, "It certainly came at an opportune time. Print magazines are a dying breed and these days practically anyone with a keyboard and an AI program can write an article for an online publication."

"I wasn't aware things were that bad for writers now."

"I am a freelance writer," Laurel explained. "Mostly magazines, sometimes websites. I tell people the best hot spots in a city, where they should eat—what they should eat—where to stay, what to do."

"Sounds very exciting," Janice smiled.

"It is. Or was," Laurel replied. "But as print media dies, and websites utilizing artificial intelligence to generate articles, there is little need for people like me."

"Surely, even the internet needs—"

"Media pays what they can get away with paying these days," Laurel explained. "I used to sell an article or two a month and live well. Now, I read reviews written by writers I've never heard of—not even sure if they have been to the places they are writing about. So, I am basically out of money with no propositions. Inheriting a place to live for a while, and a bit of money, is saving my life."

Laurel had sensed Janice's eyes on her from the moment she came in. It was even more noticeable now, although Janice was trying to not be obvious about it. It was as if she was studying a famous painting she'd only ever heard about. Janice must have sensed Laurel taking notice, because she quickly lowered her eyes, blushing. "I'm sorry for staring. I've often wondered what you look like. You have your grandmother's eyes."

"Do I?" Laurel asked. It was not something she'd ever heard before.

Then again, why would she? She wouldn't have known Bessie Hogue if they'd passed each other on the street. "Frankly, I am shocked you know anything about me," Laurel admitted. "It has been my understanding that my father was pretty much erased from his family's minds."

"Oh, honey," Janice said with a light chuckle. "Everybody knows everybody in Scroggins. You may not have been born here, but it was no secret Charlie Hogue had a daughter after he moved away. Don't try to keep anything private in a small town. It ain't gonna happen." Janice shifted the conversation with a hopeful tone. "So, do you plan to stay in Scroggins?"

Laurel hesitated, an uneasy look on her face, "I wouldn't say *stay*. More like to get my bearings and figure out my next step in life. I am toying with the idea of writing a book. But I have no idea what it would be about. Right now, I am just grateful to have a roof over my head, and a little money to live on for a few months."

Janice smiled sweetly, patting Laurel's leg. "Well, I am saddened to hear about your career troubles, but pleased to have you in Scroggins for a little while."

Laurel hung her head with a sigh, then apologetically added, "I am sorry. I'm not usually a chatty person. You don't even know me, and here I am telling you my sob story."

Janice released a genuine and comforting laugh. "Don't apologize, Laurel. And I'd hardly call that a sob story. There's no shame in having hard times, and nothing to gain by covering them up. As for your feeling comfortable with me...well, your grandmother was my dearest friend. I don't find it so strange that her granddaughter and I would hit it off. I think it would make Bessie very happy. After all, leaving you this house was her way of calling you home."

Janice declared it was time for her to give Laurel some privacy. Laurel was ready for some quiet solitude but didn't want to say so. "You need to connect with this place. And Bessie. But tomorrow I will pick you up around 10 and show you Scroggins."

Any other time in her life, Laurel would have come up with a fast excuse to dodge the invitation. Her response, "I'd like that," surprised her.

"I'll go out the front door," Janice said turning to leave. "On my way, I'll show you the best bedroom to sleep in. It gets the best air flow."

She led Laurel to a room painted a delicate shade of pink. The linoleum floor featured sprawling pink and white roses, reminding Laurel of the drift roses growing around a cottage she'd once written about in Asheville, North Carolina. A lacey coverlet, clearly handmade from varying shades of white and pink yarn, covered the bed. A folded quilt lay neatly at the foot of the bed, although the weather for quilts ended months ago.

"This was Bessie's room," Janice revealed. "If you place that floor fan in the doorway, it'll bring the cool air in here at night from the living room."

As Janice made her way to the front porch, she turned to Laurel with one final thought before leaving. "Are you set with something to eat tonight? You got any groceries?"

Laurel shrugged. "I haven't really thought about that. I'll just pick something up somewhere."

"It's *the somewhere* that will be the problem," Janice grinned. "I got a big pot roast in the oven. I'll run you down a plate in about an hour. Have a good night, and I'll see you tomorrow."

Laurel returned to the yet explored kitchen, pleased by the functionality of it. A long metal countertop with integrated drawers, cabinets, and a sink sat beneath the row of windows looking out to the meadow. Beside it sat an old stove with four burners and push-button controls. One button was missing, but the metal post remained. She imagined her grandmother pressing it for years without bothering to replace the stove.

On the back wall stood a tall wooden cabinet, thickly painted in glossy white. Dried drip marks showed the amateur paint job, probably applied countless times over the years. Inside were bowls, sifters, and old sacks of flour and cornmeal—long expired.

On the adjacent wall was a large chest freezer—the kind big enough to hide a body. She lifted the lid and found it packed with Ziploc bags of peas, beans, corn, and okra. Her grandmother had shelled, shucked, blanched, and frozen it all herself. Thankfully, the power had never been shut off. Otherwise, the smell would have been unbearable.

The center table was covered in a plastic tablecloth with a fruit and swirl design. Lifting the edge, Laurel discovered the table itself had been painted in the same glossy white as the pantry. It was heavy, as were the six matching chairs. Sitting down, she traced the raised fruit patterns with her finger, wondering how many meals had been served here.

The Hogue family had always been a mystery to her. Laurel's father had run out on she and her mother before Laurel was old enough to remember him. Her mother had known little about the Hogues, having never met the family either. Laurel hadn't learned her father was even dead until she pressed her mother for answers as a teen. Only then did she learn he'd "taken up with" some other woman after he'd left them. It was something of a habit for old Charlie Hogue apparently. According to Laurel's mother, he'd run through quite a few women before he died. It was alcoholism that killed him, her mother said, but it had been wrapping his truck around a light pole at full speed that did it. Though it was not a story that made her proud, Laurel came to understand her mother's questionable behavior and neglect after learning it.

Being abandoned with a small daughter to take care of left Laurel's mother with an insatiable need to find a man who might stay. Of course, none of them ever did. And Laurel's mother, being so preoccupied in the revolving door of men in her life, neglected to take notice of her own health until the cancer had consumed her. She'd given her daughter about the same amount of attention as she'd given cancer. Laurel grew up alone most of the time, too scared to fall asleep until she heard her mother's voice coming in at 2 a.m., usually with whichever man was with her that night.

The Hogue family's silence and disinterest in her life had been something Laurel grew up resenting. Her mother claimed there was "bad blood" between Bessie and her father, and that animosity, it seemed, had trickled down to Charlie's daughter. Yet now, having inherited everything from a woman she'd never met, Laurel had more questions than ever. And there was no one left to ask.

She decided to unpack but quickly realized the dressers were still full of Bessie's belongings. No one had cleared them out. Every chest, every drawer, held clothing or keepsakes. Laurel folded her clothes back into her suitcase. She'd live out of it for now. She did pull out her makeup bag and toiletries but paused suddenly. *Where is the bathroom?*

Retracing her steps through the house, Laurel found no bathroom anywhere and started to get worried. With the lack of a toilet now at the forefront of her mind, her bladder woke up and she needed to find it fast. *Surely, there isn't an outhouse. My grandmother was not that old.*

Laurel decided to check, opening the only other door she'd not yet checked...the one leading from the kitchen to the back porch. To her delight, she discovered the roomy back porch was screened in and contained a final door. *Please be a bathroom, please be a bathroom.* It was. Small, but containing the necessaries, Laurel was relieved in more ways than one. She wasn't sure why a bathroom would be outside of the house on a porch, but at least it existed.

True to her words, Janice brought down a plate of pot roast, peas, carrots, and cornbread. She also provided an explanation for the bathroom. The kitchen, bathroom, and back porch additions were made in the early 1960's. Before, the house did have an outhouse, and the den was where the old kitchen had stood. Janice left Laurel to her meal which Laurel ate heartily in front of the television. Accustomed to streaming her programs, Laurel realized she would have to get Wi-Fi installed as soon as possible.

As the house grew darker with night, Laurel felt increasingly disconnected from her world. Though the house was small, the empty rooms loomed around her like ghosts. The bedroom window was equally unsettling, with only blackening darkness pressing in on her. Anything could be outside there, obscured by the opaque night. She'd felt safer walking alone at night in Manhattan than the one peek she took through the curtain.

Laurel had chosen the pink room, not only on Janice's advice, but because it was the cheeriest, which helped at night. The humidity in the house was still a little much for her, but hopefully with the air units all running, and the sundown, it might be livable by morning. Distracting her from the temperature, was the deafening quiet outside. No traffic passing by. No hum of streetlights. Just silence and the unnerving chirp of cicadas somewhere beyond the walls, made sleep slow in coming. Sometimes another sound rang out, one she hoped with all her heart was just a dog howling. With the woods encompassing Bessie's property, coyotes were not out of the question. Focusing her mind on the less disturbing sounds of the whirling fan and the air conditioner helped her finally drift off to sleep.

CHAPTER TWO

An Idea is Born

Laurel slept reasonably well, once she finally drifted off to sleep. She awoke well before her alarm, squinting her eyes as the sunlight pierced the thin curtain sheers into her eyes. She tried covering her head with the bed sheet, but it was no match for summer sun. She regretted not bringing coffee but promised herself she'd grab groceries today. The house was far too quiet. It was a sound Laurel was not accustomed to. She turned on the television in the den, just to fill the air. An old *Andy Griffith* episode was playing. *If I start to relate to Mayberry, I'm in trouble.*

Janice showed up right on time at 10 a.m. to take Laurel into town. As they bumped along the gravel road out of the neighborhood, Janice pointed out details Laurel wouldn't have noticed on her own. "Your family used to own most of the land along this road," she explained. "Little by little, the Hogues sold off parcels. Farming stopped being an occupation and more of a supplemental resource for food. The coal mines paid better, so most men gave up the fields."

Town, Laurel discovered, was just a few miles down the highway past Hogg Road. The first real sign of civilization was Beacon's Gas Station. Janice explained how everyone still called it that, but the Beacon family were all gone now. Only the vintage Beacon sign stood as any indicator of its past, hanging just below a large yellow Shell logo. Beyond the gas station, a narrow road curved into a small parking lot of a modest building, about the size of a small strip mall. Two businesses divided the space. The sign over one read, **Fashion Statement** and the other said **Community Store**.

"The Community Store is our local grocery store," Janice informed her as they went by. "We'll stop there on our way home and get you can stock up. They have everything you'd need, but you'll pay less if you make the drive to a chain store in town."

"Isn't this town?" Laurel asked.

Janice laughed, "Well, for Scroggins, yes. But when you hear anyone say they are '*going to town*', they mean Tuscaloosa. It's a good half hour drive. Now I've heard rumblings may get a Winn Dixie out here next year, but they haven't started building anything yet."

"What is **Fashion Statement**?" Laurel asked, trying not to poke fun at the name.

"That's a dress shop and kids clothing store. Bootsie Taylor owns it. She has cute stuff, if you don't mind getting your clothes beside a grocery store. It is no Macy's, but when you're in a bind and need something it's a lot easier than driving to Tuscaloosa."

Further along the road Janice pointed out **The Bake Shop** in case Laurel had a sweet tooth. "Used to be most folks made their own desserts. I frankly, still do. But Delva is a pretty good baker, and her stuff is delicious. But between you and me, most people pop in mainly to hear the latest gossip in town." Janice then added with a wink, "The accurate version."

"Accurate?"

"Bootsie Taylor tells everything she has heard to Delva. Delva weeds out the exaggerations, asks around for details, then reports the truest account. If Boots is *The National Enquirer*, then Delva is *People Magazine*."

Over the next hour, Janice showed Laurel everything she'd need to know, from the post office to the one sandwich shop, and the only diner. They passed several churches on Laurel's tour of town, but Janice stopped at only one. Christ's Love Baptist Church was not an impressive structure by any means but appeared well kept. Made of mundane red brick, the front had two tall windows flanked by white shutters, with a white painted double door at its center. The stained-glass windows on the sides featured no biblical scenes, just random pastel patterns. A covered sidewalk led to the Sunday School rooms and Fellowship Hall. Behind the church sat a cemetery—unfenced, open to all.

Janice parked the car and got out, Laurel did the same, beginning to suspect the reason for the stop. "She's here, isn't she?"

"Yes," Janice said gently. "I hope you don't think me presumptuous, but she cared about you enough to leave you her things. I thought you ought to know where she's buried."

Laurel followed her new friend through the myriads of graves until she stopped beneath a tall shady tree. "Bessie used to come here with several other ladies from the church to gather the pecans. She buried Ustus here and always wanted to be buried beneath it herself."

"Did you arrange her burial?" Laurel asked, a little embarrassed that she'd never known who took care of the details.

"I did."

Laurel kneeled to touch her grandmother's headstone, noticing the fresh flowers in the vase. She didn't have to ask who kept the grave tended. Laurel wasn't accustomed to the ritual of upkeep for graves. Apparently, flowers were an ongoing must, judging from not only her grandparents' grave but many of the others around. She didn't relate to this kind of thinking but told herself she would take up the mantle—if only to show Janice she wasn't unfeeling. Laurel glanced several feet over to her grandfather's grave. It was nearly as well tended, although it looked as if an ant bed was making its home around his headstone.

"I have poisoned that anthill twice," Janice remarked with a frustrated sigh. "It keeps coming back. Bessie would have a fit if she saw it."

"She must have loved him very much." Laurel smiled, rising to her feet.

For all the care and sentimentality Janice showed to Laurel's grandmother, she, oddly enough, did not reply to Laurel's comment.

With the little tour of Scroggins over, Janice drove them back to The Community Store for Laurel to buy what she might need for home. Pulling into the parking lot, Janice grinned and gestured ahead. Sitting on a bench between the entrance to the market and the dress shop sat an elderly couple. Across their laps were napkins and two plastic food containers. As they were eating, the man and woman seemed to be chatting happily—the woman, even dabbing the man's chin with her napkin.

"Bootsie and Renzo have their lunch together every day on that bench," Janice confided with a grin. "Afterward, she goes back inside the dress shop, and he goes back to the grocery counter."

"I like that," Laurel said, watching them from the car. They reminded her of another elderly couple she'd seen once in Rehoboth Beach. Every afternoon, they walked hand in hand, sneaking an occasional kiss like two teenagers experiencing first love. They'd given Laurel hope that real love did exist for some, even if it had never existed for her.

Janice led Laurel to the building and made a quick introduction to the Taylors, explaining who Laurel was but not wanting to interrupt their lunch. "We will start shopping and see you at the counter in a bit, Mr. Renzo."

"Now hold on a minute, Missy!" Bootsie demanded, swallowing her chicken salad. "Let me hear all this again." She addressed Laurel directly, "You're Bessie's grandyoungen?"

"Yes," Laurel nodded, correcting herself and adding "Ma'am," unsure if she were being rude if she didn't.

"How come your name ain't Hogue? You married? I hadn't heard Bessie's girl was married."

"No, I am not married."

Renzo chimed in, "Young gal, don't mind Boots, here. She's got to have ever'bodies business."

"I ain't tryin' to seem nosey," Bootsie replied, apologetically. "Just I heard Bessie's granddaughter's name was Laura Hogue."

Janice patted Laurel's arm sympathetically, answering for her. "It is, Bootsie. But our Laurel here became a writer. She's been in magazines. I'm sure she changed her name to Laurel Holden for writing purposes."

Surprised Janice would even arrive at the correct conclusion, or suspecting perhaps her grandmother Bessie had kept closer tabs on Laurel's life than she ever knew, Laurel replied. "That is exactly it. Laurel Holden conveys a more authoritative impression for readers. Hogue, didn't roll off the tongue very well."

Slapping his knee, Renzo chuckled. "Better 'n hog."

Narrowing her eyes in confusion, Laurel asked what he meant.

"Gal, don't you know your real name is Hogg?" the old man found this very amusing from his wide grin. "Original name of your family was Hogg. But somewhere down the line somebody changed it. Guess you just did the same thing they did."

"It was a grade school teacher," Bootsie said, sitting upright with glee at being able to share unheard gossip. "Miss Benson. She taught me and Ida Hogg when we was in 3rd grade. Ida was your granddaddy's sister. She's long dead now. But as I recall, Tater Goolidge used to make fun of all the Hogg kids. Goin' round shouting' *here piggy here piggy*. Now, why a boy named '*Tater*' would make fun of anybody's name is beyond me. But Miss Benson was a sweet little thing. She changed Ida's name on her registry to Hogue and told Tater it always was and he was the fool for saying it wrong. After that, all the Hogg kids started going by Hogue."

Renzo waved his finger pointing down the road. "You go out to any a'them cemeteries we got and you'll find a bunch of Hoggs, but after that you just see Hogues."

Laurel thanked them for the unexpected, yet welcome, history lesson then joined Janice inside to shop. It made Laurel feel untethered to discover how many strangers knew things about her family that she never did. It was almost like waking with amnesia, although she was enjoying the feeling of belonging. It was something she'd never had before. Her mother had no family. Laurel had no siblings. She'd lived 33 years unattached to anything or anyone. An island. Now she was beginning to learn for the first time, she had history—even if it wasn't necessarily her own. In Rehoboth, or San Diego, or New York, she was simply Laurel Holden, food writer. But here in this nowhere town called Scroggins, she had history. She was meeting a community she'd been tied to all her life, whether she knew it or not. Laura Hogue, Laura Hogg, Laurel Holden was a thread in a broad and complex tapestry.

Both she and Janice pushed separate carts (which Janice called '*buggies*') as they perused the small store together. The selections were greatly limited compared to chain supermarkets, but there was enough to do for now. While Laurel deliberated over a package of ground beef in the meat section, something she felt was simple enough that even she couldn't ruin it, Janice pushed her cart into another aisle to get something from her own list.

Laurel was still deliberating between the ground beef or trying her hand at making chicken when Janice returned. "I thought you said you were going to get Coke?" Laurel asked, glancing into her friend's shopping cart.

Janice gave her a funny look. "I did."

Laurel still seemed confused. "You must have grabbed the wrong one."

Looking down into her cart, Janice replied, "No, I got it."

"Pepsi?"

"Yes, Pepsi," Janice answered. "I know these drinks are terrible, health wise, but it's my one vice."

Laurel still didn't understand. "But you said you needed *Coke*."

Janice's eyes flashed with laughter now, exclaiming, "Oh, I see! It's

SOMETIMES IT'S THE FORK

just a phrase. We call every soft drink 'Coke."

Laurel let it go, still not following, but she was about to have one more lesson in regional colloquialism before leaving the little country store. Renzo, back from his lunch break, joined them at the meat cooler pushing a rolling rack stocked with packages of chicken.

"I'm fixin to throw out some new chicken, less you ain't studyin' no chicken tonight?"

Laurel stared blankly at the kind old man. She had no idea what he'd just said to her. Thinking that perhaps she hadn't heard him, Renzo repeated himself. But again, Laurel looked back at him in complete confusion. Glancing at Janice for help, her friend suppressed a laugh and placed her hand over Laurel's.

"He is asking if you would like to buy any fresh chicken or are you not in the mood for chicken tonight."

"Oh my God," Laurel whispered. "Is that what he asked me?"

She thanked Renzo for the offer but admitted she did not know how to prepare chicken as of now. Once she learned, she would buy some. As she and Janice headed for the register, Laurel shook her head and confided, "I never expected a language barrier when I came here," sarcastically adding, "It is still America, isn't it?"

"You are familiar with a whole other side of America, I'm afraid." Janice teased. "You'll figure Scroggins out eventually."

Turning off the highway onto the dirt road, Laurel saw the Hogg Road sign again, appreciating it a little more than before. Once they were back home, Janice helped Laurel put the groceries away. From her own bag, she popped open two cans of Pepsi and poured over ice as they sat at the table. "I guess I will have to do a lot of cooking while I am here," Laurel commented. "With no real restaurants around."

"Tuscaloosa isn't that far away if you want to dine out."

Laurel frowned, stroking her finger across the condensation on the glass as the hot drink hit the cold ice. "I'm afraid dining out is probably not wise, now that I think about it." Laurel looked up into Janice's eyes and somehow didn't mind sharing. After all, only yesterday Janice had said herself there is no shame in struggling. "My grandmother left me around $30,000 along with the house. Now that I am unemployed, that money won't stretch very far if I splurge on restaurants."

"Do you know how to cook?"

"Well," Laurel sighed with an uneasy grin. "I do, but when we were at The Community Store, I did not see many of the ingredients I would need for my kind of cooking. Because of my job, the recipes I know are a bit more exotic than anything I saw in the store."

"Then you gotta learn to cook our way," Janice laughed. "Oh, the ladies around here, some of the men too, are good cooks." She emphasized and stretched the word *good*. "Fried chicken. Corn bread. Chicken and dumplings. Apple pie. Peach cobbler. Bread pudding. Meatloaf. Casseroles. Pork roasts. Beef roasts. Deer steak and gravy. Oh man, it's some good eating."

"Sounds fattening," Laurel said.

"My mother used to say, '*If it don't make you fat, it don't make you feel,*'" Janice quipped. "And food should make you feel something. Something deep down in your soul. I bet that's how you feel when you taste some of those exotic meals you write about."

"Sometimes, yes."

"Well, in the country, you always *feel* when you eat. It's part of what keeps us going. Meals are the best part of the day. It's how we show off. Nobody around here has a fancy car or a big house. We don't have impressive jobs. Our men take pride in how well their yard is tended, or their garden, if they have one. Our women show off in the kitchen. You make some delicious, heart-filling meal, then sit around with your family or your neighbors and take your time enjoying it."

"Eating isn't so ceremonial in the city. We eat and go. Of course, when I am writing about food, I take the time to savor it."

"That's every meal around here," Janice smiled. "And the best conversations—the best fellowship—comes from sitting around a big table with people you care about, talking and eating. The table is the most important thing in the house."

Laurel laughed at her friend's enthusiasm. "Maybe I should write a country cookbook," she joked.

After Janice went home, Laurel busied herself for the remainder of the day by finishing her cleaning. With the temperature in the house stabilized, it wasn't very taxing. Late afternoon, she gave the ground beef a whirl, dicing in a few bell peppers and onions as she boiled a bag of Bessie's frozen peas she'd found in the freezer. All in all, it wasn't a terrible meal. She slept more soundly than she had on her first night, figuring that since coyotes or cicadas hadn't swarmed the house to kill her last night, she'd probably survive this one.

When morning dawned, the pesky sunlight attacked her face once again, stirring her awake well before she'd planned to get up. Over coffee, she checked emails to see if any job offers had come in. There were two requests from hotels asking for a review, but it wasn't worth her time. The hotel stays and meals might be free, but the airfare and car rental wouldn't be. Laurel would soon have to come up with a plan for what she was going to do next.

It seemed as if Janice had already decided it for her, shouting from the kitchen as she came in to see Laurel that morning. "I have been thinking about nothing else but your cookbook idea."

"I was kidding," Laurel told her as Janice sat down at the table.

"Well, why not?" Janice asked. "You're here. And we have lots of great cooks in Scroggins. Folks who would love to share their recipes, especially if it gets them in print. You wouldn't even have to pay them. They'd give you recipes just for bragging rights."

"Brag about what?" Laurel scoffed.

Janice shot her a fisheye, and chuckled. "You have no idea how competitive Southern women can be over who makes the best…fill in the blank. For someone like you, Laurel, who has been everywhere and seen everything to say their dish is book worthy…I'm telling you, these ladies will boast about that the rest of their lives."

"I wouldn't even know where to begin," Laurel said with a dismissive wave of her hand. "I know nothing about Southern cuisine."

"You wouldn't have to," Janice argued. "You know what tastes good. That's enough. And you can start right here! Your grandmother was one of the best cooks I ever knew. She made elaborate meals whenever she'd have her Sunday School class over, or her Bible Study group. And every week when her quilting bee was here, she'd have three or four different desserts on hand for them. All her recipes are stored in that cabinet over the freezer."

It was a silly idea, Laurel thought. Yet, Janice's words sparked something inside her. The paradox of her life and career. She was a food writer who couldn't create. Oh, Laurel could prepare a meal from a recipe given to her by a renowned chef, but she didn't possess the insight to concoct her own. Her career had only been in telling others where to dine. Describing the food, the chefs, the locales and their atmosphere was her only contribution. Wouldn't Janice's idea be almost the same thing, though? Laurel might write about these Southern people. Their families and the recipes rich in their culture. She'd once written about a chef in Provance, Italy who grew his own ingredients and procured his meat of local pastures and dairies. A book written in Scroggins could follow that same outline.

After Janice went home, Laurel pulled the old recipe books down from the cabinet over the freezer and spread them across the kitchen table to examine. Some pages were very worn and quite fragile. Tucked between pages were more recipes, written on the backs of envelopes, note cards, and scraps of yellowed paper. Laurel flipped through page after page, some written in her grandmother's hand, some by others. She could determine from the aged condition of paper or the faded writing of pen or pencil, that many recipes were from several generations, not only Bessie. *Bobbie Sue's Coconut Cake. Mertle Dean's Rhubarb Pie. Granny Roger's Apple Butter Bread. Mother Hogg's Chocolate Chip*

Cookies. Mama's Mama's Chicken and Dumplings.

Laurel hadn't actually been serious about writing a cookbook on these dishes, but the more she read, the more she wanted to try to recreate some of them. She discovered herself making a long list of needed ingredients which she took with her when she drove to The Community Store.

Checking out at the counter, Renzo asked, "You fixin' to do a bunch of cooking?"

"Yes, sir," Laurel smiled. "I found my grandmother's recipes. I want to see what I can make. They all sound so delicious."

"Your Grandmaw was a fine cook," he grinned. "You follow what she wrote, and you'll be having some scrumptious eats tonight."

CHAPTER THREE

Tear Moistened Oatmeal Raisin Cookies

U nable to shake Janice's idea about writing a cookbook, Laurel experimented with some of her grandmother's recipes. While she certainly couldn't claim victory in her culinary skills, she did experience some modest success. Laurel was beginning to find the notion less outlandish and more intriguing. The clincher was her grandmother's Chicken Noodle Soup. Laurel had followed the directions meticulously, even down to boiling her own whole chicken for the broth when she could have bought broth at the store. The result was perfection. It was, shockingly, the best she'd ever tasted.

Sitting now at her laptop, about to send the lone article she had left to sell, Laurel knew the pitiful pay it would garner. It was for an airline magazine. Disposable. Forgettable. Nothing posh or impressive to up her value as a writer. In truth, it was probably going to see more chewing gum stuck on its page than any human eyes reading it. However, the pay—low as it was—would probably cover a month's utilities, which was better than nothing. That seemed to be her career now; reduced to writing content for periodicals people spit their gum into as their plane lands in Shreveport. It somehow made the idea of writing a real book not easily dismissible.

But could a plain Southern cookbook sell? That was exhausted territory in the world of food publishing. If she decided to do it, she would need a hook. Something setting it apart from the rest. And this wasn't Martha's Vineyard or the French countryside. This was Scroggins, Alabama. There wasn't enough "charming Southern magic" in the world to make that sell. She would have to let the idea marinate for a while; pun intended.

Remembering that Janice mentioned Delva Hopkins at The Bake Shop was the town's go-to gossip, Laurel decided to pay her bakery a visit. If anyone could tell her whether people would be willing to share their treasured family recipes, it would be this Delva person. Delva may even be able to direct her to specific people.

The Bake Shop was not the most impressive pastry shop Laurel had ever seen, but from the moment she stepped from the car, the smells wafting outside hypnotized her. Sweet and rich, like buttered memories. Strangely, the display window didn't feature pastries. Instead, it was lined with a dozen potted plants—each holding nothing more than a single, leafless stick. As Laurel stepped inside, the aroma of bread and cake lifted her by the nose, drawing her to the counter.

The woman behind the counter must have seen Laurel examining the potted sticks, because it was the first thing she referenced when she said hello to Laurel. "If you know anything about orchids, I'm all ears," the woman said. "My daughter-in-law gives me an orchid every Mother's Day. I ain't never got one to bloom again after the first one falls off."

Laurel smiled. "I'm afraid I'm not an expert on orchids."

The glass counter revealed where the delicious smells were coming from. Cupcakes, sheet cakes, pies, breads, cookies, filled the shelves. There wasn't much to choose from, but Laurel immediately understood the market here was probably limited. Most women made their own. The Bake Shop was most likely a special-order kind of place.

"You are Bessie Hogue's girl, aren't you?" the woman asked, stepping around the counter to get a better look at Laurel. She was plump, cheerful, and moved towards Laurel as if she were a cheek-pinching aunt on Thanksgiving. She gave Laurel an unexpected hug.

"Uh, yes, I am. Her granddaughter."

"Well, 'course you are!" Delva smiled. "I can see your daddy in your face."

"You knew my father?"

"Oh, child everybody did. My kids growed up with Charlie Hogue." The kind woman must have realized the hug knocked her wig askew slightly, because she righted it without missing a beat. "My boy Owen and Charlie used to run around together like two peas in a pod. Your daddy practically grew up at my house whenever he and Owen weren't at Bessie's."

The comment caught Laurel off guard. Like so many others who call more metropolitan areas home, Laurel just naturally assumed the south was still steeped in racism, at least socially. But here stood this delightful, African American woman, owner of the only bakery in town, reminiscing about Laurel's white father and her black son hanging out at each other's houses as teens. It was an unexpected, but happy, surprise. Laurel now felt a little ashamed. She'd automatically assumed that by her grandmother growing up here and living her whole life in Scroggins, that Bessie was likely a racist.

"I didn't really know him," Laurel said. "My father. Or his mother for that matter."

"Well, that's a shame," Delva said.

"What was he like?" Laurel blurted, surprising herself to have even asked. Why did she care? She had not cared her whole life. Laurel was a determined, tough, single-goal woman. What was it about coming to this place that was turning her into a sentimental sap? She had zero feelings for her father, so why did she ask that question? More than that, why was she still hoping the lady would answer?

Delva appeared somewhat uneasy about answering, seeming to be weighing her words before responding. "When I knew your daddy, he was a pretty good fella. Little wild, but what boy ain't at that age." Delva had supplied a careful answer. Respectful. Honest. But also masking a lot in what she wasn't saying. "My Owen had his moments too," Delva laughed. "Charlie was quick with the jokes. Had a grin that could charm the stripe off a skunk."

The remark brought a faint smile to Laurel's face. It was the first time in her life she'd ever heard anyone say anything flattering about her father. Her mother never held a very high opinion of him.

Delva sensed Laurel's disconnection with her father, and continued. "I thought they was getting married too young, but wasn't my place to say. When Charlie wanted something, he wasn't gone be stopped from getting it." Delva eyed Laurel as if she were inspecting her. "I guess you are the proof I was right. He wasn't ready for that kind of life. But enough said about that. Even the dead are entitled to their mistakes, even if they did die before setting them right."

Laurel did not press for more. The old lady was correct. Her parents were too young. The first sign of real responsibility sent her father running. Likewise, her mother was not cut out for motherhood. Shifting gears, Laurel changed the subject to the reason for her visit.

"I'm a food writer. I don't really know if I will go through with it or not, but I was thinking I might write a cookbook about rural Southern cuisine."

Delva let out a hearty laugh, "Girl, then don't call it that. It's just good ole' country cooking. The kind that'll keep you healthy and strong. Food for real people. Food you can bring up your youngens on. We don't make no *cuisine* round here."

Laurel grinned and explained her background in the industry—how she'd traveled the country, and sometimes Europe, writing about the community, its culture, its landscape, its natural food resources. Her writing wasn't just about food. It was about the experience.

Delva listened politely, but didn't seem impressed. Once Laurel was finished, Delva shook her head as she placed her puffy hands on her hips. "Girl, don't nobody care about that boring stuff. I don't need to know *why* a pecan pie is delicious. I don't care how long the tree's been growing or what minerals the soil's got in it. Just tell me how to make the pie and then I will. Now if you want stories, the stories are in the cooks."

"In the cooks?"

"Sure!" Delva cried. "Don't nobody care how long the apple trees have been there or how the region uses them in their daily diet. Tell me about the men balancing on ladders who picked 'em. Tell me about the woman who made up the apple pie recipe, and what all has happened in her life."

Laurel was confused. "I don't understand?"

Delva took hold of Laurel's elbow, guiding her to the cookie case. "See this oatmeal raisin cookie?"

"Yes."

"You want me to tell you about where the raisins come from? Or how that flour was grown? Or would you rather hear me tell you about how my grandmomma sat at a rickety table and made up this recipe one day, because she was trying to keep her mind busy after her two boys got called up to war in France? Her daddy got killed in World War I. Grandmomma knew what war meant for colored boys. Colored boys go to the front. When the first shot fires in war, it's a colored boy's blood that spills on the ground first. Colored blood splattering back on the white men who get to march in last."

Laurel's eyes were wide, her attention captivated. Perhaps Delva was the one who should be writing a book.

"When the Second World War started," Delva went on. "My grand-momma prayed night and day America would stay out of it. But the day came when her boys got called up to go, and my grandmomma knew when she kissed her two boys goodbye, she wasn't never gone see them again. And she didn't. She got out her sack of flour. Her sack of sugar. Her salt and her spices, and she commenced to making cookies. Every egg cracking was like a bomb dropping in her heart, wondering if her boys were safe. She cried over that dough, and she squalled over those raisins. Those tears made about the best dang oatmeal cookie I done ever tasted."

Delva reached into the case and removed a cookie for Laurel to taste. It was perfect. Chewy, rich, with a hint of lemon and spice. Not too sweet. "This cookie is amazing!" Laurel exclaimed. "It's not like any oatmeal cookie I ever tasted."

"Course, it's not!" Delva exclaimed. "That cookie stands for something. So many somethings, I can't even begin. War. Prejudice. Loss. Emptiness. That cookie is the last memory a mother had of sons who never came home. That cookie is their headstone, to a grave that never got dug."

"Wow," Laurel sighed, a lump in her throat which was not produced by swallowing the cookie.

"Now that's something a person won't forget when they read it." Delva seemed pleased with herself, and her example. "Don't nobody care about who grows the raisins."

Laurel had her book. This remarkably wise and compassionate woman had just outlined Laurel's new purpose. How many stories were hiding behind all those scribbled scraps of paper tucked into every woman's recipe book in the South? If she could find more tales such as this, she wouldn't only have a cookbook, she'd have a history showcasing the joys and struggles in the unseen lives of forgotten women.

Delva proved to be even more helpful with Laurel's book endeavor, suggesting she accompany her that very night to her prayer group meeting. Laurel balked at the idea, but not wanting to appear rude, apologized and added, "I've never been much for prayer. I'm not sure I even believe in God. It'd be disrespectful for me to join your group when all the ladies are there to pray."

Delva waved her hand as if shooing a fly, "Oh Child, it don't matter if you believe in God, He still believes in you. Besides, we just pray a little while, then we sit around and talk. It's better than any big city therapist you'd ever go to. And sometimes we talk food and share recipes. You should come with me."

"You are kind to offer, but..."

"Now what else do you have to do tonight?" Delva snickered. "I know you don't know nobody. Here's a chance."

Against her natural inclinations, Laurel accepted the invitation. For the next several hours before she was to meet Delva back at the bakery, Laurel continued with her house cleaning. She cleaned the house reasonably well already, but hadn't begun sorting through the many drawers and boxes under beds. It was difficult to know what to throw away. None of it belonged to her, and though she had no sentimental connection to any of Bessie's things, it seemed cavilier to toss it all out. After all, this was Bessie's house and whatever the old woman had chosen to save over the years must have been important to her.

Laurel gave a cursory inspection to a few of the boxes, finding they contained old letters, menial keepsakes, and old black and white family snapshots. She decided to save the boxes for another day, still uneasy about tossing anything out. With Delva's oatmeal cookie story still rattling around in her brain, Laurel opened her laptop and typed out an abbreviated version of the tale, knowing she could go back and add the flourishes later—if she did decide to move ahead with the book.

Laurel met Delva at the bakery after closing, hoping to follow her in her own car to the prayer group, just in case she wanted to make a sudden getaway. Delva squashed that idea, insisting they ride together. The meeting was being held at the home of Cordelia Corder, who was affectionately called Puddin, by everyone who knew her. Puddin's home was in what was properly considered the official town of Scroggins. In a neighborhood located near the elementary school, Puddin Corder lived in a modest two-bedroom house tucked away on the street behind the fire station.

As they went inside, Puddin greeted them at the door. She was a heavyset woman with almost bluish gray hair swept up into a tight swirl that curled like whipped frosting on the side of her head. When she saw Laurel, she squealed with delight.

"Oh my stars! Another young person!"

Puddin immediately dragged Laurel by the wrist to meet the others. In a sea of older faces, Puddin led Laurel first to the only person near her own age. Angela Peterson looked to be in her late twenties. It was hard to gauge accurately. Her box-dyed blue-black hair and exhausted eyes hinted at a life that hadn't been easy. The lack of dimension in her hair color screamed bargain dye aisle, and yet, there was a sweet innocence about her. Angela was friendly, although, judging by her grammar, was obviously poorly educated.

"See Laurel," Puddin gleefully proclaimed. "We aren't all old biddies around here. I bet you and Angela will have a lot in common."

Laurel could not imagine what that might be, other than neither of them needed wrinkle cream yet. However, Angela was genuinely nice and welcomed Laurel to their group. The next woman she met was a startling contrast.

Obedience Daniels was a stern looking woman, with a hard lined thin face and pinched nose. Her hair, once naturally black, was now dramatically streaked with gray on the sides where it was pulled tightly into a tidy, perfectly round bun in back, making her natural scowl even more severe. She looked like Ichabod Crane had a twin sister who became a Puritan Librarian.

Her sister, Patience, was the polar opposite. Pudgy, but not fat, her round face and bright eyes revealed an inner kindness that, by appearances' sake, skipped her older sister. Bootsie Taylor, from The Fashion Statement, was also in attendance, which helped make Laurel feel less like an interloper even though she only met Bootsie yesterday.

"Oh, Puddin!" Bootsie exclaimed, as she took a seat on a cushy, low back chair donning a peach-colored glossy fabric. "The room looks so nice."

"Do you really like it?" Puddin asked with a proud smile.

"Oh, my yes," Bootsie replied. "I think it's my favorite so far. I love the sheen on this fabric. It really shines."

"And the wallpaper is real nice too," Angela noted. "I love the pastels in those flowers."

As Puddin disappeared behind the swinging door to her kitchen for a tray of coffee, Patience leaned over to Laurel and whispered, "Puddin redoes this room every few months. Last time it was pale blue. I like the peach and turquoise this time much better."

"Why does she redecorate so much?" Laurel whispered.

Angela leaned close and confided, "After Mr. Corder died, Puddin needed something to focus on. Her kids don't live here no more. So Puddin redecorates her living room about twice a year. Gives her something to do."

"And it helps her socialize," Bootsie added. "I, for one, enjoy going wallpaper and fabric shopping with her. I can't get Renzo to let us change a thing around our place. It's looked the same for 30 years."

"40." Obedience snorted.

"Then once it's all done, she has the fun of having friends over to see the new look." Angela concluded.

Delva, who was seated on Laurel's other side, leaned over to whisper into Laurel's ear. "Girl, one time she had little lawn jockeys flanking the fireplace and a few Mammy jars scattered around. I didn't have the heart to tell her. She didn't even think about what it all stood for or looked like."

Laurel snickered at the confided joke, taking a second glance around the room for any other decorating mistakes. She didn't see any, although she saw a multitude of framed photographs of the same man, undoubtedly Puddin's deceased husband.

Puddin returned with the coffee and the prayer meeting officially began. Laurel couldn't help but notice the loaded table in the dining room where snacks and desserts waited for after prayer. Puddin started the session off with prayer requests for her grandson and his wife as they try to begin a family. She also had a second prayer request, "And of course, please pray that my sweet, wonderful Hershall stays happy and well in Heaven. And that he knows I think of him every day until we see each other again."

Laurel thought the prayer was sweet, although silly. Then again, she thought all prayer to be silly. But if there really was a Heaven, would Puddin need to pray for him to be happy there? Could sadness even exist in heaven?

Angela was next, and her prayer was equally unimpressive. She asked the ladies to pray for her father and brother to get along, and for her boyfriend to finally propose. Obedience made no prayer request of the women, opting to spend her moment chastising Angela on the selfishness of her praying for a proposal.

Delva chuckled. "It ain't so selfish. The girl don't want to keep living in sin. Besides, it is a public service cause don't nobody else wanna marry her man." Laurel appreciated Delva's style of humor, even if no one else appeared to.

Angela gave a good-natured smile at Delva's remark, before turning to Laurel as if to explain. "I know we'll marry up one day. He had went to the jewelry store up in Jasper, where the outlets are. Said he found a good ring but needs a few more paychecks."

Realizing her face was stuck in a bewildered expression, Laurel quickly flashed a smile of support. But inside, her thoughts were asking "how can you *had went* somewhere?"

Patience followed Angela, asking for prayers for her sisters' continued good health. Delva asked for everyone to remember her daughter-in-law in their prayers as she transitioned to a new job as head of payroll for the coal mine. Once everyone made their requests, they all turned to

Laurel, awaiting one from her.

When met with a blank stare and silence, Obedience asked Laurel, "Child, what are your prayer requests?"

Blushing mildly, Laurel felt embarrassed. "I don't really have any."

"Surely there is someone you want to pray for?" Obedience replied. "Your mother? A friend. Your grandmother's soul, perhaps?"

Laurel narrowed her brow, replying, "If my grandmother was a Christian, wouldn't she already be in Heaven? I don't really see the need to pray for her."

The room went still. But then Puddin asked, gently, "And what of your mother, sweety? Has she passed?"

Passed? Like what, a sobriety test? Laurel mused to herself, then adding, and she would never have passed one of those at all. But aloud, she responded, "She is also dead."

"That is a shame," Patience replied, before asking innocently, "What was your mother like? I never knew much about her except—"

"Except that she lived in Tuscaloosa when your father met her," Obedience interrupted. "They moved away shortly after."

There was something telling in the way Obedience cut her sister off. Laurel couldn't help but notice the tension which followed, as if a story lay in the unspoken which no one wanted to tell her. Laurel was about to address it when Delva announced to the group how Laurel wanted to write a cookbook. From that moment into the next hour, Laurel was bombarded with recipe suggestions. Each woman expressed an excited willingness to contribute one of their own dishes. It was as Janice said to Laurel a couple of days ago, having their names or the names of a relative who created the recipe in a book, would be a thrill enough for compensation.

Once the ladies in attendance finished talking up their own culinary delights, several began naming other people around town whom Laurel should talk to, who apparently made the best ___ ever tasted. By the time things wrapped up, Laurel had a fistful of paper scraps with the names and phone numbers the ladies insisted she reach out to.

As the meeting wound down, a fascinating social ritual unfolded. Without warning to anyone else, Patience and Bootsie sprang up, making an exaggerated display to "help clean up." Only, as Laurel's investigative eyes observed, the moment Puddin politely declined the offer, both women immediately returned the dishes back to their original resting places. Then, when Puddin picked up a couple of empty plates, Bootsie leaned forward with a half-hearted attempt to, once again, pitch in, but without actually touching anything this time. It was a choreographed dance of social etiquette, Laurel concluded. A long-established ritual of offering to help, but with the pre-established guidelines the offer would be refused. Here, hospitality was theater. Laurel marveled at the pretense and how those involved knew the rules. She was learning more about the South in one prayer meeting than she had in a lifetime of travel.

Delva's Recipe...known in real life as...

SARA K'S OATMEAL RAISIN COOKIES

Ingredients

1 cup unsalted butter
1 cup light brown sugar
¼ cup sugar
2 eggs
1 tbsp vanilla or almond extract
1 tbsp molasses or syrup
1 tsp lemon juice

1 ½ cup all-purpose flour
1 tsp baking soda
1 ½ tsp cinnamon
½ tsp salt
3 cups rolled oats
1 ½ cup raisins

1. Cream butter, sugar and brown sugar in a mixer until smooth
2. Add eggs and mix well
3. Add extract, lemon juice, and molasses (or syrup) and blend for a couple of minutes
4. In another bowl sift flour, soda, salt, and cinnamon together
5. Add flour mix to the sugar/butter/egg mix and blend on low
6. Slowly add in oats and raisins
7. Place mixing bowl with dough in fridge for at least an hour to firm up
8. Preheat oven to 350 and grease 2 baking sheets or line with parchment paper
9. Spoon cookie dough on pan keeping cookies apart enough to spread
10. Bake 15 minutes then let cool thoroughly (cookies will harden as they cool)

CHAPTER FOUR

Chicken and Dressing and Acceptance

s Laurel soon found out, Delva's prayer group spread news through Scroggins faster than they sent up prayers. The very next afternoon, the landline phone sent its shrill reverberating ring all through the house practically all day long. Laurel had not heard a landline telephone ring in years, but apparently everyone in Scroggins knew Bessie Hogue's phone number and that Bessie's estranged granddaughter was living in the house and writing a cookbook. Well, *maybe* writing one. Laurel tried to explain that part repeatedly. Most callers brushed off her uncertainty, saying, "Oh, sure you will. It'd be great for the town." Laurel scribbled a few names and numbers down, promising to get back to them, once she decided whether or not to do the book.

Between wrangling calls, Laurel spent the next couple of days making space for herself in the pink bedroom, slowly removing her grandmother's things. She hesitated over the clothes—discarding them felt wrong, but keeping them seemed pointless. In the end, she packed them up in boxes, telling herself she'd figure it out later. The room, though small, was enough for now.

The intense summer heat was doing a good job of staying outside for the most part. The three air conditioners were adequately keeping the house cooled off. Laurel silently congratulated her grandfather on his craftsmanship. For a house with no insulation, he had managed to keep the elements at bay.

Laurel did a good bit of cleaning as well in her first days in the house. The floors were impressively easy to keep clean. A simple sweeping, then mopping, was all they required. Oddly enough, the humidity of an Alabama summer made the simple task of dusting a little fascinating, she found. The statuettes on the mantlepieces for example, made a distinctive *unsticking* sound when lifted from their place to clean. Decades of paint applications to the shelf, softened just enough under the weighted heat of summer, caused the bottoms of vases and porcelain figures to grip in place. After breaking the hind legs of a little ceramic dog when she tried to lift it to dust, Laurel learned to give these items a soft wiggling twist before removing them from surfaces. That seemed to free them from their hold without damage, and there was something relaxing about the little "click" sound things made when they released from the mantle.

The Hogue house soon gleamed with cleanliness and Laurel's list of potential recipe contributors was growing. Finally, she began setting up a few appointments. Some would come to her, and others she'd meet around town. Angela Peterson was Laurel's first real guest to visit, aside from Janice. Being the only person she'd yet met near her own age, Laurel found herself looking forward to getting to know Angela better. Though Angela had not struck her as a skilled cook, she was willing to hear her out. However, when Angela knocked at the front door, she was not alone. A younger man was with her, maybe sixteen or seventeen. Laurel silently hoped this was not the boyfriend Angela had referred to at the prayer group.

"This is my brother Cade," Angela introduced. "He's really the one who cooks."

Cade was tall and tan, with short dusty-brown hair. He was a good-looking kid. Strong in build, but there seemed to be something fragile about him too. Inviting her guests to sit down, Laurel asked the young man, "So it's really you who wants to have a dish mentioned in the book?"

"Yes, ma'am."

Bristling at the word *ma'am*, Laurel told him it wasn't necessary. She wasn't that much older than him, although she understood to a 16-year-old, a 33-year-old seems like a ma'am. "Tell me about your dish," Laurel asked him. "What exactly is your specialty?"

"Everything is Cade's specialty!" Angela remarked. "He's the best cook in our family. When he gets to."

"Gets to?"

"Our daddy says women are who do the cooking. Not men." Angela revealed. The way she pronounced the word "daddy", as if it were "deaddy", illustrated their backwoods upbringing. "But why can't a guy like to cook? I bet Cade's wife one day won't be complaining when he wants to make her dinner sometimes."

At the simple mention of a future wife, Cade flushed around the cheeks, and Laurel observed his hands clinching the arm of the chair. It was subtle, not obvious, except to Laurel. It didn't require much education or worldliness to understand Cade was gay. Clearly, the fact was lost on his sister, and probably the rest of their family—except perhaps their *deaddy*, which would explain his disdain for Cade cooking.

"What dish is your specialty, in your opinion," Laurel asked him.

Cade listed a few, from Beef Wellington to Chicken a 'la orange. It was obvious he meant to impress her; his dishes were a bit more pretentious than what other locals might contribute to the book. She could tell they were dishes that a young, gay, country boy assumed would be. No doubt he'd learned these recipes to elevate himself, at least in his mind, from the people he found himself suffocated by in daily life. In the real world of top cuisine, such dishes were considered rudimentary. A wannabe's dish.

Laurel smiled kindly. "They sound wonderful. But the tone of this book is leaning more toward country cooking and soul food. The recipes need to fit that style. More upscale dishes would be out of place in the book."

"I have some simpler stuff."

"Yes, but do you have a story?" Laurel asked. "With any dish I choose, there must be a compelling tale behind it. You see it will be the stories behind the food the readers will connect with. The recipe itself is basically, dressing."

Suddenly, Cade sat upright, seeming pleased with himself. "I have dressing."

With a bit of anxiety flickering in his eyes, Cade turned to his sister and suggested she leave to run the errands they'd used as an excuse to get away from home and pick him up after. Not possessing the depth enough to take a cue, Angela told him that she didn't mind waiting.

"Maybe you should go," Laurel remarked, understanding Cade's desire for privacy. "I'll be making notes while your brother runs me through the recipe. Boring stuff. Why not take care of your errands and pick him up in about an hour."

Once Angela was gone, Laurel led Cade to the kitchen where they sat down at the table. She looked the nervous boy in the eyes and said, "I know you're gay."

Cade's eyes widened. "How? Do I give off—"

Shaking her head, Laurel reached over and took his hand. "No. You do not come off as effeminate. But I've been around. I know. I also know that no one else knows besides me. Right?"

"Practically. A couple guys. But they—"

Laurel smiled, "Aren't about to say anything. I understand. What is this about a dressing recipe? Or did you just need someone to talk to? Because if that is the case, I'm not known for my people skills, but I'll be happy to listen."

"Both, I guess." Cade's eyes were even bluer now as they became watery. "I do have a recipe. Chicken and Dressing. I make it every Thanksgiving. It was my grandmother's. It was her mother's originally. It's a showstopper too! Best dressing ever, everyone says so."

When Laurel gave him a note pad, Cade wrote it out from memory. Laurel couldn't help but notice the change in him as he wrote. Cade displayed more vitality in just writing down a recipe than he exhibited in personal interaction. He talked while he wrote, calling out each ingredient, citing the best way to present or prepare it. It didn't take much for Laurel to tell he was passionate about cooking.

Cade first wrote out the original recipe, or more accurately his grandmother's version. Afterward, he rewrote it again with his modifications. "Every generation adds to it," he explained. Then with pride he revealed, "And only one person gets it. Whoever is given the recipe gets to choose who in the family they leave it to. A lot of my aunts and cousins were pretty pissed she gave it to me."

Laurel rested her chin into the palm of her hand, her elbows propped on the table, watching him finish his writing. She realized this would be an integral part of the story if she wrote this book. The passion, the history, the succession, and the pride attached to these recipes. A couple of times she stopped him with questions about his changes.

"Oh yeah," Cade replied, answering one of her questions. "I don't like certain textures. No matter how delicious the dressing was, chomping down on a hunk of celery or onion was gross to me. So, I started sautéing them in water and a little chicken bouillon, then once fully cooked, I blend it up into a fine puree. When I'm mixing all the ingredients, I mix the puree in with the eggs, broth, and Cream of Chicken. You get all the flavor and none of the crunchy slime."

"I like that." Laurel marveled, glancing back through the ingredients. "I share your dislike of crunchy Dressing. And what's this Mojo Chicken?"

Cade snickered, speaking behind his hand as if sharing a secret, "That is one of my changes. Bigmama...that was my grandmother...used to spend an extra two hours preparing, because she had to boil two chickens to get the broth. Then she'd have to wait until the chickens cooled before she could strip the meat off. But last year, I experimented." He blushed a little, "Well, it was less of an experiment and more of I was out too late the night before. So, I grabbed two fully cooked Mojo flavor chickens from the Publix grocery store in Tuscaloosa. Using those for meat, including the skin, the Chicken and Dressing gained a whole new added umph. It was the best yet! So, I just prebuy those and skip the boiling."

His recipe sounded delicious. Despite being the first person she'd considered borrowing a recipe from, Laurel already decided that if she did write this book, Cade's Chicken and Dressing would make the cut. The recipe itself sold her as she scanned his other unique ingredients, but she still required a story. What was Cade's story behind this dish?

"That's why I wanted Angela to go," he confided, his eyes unquestionably teary now as his voice began to tremble.

Cade recounted his early life, summarizing it as succinctly as he could without losing the impact. He'd always known he was different. By puberty he understood what that difference was. He'd been a continual source of disappointment to his parents. His mother couldn't understand why he showed no interest or skill at sports. All the other boys played baseball, or football. "Why can't you try bein' like the other boys?"

"As if I needed anybody to point out that wasn't the same," Cade said, his head low. "My whole school life has been other boys coming at me cause I'm not like them. I've had so many fights, but you can't fight them all in a group. One on one, yeah. But those assholes team up to come after you. So, I just stay low and try to get through the day. Last thing I need is Mama and Daddy on my back again about how I'm not like everybody else."

"I'm sorry you have to go through that," Laurel frowned. And she meant it. She truly did feel sympathy for him, which was very unlike

Laurel Holden. She never felt sympathy for anyone. Never allowed herself to feel close enough to another person to hold any sort of emotion towards them.

Cade went on, explaining how he knew his mother's criticism was meant to coax him into changing, but it only taught him that he was an embarrassment to her. His father was worse. He demanded Cade learn the "manly" things. Hunting, fishing, mechanics. His father was constantly working on cars, or tractors, or some sort of machinery. He never let up on Cade, forcing him to help, only to become angry when Cade lacked the skill or knowledge. Cade admitted to Laurel that he was a failure in his father's eyes, and it was painfully obvious his father wished for a different kind of son.

"I think it's funny though," Cade remarked. "Everybody wants a boy who is *all boy*, whatever that means, but then when guys grow up like that—hunters, sport nuts, working the grimy jobs with permanent stains on their hands—they all end up the same. Emotionally stunted. Knowing nothing about anything other than what their fathers taught them was all a man needs to know."

Laurel sighed. "I find that very sad."

Cade leaned back in his chair with a groan. "Nobody considers you a man unless you wanna shoot something, tackle something, of fix something. You can't have feelings. You damn sure can't talk about them. Stick to sports, chase women, and drink beer—and if you can grunt every minute or so, you're in the club."

She couldn't help but laugh at his summary. Though Cade most likely thought of this problem as strictly a Southern stigma, Laurel had encountered it before—and not merely the south. Toxic masculinity was real and perpetuated with every generation.

"Funniest part of all," Cade continued. "These girls want that man. They think a '*man's man*' is sexy. But after a couple of years when he's got a beer belly and never has any thoughts, dreams, or feelings, those same girls complain to their girlfriends how their husbands don't communicate. Don't understand them."

It was intriguing for Laurel, hearing this bright young man recognize the trajectory of so many people's lives, rural or not. And he was right. Simplistically so. Everyone wants a man to be a man. Yet they also want a man to be authentic and real. They want cuddles and shared confidences. They want him to be soft on the inside when with them, but to the world be rugged, hard, and tough. The only problem with it, by definition alone: to become hard means you must lose your softness.

Cade was obviously a sensitive and caring young man, and very wise to have figured it all out so early. Did his parents really want to kill off that sensitive, thoughtful part of him just so he could spit, fight, and replace a transmission? It seemed so regrettable to Laurel.

"My Bigmama was all I had." Cade shared. "She didn't care if I could hit a baseball or change a tire. She just liked me for me. We'd sit and talk about everything in the world. Her sons grew up to be the men who never interact. Men who pay no attention to a woman until they want to get some. Then when the deeds is done, it's back to ignoring them. And her daughter, my mama, just married a man exactly like the rest of them. But Bigmama appreciated my mind. She liked hearing what I thought. She respected what I wanted for myself because I mattered to her."

"Sounds like she is a lovely person," Laurel smiled.

"Was," he corrected. "She taught me to cook. We spent hours together in the kitchen, making all kinds of things. Pissed my dad off, but he couldn't very well complain about me helping my elderly grandmother."

"Did she know about you?"

Shrugging he said, "I don't think things like that were in her mind. She knew I was different. *Sensitive,* as she put it. But gay...she never mentioned even thinking it...till the end."

"Tell me."

"We were making the Dressing. We always made it two days before

Thanksgiving because she said the flavors had to *marry up* in the fridge before we cooked it. It was when she said that, '*marry up*', that she asked me if I ever thought about getting married? She said she had never known me to go out with any girls and wondered about that."

Cade had done a fair job before now holding back his emotions, but now as he reached this part of his story, his tears streamed like rivers down to his chin. He wiped his face with his shirt. "She knew. And then *I knew* she knew. I started crying. Right there in her kitchen I started bawling like a baby. I just knew she was gonna tell me I would go to hell. Or I had to fight my feelings and be like everyone else."

"But she didn't?" Laurel asked, feeling confident in his Bigmama's love.

"No," he grinned. "She hugged me, kissed my forehead, and told me she knew life had been hard on me and was always going to be. Bigmama said I should keep listening to *me*, to my own inner voice. She said I was a good person, and nobody had the right to tell me different." Cade looked up into Laurel's eyes, smiling proudly. "She gave me the recipe that morning. Told me, 'It's yours. You're the only one who deserves it. You will make it for your family one day. The family *you choose* to be with."

Pressing the bridge of his nose with a sigh, he revealed, "Bigmama died in her sleep that night. And I made the Dressing for her funeral."

Unable to reign her own emotional state in, Laurel pulled Cade into her arms, holding him for several minutes. She wanted to cry. She gave herself permission to cry, this one time, but no tears came. Laurel wasn't a crier. But that did nothing to lessen the empathy she felt in her heart for the boy.

"That is a beautifully uplifting story," she told him. "But I must caution you. If I put that story in my book...it will cause you problems at home."

"I don't care. Put it in," Cade demanded. "If only so thousands of other people will know what a special lady my Bigmama was."

Still feeling hesitant about such a step, Laurel pointed out, "Writing it will basically out you."

Cade let out a chuckle which sounded half afraid and half rebellious. "Hey, maybe that's how I'll come out! If it teaches one person what it's like...if it shows somebody how they should respond to their gay kid, it'll be worth it."

Laurel stared at her laptop screen long after Cade had gone. She'd typed the recipe, adjusted the ingredients, and added the measurements to make it reader friendly. But the real story, Cade's memory of his grandmother, lingered in her mind. It had weight. It had pain. It carried a heat that simmered deeper than the dish. Then she thought back to Delva's tale about the "colored" soldiers who never came home.

Was this still a cookbook?

She didn't know.

And she wasn't sure it mattered. She was writing something honest. Something real. Human troubles. Human experience. Whatever this book became, it might feed something more than mere hunger. It might feed the heart

Cade's Recipe known in real life as...

MAMA HOUSE'S CHICKEN & DRESSING

Created by my great-grandmother Sydney House, passed down by my grandmother Louise House, added to by myself and my son Britton House

(Requires 3 days, but most work is Day 1)

Ingredients

1 iron skillet of Cornbread (recipe follows after this)

White bread loaf

1 whole chicken

OR 1 store bought precooked chicken, and in that case also add Chicken Broth to this list

Celery diced

Onion (yellow or white) diced

1 stick of melted butter

Milk (whole milk. You can use 2% if you INSIST but nothing less)

3 eggs

1 can Cream of Chicken soup (this is what the recipe says. It's wrong. I have discovered 2 cans makes it even better)

Sage

Pepper

Salt

NOTE: The above list of ingredients is fine, if no one likes you. But if you have a large family or are making this for Thanksgiving, you're gonna be doubling and tripling these ingredients.

DAY ONE

1. In a large pot, boil the chicken until done. Save the broth. OR if you purchased a precooked chicken, remove meat from the bones and place it into a bowl, set aside for later. (If you do buy a precooked chicken, get plain flavor or Mojito—which is my fave to use)
2. Crumble the cornbread into a bowl of its own (Not the chicken bowl).
3. Tear the white bread into pieces and toss into cornbread bowl. Mix together with your hands. (I use a large pot with a lid for the bread, so I can dump everything else into it eventually as it all comes together.)
4. In a skillet, sauté celery and onion together in water until soft. (this is when the kitchen starts to smell good!)
5. Add chicken to the bread bowl and mix together with your hands
6. Pour 1 can of Cream of chicken into the bread/chicken mixture and stir.
7. Add a little broth and half the melted butter (you want this moist but not watery)
8. Drain the celery and onion of the water it cooked in
   NOTE: Before the next step is where personal taste comes in. For generations the recipe's next step is to add the sautéed celery and onion. HOWEVER, I hate crunching down on celery and onion in a dressing, and most people agree with me. So years ago, I started pureeing the sautéed celery and onion in a food processor, or blender until it is a thick pulpy liquid.
9. Pour the celery and onion pieces or liquid pulp into the bread mixture.

10. Add the eggs, one at a time, stirring between.

    NOTE: Now this is where, depending on how much you are making (I make triple batches at a time) you need a thick unbending spoon, or do as I do and use my hands.

11. Sprinkle a lot of sage, and a little salt and pepper, and mix all of this thoroughly, sprinkling more as you mix. It is rare to use too much sage. I'd say 1/3 of a bottle sage for original Ingredient list and an additional 1/3 every time you double your amounts. but don't over salt or pepper.

12. Add a little milk, a little more broth, and if you need it, an extra bit of Cream of Chicken soup. You want the mixture to be moist but not soupy. (Think of oatmeal.)

13. If it is too wet, add more bread or cornbread.

    NOTE: It is perfectly safe to taste this mix to check flavor. The chicken, bread, onion, and celery are cooked and nothing else in it will hurt you.

14. Once everything is all mixed together (your hands and arms are covered with goo) you want to refrigerate overnight. (This marries the flavors together. You don't have to do this, but it makes a difference in richness if you don't.) If you have room, you can just put the whole pot in the fridge. If you don't, you can skip to the next step of spreading into pans before refrigerating.

DAY TWO

15. The next day, (if you haven't already) spread mixture into a long casserole dish or metal pan. (I use those disposable Reynolds aluminum pans from the store.) If you've made a double or triple batch, you'll have 2–3 pans worth.
16. Cover pan (or pans) with foil and partially cook on 350° in oven for about an hour.
17. After an hour, remove the pan (or pans) and again refrigerate what you plan to serve the following day overnight. (If you made extra for another date down the road, this is the time to freeze those. Cover in foil tightly, and freeze. It will last up to a year.

DAY THREE

18. The following day (the day of your meal) remove from fridge and cook again on 350° for another hour. (If mix got a little too dry overnight, just add a little broth to rewet top)
19. Remove the foil and cook an additional 15 minutes or until the top is golden brown.
20. FOR FROZEN PANS Thaw in fridge overnight and cook on 350° until done.

MAMA HOUSE'S CORNBREAD

(for the dressing, or just to make cornbread)

Ingredients

Vegetable oil
1 egg
Whole milk
Self-Rising Flour (Not All Purpose)
Self-Rising Cornmeal (Not regular, must be self-rising)
Tiny bit of sugar (if you like a touch sweeter cornbread)

1. Grease iron skillet with oil and place in oven as you preheat to 350°.
2. In a mixing bowl, add 2 cups flour, 1 cup cornmeal, egg, a little milk bit by bit just to make the consistency of batter.
3. Remove skillet from oven and pour some of the drips of oil into the batter, then discard the rest but keep the coated pan ready
4. Blend the mixture well before pouring into the skillet.
5. Cook on 350° until done, about 20 minutes.

CHAPTER FIVE

What Hides Under Beds

With the house in order, Laurel's attention shifted to the shed on the other side of her gravel driveway. Quite the eyesore, it stood as a testament to time's erosion. A rather gray and weathered structure, its unlevel door looked to have been made from mismatched boards held in place by three hinges bearing the rust of countless seasons. Tall, unkempt grass surrounded the structure punctuated with patches of scruffy dandelions.

Since moving in, Laurel had avoided going near the shed because there always seemed to be a cluster of big, winged fluttering things around the doorway. They weren't bees. They weren't moths. But they definitely freaked her out. But curiosity, as it so often does, finally won out. She wanted to know what might possibly be inside that rickety shed under that tin roof.

Feeling especially brave, Laurel ventured from the porch towards the derelict eyesore. The moment she reached the door, a loud buzzing erupted as oversized hornets shot toward her head. Flailing her arms in defense, she stumbled backward. As if the attacking insects weren't enough, something slithered across her foot, prompting an exploding scream from her lungs! Looking down she saw a long, black snake weaving through the weeds. Instinctively, her feet bolted for the road in a swell of adrenaline-fueled urgency. It was illogical, considering the back door to the house was much closer than the road. But the snake had gone in the direction of the house, so Laurel ran the other way.

Panic isn't usually accompanied by rational thinking, but perhaps her instincts drove her to the road because it was nothing but barren pebbles and sand, clear of brush and grass where snakes might hide. A white pickup truck was slowly approaching. The driver, noticing her standing in the road, came to a stop beside her.

"You okay, Miss?" asked a man not too much older than Laurel herself. He wore a blue baseball cap with a logo she didn't recognize.

"There is a snake! It's huge. It came at me!" she cried excitedly. "And there are these big flying things trying to sting me."

The man gently motioned her out of his way so that he could pull into her driveway. He parked and got out, introducing himself as Leon Davis, her neighbor "down the road a piece." Having no clue as to how far "a piece" was in distance, she was still very grateful he happened by. Leon pulled a pistol from his truck as casually as if she were grabbing sunglasses. He led the way towards the outbuilding.

"You seen that snake come outta the crib?"

Laurel looked at him, unsure how to respond.

He repeated himself, "It come outta the crib?"

Laurel blinked in confusion. "Is there a baby crib full of snakes in there?"

Leon laughed, then readjusted his hat. "No, ma'am," he smiled. "*This* is a crib. The *shed*."

"Oh," Laurel replied. "I did not know that. But I think the snake may have come from inside. I don't know. I was fighting those wasps."

"Those are dirt daubers," he said, pointing to a cluster of mud-colored cones clinging to the weathered wood on the outside wall of the crib. "They won't hurt you," Leon explained. "They just didn't want you to knock down their house."

He asked her to describe the snake and the direction it went. Laurel walked him along the path it had taken. As if he could only speak by fidgeting with his hat, Leon removed it and then put it back on again before saying, "Sounds like that was just an old rat snake. He won't hurt you. In fact, he keeps worse critters away. Probably got up under the crib to cool off on this hot day."

Leon went to the crib door and pushed it open. The rusted hinges squealed. Inside it was dark, covered with dust and cobwebs. From the thin strand of light casting from the door, it appeared to be filled with a few pieces of old wooden furniture, iron cog wheels of some sort, metal buckets, and a coiled mattress frame leaning against the inner wall. She couldn't see much else.

"You need something outta here, ma'am? I can get it for ya."

"No, no," she said apologetically. "Don't bother. I was only curious what was inside."

"Well, I'll tell you, Miss Laurel," he said revealing he was aware of who she was. "You got a few cribs on your property. If I was you, I'd wait till late Fall before I looked through 'em. Spring and summer, ain't no telling what's making a home in there. When it gets cold, you're pretty safe."

Laurel thanked him profusely for coming to her rescue and asked if she could get him a glass of water or something. He thanked her for the kindness but assured her he was fine. He was almost home. Walking him back to his truck, she asked if he had known her grandmother.

"Oh, we all knew Mrs. Hogue," he answered. "She was a fine woman. My mama lives with me and my wife. She was real fond of your grandma. I believe they growed up together."

He pointed down the road where the path disappeared around a bend obscured by trees. He told Laurel he lived two houses further down and if she saw another snake or needed anything, just run down there or look up his name in her grandmother's phone book.

Laurel waved goodbye as he pulled away, half embarrassed to have become so flustered by what apparently were every day, normal things in Scroggins. Still, she was very grateful to know Leon was nearby just in case.

* * *

Later that afternoon, after she had come home from work, Janice telephoned to check on Laurel. She also invited Laurel to accompany her to church on Sunday. Laurel did her best to explain her agnostic views without offending her new friend and neighbor. But Janice was not the least bit bothered by Laurel's lack of religious belief, still insisting she come to church with her, if only for something to do. To avoid answering either way until she gave it a little consideration, Laurel recounted her experience with the snake, the wasps, and Leon Davis.

Janice thought the entire scene amusing, assuring her city friend, "You will get used to country life. And Leon? That's Dean Davis's son. Dean and your grandmother grew up together. Bessie always helped her out when she could. Used to give her gently used clothes, pretending she'd put on weight and couldn't wear them anymore. Of course, Bessie never gained a pound. Dean knew that too. It was just Bessie's respectful way of helping."

This gave Laurel an idea. "Do you think it would offend Mrs. Davis if I took Bessie's dresses and shoes and blouses and things to give her? I have no use for them, and I feel guilty throwing them out."

"I think it would be a splendid idea. And Dean can use them."

After hanging up, Laurel began gathering up the clothes she'd packed away. She wouldn't take them to the Davis's yet, still needing to go through the other rooms. There might be more items in the other bedrooms Dean Davis could use. Laurel made a note to get on that task in the coming days.

Laurel thought more about Janice's invitation to church. Sitting in the quiet of the front parlor, Laurel sprawled across the couch, flipping through a few of her grandmother's *Guideposts* magazines. It was all such nonsense to Laurel. The very idea of God always seemed childish to her. Of course, it was natural for people to want to believe in something. Life is a tricky little prankster, who loves to pull the rug out from under you time and time again. She imagined the belief in God probably made people feel protected, safer. But she had never needed it. To Laurel, God and Santa Claus had long been retired to the same imaginary retirement village in the back of her mind. Not once in her life had God ever provided her with protection or ever made her feel safe. God and the Devil, Heaven and Hell, were man's way of avoiding their own responsibility for how their lives turned out. It was so much easier to blame misfortune on devils and attribute good things to blessings. Though Laurel found it all quite ridiculous, she would never want to offend someone else for their belief. Obviously, they needed the fairytale. But she'd never had any use for fantasies.

Perhaps, as a child, she may have believed in God, but it never served her well. She used to pray for all sorts of things. She prayed that the strange noise outside wasn't a burglar. She prayed her mother would find a good guy who would marry her and be a dad to Laurel. Then later, when she got a little older, her prayers segued into hoping that the looks her mother's boyfriends gave her didn't mean what she feared it did. If there was a God, He'd never given Laurel a second thought. In fact, He'd thrown more obstacles at her than blessings. All the clawing and scratching her way out of her circumstances had come from her own determination. But she didn't want to insult Janice. She would rethink Janice's invitation and decide later. If nothing else, it would be something to do.

The afternoon was passing slowly. She considered watching a movie on her phone, but the Wi-Fi tech wasn't scheduled to come out until the next morning. She was already nearing her maximum data usage for the month. Skipping Hollywood entertainment, Laurel popped in her earbuds and listened to her Spotify playlist while packing up a few more of her grandmother's things. Any clothing she found she laid out on one of the spare beds to give to Leon Davis' mother. As for everything else, she'd assess them one by one.

Bessie Hogue was the definition of an old lady, and that fact was proven drawer after drawer. An envelope of something identified as trading stamps was the first thing tossed into the trash. Whatever those were, they dated from the 1970's. If they hadn't been redeemed back then, it was unlikely they could be now. There were a few brooches and decorative pins in a velvet box Laurel admired. Nothing she would ever wear, but it didn't feel right to toss them out. She left them where they were. She opened the next drawer and found two boxes of greeting cards, one opened and one still sealed. Each box contained a series of miscellaneous announcements from Happy Birthday cards, Thank You cards, Condolences, Graduation and Birth congratulations. All blank. *Bessie must have been quite the card sender. Never sent me a card.* The drawer also contained a small stack of newspaper clippings held together by a pink rubber band. She didn't unbind them, but did casually flip through the top portion of a few. Some were wedding announcements of people Bessie must have known. Some were baby announcements, graduation write-ups, and a disturbing number of obituary clippings. Of course, a woman Bessie's age would have known many people who died. A few names amongst the articles were Hogue. A couple were even Hogg.

The bottom drawer, when pulled, fell downward off its track. Laurel removed it completely, reinserting it to try and correct the problem, only to find the track wasn't broken, but missing entirely. Broken off sometime long ago, Bessie undoubtedly didn't let it bother her. Laurel slid the drawer back in. But while trying to fix the drawer, she'd spotted two boxes under the bed, shoved deep against the wall. Laurel got the broom and guided them out within reach.

Both were large, possibly coat boxes from some place called Gayfers. The first, when opened, contained more greeting cards, only these had been used. From Christmas Greetings to Mother's Day, each card had a personalized note scribbled inside. Many were Thank You cards from friends and neighbors. A few were signed, "your secret pal" which raised several questions until Laurel figured out those were church related.

Opening the second box, Laurel found the oddest collection of all. Calendars. Years and years of Calendars. One was bird themed, with a different bird featured every month. One had prints of The Washington Post Covers that whatshisname got famous for painting. A couple had flowers. Some had sayings or mantras. Some were religiously based. But as Laurel was flipping through one, a slip of paper clung to a page. It was a newspaper article.

Laurel recognized it immediately. It was hers. She'd written 15 years ago. It was all about Seattle. From the music scene to fine dining, to the best place to stay...written by Laurel Holden. She made a quick search of the other calendars. In almost everyone, a print article from a local paper or a magazine was tucked into the month corresponding to its printing. *My grandmother followed my career.* It gave her a surreal feeling, seeing her past work flip by month after month, year after year. And not only her articles, sometimes there were photos. Laurel's senior portrait printed in her high school newspaper. The write up from her college graduation. A tiny mention of her new job with *Travel Heart Magazine.* Dozens of clippings depicting Laurel's achievements. Bessie Hogue *had* kept up with Laurel all through the years.

CHAPTER SIX

Sunday is For Secrets

Sunday mornings, in Laurel's world, were usually reserved for sleeping in or recovering from Saturday's excesses. But this Sunday was different. She was up by 7:30—showered, put on makeup, and slipped into a modest dress that, by Scroggins' standards, likely leaned too risqué. As she zipped up, even she wasn't sure why she was going. Janice had asked again. Laurel had said yes.

The women she'd met so far in the community had been beyond gracious in welcoming her to the fold, and many went to Janice's church. Laurel felt it would be rude to turn down the invitation. Her views on religion were not going to change, but she could keep her opinion to herself. Perhaps somewhere in her heart or mind, or both, she wanted her grandmother to know she was going to her church—for at least one visit. Maybe it was Laurel's way of saying *Thank You. Thank you for the house and thank you for at least keeping up with my life.*

The church was not as full of parishioners as Laurel expected a Southern church to be. With three rows of 12 pews each, she estimated maybe 65 people were in attendance. There was a small rectangular number board over the church organ listing the numbers of attendees from the prior week. The number read 67, and above it another figure displayed the total number of church members, 187. She asked Janice about it as they took a seat in the fifth row.

"Oh, 67's a good number!" Janice remarked. "There are several churches around. Two or three Baptist ones alone. In a town of maybe 2000 people, we do pretty good."

As they settled in, several congregants approached to introduce themselves. No one asked who Laurel was—everyone already knew. Scroggins wasn't the kind of place where anyone remained anonymous. Laurel returned their cheerful greetings with what began as a practiced, polite smile, but softened into something more real. For someone who normally loathed small talk and obligatory friendliness, she found herself disarmed by the warmth in the room. Most of the acquaintances in her life were connected to her work, but with each welcome from these church members, she found their smiles contagious.

A man entered the church, drawing a ripple of attention over the pews as people reached to shake his hand coming down the aisle. Janice pointed him out as the preacher, whom Janice and everyone else addressed as "Brother Daws." He greeted nearly every parishioner on his way down the aisle, but his gaze never left Janice and Laurel, making his way directly toward them. He was a towering man, anchored by his overly round midsection. He was wrapped in a white button-down and wrinkle-free polyester suit that, due to his girth, lacked creases, wrinkles, or cinches, giving Laurel the impression it was painted on. He was like a living, breathing, Humpty Dumpty. Other than that, he was a handsome man, probably in his 60's. His gray hair was styled into a fusion of pompadour and flat-top, a holdover from a bygone era. Beneath the silver gray clung a few streaks of the black it once had been. He wore big square glasses which magnified his beautiful azure eyes, that shined in delight as he approached Janice and Laurel.

He reached for Laurel's hand with a firm, warm shake. "My, my, my. So glad to finally meet you, Miss Laurel."

Behind him stood a woman, equally behind the times, with a towering beehive hairdo—a toned-down Marge Simpson, still clinging to a shade of reddish brown that had long ago given up the fight. "I'm Lottie Daws," she said, mirroring her husband's genuine warmth. "Welcome to our church."

Lottie took a seat up on the first pew, as Brother Daws made his way to the pulpit to begin services. Brother Daws must have either started early, or several congregation members arrived to church late, because the pews filled in a little more during the first minutes of his sermon. Laurel missed much of the beginning, too busy looking around at the other church members. Yet again, her preconceived notions of the south were being tested as she saw Delva Hopkins sitting a few rows back with her family.

Laurel would not have expected blacks and whites to go to the same church in Alabama. The distinguished gentleman next to Delva had a woman next to him, most likely his wife. Laurel wondered if he was Owen, the man who had once been friends with her father. Next to them sat another man, younger. He was handsome enough to hold Laurel's attention longer than she should have stared. When she realized he was looking at her too, she turned back to face the pulpit, her face blushing.

Brother Daws' message for the day, what pieces Laurel paid attention to, sounded like it was on *the generosity of spirit*. She wished she'd paid closer attention because she suspected it was meant for her, and how he expected her to be received in Scroggins. The service was low key in scale, with only occasional fluctuations in Brother Daw's voice to emphasize dramatic impact. Laurel quickly saw the pattern in the melodic rise and fall of how the preacher gave his message.

"*JESUS...*," he stressed firmly, "was the Prince of generosity of the spirit. *JESUS* is the light in all of us that wants so desperately to shine. And Jesus..." and with the lowering of his voice before his impactful rise at the finish, "Jesus, ladies and gentlemen of this church...is begging us to share our kindness...our *GENEROSITY OF SPIRIT*, with those among us our eyes prefer to not see. *LOVE THE DESPAIRED*...and

He will remove our own disparity."

Just as the room stilled, a booming voice from the back burst forth with quickened exuberance. "We walk by the homeless, walk by the desperate, walk by the hungry, and Jesus shouts 'throw out your love!' We take it to the 30, we take it to the 20, we take it to the 10, and touchdown! We fill our fallen brothers and sisters with the spirit!"

The man's words were jarringly loud, over emphasized in a familiar way Laurel couldn't place, until Janice leaned over to her ear.

"That's Bud Rawlings. He's a sports announcer on the radio station in Tuscaloosa. Really nice man, but everything he says sounds like he's calling a football game."

Laurel snickered into her hand as Brother Daws thanked Bud for the assist and wrapped up his sermon.

After the service, Brother Daws took position at the door of the church, with his wife on the other side, wishing their church members well in the coming week. As Janice and Laurel edged slowly closer to the front, overhearing the many "Good sermon, Reverend," and "Enjoyed the message today, Brother," she felt a tap to her shoulder.

"Good Sunday, Miss Laurel." Delva said with a bright smile. "I sure do hope we see you back again next week."

"I don't know about that," Laurel replied, catching eyes with the younger man behind Delva who she'd been staring at earlier. "We will see, I guess."

The man stepped more into view, edging Delva gently aside. "You really brightened up the place. If you come back, I may be persuaded to myself."

The woman beside him made a disapproving face and pinched his arm. "My son is not a regular church goer. Something Miss Delva and I are working on. I am Maple Hopkins. This is my husband Owen, and our son, Linc."

Laurel gave another smile to the handsome Linc, who she now estimated was near her age. She then turned to his father. "Mr. Hopkins,

I understand you knew my father. I wouldn't mind hearing about him sometime."

Owen exchanged an awkward glance with Janice. Once again, Laurel was given the impression there was some secret about her father everyone, but she was privy to. But then, Owen replied. "I grew up with Charlie, but we didn't stay close after he moved away. Happy to tell you what I can, though."

As everyone continued moving towards the door, Linc took advantage of the brief time he and Laurel stood shoulder to shoulder. "If you come back, I'll come back."

Blushing at his flirtation, but thrilled when he made it, Laurel was about to reply when someone grasped her arm, pulling her sharply sideways towards them. Startled by the rude gesture, Laurel found herself facing an old woman with round shiny brown eyes and a big grin on her face. She had an old lady perm drawing her hair very close to her head. The hair was tinted somewhere between lavender and periwinkle; it was hard to tell.

"I am Flossie!" she exclaimed, as if the name meant something to Laurel. She pulled Laurel into an exuberant hug. Over the old lady's shoulder, Laurel saw Linc's amused reaction to Laurel's reaction.

"I'm sorry," Laurel replied, pulling herself back from the elderly—but surprisingly mighty—woman's hold. "Should I know you?"

Flossie slapped her hand onto Laurel's shoulders, "Honey, I am your great aunt. Bessie was my sister. Guess I'm 'bout the only family you got left in this town."

Before Laurel could process the revelation, the crowd carried them out onto the steps. Janice stayed behind to help Flossie down, prompting Laurel to rush back in guilt. One by one they traversed the steps. "You are a sweet little thing," Flossie remarked, clutching her hand. "I been wantin' to meet you, but my drivin' days are over." Flossie then pursed her lips and nose into a pretend mad-face as she scolded Janice. "Why ain't you brung this girl out to see me?"

Janice, looking guilty, apologized to the old woman. "I was planning to Miss Flossie, but she has only been here a few days. I thought I would give her time to settle in. I've been doing my best over the months to keep Miss Bessie's place up, but with my own house and job, I'm afraid I wasn't able to keep it move-in ready. Laurel has had a lot to do."

"I guess so." Flossie nodded. She continued holding Laurel's hand, swinging it back and forth with her own as if Laurel were a little girl. "You come see me though," she told her niece. "I live in the little green house down that hill right yonder." Laurel followed her finger to the thin dirt road across the street. It moved down a gentle hill to an olive-green house in the distance. "Now you know where I am. So, you come see me, hear?"

"I will." Laurel promised. "What is the best day to visit?"

Flossie let out a raucous chuckle, "Honey, I am about a hunnerd and sixty years old. I ain't doin' a blame thing ever but watching my shows. You just come on anytime you want. But I watch Wheel of Fortune at 6, don't come then."

Laurel assured her she would visit soon, adding she was very happy they had met. Flossie kissed her cheek, then did the same to Janice, telling Janice, "I think you are as good as gold. Bessie'd be smiling big knowing you are looking after her grandbaby."

They watched Brother Daws and Mrs. Daws come forward, escorting Flossie to their car. Undoubtedly, it was their habit to pick the elderly lady up before church and bring her home after. Laurel wished she'd had the forethought to ask if Flossie needed help getting home. Frankly, it, like helping her down the church steps, never occurred to her. Laurel was not accustomed to being around frail people or anyone requiring assistance. And she certainly wasn't accustomed to being someone who supplied it. She kept to herself and allowed others to do the same. Clearly, this was not that kind of town.

Janice drove Laurel back to her own house where she'd pre-prepared lunch before church, keeping warm in her oven. They entered Janice's house through the kitchen door, causing Laurel to wonder if every front door in Scroggins was just for show. It was Laurel's first time in her new friend's home, but she was not given a tour. Janice immediately retrieved lunch from the oven. The kitchen was small, connected to a similarly sized dining nook where they ate a delicious lunch of fried pork chops, roasted potatoes, and green beans. While they were eating, Laurel found she could basically tour the entire house by sight alone. Just off the dining area was Janice's living room, which could be seen in its entirety from the table. It was nothing special. Perhaps more updated than Bessie's. But of course, Janice was far younger than Laurel's grandmother had been, plus she had a job in Tuscaloosa as sales manager of a furniture store. Janice's house was bound to be slightly more modernized. Politeness dictated Laurel say something positive about her friend's home, but with everything being so lower middle class ordinary, she didn't know what to say. When a certain settee caught her eye, she commented on it. "I love the fabric on that couch. Such a lovely shade of turquoise."

"Recognize it?" Janice grinned. "It's the same one Puddin has, only the fabric is different."

"I see it now, it is!"

"Puddin usually comes to my store to buy her furniture when she redecorates. I give her 35% off everything, even sales prices. If you decide to buy some things for Bessie's...excuse me, old habits...*your* place, I can do the same for you."

"Thank you! I will keep that in mind. Unfortunately, right now I am pinching pennies until I figure out what I plan to do."

With a confused look in her eyes, Janice remarked. "I thought you were going to write a cookbook?"

Shrinking a little from self-doubt, Laurel answered. "I never said for sure on that. I just write about food; I don't cook it."

"No one expects you to cook it. Just tell other people how to." Janice bit into a slice of the pork chop. "Look at yourself. You just admitted you can't cook. Well, I couldn't either till someone taught me. Around here recipes are as good as currency if the dish tastes good enough."

Laurel had to admit she had a point. But was cooking really so important anymore? "In today's world, Janice, it's easier to have food delivered than it is to make it yourself. People don't have time for that." She didn't realize she'd made a joke until Janice started laughing.

"It is plain to see you have lived a much different kind of life than most of the rest of us, Laurel." Janice wiped the edge of her mouth with a napkin, then finished her thought. "Not everyone can afford to order in or dine out much. Around here, and I'd bet it is no different across the rest of country, way more people make their meals at home than get it brought to them."

"Okay," Laurel conceded. "But the book industry is flooded with cookbooks. I can't see how mine would appeal to publishers. Even if I work in the hokey stories. Will people be interested?"

"They will," Janice smiled reassuringly. "Trust in the stories you're being given and trust your ability to tell those stories the right way. I think people out there could benefit from some of the messages behind the creation of those recipes."

"I don't know. Down home, wool spun tales aren't very in style right now."

"I disagree," Janice said. "People, no matter where they live, share basically the same triumphs and tragedies. We all cope best we can. People crave connection."

Elbow on the table, her chin resting on her fist, Laurel commented, "Will the public at large believe they stand to learn anything from a rural community?"

Janice might have been offended by Laurel's question had she not understood the irony that even Laurel was not yet wise enough to see. Laurel was *the public at large*. Her fast-paced, coast-to-coast life had given her the same predetermined idea everyone else carried who lived with sidewalks and streetlamps. The notion that rural life—country people, more specifically—was something to be laughed at on television or ridiculed in movies. Laurel was unaware she was her own living test case. Only a week in Scroggins and Janice had already seen a break in Laurel's façade.

"Personally, I think people could learn a lot from us down here." Janice professed. "We don't rob each other. Most of us never even lock our door. Nobody we know goes hungry. If we don't have money to buy it, we know how to grow it. Nobody cares if Jane got a Fendi bag or if Jack drives a Porsche. What we care about is if Jane will come over to take your kids to school when you have the flu, or if Jack is willing to help you cut up the tree when it falls over your driveway."

"Sweet point."

Janice patted Laurel's arm. "I know we talk funny, and historically we all seem behind the times," Janice continued. "But we all have Google now. And Amazon. If we wanted a Fendi purse you better know we could get one delivered out here. It's only that things like that aren't as important to us as peace and connection are. A connection to the earth and to the neighbors we share it with. Those will be the stories you'll collect. Sometimes it is beautiful, and sometimes it can get pretty ugly. But there is much to be learned in someone else's kitchen."

"I suppose I worry the average book buyer will look down their nose at rural life." Laurel's eyes fell with remorse as she admitted, "I always have. To be honest, I still find this way of life more funny than fulfilling. I wouldn't want to write anything that disrespects any of you. But if I can't relate to you, how to I portray you fairly?"

Janice rose from the table to place their dishes in the sink. She gave them a quick rinse before setting them down, then turned back to Laurel with her arms folded and a tender smile. "I highly doubt you related very well with the goat farmer in Calabria that you wrote about. But you wrote about his lifelong devotion to his herd as if they'd been children he personally birthed."

Laurel looked back at Janice in astonishment.

"Yes, Laurel," Janice grinned. "I've read your work. You made me feel like I knew that old goat farmer. You had me there, seeing it all for myself when he buried his favorite goat, Francesca. All that love and respect you poured into two paragraphs explaining where the hotel acquired its fresh daily milk."

Laurel was speechless, and a little humbled, "Wow."

"These recipes, these people in Scroggins," Janice explained. "You'll depict them with the same reverence. It's who you are. How you write. And readers will relate to them because there is a lot to be learned from them. These aren't women who had the luxury of therapy. They don't down a bottle of wine every night after a hard day. These recipes are from women who had farms to work, children to raise. Children to *bury*. And unworthy husbands to wrangle. There was no such thing as a weak Southern woman—still isn't."

Unsure if she'd been reproached for her thoughts or not, Laurel had to admit that Janice showed her there could be value in the perspectives this book might provide. And even if no one read it but Southern women, that was still a market unto itself.

Laurel asked if she could help wash the dishes—a sincere ask, not one like Bootsie and Patience had given Puddin. Janice declined however, but offered to drive Laurel home, but it was such a nice afternoon she preferred to walk.

Laurel began her short journey along the red dirt road, second guessing her decision when she saw how dusty her shoes were getting in the soft powder. Birds were singing on treetops hidden behind leaves and vines. A few squirrels scurried across the road with acorns in their mouths. The hot day was delightfully tolerable along the walk, thanks to the heavy canopy of overhead tree limbs. Laurel stopped once, allowing a maroon pickup truck to pass. Respectfully, the man slowed to a crawl, as to not engulf her with dust. He waved a friendly hello from his cab, which she returned.

Passing by the center house between where she and Janice lived,

Laurel saw two children playing in their side yard. Though it was a badminton net dividing the boy and girl, it appeared as if they were tossing a basketball back and forth over it. At the foot of their property, beside the children's driveway, stood a long row of mailboxes affixed to a long log rail. Glimpsing the boxes as she passed, Laurel saw the name Hogue painted in faded red across one. She stood, pressing her palm to her forehead as she sighed at her own stupidity. Not only had she driven past these mailboxes at least 6 or 7 times and not noticed them, it had also never occurred to her to check the mail. Not once in her week here had Laurel given any thought to where her grandmother's mailbox might be or if she might need to check it.

Laughing at her ridiculousness, Laurel opened the metal door to find the mailbox empty. She reminded herself to check it every few days. After all, her own mail would be forwarded here now. Resuming her walk home, she glanced absentmindedly at the other mailboxes, hoping to familiarize herself with her neighbors' names. There were nine boxes in all, sparking another mental reminder that this road did stretch further than Bessie's house, including Leon Davis's home somewhere down the way. She still hadn't taken those clothes to his mother yet. It was then that her eye caught sight of another box, raising her curiosity. Another Hogue, this time spelled out in adhesive letters, not paint.

Laurel opened the mailbox, discovering it was nearly half full of mail. She removed one of the envelopes. Her name was on it. It was only a response from one of the magazines she'd reached out to asking for a staff writer position. The answer was no. It was a polite no, dressed up with all the required respectful flattery, but still a no. She lifted out the other mail, skimming through. Her name appeared several times, along with Bessie's. This was Bessie's mailbox. But that begged the question, *who is the other Hogue?*

Laurel examined the row of boxes, mentally assigning them to the houses along the road, counting backwards from Bessie's. Assuming the placement of each mailbox correlated to the order of homes, then it appeared the first Hogue box belonged to...Janice. Laurel almost turned around to go back to Janice's to ask, but she didn't. There could be a variety of reasons for the second Hogue mailbox. Perhaps one of the family who died or moved, sold Janice the house—or was renting it to her. Just because the box read Hogue did not mean the Scroggins mailman didn't know who really lived there. Or maybe Janice was a Hogue. Laurel was not aware of all the Hogues she was related to. Janice could be a distant cousin. Or close cousin. But why wouldn't she have said so when they first met? Then again, hadn't Flossie mentioned at church how she was Laurel's only relative in town. It then dawned on her that Janice had said herself that the Hogue family once owned the entire stretch of road. It was entirely possible that Laurel's grandmother had also owned Janice's house, possibly leaving it to her just as she'd willed her own to Laurel. It wasn't important. She would ask about it later. Right now, she had a new concern as she continued her way down the shady lane. Did snakes ever slither across the road? Leon said the big black snake had been sheltering under the crib to cool off. Much of this dirt road was well-protected from the sun. With the thought now the only thing in her mind, Laurel began hurrying along, scanning left and right for any signs of reptiles.

When she made it home with her mail, she was happy to be back inside with cool, crisp air flowing around her. Despite her body heat and the sweat on her face and shoulders, the cold air hitting it brought an uncomfortable chill until her temperature regulated. Still curious about the mailbox, Laurel sat down in the front parlor and picked up the telephone, scanning the notepad beside it where she'd written new names and numbers. As she began dialing the decades old landline phone, she paused. *What is happening to me?* Laurel's entire life was one lived on the go. She had not dialed on a landline since she was a little girl. How was it that now it felt perfectly natural. Her own cell phone was still in her pocket, she could have used it at any time on her walk home. *I am getting too accustomed to this way of life.* Replacing the receiver back on the hook, Laurel pulled her phone out and dialed her friend and neighbor.

"Hello?" Janice answered.

"Hey, its Laurel. I have a question."

"Go ahead."

"Are we related?"

CHAPTER SEVEN

The Family Tree is Choked with Vines

J anice came through the back door, finding Laurel at the kitchen table with a couple of old boxes opened before her, photographs spilling out. Some had handwritten notes identifying the people and occasions captured in them, while others were frustratingly blank.

"I found these the other day but haven't looked at them yet," Laurel told her friend. "These are too old for you to be in them. I don't know who any of these people are."

Janice smiled, pulling out a chair beside her. She reached into the box and picked up a worn photo. "That man was your grandfather's brother, Edgar. I met him once, right before he passed." Her eyes lit up as she spotted a familiar image beneath the top layer. "And this fine young lady here—that's your grandmother."

Laurel studied the black and white snapshot. Her grandmother had been striking in her youth, wearing a dark dress with white cuffs and a rounded lace-trimmed neckline. Her dark hair, pulled back with a band of heather, curled neatly under at the shoulders. She looked like someone from an old Hollywood film—though less glamorous, more real.

Janice reached for another picture leaning against the box's edge.

"That was Mr. Hogue—your grandfather."

Laurel let out a small, involuntary purr. "Well, he was hot!"

Janice burst into laughter. "He cut quite a figure in his day, or so I've heard. I think their wedding picture is here somewhere." She dug deeper into the box and found it.

Laurel raised a brow. "That's a wedding photo?"

"It is," Janice confirmed. "You've got modern wedding brain. Back then, people didn't have big ceremonies. No gowns, no flowers—just a preacher and the fanciest dress you owned. Most women only had two or three to choose from."

"They aren't even touching," Laurel remarked. "Did they love each other?"

Janice took the picture back, returning it to the box and replacing the lid. "I think they did. Then." The way she said *then* spoke volumes about Laurel's grandparents' marriage. Janice pushed the box aside and rose from the table. "What you are looking for isn't in these boxes. Follow me."

Janice moved from the kitchen, through the den, to the bedroom behind it. As Laurel followed, her mind raced with questions about her grandmother's marriage. "What did you mean, they loved each other *then*?"

"You need to keep in mind I was not alive back then," Janice reminded her. "I only met them later."

Laurel felt foolish now. Of course, she met them later! Janice was significantly younger than her grandparents. It was a distinction easily forgotten considering everything Laurel had so far learned about her grandmother had come from Janice.

"How did you meet my grandparents?"

Janice opened the chifforobe in the yellow bedroom. Laurel was about to tell her she had already looked in there when she first moved in, finding it only contained quilts, sheets, and towels. However, Janice proved far more familiar with this house than Laurel once again, when she removed the quilts from the bottom of the cabinet. After placing the quilts lovingly on the bed, Janice lifted a small latch in the bottom panel.

"There is a hidden compartment!" Laurel cried out.

"Not so much hidden as covered by blankets."

Janice lifted a brown leather-bound family photo album. Others lay beneath it, but only the brown one was what she wanted. Ushering Laurel to sit on the edge of the bed with her, Janice went to the page with a familiarity showing she knew exactly where the picture lay.

"I met your grandparents as a teenager. I liked them very much. Here I am with them at my wedding."

"Your wedding?" Laurel gasped. "I didn't know you were ever married."

"I was," Janice smiled gently. "To your father."

Laurel sat stunned, leaning back against the stack of quilts, her legs folded under her. Janice scooted back with her, only the muffled rumble of air conditioners at the other end of the house, breaking the silence until Janice began to share the story of her life. One Laurel never knew.

She'd met Charlie Hogue in school and had been smitten from the start. "If it helps you picture it, he looked very much like his father did at that age."

"He was a stud," Laurel grinned, teasingly.

Janice said, a wistful smile tugging at her lips. "Yes, he was."

She went on to say that though Charlie was not exactly her beau, she lived as though he were. While he ran around cavorting with other girls, she remained true to him, knowing he'd always come back around to take supper with Janice and her family a couple of times a month.

"I have no idea what *cavorting* or *take supper* mean, but I get your point." Laurel mused. "Didn't it anger you for your boyfriend to be out with other girls?"

Janice's gaze drifted into the distance, most likely where she kept her memories. Perhaps pleasant ones, judging from her expression. "He wasn't officially mine," she clarified. "And things like that weren't worried over back then. *Boys will be boys.* You know the saying."

"Yes," Laurel quipped. "Misogyny 101."

"You young people, with your rules and characterizations." Janice seemed to display no offense or outrage by the disparity, but Laurel found herself processing it much differently. "Charlie always told me," Janice continued. "When I get ready to settle down and get married, it'll be you. I'll let you know when the time comes."

Laurel grimaced, slapping her hand to her forehead. "That is revolting!"

"I thought it was sweet."

"Janice! It's egotistical!" For a moment, she forgot they were discussing her very own father, although she felt no special connection to him.

It was clear by Janice's contrasting view, and how dreamy eyed she looked even talking about Laurel's father, that she'd deeply loved the man. Maybe she still did. Far more charmed by Charlie's personality than his daughter, Janice went on with her reminiscence. She told Laurel how the day arrived when Charlie Hogue was ready to marry. True to his promise, he showed up to her house one Saturday afternoon, picked her up in his truck, and drove to the preacher's house. After the ceremony, they came back to Bessie and Ustus' home for a small dinner Bessie prepared for them.

"We lived here with your grandparents for the first year while Charlie and his brothers built my house."

"You lived here?" Laurel gasped.

"In this very room," Janice smiled, caressing the bedcover with the palm of her hand. "Your uncle Dave was a contractor and had started a business. Your uncle Vern and your dad worked for him. When they weren't on a job, they worked on building our house. It wasn't fancy, but it's still standing, so I can't complain."

Laurel was astounded by it all. Her mind was sent reeling into all sorts of terrain. "I am so full of questions. Like what happened? Was he ever really married to my mother?" Suddenly, Laurel grew quiet, her trembling hand hovered over her mouth. "Oh my God! Janice...are you actually my mother?"

Bursting into laughter, Janice wrapped her arm around Laurel's shoulder. "No, sweetheart. I'm not. And yes, he did marry your mother. As far as I know."

This brought new questions to Laurel. She wanted to know what happened to Janice's marriage. How could Janice stand living in the same house after that? Janice shushed her friend and went on with her tale. She explained how after marrying Charlie, Janice blended into the Hogue family with ease. Bessie was not one of those bothersome mothers-in-law you hear about. Bessie was a loving woman and delighted with Janice joining the family.

"We became fast friends." Janice paused, pointing to another picture in the album lying across her lap. A pretty girl, but she refused to smile for the photographer. "Bessie and her daughter Lindy did not get along very well. Lindy considered herself a modern woman. Funny, considering how very unmodern those times were. Bessie did not approve of Lindy's choices, and Lindy adamantly disapproved of Bessie's *decisions*."

Again, the simple phrasing of a word hinted to a backstory no one would tell. Laurel was on the point of asking Janice up to elaborate, but Janice had moved ahead with the story she was telling. "Eventually Lindy left home. She married someone later, I heard. I never saw her again once she left. None of us did. I think your Aunt Merle kept up with her. But Merle died years ago."

"Merle?" Laurel repeated, "I have never even heard of her."

Janice turned to another photograph of an older girl, much more serious in demeanor with eyes like that of someone decades older than she was. "Your Aunt Merle was an angel. She helped a lot during the hard times before I married into the family. Kept the family going. But by the time I married in, she was living in Birmingham with her husband. She died a few years back."

"What hard times?" Laurel asked. "And why did you and Charlie break up?"

Letting out a hesitant sigh, Janice turned to face Laurel eye to eye. "This is all ancient history. Why dig it up now? You're here. That's what matters. We should be focusing you and your book and restarting your career."

"Don't do that. Don't deflect," Laurel asked. "I want to know Janice."

"Why does any of it matter?"

Laurel grasped her friend's hand, intertwining their fingers as she squeezed. "My father hurt you. I can see that without you spilling a word. If it's something you'd rather not relive, we can stop, but don't stop because of me alone. You have been nothing but kind to me since I came here. Kinder than I think I would be in your situation. I'd like to know how a woman can be so badly hurt by a man yet still treat his daughter like family."

"You are family," Janice smiled. "To me, you are. I don't have any others. Bessie was my family and now you are. Blood doesn't mean as much as people make out."

It was evident she didn't want to relay the rest of the dismal tale, but Laurel wanted to know. And Janice understood Laurel had a right to know. Up until now, these were all simply long dead memories of Janice's life. With Bessie gone, they were now Janice's alone. But Laurel had come home, whether she considered it home or not. And Janice knew she had a right to know who she came from; however unpleasant it could be in places.

"Once our house was built, Charlie and I settled into our own home. It was fun at first. Bessie and I sewed curtains for the windows. She gave us a few pieces of furniture she had out in the crib that once belonged to Ustus' parents. Bessie and I would sit on her porch Saturdays shelling peas and butterbeans, shuck corn, snap green beans...all to store in the freezer for winter. It was a nice time in my life."

"Until it wasn't?"

Nodding, Janice said, "Until it wasn't. Your father had almost doubled his workload, coming in late only to disappear in the morning back to the job. Had it not been for Bessie and Ustus, I'd have been totally alone. But you see, Charlie owed quite a bill from building our house, so I understood his working so much."

"You didn't have any time with him at all?" Laurel asked.

Her face growing pink around the cheeks, Janice confessed, "Well, sometimes he'd wake me up at night. That's when I got pregnant."

"Pregnant!" Laurel shouted. A sudden wave of exhilaration filled her. Could she possibly have a sister or a brother she never knew about? The question was on the edge of her lips when she stopped herself. *Janice lives alone. And Bessie gave me the house. Something terrible happened.*

Janice continued, drawing her heartbreaking tale to its conclusion. "Charlie acted pleased by the news, but...a wife knows. Something didn't seem right with him. Then as my due date got closer, something went down with the Hogue brothers. There was a huge falling out. I didn't get the real story until it was long over."

She told Laurel how Charlie had not been working extra hours as she believed, he'd been seeing some girl from Tuscaloosa. His brothers knew about it but said nothing, because men never told on each other, even if they disapproved. It was only once Dave figured out Charlie was stealing from his company that he fired Charlie.

"Oh my God," Laurel exclaimed. "What happened then? How did my father tell you?"

With an insincere grin, attempting to be humorous, Janice revealed, "To this day he never has."

She closed the photo album, but not before she discreetly touched her finger to Charlie's picture. Laurel caught it out of the corner of her eye. Janice still loved Charlie, despite everything.

"Dave fired Charlie and demanded he pay back the money. Charlie left. Left town, left me, left his parents. He didn't even stop by the house to tell me about it or say goodbye. He went to Tuscaloosa, picked up his girl and ran away."

Laurel was never the type of person who cared much about other people's turmoil. She always had her own that required her attention. She couldn't count the times she had selfishly ended a conversation the moment it turned unpleasant because she couldn't muster the energy to pretend to care. Yet now, she genuinely felt something. Maybe it was a form of inherited guilt, because the villain who'd wrong Janice was Laurel's father. Although why she should feel responsible for his actions was a mystery when he had wronged Laurel too. But above all the thoughts hovered the haunting question Laurel could not ignore.

"Where is your baby?"

For as well as Laurel perceived herself to be a master at cloaking her thoughts, Janice saw right through them. Presenting an authentic laugh this time, she nudged Laurel with her shoulder and said, "No, Laurel. I already told you. I am not your mother. I wish I were." Her face turned solemn now as she offered the last detail of her sordid history. "My baby died inside me. Stress I suppose. Who can say? It stopped kicking a couple months before it was to be born, so I carried my baby to term, and then we buried her in the churchyard."

As abnormal as it was for her to be so affectionate, it felt completely natural to Laurel when she pulled Janice into her arms. She wished she could hug all the pain out of Janice's life. The rest of Janice's life story was uneventful. She continued living in the house Charlie built for her and found a job at a furniture store. As time went on, she helped Bessie look after Ustus after his first stroke. After his death, Bessie and she kept busy with their clubs and church friends. Once Bessie became ill, Janice took care of her until the end.

"Why didn't you remarry? Make a new life for yourself?"

Janice shrugged. "I liked the old one too much I guess." She could see Laurel disapproved of her choices. "It's easier to have life behind you," Janice explained. "You get a nice sense of peace knowing there is nothing ahead to worry over."

It was Laurel's turn to pick up Charlie's story, filling in whatever blanks for Janice she could. "He married my mother after you," Laurel said. "At least I think he married her. When she got pregnant with me... well, at least he hung around for almost a year after my birth. Then he was gone. Another woman...again, I suppose. When he got drunk and died in a crash, he was with whatever unfortunate woman he'd most recently convinced to ruin her life for him."

"And your mom?" Janice asked. "Was she nice?"

"My mother was little more than a tramp," Laurel answered with bitterness. "I always thought he'd done that to her. Left her desperate enough to do the things she did. Maybe she was always like that." With an angry shake of the head, Laurel added, "She had no qualms stealing your husband, and with you expecting a baby. What kind of awful person can live with themselves after they try to make someone else's husband belong to them? My mother deserved the kind of life she ended up having. Whatever hell she lived in, or went to after, she deserved."

"Don't say that," scolded Janice. "She was your mother."

Laurel went to the window, pulling back the curtain and staring outside. Or perhaps it was she now gazing off where she kept her own memories buried. "My mother wasn't a mother. She cared too little about other people. She was willing to degrade herself to steal another woman's husband, and the result left everyone involved destroyed."

"But we are not destroyed," Janice offered, grabbing Laurel's hands. "I don't feel destroyed, and you certainly aren't. Maybe I have had a boring life. Maybe I chose to keep myself walled off. But you know, I still liked my slow-paced life. And your mother and father, despite their best efforts or their thoughtless mistakes, turned out a bright, beautiful, powerful woman who I suspect is discovering her own walled off heart isn't as walled off as she thought."

CHAPTER EIGHT

Chicken Batter, Add Tears

Perhaps some people who move to a new town have difficulty making friends or maybe that is only the case in larger cities where someone can live alongside their next-door neighbor for years and never know their name. This was not Laurel's experience since arriving in Scroggins. Her second week in town was filled with invitations. Primarily the invites had less to do with getting to know her than it was women wishing to be included in her cookbook. Word of the big-time writer moving to town planning to write a cookbook featuring Scroggins, spread like wildfire. The landline Laurel had forgotten to cancel on Monday, rang hourly with someone on the other end asking her over to sample their coveted dish. Each caller felt assured she would want to include their dish.

"Do you know you're the first person I've called on my cell all week?" Laurel confessed to her longtime friend Daniel over the phone. "Everyone here uses the old landline. I guess they all had my grandmother's number saved."

Daniel Threshton, a celebrated restaurateur with establishments in Boston, New York, and Chicago, met Laurel years ago when she reviewed his first Boston venture. Since then, their friendship had grown close, especially after she came to know his wife and family.

"Sounds like you've struck gold, at least in terms of material," Daniel said. "If you really want to do this. It's a departure for you."

"That's exactly why I wanted your opinion. Does anyone even care about this kind of thing anymore?"

"There's a market for just about everything," Daniel said. "Low country cuisine is trending."

"Funny—I've never considered any of this low country."

"It's just what self-important chefs like me call Grandma's peach cobbler when we want to sound inventive. But seriously, Laurel, why not go for it? Even if it only sells regionally, it could buy you time while you figure out your next big thing."

Laurel smiled, feeling the tension melt away. "You think it's worth it?"

"I do. In fact, Denise and I have talked about opening a place in Charleston or Savannah. Who knows—maybe I'll end up serving your finds on my next menu. You've got nothing to lose."

"And maybe a story to tell."

"Exactly. Just don't leave out the sappy ones. The emotion, Laurel— that's what makes it sing. You're a storyteller. Usually, it's cities you bring to life. Now, maybe it's people."

Daniel's words echoed through her thoughts as Laurel pulled into the driveway of Brenda Rawlings, one of many fried-chicken hopefuls. Brenda had called earlier that week, swearing up and down that her mother's chicken recipe was the best Laurel would ever taste. Judging by the number of similar claims from other women, fried chicken was evidently sacred ground in Scroggins.

Brenda greeted her warmly at the door. Laurel recognized her vaguely, but it was Brenda's husband, Bud, who jogged her memory. He was the loud churchgoer who echoed the preacher's sermon with enthusiasm last Sunday.

Their home was a far cry from Laurel's aged farmhouse. Brick, modern, carpeted, with a large kitchen island. It was the first house she'd been in that made her feel like she was living in the present day.

The cook got to work quickly, showing Laurel her arrangement of ingredients ready to use on the table. Brenda clearly watched a lot of cooking programs on television judging from her immaculately laid island. Every bowl, large or small, was matched with its ingredients, from flour to whisked eggs to paprika poured into them. Not a stray spice bottle or sack of meal was in sight. Brenda was camera-ready!

Bud, grabbing his keys, leaned in with a theatrical tone, kissing Brenda goodbye. "We got flour—UNBLEACHED—heading into cornmeal. CORNMEAL's been sifted, folks! And next up... that's right! We got the EGG DIP!" Laurel chuckled. He was a character, clearly beloved for antics like these.

Once Bud was gone, Brenda got down to business. "Now, I cheated a little, just for time's sake. You gotta soak the chicken overnight in a brine, then let it stand 20 minutes drying on a towel before you get started. I did all that already." She continued, moving from bowl to bowl pouring various spices and herbs into her flour bowl, which she combined with a bit of cornmeal before using her sieve to grind them together into a fine powder. Lifting a chicken leg, she explained, "We dip the chicken into the flour mix. Twirl it around good to cover it."

"Then we put it in the oil to fry!" Laurel smiled, glancing at the preheated oil in a skillet on the stovetop. She had to admit she was quickly developing hunger pains and the taste for fried chicken.

"No, no," Brenda corrected, showing her the proper way. "It's not time for that yet. That, Miss Laurel, is where a lot of people make their mistake. We take this floured chicken and dredge through the eggs. Then we let it rest on this plate for about half an hour." She went through a few more of the chicken pieces, showing Laurel again the procedure, and then let Laurel handle the final three pieces herself. "You see, the egg will dry, locking in the batter under it. This is going to keep your crust from slipping off while cooking. So, we just wait a bit and move to the next step."

While the egg coated chicken was drying, Laurel asked Brenda about the recipe's creation and if it had a special story behind it or behind the person who wrote it. Brenda seemed confused at her meaning. "You see, Mrs. Rawlings, this isn't only a cookbook. It's more like a collection of stories—with recipes attached. I'm hoping to capture not just the food but the history behind the dish."

Brenda didn't seem sure she quite understood what Laurel was after, admitting, "I can't think of a thing regarding my mother in relation to her fried chicken. I can tell you something interesting that happened with me once when I was making this chicken. But you'll think it's silly."

Laurel forced a smile, beginning to think Brenda Rawlings chicken probably wasn't going to make the book. "Tell me anyway. I'm already here, and you never know."

Brenda, a shy woman, wavered a little more on the value of her story. Only after a little more coaxing, did she agree to share it. It was not about her as it turned out, but her daughter Emily. It happened a few years ago after Emily had been married a couple of years.

"We were anxious for grandchildren," she confided to Laurel. "So was Vince's momma and daddy. Vince is Emily's husband. His momma and I are friends. We talked a lot in the beginning about how we couldn't wait for grandchildren. But none ever came. Soon we stopped mentioning it to the kids because we could tell from their avoidance of the subject, something was wrong. Turns out Emily wasn't able to get pregnant easily." Brenda's frown seemed more for emphasis on the disheartening part of the story than any actual anguish. Then she went on, "Emily and Vince loved each other so much, and they really wanted a baby. One day, it was the night before Easter I think, Emily was here with me prepping this chicken for us to fry Easter day. It was the first time she spoke about her problem to me. Oh, Miss Laurel, you should have seen us standing here in this kitchen, squalling our eyes out over the chicken. Didn't even need any salt thanks to us."

Laurel, understanding when it was appropriate for her to appear as if she felt a stir of emotion, gripped her hand over Brenda's sweetly. "I am sure it was a difficult conversation."

"It really was," Brenda continued. "I kept cutting up the chicken and putting the pieces in to soak overnight, while Emily made up the flour mixture, so it'd be ready the next morning. Save time, you know. We had church services Easter morning, so for the chicken to be ready to fry we had to pre-make the batter."

It wasn't necessary to explain that part to Laurel, but Laurel allowed her to recount her memory as she wanted because it was obvious this chicken was going to take some time to fry.

"We prayed together. Prayed right over this countertop. Me, with wet hands dripping in egg yolk, and Emily's fingers coated with flour and cornmeal. We pretty much made a paste together by the time we was done. But we held hands and gave it over to God."

Laurel had to remind herself to freeze the sympathetic smile on her face, and not roll her eyes as she would have previously done before moving here. In Scroggins, religion was not to be scoffed at, and Laurel was in the minority.

"We finished praying and went back to our chicken," Brenda said, moving on. "We heard a scratching on the door right after we loaded the chicken in the fridge to soak. Emily went to the kitchen door and found the skinniest little cat you've ever seen. It was gray and its tail was missing. We could tell from the looks of it, it hadn't ate in days."

Laurel maintained her polite smile, but mentally began asking herself, *has this been about saving a cat the whole time?*

"Usually, wild cats are skittish," Brenda explained. "But that cat let Emily pick it right up. She gave it some milk and then that crazy cat let her hold it like it had always belonged to her. Emily ended up taking it home with her. And that cat never left her side. My Emily fed it, and took care of it, and it got to be a real healthy-looking cat. She named it Justine. Emily always said if they ever had a son, she wanted to name it Justin, but since this was a girl cat she named it Justine."

Realizing this story was not interesting enough for a book, Laurel had to say something to the sweet woman. "Did the cat help her work through her sadness over not being able to have a baby?"

Suddenly Brenda produced a big toothy smile. "That's where it gets weird, Miss Laurel. And silly on my part to think what I thought...what I still believe. It wasn't a month later Emily found out she was pregnant! We were all excited but scared to death too because even the doctor kept saying he didn't think she'd carry to term. Emily quit work so she could take things easy, and we just waited and prayed."

"What happened?" Laurel asked, genuinely interested now to know. "Did Emily make it to full term?"

"It was that cat," Brenda's eyes widened as she stifled a giggle. "That cat, Justine, laid on Emily's stomach, purring and purring every time she sat down anywhere. There was nowhere Emily went that that cat didn't go with her. The store, over here to my house, nowhere." Brenda clasped her hands together in thanks as she revealed, "Emily carried that baby to full term. Vince called us one night, all excited, telling us to meet them at the hospital. When she went in to deliver, we were all so thrilled and excited. Emily gave birth to a perfectly healthy boy!"

Laurel found herself relieved to hear it. "Did the cat get jealous of the baby?"

Brenda leaned in over the counter, a fanciful look in her eye as she answered, "Vince went home late that night to feed the cat, but he couldn't find it. So, I went over the next morning to feed it and I couldn't find trace of it nowhere. Last time Vince remembered seeing it was laying on Emily's stomach when her contractions started. He said it was in the window looking out at them when he got Emily in the car to go to the hospital. None of us ever saw Justine the cat again."

Furrowing her brow in confusion, Laurel didn't understand the importance. Not being a person of faith, or holding any spiritual or fantastical beliefs, Brenda's story was lost on her until the woman explained.

"Emily came home with our grandson the next day, but the cat was gone. I believe, and so does my daughter...silly as it may sound...our prayer got answered that day before Easter. Right after we prayed for Emily to conceive one day, that cat scratched at the door."

"You don't mean..." Laurel hesitated before even saying the words. "You don't really believe the cat had anything to do with it, do you?"

Brenda nodded her head with faithful certainty. "I do. We all do. That cat...Justine...brought the baby. And she stayed with my daughter all the way through like an angel from Heaven, protecting it and giving it strength until it could get born. And so, when the baby came, Justine left. Her job was done. My Emily named her son Justin, so we wouldn't ever forget our miracle."

Laurel didn't say anything for a moment. Searching for a proper response but falling short. Brenda understood how difficult her tale would be for less spiritual people to believe and was even kind enough to absolve Laurel from any expectations.

"I know that isn't really book-worthy. I don't expect to see it in your cookbook." Brenda smiled sweetly and added, "But that's my chicken story."

Laurel looked at her across the island and found herself smiling—legitimately entertained by Brenda's story of hope and mysteriousness. "Mrs. Rawlings, I think that may be the most moving story I have ever heard."

The response came as a surprise to Brenda Rawlings. "You think I may be right?" she asked excitedly. "The cat somehow brought baby Justin to us?"

"No, I don't actually believe that," admitted Laurel. "But there is absolutely nothing wrong with you choosing to. And it doesn't really matter if I believe it. What matters is your story stirred emotion within me. Mrs. Rawlings, I am not an emotional person. But when you told me Emily successfully gave birth—I felt as if it were my moment too. Your tale is one of innocence and hope. I want to use it in my book."

Brenda was almost giddy with the news. Laurel's approval of her tale gave Brenda the validation she'd needed to justify her treasured belief in how she got her grandson. Putting her joy aside for the moment and returning to the serious art of fried chicken, Brenda announced, "Okay. Now let's prove to you how delicious this chicken is. The pieces have rested enough. Now pour the remaining flour in this sack."

Looking at the brown paper grocery bag, Laurel did not understand. Brenda demonstrated for her, explaining how the final step was recoating each piece with flour again, but instead of dredging it this time, shake it in the bag so only the amount of batter needed would cling to the chicken.

After Laurel shook the bag vigorously, she placed a piece in the hot cast iron skillet to fry. "Never put more than three pieces in at a time," Brenda cautioned. "And turn only when it looks like the bottom is starting to brown. We only turn it twice."

"Is the iron skillet important?"

Laughing as if now it was Laurel saying something silly, Brenda answered, "My dear, the skillet is the main ingredient."

Brenda's Recipe known in real life as...

MICAH'S FRIED CHICKEN

(This takes two days)

Ingredients

Pickle juice (dump the juice out of a jar, then refill jar with vinegar to save your pickles)

Sugar

Chicken (cut up, WITH skin) (you can use boneless breasts if prefer. Good, but not as good)

Flour and Cornmeal (OR omit both if you can find Autrey's chicken flour, it's the best)

Water

2 Eggs whisked

Salt

Pepper

Paper sack (small, and you might need several. They tear when wet)

Oil (Vegetable is best, or if you're rich, peanut oil...but that costs a lot)

1. Pour jar of pickle juice into a pot or plastic container (either works as long as you have a lid). Add equal parts sugar and water. (Usually 1 cup each, but if you are making a lot of chicken for a big gathering, like Homecoming or Thanksgiving, add more as long as it stays equal parts. You may want a second jar of pickle juice too if using more than one chicken.) Stir well to marry up the sugar and liquid.
2. Put chicken pieces in liquid (this is called a brine). Make sure chicken is covered in brine and stir up well to get sugar and pickle juice mixed with the water. Refrigerate overnight and until you are an hour from cooking.
3. Remove chicken from liquid and let air dry 15 minutes. (You can pour the liquid in the sink now.)

4. While chicken is drying, salt and pepper both sides. (If you found Autrey flour, don't salt. It has it in the flour)
5. Pour oil into a skillet. (It doesn't have to be a cast iron skillet, but if you have one it adds extra Umph!) Pour enough oil to cover half of the chicken pieces once you insert. (Do not let chicken be covered in more oil than that.)
6. Heat oil to a good medium temp. Hot enough to start frying right away, but not too hot to overcook the outside of the chicken too fast.
7. In a bowl pour your Autrey flour, or the flour and cornmeal (use a ¾ cup flour to ¼ cup cornmeal ratio). Then do the same in a paper bag, set aside for later.
8. Place chicken, one piece at a time, into flour. Press firmly, turning a few times to make sure it is fully coated. (Even slightly lift skin a little to make sure all under there is floured too. It makes it even better.)
9. Dredge chicken through egg coating and let dry a few minutes while coating 2 more pieces
10. Once dried some, shake 1 piece at a time in the paper bag flour.
11. Place chicken in skillet, but pieces should not touch. (This means only three pieces at a time. So, if cooking a lot, you might want two skillets going at once.)
Let chicken fry about 5 minutes, then turn.
Okay, here's a tip. Use a fork, not tongs. Tongs sometimes scrap the batter off, whereas a fork you just puncture through and turn. Keep a spoon near to help you press the piece off the fork without removing batter.
Now, if at any time some batter comes off, don't panic. Take your spoon and dip into the flour mix you had the chicken in, and sort of sprinkle onto the messed up place.

It'll be yellowy and powdery on the skin when the rest of the batter has cooked some already. Dip the spoon into the hot oil and kind of splash up on the new batter area, until it is oil soaked like the rest. It will be fine.

Turn chicken every 5 minutes or so until done.

IF the skin is browning too fast, lower your heat and cover with a lid.

IF using a lid, open with lid towards you like a shield to avoid oil splatter on you. Remember, moisture has collected under the lid which will drop into oil when you lift it. It's gonna splatter.

Chicken is done when the skin is a golden brown AND you can stick a pointy knife into the piece and no red juice bubbles out. Clear juice means done. Red juice means its still raw inside. Check BOTH sides for clear juice before removing.

Remove pieces to cool on a paper towel

Repeat your flouring process to next batch of chicken and follow same steps as before.

Now, by the time you have used the skillet twice, that oil needs to be changed. Some of the excess batter has flaked off a bit by now, and if you don't use fresh oil, you're going to have some scorching and old oil taste.

If making a lot of chicken and want to keep the completed pieces warm, turn your oven to the lowest setting and place on a plate or pan in there. Do not stack chicken. Each piece should not touch any other.

Also keep in mind if making a lot. You probably want to use fresh flour mixture after 3 or 4 batches.

CHAPTER NINE

Human Driving Hazard

S ummer rain carries a kind of magic often unnoticed in cities or suburbs. Laurel had never recognized anything remarkable about rain in the summer. Rain was rain, no matter what time of year it fell. Wet, inconvenient, and often bracing. The hard pounding against the roof made dressing feel like a race against the storm. She was heading to visit Althea Roberts, someone she'd never met, whose home was tucked somewhere near the high school. With any luck, GPS would cooperate.

Stepping out onto the front porch, Laurel paused beneath the overhang. Water rushed from the roof in thick, silver sheets. The porch swing swayed gently, beads of rain glistening on its wooden slats. A ribbon of moisture crept along the edge of the porch floor, just inside the safety of the eaves. She stopped for a moment and took in the world before her.

Clouds veiled the sun, but the trees and grass looked richer, more vibrant—like nature had been freshly painted. The kudzu tangled along the roadside shimmered like an emerald curtain, beautiful in its wildness. It almost made you forget the way it slowly strangled everything beneath it. The air was just as heavy and humid as it had been since she came to Scroggins. She always thought rain cooled things off, but this storm seemed to amplify the heat turning the air to steam.

By the time she got into her car, the downpour had softened to a drizzle. The drive down Hogg Road felt smoother than usual—no plumes of dust kicked up beneath her tires. The rain had pressed everything into stillness. Her GPS guided her without issue, and she pulled into Althea Roberts' driveway just as the rain picked up again. Thankfully, this rainfall was much lighter than the earlier downpour, and the clouds were thinning. A middle-aged woman was waiting at the door when Laurel pulled up. She waved for her to remain in the car until she managed to open an umbrella. Rushing out to meet Laurel, she escorted her to the house under dry cover, identifying herself as Althea.

Once on the porch, Althea lowered the umbrella, closing and reopening it several times to shake the excess water free. She looked up to the sunny sky and declared, "Well, looks like the devil is beating his wife behind the door again."

"I'm sorry?" Laurel replied, unfamiliar with the term.

Althea laughed, explaining, Just something my granddaddy always said whenever it was raining with the sun still out."

They went inside where Laurel discreetly sized up her hostess. Althea, possibly in her forties, wore her salon-highlighted hair with visible roots, betraying she'd missed her last appointment. Her home was rather nice, much more upscale than Bessie's house. And with the cool indoor air and absence of a familiar hum, Laurel knew Althea had modernized central heating and cooling. No rattly window units in sight.

After a few minutes of polite small talk (which Laurel despised), she guided the conversation toward her purpose for visiting. Althea leaned in with barely contained excitement. "I'd love for you to include one of my recipes in your book! Puddin' Corder said you were looking for dishes that come with a story."

"That's right," Laurel said. "Although it will be a cookbook, it is primarily a collection of Southern tales about life here and the experiences of those who live here now or lived here long ago."

Althea's eyes lit up. "Well, I got two or three I can tell you. If you don't want to put them all in, I am sure there's one you'll like."

Her over anxiousness made Laurel slightly uncomfortable. Clearly, Althea wanted to be featured, but Laurel dreaded the possibility of poor storytelling—or worse, mediocre food. But she reminded herself, for some people, this was their only shot at being in print. She wouldn't judge too quickly.

"Where do we begin?" Althea asked her guest. "Do I show you the recipes? Or should I have cooked them for you? Or do you want to hear the stories first just to see if it's what you are looking for?"

"Why not show me the recipe first," Laurel answered. "If it seems like a good fit, then you can tell me the story about it."

The first recipe Althea presented for consideration was for sweet potato casserole. It appeared to be a unique take on the dish, although Laurel had very little knowledge to go on. It seemed a little complicated, which in her mind must equate to being better than a customary interpretation. However, the story accompanying it turned out to be one of the craziest situations Laurel ever heard.

"It happened on my way to my sister's 50th birthday party," Althea began. "My husband Curtis had recently had a knee replacement." She could have ended it there, having already set up the moment. But as Laurel was quickly learning, Southern people find it necessary to supply backstory—no matter how irrelevant. "He played football for Alabama in college and tore up his knee way back then," Althea informed Laurel, layering in the pointless background. Had problems with it for years after, until he finally had to get a new one. Probably didn't help matters when he decided to get back in shape in his 30's and took up running every afternoon."

Althea circled back to the beginning of her tale now once she'd illustrated the legitimate need for a knee replacement—as if Laurel might be under the impression people sometimes got knee surgery without cause. "Curtis was about 2 weeks into recovery, when my sister had her 50th birthday party. He wasn't cleared to drive yet by the doctor. That's why I was driving us to Linda's 50th surprise party."

Laurel wondered for a moment why it was necessary to explain that Althea was driving unless it was a cultural dictate in the south that men were never driven by their wives if they were capable. She dismissed the thought and tuned back in to Althea's story.

"My niece doesn't have much money," Althea confided. "And she asked guests if we would bring a dish for her mother's surprise party."

"Hence, your sweet potato casserole?"

"Right!" Althea exclaimed, slapping Laurel's knee. "Anyway, I was driving along the highway, headed for the interstate. My sister lives in Cottondale, you see. And I came up behind a truck, transfer truck, you understand."

Laurel nodded.

"Well, you must know even from your short time in Scroggins, when you're on the highway, especially moving towards the interstate onramp, there aren't a great many stops along the way. It's a straight shot and most houses or turn offs are back this way more towards Scroggins, proper."

Laurel was beginning to see where this was going now.

"Some blame fool must have braked abruptly to turn off somewhere..."

Yep, Laurel thought, *I see where it's going.* She also made a mental note to remember that "blame" must be the word proper Southern ladies use in place of "damn". She'd heard it several times now.

Althea continued, "That 18-wheeler was just as surprised as me by the car suddenly braking to turn. He slammed on his breaks, and so did I." She paused a second, adding in, "Now Curtis always says I follow people too close when I drive. Even though he is wrong to assume that, in this case I guess he was right because I slid up into that transfer truck's trailer. I didn't crash, you understand, just tapped it. It was so light even he didn't seem to take notice."

Laurel grew confused now, having expected this story to be about a car accident.

Things became clearer a few seconds later. "Well, when I tapped that trailer, I must have hooked my car's bumper to a hitch or something on it. Because when he took off again, we did too."

Laurel gasped. "You mean you were stuck to the back of his cargo?"

"You better know it!" Althea laughed, slapping her guest's leg again. "Well, there we were, me and Curtis, hooked onto this 18-wheeler, going everywhere he went. I tried honking, but every time I did, he swerved a little to the right. I finally figured he couldn't see me in his rearview mirror because I was so close up on him. I guess he thought somebody was trying to pass him and he would move over a little so they could, but then they never passed. We got on the interstate, and you wouldn't believe how many cars went by us honking and trying to get that driver's attention, but he never stopped. Curtis was scared to death, shouting at me about what a terrible driver I am, but it was not my fault. No matter how many people honked, that driver paid no attention. Maybe they get honked at enough they tune it out. I don't rightly know. But he never figured out we were stuck to him."

"How long were you attached?"

"When we passed through Cottondale and started moving into Tuscaloosa, I figured we were in it till that trucker pulled into a truck stop for gas. Up head a few miles, I knew there was a truck stop, but blame if that man didn't pass it by! By now I figured we may get all the way to Detroit before this fool understood a car was attached to the back of him! We were riding it out for about an hour until he turned off onto Highway 43, out there near Fosters."

Althea stared at Laurel as if she were expected to know what or where Fosters was. Finally, Laurel just nodded and that was enough for Althea to pick back up with her story.

"It was dark now," Althea explained. "And most people had already come home from work, so 43 was fairly deserted. Then as we were hustling down the highway, the truck must have hit a good-sized pothole, that road is covered with them. But when we hit that pothole, my car sorta bounced free of whatever it was hooked on."

"You were finally safe!" Laurel cried.

"You'd think so, wouldn't you." Althea teased with a grin. "Understand, we'd been chauffeured by this 18-wheeler for over an hour. I gave up attempting to steer my car's wheels free, so my hands weren't on the steering wheel when we popped loose."

"Oh, no!"

"Oh yes! Well, we went barreling sideways off the road." Althea was perched on the edge of her chair now, as if living the rush of the experience again. "Now out there in Fosters it's nothing but farmland and grown over fields. When we went sailing off the highway, we popped over the ditch on the side of the road and lost one of our tires. Then we kind of coasted a little ways, until we slid up under a road sign with one of those candidates running for office. Can't remember now which one it was, some ridiculously made-up sounding name like Flip, Chip, Kip. That's it! Kip Bleeker. Anyways, the car was basically stuck right where it was."

"I have a question?" Laurel asked. "At any time did you think to use your cell phone to call for help?"

"I tried that, but my phone at the time wasn't good about holding a charge. I had a new one on the way but it hadn't been delivered yet. Curtis never saw the use in him having a phone because nobody ever calls him anyway, and he said if I ever needed him, I was either in the house with him, or he was at work, and I could call him there."

Laurel then asked, "What did you do?"

"We knew Nick's in the Stick's wasn't too far back down the road a piece."

"Nick's?"

"In the Sticks," Althea answered. "It's a famous steak house out there. Big tradition around here. Anyway, I figured we'd walk to Nick's and call a tow truck. Now wouldn't you just know it was a Monday! We walked about half a mile, and they were closed. The one or two houses we passed didn't have any lights on, so we went back to the car while I poked around with my phone trying to get the charge cord to work. Something was wrong with where it goes into the phone. The post or something. Whatever it was, it wouldn't work unless it was completely still and pinched between my fingers to the port. We finally got it to charge enough to call for help. By then, we were so hungry we just ate that sweet potato casserole ourselves with our fingers."

Laurel found the story charming, liking the humorous slant it would provide. "I may punch it up a little here and there," she warned Althea. "Add a few more moments of peril or expound on the comical tones."

The woman gave her permission to do whatever she liked to "juice it up" for her readers. She then asked if Laurel was pleased enough with the story or if she wished to hear the other one. Though Laurel felt comfortable using the first story, she allowed Althea to tell the other. It was much shorter, but possibly even funnier than its predecessor.

Althea began once more, by explaining another medical happenstance regarding her husband Curtis. In this story, he was recovering from shin splints. However, the moment she told this to Laurel, a man's voice called out from the hall. Curtis was home. Judging from his freshly combed, but damp hair, he must have been showering. "That is not what is was, darling."

"Oh, hey!" Althea exclaimed upon seeing her husband enter the room. "Miss Hogue, this is my husband, Curtis."

"It's Holden," Laurel corrected. "But you can call me Laurel. It is nice to meet you." Curtis shook her hand, still drying water from his ear with a towel even though he was fully dressed. "I was just hearing about your adventure with the 18-wheeler."

"Wasn't that outrageous!" Curtis chuckled. "My wife is a splendid woman, but we try to keep her in the passenger seat as often as we can."

Althea asked him if it wasn't shin splints he had when her other story took place, what was it? He answered that it was planters' fasciitis.

"See what running gets you?" his wife quipped. "Anyway, that's why I was driving that time."

Surprised by the comment, Laurel gazed incredulously at Althea. "Please don't say this was another automobile accident!"

Blushing, Althea declared, "Guilty as charged. But this one also was not my fault."

"Darling both were your fault," Curtis teased, walking to stand behind her chair. "Which is why our insurance premium is so high. But it's okay," he said, patting her shoulder. "It could have happened to anybody."

Out of his wife's line of sight, Curtis shook his head at Laurel, *mouthing it was all her fault.*

"Curtis had feet issues, I guess," Althea went on. "Anyway, we were due at Training Union."

Laurel paused the story to ask what that might be. Curtis explained it was basically Sunday School, but at night, as Althea continued. "We just got a new car. Automatic. But you see, Miss Laurel, I learned to drive on stick shift. I was used to having a gas pedal, a brake, and a clutch. Three pedals. This new car only had two."

Curtis took over with a highly amused look on his face. It was obvious he'd told this a multitude of times over the years and greatly enjoyed the telling. "My darling wife here," he began. "Was trying to back out of our driveway."

"I did back out of the driveway!" she chirped.

"Yes, you did, darling. With gusto." Curtis stifled a grin as he looked down at Laurel. "You see, Miss Laurel, being used to pressing a clutch first, my wife depressed the gas pedal quite firmly. That car went flying backward at full speed."

A gasp escaped from Laurel's mouth.

"Althea was a little confused, at first. Shocked maybe," Curtis explained. "Anyone else would have snapped to and hit the brake.

But my Althea froze up, and we zoomed out of our driveway, through the neighbor's yard across the street, and smack into *and through* their living room wall!"

"You didn't!" Laurel shrieked.

Shrinking slightly in her chair, his embarrassed wife replied, "Well, yes I did a little."

Curtis sent Laurel a subtle wink, explaining, "Our neighbors are good friends of ours. They were at their dining table having their supper. Oh, you should have seen it, Miss Laurel!" Curtis erupted in excitement, "I mean, the living room window blew out, the wood and siding exploded in, the ceiling joists buckled from the load bearing wall punching out! Nothing but wood, vinyl, glass, dust, and sheetrock hanging. She ran over their couch, their coffee table, and knocked their bird cage down. Our neighbors are sitting at the table, trying to have their dinner and our car is sitting three feet away from them. Not to mention their pet cockatiels are now fluttering all around, scared to death. It was a sight to remember!"

"What did they say?"

With the timing of a professional comedian, Curtis Roberts answered, "Althea just rolls down the car window and asks, 'what are we having for supper?'"

Laurel broke into laughter. Normally, laughing at another person's misfortune would be bad manners, but seeing how much Curtis Roberts enjoyed telling the story lent her permission. Once she caught her breath, Laurel asked the ever-important question, "What did your neighbors do?"

"They asked us to join them," Curtis said. "You know, once they realized we were okay, and they got over the immediate shock."

"They weren't angry?"

"If they were, it would be rude to say so." Curtis explained. "Their son once accidentally backed over our dog and broke his leg, and we were real good about it. Accidents happen and neighbors forgive.

Besides, we had insurance."

"And Clara was able to get all new drapes, carpet, and furniture!" Althea pointed out. "She was thrilled." Picking up the end of the story, Althea presented a handwritten note to Laurel, "They were having 10 Bean Soup and asked us if we'd eaten yet. So, we tromped over the mess and had dinner with them while we waited for the insurance man to come over. She gave me the recipe. It was mighty good soup."

Laurel locked eyes with Curtis and asked, "Please tell me you have taken her keys away?"

Althea's Recipe known in real life as...

COUSIN DAWN'S SWEET POTATO CASSEROLE

Ingredients

3 medium sized sweet potatoes

1 ½ cup All Purpose flour

¾ cup Crisco

Buttermilk (you'll eyeball the amount)

Wax Paper (Not necessary, but saves a mess)

Sugar

1 stick Butter cut into 1 tbsp squares

1. Slice potatoes into ½ inch round slices

2. Boil sweet potatoes until tender but not broken (save water)
3. Grease a round casserole dish
4. In a bowl add flour and Crisco. Cut Crisco into the flour (take two butter knives and cross slice, kind of mixing the shortening into the flour but not exactly blending it)
5. Add buttermilk until mix is moist but still thick
6. Whip dough in a mixer or by hand until smooth
7. Roll out wax paper and divide dough into 1/3 parts
8. Take 1/3 of the dough and roll out wide enough to cut into strips to line the side of dish
9. Place the strips along the sides of the dish (Just the sides, not the bottom)
10. lace a layer of cooked sweet potatoes on the bottom of dish (use half of your total amount of potatoes, you're making two layers)
11. Pour a cup of sugar over potatoes (1 ½ cups if you prefer)

12. Lay 4 tbsp of butter across
13. Pour in a little of the reserved water to just lightly cover
14. Roll out another 1/3 dough and cut into 1" x 4" strips
15. Crisscross dough strips over the potatoes and butter
16. Repeat layers of potatoes, sugar, and butter
17. Cover again with a little reserved water
18. Roll last of dough to cover the top of dish and poke small holes in top of dough
19. Cook on a small stove top eye on medium low for 25 minutes (bubbles should pop through the holes some)
20. Preheat oven to 425° while casserole is cooking on stovetop
21. Move dish to the oven and cook another 25 minutes
22. Once done, run a knife around the edge of one side of the top to pour out the excess water. Then it's ready!

CHAPTER TEN

Barbeque Sauce and Buckshot

Janice Hogue knew at once when Laurel phoned to ask if she could join her for church again, it wasn't the Holy Spirit stirring within her, it was the hope of seeing Linc Hopkins. Laurel feigned ignorance at the accusation, but Janice was not fooled. When Laurel stepped off the porch, in a slim-waisted lime-green dress that hit just above the knee, Janice raised an eyebrow. Her hair had more glisten than it ever had before, causing Janice to think maybe Laurel used a little highlight rinse the night before.

"Look at you, all dressed up, and giddier than I have ever seen you be before."

"How do you know I am not naturally lighthearted?" Laurel replied with a grin. "You've only known me for two weeks."

"Two weeks of which I have spent a lot of time with you." Janice smiled. "I think you are a little smitten on our High School Principal."

Laurel's coy expression shifted to one of surprise. "Is that what he does? He seems far too young and easy going to be a school administrator. My old Principal was a quick-tempered bald man with a toupee."

Janice laughed, reminding Laurel things have probably changed some since her school days. Walking into church, several people waved showing their delight in seeing Bessie's granddaughter return. Janice led Laurel to the same place on the same pew as they had sat last Sunday, telling her quietly that it would always be her seat from now on.

"It's a huge show of disrespect to sit in someone else's spot," Janice whispered. "Where you sit that first time, is where you sit forever."

"What if it's a bad seat?" Laurel asked.

"Well, this isn't exactly a rock concert," Janice quipped. "There are no bad seats, only ones of prominence." It was clear Laurel didn't understand, so Janice explained. "Old Mrs. Conway has owned that second pew, right-side aisle seat since before I was born. If anyone tried to sit in her spot—well, let's just say there'd be an uprising."

"What if she doesn't come one Sunday?"

"Unless she dies," Janice smirked. "You best keep your tail out of her seat. You're lucky, you inherited Bessie's spot. Where you are right now is yours fair and square for life—as long as you live in Scroggins."

Laurel understood the message Janice's tone implied. It was her new friend's subtle way of trying to sweeten the deal and convince Laurel not to move once summer was over.

"Your church pew is sacred," Janice continued. "I used to be four rows back. I had to wait until Ustus died to move up here by Bessie."

Brother Daws had taken his position in the pulpit by this time and began his Sunday welcome before turning things over to the choir for a few hymns. During the ritual of most parishioners standing, hymn books open, pretending to sing along with the choir, Laurel tried to casually scan the pews behind her. Janice had practically given her a map of where Linc would be. The high school principal wouldn't dare sit in a different place. Laurel's eyes found him. Linc was with his grandmother and parents again, and he was looking directly at her with a grin. Delva, seeing the exchange between them, sent an accepting wink Laurel's way.

Once services were over, Laurel waited a moment by herself before following Janice out of the church, pretending something fell out of her purse on the pew. The pause gave Linc time to come to her.

"I told you I would come back if you did," he said playfully.

"And I did." Laurel smiled, but then realized she had no idea what to say next, relying on the obvious, "I take it you are not a regular church goer?"

"I come when I can, mostly for Granny." Linc said, then felt the need to clarify. "Don't misunderstand, I'm a believer, I just don't enjoy my faith tied up in someone else's box. Normally, I am in far too much need for a day to myself after my work week. But in summer, I have less demands." Then with a coy smirk, he added, "Plus it never hurts to keep Granny happy."

"I like your grandmother. She's a nice lady."

"I suggest you don't get her riled if you want to keep thinking that."

Laurel smiled, "It is good of you to give her your Sunday morning. I am sure Principal duties can wear you out by the end of the week."

Linc clapped his hands together with a cunning grin, "You've been asking about me?"

Laurel's cheeks flushed. "I haven't been *asking* about you. Your name came up, and they mentioned what you do. That's it."

"A white woman, surrounded by other white women, was told about what a black man does for a living without provocation? Doubtful."

She was surprised by the candor. "Seems to me Scroggins is reasonably liberal considering."

"Don't let church fool you," Linc cautioned. "My family has been coming here for generations because my great grandmother took care of one of the founding members. It wasn't so much integration that put us here, as it was years of servitude. By the time my great grandmother and the woman she looked after both died, we'd been here so many years it would have been stranger for us to stop."

"And here I was believing Scroggins was a surprisingly evolved place. You've blown my fantasy to bits."

Linc gave another devilish smile and said, "My apologies. Maybe you will allow me to supply a replacement fantasy. So to speak."

His flirtation was suggestive, but in a gentlemanly way Laurel found charming. Apparently, he wasn't used to someone like her, and it showed when she said, rather bluntly, "I want to go on a date with you. Would you like to go out with me sometime?"

Stunned, Linc muttered, "Yeah. I'd really like that."

"Great," Laurel said. "Let me give you my number."

Linc Hopkins narrowed his brow with an amused chuckle, "It's okay, Laurel. Everyone in town has your phone number. Your grandmother was a friend to practically everybody. I used to cut her grass every week when I was a kid."

"How industrious," Laurel teased. "Please don't hold it against me if she wasn't nice to you."

"Bessie?" Linc replied with a bright smile. "Bessie Hogue was never *not* nice. In fact, she paid me twice what anybody else did. Course, she had a lot of yard."

"I didn't know her," Laurel admitted. "I'm glad she was good to you."

Linc suddenly shifted awkwardly, looking down to the floor a couple of times as if in search of words. "Speaking of Bessie's yard...you are new. So...no one is going to tell you this. They are all just waiting to see when you figure it out."

"Figure what out?" Laurel replied.

"Your grass is getting pretty high," Linc smirked with a boyish grin. "That field outside your kitchen window isn't supposed to be grown up like that. You are going to need to hire someone to handle your maintenance, unless you know how to run that tractor in your shed."

"I have a tractor and a shed?"

Linc leaned back registering her remark with great amusement. "Laurel, you own 100 acres around you. I think our first date is going to be me showing you around your property."

Delva motioned to her grandson to hurry up so they could leave, shouting across the now nearly empty church. "Boy, I got a roast in the oven."

Linc rejoined his family while Laurel moved outdoors to locate Janice, and her Aunt Flossie. They were standing at the bottom of the church steps chatting with Brother and Mrs. Daws. As Flossie saw her approaching, she shook a shameful finger Laurel's direction. "You never did come see me."

Smiling, and giving a friendly wink at Brother Daws, Laurel replied, "Yes, ma'am I know. That's why I called Reverend Daws last night to tell him not to worry about driving you home today. I am taking you to my house for lunch and I'll take you home this afternoon."

The news lit up Flossie's face. Invitations were rare for women her age, and the chance to spend time with her great-niece was an added joy. On the drive to Hogg Road, Flossie admitted she hadn't been back inside her sister's house in almost a year. Bessie normally came out to visit her. During Bessie's final weeks, she hadn't been able to visit at all. Janice declined the invitation to stay for lunch, understanding the two women needed time alone together. Janice let them out in Bessie's driveway and went home.

As Laurel helped her elderly aunt along towards the porch, Flossie advised against it. "I ain't young and spry as you, honey. Best get me in through the kitchen. Fewer steps."

"Seems like everyone around here enters homes through the kitchen," Laurel commented. "Why did anyone even build a front door?" Her own remark sparked a thought, a question she'd never asked but wondered about since she'd moved into her grandmother's house. "Aunt Flossie, why are there two front doors so close to each other on the porch?"

"Oh, baby, that's just practical," Flossie replied. "Weren't no such thing as a air conditioner back when we was raised. Shoot, my Norman didn't put one in our window till about the late 60s. Folks needed two doors open in front, with two doors or windows open in back to channel the wind in and cool things off."

Laurel couldn't help but smile at the simplicity of the answer. That probably also explained why there was no hallway in Bessie's house and each room opened to the next. As they drew nearer to the back porch, and the back yard came more into view, Flossie looked around and said, "Honey, you got to get this grass cut."

First Linc, now Flossie. Laurel was becoming thoroughly embarrassed. But Flossie wasn't finished with her assessment. "And put some livin' plants in those hanging baskets out front. Your grandmaw would roll over in her grave if she knew her porch was such a mess. Bessie always had flowers all over that porch in summer."

"I guess I haven't thought about it," Laurel admitted. "I never go out there except to leave or come in."

Flossie's voice, weak with her years, made a pitchy whistle sound when she let out a cackle, "Honey, you don't know what you're missing! Bessie and me would sit out in that porch swing for hours just chatting away. When you got those baskets brimming over with pretty things, smell-good things, and the breeze gets to blowin' through. You ain't never felt nothing more peaceful."

They reached the screen door to the back porch and went inside. On more stable footing, Flossie let go of Laurel's arm and headed to the door. Twisting the knob and finding it locked, she moved to the door of the bathroom. When Flossie pulled it open, Laurel cautioned her. "I think the door is hung at an uneven slant, it…"

The knob of the opening door swung out of Flossie's hand as the door made a continuous swing until it smacked into the outer wall. "I know this house, honey. This door always gets away from you if you ain't holding tight." She then added with a huff, "There used to be an old wool sock hung up here by a nail to keep the knob from smacking into the wall. But I guess somebody must'a pulled it down."

Laurel, assuming her aunt needed to use the bathroom, reached to close the door for her as she went inside. But Flossie wasn't going into the bathroom for that. Laurel observed with surprise, when Flossie lifted the aloe vera plant from the back of the commode, removed a key from the saucer, then made her way out of the bathroom, across the porch, and unlocked the kitchen door.

"Does everyone know about that key?" Laurel gasped.

"Yep."

"I guess that's how Janice came in my first day," Laurel realized. "I assumed she had her own key."

"Nobody ever needed their own key to Bessie's. Ever'body knows it's under the pot...on the pot!" she tickled herself at her little joke. "Round here folks gotta be able to let themselves in, 'specially if you're an old lady. If you was to fall, how's any'body gone get to you and help you up? And if a neighbor growed a heap of okra, they gotta be able to drop it by, even if you ain't home."

"Then, why even have a lock in the first place?" Laurel asked.

"Cause don't nobody's doors stay shut reliable. Your grandpaw built this place and these doors are a bit crooked and the floors are too. We got locks to keep 'em closed, not shut people out."

Flossie made herself comfortable in a chair at the table, while Laurel went about heating up lunch. Laurel was nervous about her cooking, having practiced a couple of times over the week before feeling confident enough to have a guest. She'd cooked everything early that morning, as Janice had advised, and left it simmering in the oven during church. She only hoped she hadn't dried it all out. As she readied lunch, Flossie continued rattling on with her tips for how Laurel could adjust to country life.

"Now anybody who you know is gone come in through the kitchen," Flossie explained. "They'll likely knock though, knowing you're a young gal livin' alone. But if somebody comes a'knockin' at the front door, don't even bother goin' to it. You don't know them. They are a'sellin something or deliverin' something. Anybody you know is gonna come through this kitchen door."

Giving her meal a final inspection, Laurel felt proud of herself. It at least looked delicious, but whether it was or not was left to be seen. She had followed Mrs. Rawlings fried chicken exactly as she was taught, even the overnight buttermilk soak. As Laurel began placing everything on the table, Flossie's eyes sparkled with anticipation.

"My word, Laurel. This looks mighty scrumptious." Flossie took it all in, a stray tear escaping the corner of her eye. "You got Bessie's green tea pitcher. Her brown and yellow plates. It's like she ain't even left. And is that her black-eyed peas?"

Laurel nodded, "Yes, ma'am. I found them in her freezer and cooked them this morning."

"Use a hunk of ham hock?"

"No," Laurel frowned. "I don't actually know what that is. But I put a slice of bacon in. Does that count?"

"Good effort," Flossie said, tasting the peas. "Next time use ham, but these is good. 'Specially for a beginner."

Laurel watched as Flossie lifted a golden-brown chicken thigh from the platter. Before placing it on her plate, she turned it over in her fingers, inspecting it. Nervously, Laurel asked, "Is it okay?"

Flossie placed it on her plate where she stuck a fork into the tender meat. "This ain't Bessie's chicken. This looks like Brenda Rawlings chicken." Tasting it, Flossie smacked her thin lips together, "Yep, that's Brenda's. Good choice. Bessie's chicken wasn't as good. Hers was always a little doughy for my taste." Flossie licked her lips, "You didn't use the bag though, did ya?"

Laurel jumped up, pulling the bag from the top of the trash. "I did! Just like Brenda told me."

Flossie waved her back to the table. "Calm down, honey. It's mighty good. You did real fine. But you used a plastic bag. That's all it is."

"Is there a difference?"

Cackling again, Flossie replied, "Baby, every change—no matter how minor—changes everything. Always use a paper bag to shake flour.

Never plastic. But you got this so close to right it ain't much different. Still miles better than Bessie's or half the women in Scroggins. You're doing good kid."

Throughout her adult life, Laurel Holden experienced the feeling of pride in her work many times. From emails received from restaurant owners and hotel managers, and even city council representatives, thanking her for her glowing article. Yet somehow, this frail old woman, covered in wrinkles and liver spots, with her lavender perm, praising Laurel's meal eclipsed any recognition she'd ever known before. Laurel raised her shoulders triumphantly, hearing her grandmother's sister tell her she'd made a nearly perfect batch of fried chicken.

Digging into her third piece, with an extra helping of mashed potatoes and peas, Flossie shocked all Laurel's sensibilities when she asked, "So do you prefer colored fellas?"

Laurel nearly choked on a piece of chicken skin as her ears registered the question. "Excuse me?"

"I seen you flirtin' with the Hopkins boy. Ain't nothing wrong in it. Just wondered."

Laurel didn't quite know how to respond. "I have dated a couple of black men before. I've dated Asian men. White men. Even a Lebanese man. He was by far the best looking, but had an unwavering devotion to romantic comedy films."

Flossie let out another cackle. "Lord girl! Is that what you young folks consider a problem?"

Laurel grinned across the table. "It was all he ever wanted to see. "Sometimes you just want a car chase! Or an exciting little murder!"

"Sounds like you're a little picky to me," Flossie remarked. "You sure that was what you didn't like about him?"

"Well," Laurel sighed. "He expected too much from me, emotionally speaking. Most of the men I dated were like that. I traveled far too much to be someone's comfort animal."

"Sounds like you run through roosters faster than it takes to lay the egg." Flossie chuckled. "That Hopkins fella is a good one. You can do worse."

Laurel wasn't exactly sure if *good one* was a racial slur or not. Flossie could have simply meant *men*. She decided not to find out.

The remainder of lunch was spent with Flossie telling Laurel about her own family. Her late husband Norman. Her daughter Rachel and Rachel's husband Ernest. Flossie also had a son named Wyatt, whose wife she only referred to as "that sorry woman he married."

Once lunch was over, Laurel brought out Bessie's photo boxes and albums, asking Flossie various questions about the people in the pictures. Flossie was very helpful identifying faces from her branch of the family. She was even able to show Laurel who Rachel and Ernest were. "And this one here," Flossie beamed. "That's me and my Norman."

Laurel looked it over after Flossie handed it back to her. "You were a looker! And your Norman was very handsome."

"That he was," Flossie replied. "And a good man too." When Laurel placed another picture Flossie had identified back in the box, the old woman tapped Laurel on the hand. "Get a pen and write these names on the backs of these pictures when I tell 'em to you. After I'm dead and gone, how you gonna remember?"

"Why would I need to?"

Flossie clicked her tongue disapprovingly. "Laurel, honey, family ain't something you let slip out of your memory. You come from these people. Whether you know it or not, they are in you. One day your youngens will want to know where they come from. What are you gonna tell them if even you don't know?"

Laurel scoffed, blushing a little at the thought. "I am not a mother type. There won't be any added limbs off my branch of the family tree."

Flossie snickered, mostly to herself. "I ain't never heard of a woman who didn't wanna have children. Not really." She cackled out another laugh, adding, "Oh, I heard some say they didn't, but that was mainly because they were too blame ugly to think they'd ever find a man fool enough to wanna make babies with them. But that ain't your problem honey. So it can't hurt none just to jot down some names. You never know."

Continuing through the box of pictures, Flossie identified her parents, Laurel's great grandparents. She also found their parents among the very old and umber colored photographs. There were also cousins, great aunts and uncles, and photos from various family events Flossie recounted to her. She even knew quite a few names of Laurel's grandfather's people. "It's a small area here," Flossie reminded her. "Ain't got to be blood related to know who most of these people were."

Taking a serious turn, Laurel wanted to know something, and it was a question she felt uncomfortable asking Janice about. "Aunt Flossie," Laurel began, then paused. Only now had she realized she'd been addressing her this way. Laurel took a moment to let that sink in. Never in her life had she known anyone she addressed with a familial title. Laurel felt good saying it. It made her feel connected. Snapping back from her silent tangent, Laurel finished her question. "Why did my grandmother never try to get in touch with me?"

Awkward silence fell between them for a moment and Laurel could see sympathy glistening in her aunt's eyes. And regret. Someone else's regret. Flossie seemed to carry her sister's mantle now and Laurel could tell that had Flossie been her grandmother, different decisions might have been made.

"I know my father was not a standup man," Laurel went on saying. "But how could she shut him out of her life that way? My mother never even met my grandparents. Why would Bessie not reach out, especially after my father's death. Did she hate my mother that much?"

Flossie's tender hazel eyes fluttered a few times as she attempted to find the words to explain something even she didn't fully understand. "Laurel, your grandmaw never hated nobody in her life, not even when she had damn good cause to. She didn't hate your momma. She didn't hate you neither even though I bet you must have thought that growin' up."

"I did," Laurel admitted. "I felt, empty. Like, what was wrong with me for my father to have left and his family to want nothing to do with me."

Flossie lifted one of the pictures of her sister from the photo box. Staring at it with an air of judgement in her tone, Flossie did her best to make sense of it for Laurel. "My sister was wrong in what she done. Bessie should have acted different. But she lived by a set of beliefs and morals that sortta locked her into a cage she couldn't get out of."

"I don't understand."

"I know you don't honey," Flossie smiled gently. "I can't hardly understand it much myself. Me and Bessie were close friends, not just sisters. Hell, we didn't even like our other sisters. It was me and her always. And I guess I knew her better than she knew herself, but I still don't get it all."

Flossie picked up the brown leather album Janice had shown Laurel last week. Turning to the photo of Janice and Laurel's father on their wedding day, Flossie pointed at it. "What do you see that's missing in this picture?" Laurel, scanning the page, could not see anything out of place. Janice and Charlie were in the center, with Bessie on the other side of her son Charlie and another couple, presumably Janice's parents, beside Janice.

"I don't see anything strange," Laurel said.

Flossie hung her head, "I forget you grew up without one, but where is Charlie's daddy? Your grandpaw ain't in this picture."

Wondering how she could have missed something so simple, Laurel gasped. "He isn't!" She flipped through the few other photos from the day, not finding a single one of Ustus Hogue. "Why wasn't he in any pictures?"

"Cause he wasn't there," Flossie revealed. "He stayed home, and my husband Norman stayed here with him."

"Why?"

Flossie set the album aside and lifted another one, one Laurel had not yet looked through. She turned to a page showing a middle-aged man sitting on the edge of a couch. It was the same couch in the next room, the one in front of the air conditioner. Everything was the same. The gas heater, the curtain sheers, the linoleum. The picture was worn, maybe it had been folded a few times in the past because faint lines crossed in places over the man's forehead and cheeks. He was sitting with his eyes closed, making it difficult to recognize him. It was not a very good picture of whoever it was.

"This is Ustus."

Laurel couldn't believe it. The pictures Janice had shown her depicted him as quite handsome, *hot even*, as she initially remarked. "How old is he here?" Laurel questioned. "His hair is thin, and he's thicker. It's hard to tell with these folds in the paper and his eyes closed."

"There ain't no folds, honey. That's his face." Flossie explained. "And his eyes ain't closed. They ain't there anymore when this picture was took."

Laurel clutched side of the table, unable to believe her ears. "What happened to his eyes?"

"Got shot out."

As Flossie went through the entire traumatic affair, Laurel sat with unbreakable attention. Flossie's account of the event was like something out of a high drama silver screen movie. Listening to her go through it, Laurel envisioned Edward G. Robinson or Humphrey Bogart in the role of her grandfather.

According to Flossie, Ustus Hogue was not a generally affable man. Those who he liked, liked him back and thought him to be a pretty good guy. Those Ustus wasn't as nice to, thought him to be, as Flossie put it, "a horse's ass." One day, while acting like a horse's ass, Ustus began picking on another man in front of a group of other men.

"You know that bridge you come over driving in to Scroggins?" Flossie asked Laurel. "That bridge wasn't built yet. County work crews were down there digging out where it would go. See it was just dirt road out here till they put in that bridge and highway."

Laurel knew the place along the highway Flossie was referring to. She'd driven over that bridge a few times and noticed that in the gulley below, there appeared to be much older, gravel road which was now almost overtaken by nature.

"Bunch a men went down there to see the construction going on," Flossie continued. "Sounds dumb now days, but back then nobody had nothing else interesting to do. Watching machinery dig a road was high entertainment. So, my husband Norman went down there with Ustus and bunch of other fellers to see the progress. There was this man, ole' Jugger Dooley. Ustus had been pickin' on Jugger ever since they was kids. Lots of folks picked on poor Jugger. Now I ain't taking up for Jugger. He was downright frustrating. He weren't right, see. You know what I mean. They called it *retarded* when my kids were young. Not supposed to say that now. Now it's *challenged* or *differently abled* or some nonsense like that. But basically, Jugger was messed up. Had tantrums. Couldn't speak right. We all pretty much avoided him. He was a pestering soul. But your granddaddy liked to pick on Jugger every chance he could. So, when he started in on Jugger that day down there at the bridge, Jugger threatened to kill Ustus."

"Kill him?" Laurel gasped. "And no one did anything?"

"Now you got to remember, didn't nobody take ole Jugger serious. But he said he was a'goin home and getting his papa's gun and coming back to kill Ustus." Flossie took a sip of tea, coating her drying throat. "Nobody thought nothing of it. But sure enough, here comes Jugger running down the road about a half hour later. Got his daddy's shot gun aimed up on his shoulder."

"Oh my God!" Laurel cried.

"Jugger got on the side of that embankment and unloaded a load of buckshot right at Ustus. Well, the men went scattering and Jugger threw his gun down and ran back home. My Norman got over to Ustus and saw what had been done to him. Your granddaddy's eyes were ripped to pieces, some pieces just gone and some hanging by threads down his cheek. His face and forehead was tore open with shrapnel."

Laurel felt queasy just imagining it. It was a terrible story to think about happening to anyone, but it had happened to her own grandfather. That in itself was hard to comprehend for a woman who had never felt as if she had any family at all.

Flossie continued, taking a moment to illustrate how needless the whole tragedy had been in the first place. "Everybody told Ustus for years to stop messing with that retarded boy. But your granddaddy thought it was a bunch of fun to rile ole Jugger up."

"But get back to that day," Laurel urged. "What happened after Ustus had been shot?"

"Well, Norman got him to the hospital in Tuscaloosa and called me at home. I went running over here to Bessie and told her what happened. She was right in the middle of canning her barbeque sauce to store up for winter, when I busted in. She dropped everything, and we hightailed it to Tuscaloosa."

"I can only imagine what she was feeling on that drive," Laurel commented. "Not knowing if he would live."

"Dying would'a been easier," Flossie remarked solemnly. "Ustus was totally blind from then on. Wasn't nothing any doctor could do but clean out what was still holdin' on in his eye sockets. His face healed up pretty good except some scars. But it was like he got meaner after he couldn't see no more. He would get so mad, especially at the kids. If they was too rambunctious he'd get after them with his walking stick. I'd come in this kitchen and they'd all be hiding under the table while their daddy was stalking around trying to find 'em."

"That's terrible!"

"He'd be frustrated with Bessie too, even though he couldn't do a blame thing without her. She had to do everything for him. Couldn't hardly leave the house that first year. Your Aunt Merle went to work in Birmingham as a secretary. Took a bus all the way there and back every day. She left here about 5am and didn't get home till 9 that night. Did it every day to help the family. The boys all had to get work. The farm went to weeds cause they needed money faster than a crop could grow. Took jobs in lumber and construction. That's how your uncle Dave started his business."

Letting it all sink in, Laurel's thoughts went back to their original starting point, before Flossie's history lesson sidetracked Laurel's brain. "But how does it relate to me and my mother?"

Folding her wrinkled arms against her chest, Flossie said, "Don't you see the connection? Your grandmaw had every reason to leave that man but she never did. She stayed and took care of him till his dying day."

"She must have loved him very much."

"Naw, she didn't love him!" Flossie bellowed, as if it were a ridiculous thing to say. "She couldn't stand Ustus! He'd done her wrong for years. But she had married him. And married was married, least to Bessie. You didn't run out on your marriage just cause things didn't end up how you expected. She used to say, 'I said death do you part. Rich or poor, sick or not. Said it to God. God. You can't break your word to the Lord."

Laurel crinkled her nose. "I think the Lord would understand if you were being treated like shit!"

"I don't disagree, but not to Bessie. Our folks were devout. She learned it good from them. She viewed it like a test from the Lord. No matter what she went through with that piece of shit husband, she never left him. But don't you see, Laurel. Your daddy did. He left his wife, and it was a wife who was good to him."

It was making more sense now. Convoluted as it may be, Laurel was beginning to understand her grandmother's way of thinking a little better.

"Janice helped out with Ustus when she married up with your daddy. She saw what all Bessie suffered through. Janice was, and is, a good woman. But your daddy decided he didn't want her no more, took up with your momma and left. And he didn't just leave Janice. He stole money from his brother and abandoned his entire family to survive with one less pair of hands to help out."

"Bessie was angry with her son," Laurel replied. "It really wasn't about me. She wasn't rejecting me for being born."

"Honey, I don't even think she thought about Charlie enough to even know he had a kid till you was a year or two old. For Bessie, you get one marriage. The one you promise to be with is your spouse for all eternity. Mistake or not. To Bessie your mother wasn't ever her daughter-in-law because Charlie only had one wife in God's eye. Janice was her son's wife in God's eyes. All Bessie's loyalty and devotion was to Janice. They leaned on each other a lot of years."

"Did she ever talk about me?"

Flossie shook her head. "Your grandmaw never confided anything to anyone. I heard through gossip that Charlie had a daughter. Bessie never said anything to me. I didn't even know she left you her house and savings till the lawyer read her will. I guess she managed to keep up with you whether any of us knew it or not."

Laurel remained quiet for several minutes, though she gave the impression she was looking through the photo album, she paid little attention to the images. In truth, she was reeling inside from the things she was learning about her family. The Hogues, though seemingly well respected in the community, were not proving to be anything to be very proud of. She began to wonder whether it was better before she knew anything about her family history. Before coming here, she may have felt adrift in the world, but now she wasn't sure she liked what she was tethered to. The history of the Hogues carried so much anguish. So much heartache. Betrayal. Abandonment. It suddenly struck her how glad she was that her name was officially Holden.

"I have upset you, honey." Flossie whispered. "I always did have a big mouth. Maybe I shouldn't of—"

"Oh, no, Aunt Flossie," Laurel said. "I wanted to know. I'm glad I know. It'll just take getting used to. I never dreamed my family lived such unhappy lives."

"Oh girl," Bessie chuckled, as if her young niece was missing a point so obvious she was surprised she couldn't see it herself. "The unhappy things we got to go through in life, don't make our lives unhappy. Ain't nobody getting out of this world free of some kind a'misery. That's how we know when things are good. Cause they ain't like they was when they were bad."

"All I see is sadness," Laurel confided. "Look at just what Janice alone has gone through. And none of it was her own fault. And Bessie was the same. She didn't deserve all that."

Flossie shook her head in defiance, "You are pulling the wrong lessons out of the textbook, Laurel. Janice ain't an unhappy woman. When Charlie run out, he took the misery with him."

"Yeah, but she lost her baby."

"I lost two babies in my life," Flossie confessed. "One before it got born and one when it was two months old. Bad things happen. Don't mean you still can't be happy you're alive. I have seen Janice's face sitting with you in church. Just you comin' here brings her a whole new happy feeling. Her life ain't been unhappy. Just that middle part was."

Laurel leaned over, bumping her shoulder into her aunts with a half-smile. "You should have a talk show. You see the positive in everything, don't you?"

"Better than not lookin' for it at all.," the old woman cackled. "My Norman and me loved one another. Never stopped. I nursed him through the end when his heart was so weak he could barely walk to the bathroom. He died ten years ago, and I ain't never been sadder than I was then. That don't mean I'm unhappy. A person can't be unhappy if they've had true joy in their life. Even for just a little while."

Laurel drove Flossie home, taking time on the drive back to process all she'd heard. It was a lot, and she wasn't sure she could see life through Flossie's rosy outlook. Nothing had ever happened to Laurel that had ever provided her with much joy. Certainly not enough to wipe the bad out of the ledger. Once she got home, she sat for a while on the front porch swing. Her eyes drifted up to the row of empty hanging baskets. *Maybe I should put some flowers in.* Those baskets of dried, dead plants hadn't been on her radar before today, but now it was as if they symbolized something. They sent a message to the outside world from the first moment this house was glimpsed that everything there was dead. Nothing of beauty existed in the Hogue house anymore. Did that now include her too? Had she been living her life this whole time with an invisible line of dead flower baskets shrouding her?

There were so many moments in her life when Laurel had wished she'd never been born. Not exactly suicidal, but uninvested in her own existence. She could remember joking once to a boyfriend, who did not hang around very long, that if there was a button she could press which erased her existence, she would press it. That she would have pressed it every day of her life. That she had not lived a single day of her life when she wouldn't have pushed such a button.

Would I push it today?

She didn't know.

Bessie's Recipe known in real life as...

BIGMAMA'S BBQ SAUCE

Created by my grandmother, Lettie Robertson
(makes a lot, so store or share)

Ingredients

1-pint red vinegar

1 bottle ketchup (any brand is fine) (bottles used to be one size, so get what size you thing regular used to be)

2 tbsp mustard (not mustard powder, bottle mustard. Any brand)

1 lemon juiced (real lemon, not storebought juice)

2 tbsp butter or margarine

2 tbsp Worcestershire sauce

1 onion peeled and chopped finely (white onion, sweet onion, doesn't matter, but red onion is a no)

1 tbsp dark brown sugar

Salt (to your taste)

Pepper (to your tase)

Dash of hot sauce (make two or three, you decide)

1. Mix all the ingredients together
2. Cook on low till it tastes good
3. Jar it or bottle it. Refrigerate and reheat whenever you use it if you like it warm

CHAPTER ELEVEN

Never Boil a Pig for Family

With both Linc and her aunt Flossie making comments on the state of the yard, Laurel decided to hire someone who could take care of its upkeep. It wasn't something she knew how to do. Ever since it was brought to her attention, the overgrowth crowding up to the house was all she could see. It wasn't only the unsightliness of it, but the idea of that long black snake twisting and writhing somewhere out there terrified her. Whenever she went to her car, she imagined it sneaking up and coiling around her leg.

Not having a great deal of disposable funds to hire an authentic maintenance crew, Laurel wondered if any teenage boys might be eager for a summer job. The problem was she did not know any, except Cade. She decided to offer him the job and if he wasn't interested, maybe he knew someone who would be. To her happy surprise, Cade eagerly volunteered.

His father dropped both Cade and a lawn mower off at the house bright and early one morning. Laurel stepped outside to say hello, again thanking Cade for the help. The change in his behavior in his father's presence was markedly different from the Cade she'd met with in her kitchen. His eyes were devoid of their sparkle and his personality was noticeably dialed down.

After a brief hello, Cade simply said, "I'll get started on the yard. Then I'll see what I can do with that field."

"You gone have to bushhog that thing, boy," his father said.

"Yeah, I know that already." Cade replied, a little annoyed. "That's what I meant. I'll see if I can borrow a tractor—"

"Mrs. Hogue had a tractor," his father barked. Shielding his eyes from the sun with his hand, Cade's father looked across the field. "Must still 'round here someplace. Ain't no sense to borry one."

"I'll figure it out Daddy."

Cade rolled the lawnmower around the back of the house to begin work while Laurel, used her mental *English to country* translator, to deduce that *borry* was the rural pronunciation for *borrow*. Now realizing that she'd never met Mr. Peterson, she reached out her hand, introducing herself. He did not take it, but did reply, "Your name ain't Hogue?"

"No, it is Holden."

"You married?"

"No," she answered. "Holden is my pen name." She could read in his expression that he was unfamiliar with the term. "It's the name my writing is known by."

With a simple grunt, he replied. "Guess there ain't no more Hogues left then. But I'm Hank. And if that boy don't do a good job for you, you let me know. I'll come back to get him in a few hours."

"I am sure he will do a wonderful job," Laurel said with a smile. "It's probably not very complicated, although it isn't something I know how to do."

"That boy ain't got a whole lotta skill with much a'anything," Hank Peterson said with a scoff. "I'll take a look when I come get him and see if he did it right."

Laurel watched Hank pull away in his dingy white truck knowing that she did not like him already. He was the epitome of the sort of limited minded man Cade had talked about last week. Hearing the start of the lawn mower in back, she returned to the cooler air inside the house, rejoining her cup of coffee and laptop.

The roar of the mower outside might have distracted a different writer, but for Laurel it was a welcome buffer from the endless quiet of the country. She missed the sounds of trucks moving past her apartment window, or city workers jostling up and down on jackhammers, or just a normal surge of bustling traffic. Laurel's fingers were now typing at a rapid pace, feeling like the old days. She wasn't aware how much time had gone by as she sat working on the cookbook until she heard Cade open the screen door off the back porch, and yell, "Laurel! Mr. Hopkins is here to see you!"

Not expecting a visitor, especially one as handsome as Linc Hopkins, Laurel quickly removed her reading glasses and, in an act of female vanity, tucked them under the tablecloth. It was not a clever hiding place as the bulge under the plastic cloth was hard to overlook. Linc rapped at the kitchen door, despite being able to clearly see through the door's window. She waved him inside, rising to greet him.

"This is weird," he said right off the bat. "I had this whole thing rehearsed in my head about how this isn't as creepy as it appears. One of my students lives down the road and I was coming to see him. He broke his leg the last week of school and I thought I see how he is doing."

"And since I am on the same street..."

Linc grinned. "Something like that. But I knew before I left home, I was going to use that as an excuse to stop by here."

Appreciating his disclosure, Laurel smiled. "I'm glad you did."

"Kind of blows my cool image though, admitting I wanted to see you."

Laurel laughed, then confessed something of her own, "If it makes you feel better," she said, reaching her hand under the tablecloth, removing her glasses. "The second Cade said it was you, I shoved these under here."

Linc nodded with a grin. "Readers?"

"Yeah."

"I have three pairs. One at work. One at home. One in the car."

With the humbling portion of the visit over, Linc did not know what to say next. However, Laurel saved the day by reminding him, "You know, you did say you would show me around my land."

"I did, didn't I?" Extending his arm for her to take, he added, "Shall we?"

Despite his flimsy excuse to pay a call on her, Linc's tour of the Hogue property turned out to be very helpful. They began from the back porch, moving around to the back of the house, which was now freshly mowed, eliminating Laurel's worry over encountering the snake. It felt embarrassing to admit she had not been on this side of the house since moving in, but certain odd aspects forced her to as she saw a few things she'd never seen. Although, Cade had trimmed the grass in that section, several iron posts were sticking out of the ground in odd, random places. He'd been unable to position the mower close enough to take down the tall blades of grass and weed growing directly against the rusty rods.

"What are these iron posts for?" Laurel asked Linc. "Aren't they rather in the way?"

"See these holes in the top?" Linc pointed out, sticking his forefinger through an opening at the top of a post. "There used to be a long rope passing through these. It was how your grandfather navigated his way to the chicken houses. As long as he held the rope, he could get there and back to the house."

They continued across the yard until it came to a well-trodden path. Generations of Hogues had worn the ground clean along the path leading uphill past the meadow. Once on this side of the field's overgrown condition, Laurel could see the path stretching between two long-weathered wooden structures. It wasn't anything she could see from the house, not with the meadow so wild and tall. As she and Linc passed through, Laurel observed the structures more closely. Both were equal in length, raised high on posts, and had something resembling glassless windows lining them. A few of the rectangular openings still had rusty screens covering them, while the rest were empty or tattered and left flapping in the breeze.

"These were the chicken houses," Linc explained.

"I thought chicken pens were usually on the ground?"

"Normally," Linc answered. "These were built higher to be more accessible for your Mr. Hogue." Linc pointed out the shallow troughs attached to the fronts of both houses. "When the hens laid their eggs, they rolled out of the henhouse into this trough. All Mr. Hogue had to do was follow the rope up here and collect the eggs from the trough."

Laurel gave off a little sigh. "Seems like a complicated way to get something you can buy in a store rather easily."

"That's the city girl in you," he replied. "Now keep in mind, I was nowhere near being born when it happened. But my granny told me that after Mr. Hogue went blind, the chicken houses were a way to make him feel useful and earn a little money. For a while The Community Store only sold eggs from Ustus Hogue. When he died, your grandmother sold off the chickens. I was working for her then. I remember the day the chickens left on a truck."

Laurel let out a judgmental moan, "From what I hear, Ustus Hogue was a prick. I don't see why anyone should give a damn if he felt useful or not."

"Ouch!" Linc chuckled. "Don't get this girl's dander up!"

She smiled at his joke, but it didn't change how she felt. "Maybe his punishment for harassing that disabled man was to live with the helplessness. This all seems like therapy for *him*. What happened to the man who shot him?"

"He died in a state asylum," Linc answered. "And yeah, your grandfather probably wasn't a very nice guy, but a man still needs purpose. Without it, the empty time consumes him."

"This chicken business still seems too good for him."

"Who says it was for him?" Linc supposed. "The way I heard it, Mr. Hogue's little temper tantrums and attacks on his family got a good deal better once he found something to do."

Coming to the end of the chicken houses, another house came into view at the top of the hill. Linc informed her that the house and its surrounding land once belonged to the Hogues. In fact, her uncle Dave lived there for a while, but Miss Bessie sold the plot of land years ago to man who planned to raise emus.

"He never did start raising them, though? I wonder what happened?" Linc said it as more of a question to himself, possibly one to ask his own grandmother.

Just before reaching the top of the hill, Linc pointed to a gray, weathered, wooden outbuilding. It had double doors, nearly rotting off, and a roof made of red stained tin just like the building next to Bessie's house.

"Is that one of my cribs?" she asked.

Amazed she knew the term, Linc grinned, "Look at you and the local lingo! I'm impressed. But no, that is larger than a crib. That is your tractor shed."

"There *is* a tractor!" she exclaimed, noting she would have to let Cade know later.

They peeked inside where a rust patched olive-green tractor sat beside several coiled blade devices atop trailers. Linc told her the tractor still worked or was working a few months ago when a hired man came by every few weeks to chop the grass in the fields. She wondered aloud why Bessie had not sold off the other plots of land or simply let the vegetation take over after the farming years were done.

"In towns like Scroggins," Linc began. "Especially for anyone of your grandmother's generation or older, land made you king. Money was nice, but money without land to anchor you down just meant you were a generation away from being poor again. Didn't matter if you had money or not, if you had land. Land could always bring you money in one form or another."

"It seems like an albatross to me."

"In our modern times, I agree. No one uses their land now. Over generations, rural populations fall. People move to cities. And those kings and queens who used to own all the soil, just get left with a barren kingdom they don't have the resources or energy to maintain." He looked Laurel in the eye now, hoping to perhaps stir something inside her. "But this land...your land, Laurel. It may be a ghostland now, but the ghosts who walk here are part of you. An entire family line of Hogues and Hoggs have strolled these paths and worked these fields. Miss Bessie understood that. She didn't glance out her window and see a burden. She saw a history.

Behind the barn, they picked up on another trail moving into the dense treescape. Gentle ruts down the path hinted how this was once a drivable road through these woods, but nature spent recent years reclaiming it. Narrowed by fallen pine needles, twigs, and tendrils of growth, it was now only a footrail. Along the way, breaks could be seen through the wall of pines where a sunny field stood hidden by trees. The trees had not yet reclaimed the meadows once used for planting, but in time they would. Only tall grasses waving in the breeze hinted at where rich soil still lay.

Laurel's foot caught in an uneven place on the trail, stumbling her a moment until Linc caught her by the arm, then slid his hand into hers for stability. She offered a smile of thanks.

"How is your recipe collection progressing?" he asked, partly to continue conversation and partly to distract from the fact that he had not let go of her hand yet and didn't want to.

She gave him a mischievous wink, recognizing the slick maneuver, then casually answered. "It's going well. I already have a few recipes and entertaining stories. I can safely say now, I do see potential in the book. I will give it a shot."

"You haven't asked me whether I have a story or not," he teased. "Do you?"

"Maybe," he said with a light squeeze to her hand, just to let her know he intended on keeping it clasped to his own. "But I doubt it would fit with the others."

"Let's hear it."

Linc began by clarifying it wasn't truly his story. It was one his grandmother once told him, but he'd never been able to forget it. Intrigued, Laurel urged him to continue. He explained that there had once been a cherished recipe for a pork belly stew which his family held very dear. For generations, the ingredients and instructions on how to make it was closely guarded by whoever it had been passed down to.

"Granny told me it was her great aunt who was the last holder of the recipe. She'd inherited it from her mother, much to the fury of her other sisters."

"I have been hearing a lot of that lately," Laurel remarked. "You people guard the secrets to your food like a bank guards the vault." Her feet stopped in place as her face turned to Linc with a horrified expression. "By your people, I meant Southern...not black."

He laughed loudly, echoing through the trees. "I understood that, Laurel."

"Just wanted to make sure."

Linc went on with the tale, appreciative of her sensitivity. "One day that great aunt was preparing that very pork stew for a big family gathering. It was a celebration of some kind, but I don't think Granny ever knew what it was for. The stew was cooking over an open fire outside in the yard. The pot was suspended from three big posts tied together like a tripod. That's how they cooked back then I guess for big groups."

"Not inside at an oven?"

He laughed again. "Laurel this was a black family over 100 years ago. None of them had a house big enough for that many people to gather. And I doubt they even had a stove. Probably cooked in the fireplace during normal times. Anyway, for whatever reason, the stew was cooking outside, boiling up the pig and vegetables and whatever else they had in there."

He stopped his story a moment, pausing to examine the trail. It appeared to veer to the right, but it also could have been continuing straight ahead. Years of neglect and no human foot traffic made it hard to tell. "Let's go this way," he said pointing ahead. "That might be a trail, but who knows where it goes. This one should take us back to the house. If not, it'll hit Hogg Road which is just as good."

Lifting a few thin branches over Laurel's head to allow her through, Linc finished his family's story. "Granny's great aunt either went too close to the fire while stirring the pot, or maybe it was that the pig fat boiled over, spreading the fire closer to her. Whichever it was, the hem of her dress caught fire. She tried to stomp it out, but the flames engulfed her quickly. The whole family was in the yard and saw her catch ablaze and start screaming and running in a panic as the fire climbed up her body from head to toe."

"Oh my God!" Laurel cried in disbelief. "Did they put her out?"

"What could they do?" Linc shrugged. "It's not like they had fire extinguishers back then and anyone who got too close would have only ignited themselves. They watched in horror as she ran in circles. Whenever she got close to someone, they'd run the other way to avoid being caught in the blaze. Granny said her aunt screamed for a minute or two before she collapsed—her clothes gone, her skin melting under the flames. When it was over, she fell to her knees, then forward onto the ground. The fire burned out, leaving nothing but charred bone and muscle. And the recipe? It had been in her apron pocket. Lost forever. No one else knew how to cook the stew or what seasonings she used. People tried to recreate it over the years, but no one succeeded. Now, no one alive remembers the taste, even if someone managed to stumble on the right ingredients."

Laurel stood aghast, her mouth open and her eyes wide. "*That* is the takeaway from your story?" she exclaimed. "No one ever figured out the recipe! That poor woman burned to death in front of her entire family!"

Linc shrugged again. "Well, yes, it was tragic, but I didn't know her, Laurel. It's just a family story. Do you want to use it?"

"Hell no!" she gasped, half revolted and half stifling a macabre desire to laugh. "I do not want to use your family's ghastly story of the day they all let *Aunt Mary* burn to death."

Her remark made Linc laugh. Shaking his head, he agreed, "Yeah, now that I hear you say it, I guess it is a terrible story to pass down. Maybe Granny was trying to teach me not to get too close to the gas heater, now that I think about it. She was always warning us about going too close to the heater and would say 'you don't wanna end up like Aunt Bernadine!'"

"Is that how Delva gave warnings?"

Linc leaned back, chuckling, as he placed his hand on the small of Laurel's back to continue their walk. "I never thought about that before. Why would anybody tell a little boy such a graphic story?"

"And yet you told it to me," Laurel smirked. "Now I will have that image seared into my head all day."

He pulled her into his arms unexpectedly, "Since that is my fault, let me provide you with something to replace it."

Lifting her chin with his thumb, Linc lowered his lips to meet hers. They kissed passionately for several minutes before they finished their walk through the woods.

When the trail released them in the yard behind Bessie's house, Laurel stepped into the sunlight, still holding his hand. "That kiss was really something," she smiled. "But it wasn't good enough to get that story out of my head. I think you may need to stay for dinner."

"No pig though," he teased.

"You'll be lucky if you get a ham sandwich."

* * *

When Hank Peterson arrived to retrieve his son, he found Cade sitting

142

on the front porch drinking a glass of tea with Laurel and the school principal. Stepping out of his truck, Hank called out, "You done with your work, boy? Or are you just lazing on the porch wasting time?"

Laurel stood up, "He finished about 15 minutes ago and he has done an amazing job! Just look around, I can walk through the yard now. He even discovered there are blueberry bushes I didn't know were there."

Hank looked at the black school principal sitting on the white woman's porch and sneered slightly before muttering a greeting. "Didn't know you two were friendly."

"Considering you did not know me at all until a few hours ago," Laurel replied. "I don't see how you would."

She turned her attention to Cade and asked him if he would like to be paid now or if he wanted to accept her earlier offer. Cade told her she could pay him at the end of the week, like they'd discussed.

"What?" Hank asked. "You thinking of hiring him permanent? Can't think he'd be the man needed to keep this place up."

"You would be surprised, Mr. Peterson." Laurel said. "He not only tamed this out-of-control lawn, he got the tractor running and said he would come back tomorrow to start clearing the field."

With a hint of pride in his voice, hoping his father might be impressed, Cade also added, "And I'm going to paint this porch and that swing before they get in too bad a shape."

Hank snorted to the air, thanked Laurel, and helped his son load the mower into the truck bed. Laurel thought she heard him tell Cade as they got into the truck, "You may make a man yet, boy."

Once the dust settled on the road behind Hank's departing truck, Laurel turned to Linc and said, "I don't like that man."

"I don't care much for him myself," Linc confided. "I tried talking to him and his wife a couple of years ago, when Cade was being bullied. All he had to say was that I should let the boy's ass get kicked until he learns how to fight back."

"That is deplorable."

"Welcome to Southern male toxicity," Linc sighed. "But I'd rather not waste my time talking about Hank Peterson. How about that ham sandwich you mentioned?"

Smiling back at him, Laurel opened the door and beckoned him inside.

CHAPTER TWELVE

The Cactus Plant

I t had been a few weeks since Laurel arrived in Scroggins. Though grateful for the rent-free place to live, excluding utilities, she found herself in a strangely disorienting situation. The newness of her surroundings had worn off, yet she still felt as out of place as her very first day. She didn't necessarily feel lonely, in fact, she'd met several people in her time there. Janice made frequent visits and Leon Davis never failed to wave when passing by if she were outdoors. The older women she'd met in town now felt it was their civic duty to phone her every few days to check on her, as well as share whatever happened to be going on in their lives that day. It was as if she'd inherited her grandmother's vacant role in their daily socialization. And then there was Linc, who began showing up in her life a few times a week. Laurel found herself growing increasingly fond of him, sometimes even hoping he might drop by or call.

It was Bessie's house causing her to feel out of place. In the beginning, it was a quaint change in lifestyle. A vast departure from anything she was accustomed to. But now Laurel felt like a perpetual visitor in someone else's home. Every inch of space belonged to a woman she had never known, wasn't going to meet, and had monumentally different tastes than she. Her limited finances ruled out redecorating, though she did occasionally wish Puddin would decide to expand her quirky pastime into redoing Bessie's place. Laurel changed a few things up a bit. She rearranged the furniture in the pink bedroom, pushing the bed to the far wall and away from the bank of windows. It was no wonder old women woke up at the crack of dawn with the sun shining directly in their eyes. She also took out the quilts stored in the chifforobe and chose a new design for her bed. Even though these were still Bessie's quilts, seeing a new cover helped Laurel feel less like she was living in a ghost's home.

One morning, knowing it was Janice's day off, Laurel called to ask if she'd like to join her to shop for plants. Janice liked the idea, promising to show her the best nursery in the area. She drove down to pick Laurel up in her car, stating she had a larger trunk. When she arrived, Janice walked in carrying a strange, leafless plant which looked more like a sprawling cactus than anything else. Its flat, green limbs drooped downward, each lined with serrated edges.

Laurel took one look and asked, "What in the world is this?"

"It is your Christmas cactus," Janice said with a smile.

"Christmas cactus?" repeated Laurel. "I have no idea what that is? Did you buy this?"

Shaking her head as she sat it down on the table, Janice explained. "No, Laurel. This really is *your cactus*. I totally forgot I took it home with me after Bessie died, to keep it alive. It doesn't require much care. Just water it every few weeks and keep it near sunlight, but not direct light."

"It's kind of ugly, Janice."

Laughing at the critique, Janice argued. "No, it isn't. When it blooms it is beautiful. Sometimes it's pink, sometimes it's white, I have even seen it almost red before."

"Let me guess, it blooms at Christmas?"

"You would think so, wouldn't you?" Janice teased. "This thing blooms twice a year. They're only supposed to bloom once during winter. Sometimes it's around Halloween, sometimes Thanksgiving, sometimes Christmas. I think it upsets its schedule when you split it."

"Split it?"

Janice went on to explain how the root ball continues to expand in size year after year requiring propagation every other year. "Just divide the roots and separate them into two parts, replant them both, and then you have two of them. Eventually you'll have multiple plants."

"Why would I want multiple?"

Still amused by Laurel's reaction, Janice replied, "It's how you keep it alive. You can keep the extra plant or, most people, give the new one to relatives or friends." Then Janice dropped the surprising bomb. "This plant is over 200 years old."

"What?"

"Yep. Originally, this was Bessie's grandmother's plant. And who knows how far it goes before that? That is another reason to always have one or two splitting's of this somewhere, in case the original dies, you still have a piece of it going and, in a year, or two it'll be as big as this one."

Laurel appeared perplexed. "So, my family has kept this ugly thing alive for 200 years?"

"Or longer," Janice said. "And it's not ugly. Like I said, when it is all in bloom it is beautiful." Then with a stern tone Janice never used with Laurel before, she said, "And you better keep this alive."

"Don't you want to have it?"

Janice shook her head. "I have three pots of this same cactus at my house. And Flossie has a couple as well. She's been keeping hers going since she first got married and her mother gave her a splitting. This plant has been tended to and kept alive by generations of your ancestors. This plant is your family tree."

Laurel, who had never had—or considered—children, never had a pet, was now expected to keep a cactus alive or else send her entire family lineage into oblivion! She promised to do her best, and they left to go find prettier plant life at Douglas Farms nursery.

Janice must have called ahead to alert the owner they were coming, because the moment they pulled up to the nursery, a plump woman in her forties came rushing out to meet them. She wore a wide brimmed sunhat and gardening gloves and introduced herself as Lorraine Douglas.

The nursery was clearly a home operation. A sage-green house with orange shutters stood between two open-air structures covered by light-filtered canopies. Wooden tables overflowed with flowering plants, and behind the house stretched neat rows of evergreens, budding fruit trees, and herbs.

"You are Bessie Hogue's girl!" Lorraine bellowed. "Bessie was always so good to me!"

Before Laurel could even say hello, Lorraine launched into a memory of being a child during tough times and how Miss Bessie always made sure she got lunch in the school cafeteria—even when her family couldn't pay.

This was not the first time Laurel had been told about her amazingly kind and generous grandmother. These stories should have made her proud, and they did, but they also boomeranged back around causing her to wonder why this loving old woman never called or wrote to her. Of course, she knew the answer...her religious views would not allow her to acknowledge Laurel's mother being a legitimate part of her family. But did her religious views take such precedence that her own grandchild should be punished?

Pushing her resentment aside, Laurel followed Janice around the nursery selecting various flowering plants for the front porch. Lorraine's comments about how happy Bessie would be to know her porch would be filled with flowers again, almost made Laurel call the idea off. But even she had to admit, the house looked quite dreary pulling up to it. It needed plants. In addition to flowers, Laurel bought basil, rosemary, thyme, and sage. She'd typed up enough recipes in the last two weeks to know that any decent cook had to keep fresh herbs on hand.

Once back home, Janice helped Laurel put soil in the baskets and plant the beautiful blooms. For now, Laurel decided to keep her herb plants in little pots on the kitchen windowsill. The long bank of windows in the kitchen acquired almost constant sunlight. She admitted the herbs stood a far better chance of living if they were always in her sight, reminding her to water them.

When the last pot was in place in the window, Janice poured them both a glass of iced tea. Laurel's hibernating laptop was already open when Janice sat down at the table, her motion triggered the screen to light up.

"I see you are writing about Ustus."

"I am," Laurel replied. "I think it is a good life lesson. Anti-bullying, you know. Not to mention how one mistake can affect the lives of everyone else around you."

"True."

"Janice? Don't you have a story? I know you have recipes," Laurel smiled. "But what is your story?"

"I told you my story."

"You told me my father's story. You told me my grandmother's story," Laurel countered. "Yes, you were part of them, but what is *your story* Janice? Who were you before you became Mrs. Charlie Hogue?"

"Believe me, Laurel. I am not that interesting."

Laurel's eyes sent her a reprimand. "Don't say that. I don't believe it anyway. Don't you have something to contribute to the book? After all it was all your idea!"

Janice became quiet. Reflective. Laurel sensed she was reaching into a long-sealed place in her past. The writer in her couldn't help but wonder what story might be buried there. But before she could push, she stopped herself. This wasn't some passing stranger—this was her neighbor. Hell, her father's first wife. She couldn't pry just for book material.

"Never mind," she told Janice. "I shouldn't push you if you're uncomfortable."

"It's okay," Janice said softly. "It is no secret. Everyone knows about my family. I just haven't talked about it in a very long time."

Her family? It was something in the way she said it. Janice always seemed so immersed in the Hogue family that Laurel had never considered that it might be for a reason.

"I think the last time I talked about it was with...your father," Janice revealed. "At the time, he was sympathetic."

She got up and walked to the sink with her glass. Laurel assumed she was finished with her tea and going to put it in the sink, but she didn't. Janice just placed the glass onto the metal counter and stood gazing out to the freshly mowed field.

"My father worked for the sawmill. I was around 19 when it all happened. I had just married Charlie, actually." She continued staring outside, but at nothing in particular, or maybe the past. "I remember when I got married how sad my little brother was. I took care of him. Had since he was born. Mama was always a sickly kind of woman. One ailment after another."

"Hypochondriac?"

Janice shook her head slightly as she turned back around, answering Laurel's logical assumption. "Oddly, no. Poppa often thought so, and made fun of her for it, but Mama really was sick a lot. Now that I'm older and know more, I honestly believe she suffered from terrible allergies and a little asthma. But you couldn't do anything about that then, and we didn't even know what those things were."

Laurel nodded. "I can understand that."

"Tom cried his eyes out when he learned I was leaving home to go live with my husband." Janice was smiling, but Laurel could tell it was a bittersweet, pained sort of smile. "Sometimes when Mama was feeling bad, my father took Tom with him to cut trees. I wasn't there anymore to see after him, and Mama wasn't able to." Janice's hands gripped to the rim of the sink behind her, her gaze shifting to stare at the floor. "They were loading cut logs into one of those big trailers to haul to the sawmill. Poppa was driving the lift, picking up several logs at once and dumping them in the trailer. My brother usually tromped around the woods while Poppa worked."

Janice lifted her eyes from the floor and looked at Laurel. Laurel felt frozen in suspense. Not the anticipation kind of suspense, the heart-tightening, apprehensive kind. She could feel this was about to turn tragic, quickly. Janice, still holding herself against the cold metal of the counter, was teary, but not distraught. She had obviously dealt with her grief over the years.

"It was the craziest accident," she said almost smiling. "The trailer they'd been loading was full, so one of the men drove it off to take to the mill. The lift Poppa was operating already had logs ready to drop, so he rotated the arms to the next truck."

"Oh no," Laurel whispered, covering her mouth. "He didn't see your brother?"

Janice wiped her face with her hands as her wide, incredulous eyes filled with more tears. "That's the crazy part!" she said. "He did. Poppa saw Tom standing in the back of the empty trailer the second he directed the logs to it. Poppa stopped the logs directly over it, and shouted out to Tom. 'Boy get outta there! I almost dropped these trees right on top of you!'"

"So, Tom got out!"

Janice shook her head. "Tom laughed and started moving toward the tail of the trailer to jump out. But Poppa sneezed. His hand had still been on the control, you see. He was waiting for Tom to get clear of the trailer. But he sneezed, and..."

Laurel shuddered, her own hands pressing against the tabletop just as firmly as Janice gripped the sink. With a catch in her voice, Laurel murmured, "Your father accidentally dropped the logs."

Janice nodded. "They rolled down onto Tom, crushing him." Janice then channeled an almost biopic detachment as she told the rest. "Poppa and the men knew of course Tom hadn't survived. Blood was... well, they just knew. Still Poppa and the men started trying to shove the logs off him, but..."

Laurel struggled with what to say. She wanted to reach out, offer comfort, but Janice's resilience didn't seem to require anything. Laurel quietly appreciated that in her friend, because Laurel had never been very good at empathy. She said the only thing which came to mind, "That must have been the most horrible experience your family ever had. And your poor father."

"He wasn't ever the same," Janice whispered. "After that he drank night and day. Drank himself to death within a couple of years. Mama went to pieces right after the accident. She died a few months later. They said heart attack, but it was pure grief."

"How did you cope with all of that?" Laurel asked, unsure if she was supposed to go over and hug Janice or continue sitting and listening as she had been doing.

"Wasn't easy. In a lot of ways, Tom was mine. Until I left home."

"How did you get through all of that?" Laurel asked.

"I was here," Janice told her, gesturing her hands across the room. "I was living here with your father, so I missed a lot of Mama's end and Poppa's spiral. After Mama died, Bessie and I tried to get Poppa to stop drinking. When he wouldn't, we just let him go."

"I bet you felt very alone."

Breaking from her somber state, Janice smiled, answering surprisingly, "Not really." She closed her eyes as if summoning something to mind. "Ruth 1:16, *your people shall be my people.* I had your father, for a while at least. And I had Bessie and Ustus. Then when Ustus died, Bessie and I had each other. And now that Bessie is gone...here you are. I was, and am, a Hogue." Then, as if relinquishing the sadness she'd cast into the room, Janice made a joke to break the awkwardness. "Unfortunately, I don't have a recipe with that story, or I would let you print it."

CHAPTER THIRTEEN

Old Maid Brunswick Stew

L aurel wasn't sure why she kept going to Sunday church services with Janice. In a town devoid of entertainment options, maybe it was simply something to do. She was no closer to believing in God than she had ever been, but she did find herself enjoying the sermons. Hidden between bursts of fire-and-brimstone scripture were nuggets of insight she actually found useful. Little moral footnotes. Life lessons, camouflaged in biblical gibberish.

She was even considering going to the upcoming church fellowship dinner, providing Linc was planning to go. He was skipping this Sunday's service because a teacher buddy of his had tickets to last night's football game in Tuscaloosa. He must have known he would get in too late and planned to sleep in this morning. Laurel was not accustomed to this football obsession. Though she was not unfamiliar with the fandom of it, after all they have football up north too, but here in Alabama, it carried as much weight as anything Brother Daws shouted out about from the pulpit. On two separate occasions in town, she'd been asked if she "were Auburn" or "Alabama", as if she were expected to choose between two sides in a sacred blood feud. It took Linc explaining that Auburn University was the archrival team of The University of Alabama, despite their almost never managing to win against Alabama's Crimson Tide.

Church wasn't quite the same without being able to sneak glances with Linc behind her. However, Brother Daws gave another soul stirring sermon on the importance of forgiveness, or maybe it was honesty—she only paid occasional attention. Laurel was too occupied texting back and forth with Linc several times during the service, until Janice closed her hand over Laurel's phone like an admonishing mother. As the service ended, Laurel was sliding out of her pew when she noticed a man waving at her across the church, signaling for her to wait. When he made it over to her through the exiting parishioners, he handed her a manila folder.

"Am I being served?" she asked with light sarcasm.

The man did not appear to comprehend the joke.

"Are you a legal process server?" she clarified.

He grinned now, understanding her confusion. "Nothing like that. I'm Wilson Bevins. I wanted to show you some of these recipes. They belonged to a relative of mine." He shifted a little nervously on his feet, then in a quieter voice, added, "I hear you're collecting family stories too, and well...she had one. A big one. No one in my family knows what I know, and after me nobody will, unless I tell her story."

"I am not exactly following you," Laurel remarked. "Is the story already written in the folder?"

Wilson shook his head. "Some people believe family secrets should stay hidden. Protect the family name. Protect the dignity of the people involved. But if those people are dead and gone, is it better that no one remember them at all rather than taint their name nobody remembers anyway?"

"I still am not sure what you are asking me?"

Exhaling a deep breath, Wilson Bevins said, "Look over these. If there is nothing in these old handwritten recipes you think anyone would ever want to cook, or if they aren't unique enough to publish, then we will forget I ever talked to you. But if one of these hits you as good enough to print, I'll take that as a sign my great Aunt Liz's story is supposed to be told."

She felt the weight of the folder, realizing it was light and therefore could not contain many recipes. "I can glance at them now, if you like. Unless you're in a hurry."

Wilson didn't refuse the offer, so she took a look at the recipes. They were written by a very old hand, one who obviously hadn't finished school although they were still legible. Out of the four total options, two were an immediate no. Green bean casserole and monkey bread, neither with instructions, only a vague list of ingredients. The peach cobbler was interesting, but Laurel already had two other such recipes under consideration from other cooks. The Brunswick Stew seemed the logical choice. Her book would need a soup section and so far, all she had were a couple versions of chicken noodle, one beef stew, and her own grandmother's vegetable soup to choose from.

Laurel closed the folder and said, "I'll take the Brunswick Stew, Mr. Bevins. if the story is compelling enough."

He seemed pleased. "May we meet somewhere, and I can share it with you?"

"We could meet at my grandmother's house one day this week?"

Wilson's eyes darted, appearing uneasy about that. "I'm married, Miss Holden. And I have children. It wouldn't look right for me to show up to some pretty young woman's house alone. Could you meet me at the diner for lunch tomorrow? It's real public. My lunch break is at 11 a.m., if that's alright."

Laurel agreed. As Mr. Bevins walked away, Laurel felt rather good inside learning that she viewed as a young beauty in town. She would have to drop that little tidbit on Linc—just so he'd know she was apparently a catch.

* * *

When she arrived at the 2nd Street Diner, she found it held some amount of rustic charm. Slightly greasy, slightly chaotic, but undeniably popular. Of course, that is probably easy to accomplish when you are the only restaurant in town. Laurel arrived before Wilson Bevins, taking a booth table and perusing the menu. Salmon croquettes, Chicken and Dumplings, Fried or Blackened Catfish, and something called Burned Ends Pork Butt (*no thank you*), and a wide variety of vegetables to choose from. Busy scanning the menu while she waited for Wilson, she wasn't paying attention when a familiar voice called out her name.

"Angela!" Laurel exclaimed, glancing up to see the waitress standing at her table. "I didn't know you worked here."

"Every weekday," Angela smiled. "You by yourself today?"

"No, I am meeting someone. Maybe you know him, Wilson Bevins?"

"Yeah, I know Mr. Bevins. I'll go on and get three waters." Angela walked away before Laurel could ask why *three*? But all became clear when Wilson Bevins arrived accompanied by a woman.

"Good morning," he greeted Laurel before introducing his companion. "Miss Holden, this is my wife, Sheila."

Sheila was a friendly woman, shoulder length brown hair, medium build, but wore a few too many bracelets and necklaces—all appearing to be homemade with a bead kit. "I hope you don't mind me joining you?"

"Not at all," Laurel smiled.

Angela returned with the three waters and asked Laurel what she wanted from the menu. Laurel politely gestured to the Bevins to order first. "Oh, I already know what they want." Angela smiled. "It's Monday."

Sheila Bevins leaned across the table as if confiding, "We always get country fried steak on Mondays. It's the best."

Laurel agreed to have the same, although she was not quite sure what Sawmill gravy was. She glanced at the list of side dishes and chose her vegetables. Then it hit her. "Oh my God! This is what they call a *meat and 3*! I just got it."

Angela patted her back, winking at the Bevins. Though no one said it, Laurel got the distinct feeling she'd just been given a *bless her heart*, which she had come to know meant, *naive* at best, but usually *idiot*.

Moving straight to business, Wilson Bevins asked Laurel if she had changed her mind about the Brunswick Stew recipe, to which she replied she still thought it would be a good addition to her book. "But as I said, it requires a compelling story behind it."

Wilson nodded back, like her answer had unlocked something sacred. "Okay then. That's the sign I was waiting on. You see, Miss Holden, what I got to say is a family secret. Not even a family secret, being that only I, and my wife, of course, know it. It was told to me by my Daddy before he died."

Sheila jumped in, trying to soften the edge. "Wilson makes it sound mysterious, but the truth is—it would have been scandalous back then. Now? Not so much."

His face grim, Wilson admitted, "I wouldn't tell it normally, except I feel like I owe it to her. She's practically forgotten about in our family, and she shouldn't be."

"I'm listening," Laurel replied.

Wilson began his little family saga. The era from which it took place was revealed right at the beginning by his saying, "Nobody uses the term *old maid* anymore. But not too many years ago, it was a common thing to hear." He glanced quizzically at Laurel, as if estimating her age.

"Thirty-three," she revealed, already knowing where this was going. "I suppose I'd have been called an old maid back then too."

Sheila piped in, apologetically. "I think it's an unforgiveable label they used to cast on women. No one dared give a man such a label. Men were called a *confirmed bachelor*. That sounds almost *dignified*."

Laurel almost commented that she'd always thought it implied they were secretly gay but decided to keep that to herself. She did, however, feel obliged to defend womankind a little. "I've never felt as if a stigma is on me for having never been married. Women marry much later now than they used to—if they even marry at all. We do not need a man for survival."

"That is true," agreed Sheila. "But at the time Wilson's story takes place, it wasn't. It wouldn't matter much if it happened now, but back then an unmarried woman was a burden on her family."

Wilson Bevins told the story with great care. Laurel could tell he held a sacred respect for his family, even those members he never knew. He told it with almost biographical reverence. As he spoke, his gentleness towards his heroine caused Laurel to mentally collect certain turns of a phrase, or cadence of sentence, and catalogue them in her brain to recall later when and if she wrote this story.

"Everyone knew Liz Bevins had missed her time," Wilson began. "That critical window when a girl can secure a husband."

He continued explaining how Liz's sisters had all crossed that threshold a long time ago, each married with homes of their own. For Liz, the fact that both of her younger sisters were married, only made her seem all the more pathetic to any remaining men still searching for a wife. For a brief time, it looked as if she might have a potential husband on the line she began keeping company with Billy Slade. Though not an ideal match, or even a desired one, he was available, and that was good enough for Liz.

"Liz felt certain Billy would marry her," Wilson stressed, allowing Laurel's mind to fill in the unspoken blanks.

Wilson went on to explain how Liz's budding courtship was interrupted when a letter came to her parents. Liz's brother Wiley wrote how his wife Sally had fallen ill.

Sheila quickly noted, "Sally was the kind of delicate girl whose body wasn't in any shape to handle pregnancy."

Picking up again, Wilson explained. "My great grandparents sent Aunt Liz by train to stay with her brother and help look after Sally until she could deliver her baby. While Liz was two states away, Billy Slade began courting another girl. When Liz's mother wrote Liz with the news of Billy's marriage, Liz was devastated."

"I'll bet," Laurel remarked. "Her boyfriend married someone else while she was doing something nice for her brother and sister-in-law."

Sheila's face turned sorrowful as she confided, "But it wasn't love for Billy that shook her to the core. You see, Miss Holden, Sally wasn't the only one who was gonna have a baby!"

Laurel glanced at Wilson, who was nodding. "My great aunt Liz was pregnant too, by Billy," he said. "Once Liz started to show, her brother Wiley and his wife thought it was best for her to remain with them until both babies were born." Wilson's face looked sadly apologetic, as if feeling the need to explain his family's little conspiracy. "There was no way Liz could go back home in her shameful condition. Her parents would have thrown her out, anyway."

Sheila chimed in once more, "Sally was only two months further along than Liz. Wiley figured they'd pass both babies off as twins."

"Twins!" Laurel exclaimed. "Even only a two-month difference you would still be able—"

"Now, not in those times, Miss Holden." Wilson explained. "Folks didn't have neighbors living on top of them back then. It was a good mile to the next nearest house. If they just stayed to themselves a month or two, both babies would be grown enough to cover the little secret."

Wilson's history of his two ancestor's pregnancies took a tragic turn as he continued. Sally's waning health deteriorated further and both she, and her baby died in childbirth. Wiley was distraught beyond belief. It was Liz who kept him going through his grief. With his own family lost forever, Liz's unfathomable situation became Wiley's focus. He not only needed to protect his sister's name, but he was terrified she might die giving birth too. When Liz's delivery time came Wiley prayed with every breath while he delivered the baby alone, without witnesses. Both Liz and the baby survived.

With a low voice and sour expression, Sheila confided to Laurel, "Wiley Bevins wrote his parents that Sally died in childbirth having twins. He figured they could still pass of Liz's boy as his own, and by saying it was a twin, could account for it being smaller."

"From that time on, Liz Bevin's son was known as Wiley and Sally Bevin's son for the rest of his life," Wilson said sorrowfully, adding, "And for the rest of his children's lives too. Nobody knew a thing until my father told me ten years ago on his deathbed."

"Wow," Laurel gasped. "Poor Liz. What she must have gone through, never being able to claim her own son."

Wilson had a little more to say about that. "In the beginning it was a great situation for Aunt Liz. She remained with Wiley for a couple of years, under the pretense of helping out. But Wiley was still a young man. Over time he got married again, and his new wife wasn't too keen on having an old maid sister-in-law always around."

Angela returned with the lunch plates, causing the conversation to come abruptly to a halt until she left again. Then Laurel whispered across the table to the Bevins, "They kicked her out? Made her leave her own child just to keep the secret?"

"Liz became one of those relatives who got passed from house to house every few months," Wilson replied. "She'd stay with one sister for a while, then go to the next, then the next, then back to Wiley for a turn. Every time it was her turn to go to Wiley's she would see her son, how much he'd grown, and hear him call Wiley's wife 'Mamma' just like his little brothers did."

"Liz Bevins lived and died an old maid," Sheila said. "I met her once, briefly at our wedding. She died a month later. But even that brief meeting, I remember her seeming a little overexcited to meet me. Hugged me just a little too long. You know?"

Laurel nodded. "You were her grandson's wife and only she knew it."

"Exactly." Sheila said. "Ever since my father-in-law told Wilson the truth, it's weighed heavy on him."

Wilson Bevins's face now looked back at Laurel as though he were ashamed. As if he had done something so reprehensibly cruel that he could not forgive himself. "I never thought anything about her other than, Old Aunt Liz. Poor Old Aunt Liz," Wilson admitted. "She was so good to me the few times I ever saw her. If I had known Aunt Liz was my grandma, I'd have shown her more love. I don't even think I ever said I love you to that woman. She said it to me every family reunion, funeral, or wedding. And I never said it back."

Laurel looked sympathetically at the troubled man. "You will say it back. I will print your story. Aunt Liz's Brunswick Stew will right the wrongs she suffered. Anyone who reads it will know Liz Bevins was your grandmother. Letting go of the secret can be your 'I love you' to her."

When the Bevins's left, Laurel waited to say goodbye to Angela, and ask how her effort to persuade her boyfriend to get married was going. "Maybe making some progress," Angela remarked. "Hard to tell."

"What does he do?"

Angela shuffled a moment on her feet and said, "Coal mine. Around here you either work at the mine, the mill, or farm."

Laurel then asked, "Hey, before I go...how did you know to bring three waters earlier. I didn't even know Mrs. Bevins was coming."

Angela laughed. "You'll soon figure everybody out. They don't go nowhere without the other one. From what I heard, before they was married, they were each going with somebody else. Turns out his girlfriend was running around behind his back with Miss Sheila's boyfriend. So, when Mr. Wilson and Miss Sheila started dating way back when, they promised to never let the other ever worry about being unfaithful. They won't do anything unless the other is with them."

"Really?"

"Yeah," Angela said. "My daddy makes fun of Mr. Bevins for it. Says Mr. Bevins is hen pecked and can't never go do anything with his friends or anything on his own. Says he ain't a real man letting a woman control him like that." Angela sighed and glanced out of the window as if wishing for something. "But I think it's sweet. They respect each other's feelings, you know? I think it's nice."

* * *

Laurel liked it too. Wilson and Sheila's story alone, with a little dramatic license, could make a good addition to her book. But for now, all she wanted to do was get home and transcribe the story of Aunt Liz. Laurel couldn't help but wonder how many Aunt Liz's existed somewhere in everyone's family tree.

Wilson's Recipe known in real life as...

AUNT LIZ'S BRUNSWICK STEW

Ingredients

1 Whole chicken

2 quarts water

1 onion chopped

2 cups cooked ham

3 potatoes diced (Idaho or Yukon, but if you use Yukon make it 5 potatoes cause they are small)

2 16 oz canned tomatoes cut up

10 ounces lima beans (frozen is fine but thaw partially)

10 ounces black eyed peas (frozen but partially thawed)

10 ounces whole kernel frozen corn (partially thawed)

2 tsp salt

¼ tsp pepper

½ tsp seasoned salt

1 tsp sugar

1. In large pot boil chicken with onion and ham until chicken is done
2. Remove chicken and cool until meat can be torn off the bones
3. Add meat back to pot
4. Add tomatoes, potatoes, beans, corn, salt, sugar, and pepper
5. Lower heat from boil to medium and continue cooking covered
6. Once potatoes and beans are cooked, lower heat and let simmer until ready to eat

CHAPTER FOURTEEN

May the Best Cookie Win

Word about the cookbook, and the accompanying Southern stories, had spread around Scroggins like butter on a hot biscuit. Laurel was becoming overwhelmed with entries as everyone wanted in. Recipes poured in faster than she could organize them. Some were delightfully unexpected. Others? Repetitive. One dish stood out for its sheer redundancy: chocolate chip cookies. Laurel was drowning in them. An idea sprang to mind on how to address the several hopefuls at once. Laurel would host a bakeoff. It would not only be the perfect way to choose the best chocolate chip cookie entry without bruising feelings, but Laurel would invite the women to Bessie's house to battle out who would win the chapter.

Puddin Corder was emphatic that her mother's cookies would outshine any others, while Patience Daniels argued her family recipe was unbeatable. Even the preacher's wife, Lottie Daws, wanted to be considered for selection, although she was not as braggadocios as her counterparts. Janice took the day off from the furniture store, offering to help Laurel judge. Laurel had invited Flossie, but her elderly aunt turned down the invitation citing that it overlapped with her soap opera, *General Hospital*. Delva agreed to join in, pronouncing herself as an expert judge since she owned the local bakery. Obedience Daniels became a judge as well, tagging along with her sister. Of course, Obedience had ulterior motives, and the others knew it. She was not there to champion her sister, but to police, edit, or veto whatever family story Patience chose to tell the writer. Laurel suspected, however, the old woman just simply had nothing else to do or anyone else to do it with.

By midafternoon, the long kitchen table was bustling with culinary activity. Each woman carved out her station like an artist at her easel. The plastic tablecloth rippled beneath mixing bowls and measuring cups. Flour floated in the air like dust particles caught in sunlight. The window unit hummed, blasting just enough cool air to keep the mist of flour in motion. Feet scuffed over the flour dusted linoleum in a flurry of activity.

While the three competing women sifted their flour, cracked their eggs, and nibbled at their bowls of chocolate chips, Laurel and Janice were more captivated by the way Lottie Daws kept removing hairpins from her hairdo whenever she paused to check her recipe. Laurel counted at least six pins withdrawn from that beehive, wondering when that Jenga of a hairdo might collapse.

Delva, picking up on what her friends were watching, asked outright, "Lottie, how many of those pins come out before your hair falls down?"

A lighthearted laugh escaped from the preacher's wife signaling she too knew her habit was ridiculous. "I swear I pull about twenty of these things out every week after my hair gets done. The lady who does it puts way too many in. After a while they start to poke my scalp as they settle. Drives me crazy. And by my weekly appointment on Fridays, it looks like I have a deflated mushroom on my head."

"Miss Lottie," Janice asked. "Why don't you just change your look? No one says you are required to live under the assault of hairpins all the time."

Lottie placed her flour dusted hands on her hips, leaving perfect prints on her sides when she removed them. "You would think that would be the solution, wouldn't you. But ladies every time I get to thinking about cutting my hair off short, I hear my Mama's voice in my brain telling me it is a sin to cut a woman's hair."

"Is it?" Laurel asked, looking around to the other women. "I never heard that."

"Oh, there is a passage in the Bible that says a woman's long hair is her glory," Lottie replied. "But my mama interpreted that as a mighty high sin."

Puddin saw Laurel's confused face and tossed a chocolate chip at her to get her attention. "Old Testament is full of harsh laws. When Jesus came down to earth, He pretty much done away with all those rules. Jesus told us to follow His new doctrine. Basically, all He wants is for us to love one another and be good to one another."

This pushed Laurel to remark, "If the Old Testament is invalidated by the New Testament, why is the Old Testament still preached? Brother Daws was quoting it just last Sunday."

Being the preacher's wife, Lottie took the reins to answer that question. "Old Testament is still The Bible, along with the New. You must know both, but Jesus' word is less strict, like Puddin said."

"Basically, the Old Testament is God's word," Patience explained. "And the New Testament is Jesus's."

"The new generation!" Laurel laughed, although no one else did.

Looking up from her cross-stitching for the first time since she came in, Obedience Daniels scolded her sister. "I don't believe anyone requires your naive breakdown of our faith, Patience."

Delva jumped back to Lottie's original statement, "So Sister Daws, if you feel sinful cutting your hair, why don't you just wear it long and not fuss with those pins?"

Obedience coughed lightly into her hand before offering her pious opinion. "Women of a certain age do not wear their hair down their back. It would be vulgar. I have kept my hair off my shoulders since the day I saw my first sign of crow's feet."

Lottie, though disapproving of how Obedience explained it, nodded quietly in agreement with what she said. "Not to mention, when you are raising a family, little fingers and long hair bring a good many headaches."

"Well, surely you are past your raising children stage," Laurel chuckled.

Lottie chuckled back, "That's what all mother's think just as their young ones reach adulthood, but then you get grandchildren they ask you to babysit and it's yanked hair all over again."

Finished before the others in getting her batter spooned onto a pan, Puddin was the first to put her cookies in the oven. Patience followed a few minutes after, then Lottie. Handing their recipes over to Laurel to look over, she scanned them for similarities and differences. Before today, Laurel hadn't expected much deviation from one chocolate chip cookie to another, but now she realized they could be very different indeed.

Delva peered over Laurel's shoulder as she read the recipes, then with a tone of accusation, said, "Now Puddin, are you sure this is *all the ingredients?*"

Laurel raised a brow Delva's way.

"What do you mean, Delva Hopkins!" Puddin replied indignantly, with a slight squeak in her voice as everyone's eyes fell on her.

Pulling the paper from Laurel's hands, Delva gave it a closer inspection. With an exaggerated "Humphf," she tossed it across the table in Puddin's general direction, declaring "Cordelia 'Puddin' Corder! You and me go way too far back for you to expect me to fall for this foolishness. You know blame well every recipe you ever share with somebody ain't really the recipe. You always leave out an ingredient, or you add something extra to make it taste weird, or you short the egg count."

Protesting the accusation, Puddin yelled, "I do not!"

"You do too!" challenged Delva. "Anything that makes it almost the same recipe as yours, but not quite as good."

Laurel glanced at the others, gauging their reactions. Lottie sent her a playful side wink. Patience was giggling. And Obedience, who looked uncharacteristically amused, gave Laurel a single, very subtle, nod. It was clear these friends knew each other well.

Still feigning outrage, Puddin, now red-faced with embarrassment, cried, "Delva! I don't do that. Why would I do that?"

Normally a person who preferred to remain neutral in other people's conflict, the preacher's wife felt compelled to weigh in. "It's true, Puddin. Remember four years ago when you gave me your meatloaf recipe? Tasted like I made it out of those brown tubes under the toilet paper rolls. It was so dry and tasteless." Addressing the rest of the women now, Lottie confided, "It was nothing like the meatloaf she brings to church dinners."

"You just aren't as good a cook as me, Lottie Daws!"

Placing her hand on Laurel's shoulder, Delva testified, "That is not her real cookie recipe. I stood at this table and watched her add both vanilla and almond extract, but she only wrote vanilla on that list."

"So, I accidentally left almond out," Puddin sighed. "Just a simple mistake."

"What about your brown sugar?" Obedience snorted without looking up from her cross-stitching.

Laurel reached across the table to retrieve the recipe. Scanning the list of ingredients, she defended the frazzled Puddin, "No, Miss Daniels, she listed brown sugar. I see it right here."

With triumphant clarification, Obedience sneered, "Yes, but which sugar? Puddin used both light brown and dark brown sugar."

Puddin blushed again, this time her eyes held a hint of shame. They'd caught her.

"Girl," Delva chortled. "You know well as I do there is a big difference between dark brown and light brown sugar. Besides, you used a half cup of each. Not one cup of just one. I'm telling you, Miss Laurel, you can't trust Puddin's recipes. She always wants to make sure nobody makes it as good as her."

Inspecting it again, seeing both Delva and Obedience were correct, Laurel laid it aside, but not before gently asserting to Puddin, that if her cookie won and tasted the best, she would need to correct the recipe to include everything. She then looked at Patience's recipe and saw something she'd never heard of before. "Miss Patience, what is oleo?"

Delva answered for her, "That's just shortening. She used it. That stick of Crisco there."

While the cookies were baking, each woman told their corresponding story. Puddin's tale revolved around the day her late husband buried his beloved hunting dog Daisy. Daisy was his pride and joy. According to Puddin, she was the best deer hunting dog in the state and no matter how much other men offered for her, her Hershall would never sell Daisy. When Daisy was dying, he brought her into the house and put her in the guest bed where he stayed with her all night. Puddin's cookies were the only thing he ate while he sat up with his dog. It was a nice enough story about a man's genuine love for his cherished companion, but Laurel doubted it was book worthy—unless that cookie was freaking awesome.

Lottie had a death story as well, only hers involved a person. She recounted a memory of when she sat day and night with a past church member dying from cancer. It was a touching story, one Laurel thought readers may connect with, although, the personal connection lacked the depth Laurel was hoping for. Its only tie to the cookie was it having been one of many recipes the dying woman shared with Lottie during the long hours they passed together. In comparison to some of the other emotional tales Laurel already collected, Lottie's didn't quite measure up.

By this time, the three contending cookies were fully baked, cooled, and ready for tasting. Patience had not yet told the story to her chocolate chip cookie, but Laurel, Janice, and Delva went ahead with the tasting part of the contest while the entries were still warm. Puddin's cookie was delicious. There was no doubt about it. Laurel was beginning to worry about the uphill fight to acquire an authentic recipe from her if it beat out the others. Her worry was short lived as Patience's cookie knocked Puddin's out of the running. Moist, sweet, yet salty, it was everything a chocolate chip cookie should be. Laurel and Janice could tell by the other two contestants' faces, they knew they were beaten. Delva's vote was the same, that Patience's cookie was better than Puddin's. Obedience remained mum until the final cookie was tried. The preacher's wife's cookie was still untasted. Everyone bit into Lottie's cookie. It was nice, but honestly no better than store bought. The judges were in total agreement. Patience was the hands down winner and even Obedience had to begrudgingly admit it. Her sister had outshined the others.

Patience Daniels was delighted to have won the coveted spot in the cookbook. Try as she might to conceal her pride for her sister's win, Obedience was glad as well. Her sister had so few wins in life, it pleased Obedience to see this one, which meant so much to Patience.

Now it was time for her to tell her story as all eyes looked across the table towards her. She unfolded her tale with childlike reverence, made clear once she revealed it was about her mother. With a careful glance her sister's way before moving into the story, Patience saw the flicker of sentiment in Obedience's eyes. Obedience now understood what story Patience wanted to tell and approved. It was a simple recollection, yet powerfully dear to the storyteller, of how their mother used something as simple as making cookies, to educate them. As Patience wove her little narrative, Obedience seemed to be smiling as well.

"Mother believed girls deserved to be as educated as boys," Patience divulged. "Although Father did not see the purpose. I don't know how early in life she started with us," Patience paused and looked at her sister, "I suppose she did it with you and Prue before I was born." Obedience sent her a gentle nod as Patience continued. "Mother would pull me in to help make cookies. She would use the chocolate chips to teach me how to count." Patience went on to explain how in the beginning, her mother would ask her to place 5 chips in the first cookie, then 6 in the next, followed by 7, 8, etc.

"Her lessons became more complicated the older I got. She would tell me to make the first cookie have 4 chips, then on the second cookie add 6 to the 4." Pausing her simplistic story in case anyone did not understand, she said, "She was teaching me to count to 10, you see." After the others politely nodded, Patience went on. "Then the next week she would pull out the pans to make cookies and after the dough was ready, she told me to put 13 chips in the first cookie. She then asked me how many chips it would be if I put 5 less in the second cookie."

Laurel smiled at the sweet woman, "She was teaching you addition and subtraction."

Giggling, Patience exclaimed, "And more than that! It would get much more complicated as we got older. She would tell us to add the number of chips in the first row and divide the number of chips in the last cookie, saying our second row should only have that specific number chips in every cookie." Patience clapped her hands together happily and beamed, "I never knew multiplication and division could be so delicious!"

Breaking in with her own contribution to her sister's tale, Obedience replied, "Then of course with the fully baked cookies, we learned fractions and percentages. Our mother always did her best to instill a hunger for learning."

"No better way than with these cookies!" Lottie laughed, waving her almost completely devoured cookie.

Folding her stitching in her lap, Obedience took a more active role in the conversation now. Stirred by reminisces of the past. "Mother taught us something with everything in life. For example, we had a tulip garden in spring. In the mornings, we would go out with her to cut fresh blooms for our dining table. Mother would tell us about how in the 17th century, the Netherlands entire financial market collapsed over tulips."

"Tulips?" Janice repeated. "Really?"

Obedience nodded. "I don't recall specific details, but as I remember she said tulip bulbs were as valuable as currency, even traded as such for a few years. Then for some reason or another, the tulip market plummeted and sent their people into ruin."

Patience's eyes sparkled as though she were a girl again. "Mother used anything at her disposal to teach us something we'd otherwise never have learned."

The Daniels sisters' story was an understated one, much different from the others Laurel had heard, but there was an important simplicity to it which she felt was important to include in the book. Perhaps most mothers were like theirs had been. Laurel really had no of knowing. The only things she'd ever learned from her mother was how to dodge the landlord and what a blackout drunk looked like. She found herself wishing she had been one of the Daniels sisters.

Patience's Recipe known in real life as...

HOUSE FAMILY CHOCOLATE CHIP COOKIES

Created by my great grandmother Sydney House, passed down from my grandmother Louise House, and improved upon by myself and my son, Britton House

Ingredients

¾ cup shortening (Crisco butter flavor is best)

¾ cup light brown sugar

¾ cup dark brown sugar

2 tbsp whole milk (not 2%, and definitely not skim...what's wrong with you?)

1 tbsp vanilla (if out, don't sub almond, go buy vanilla. Almond is just nasty!)

1 egg

1 ¾ cup all-purpose flour (not self-rising, you'll mess it up)

1 tsp salt

¾ tsp baking soda (baking SODA, not baking powder!)

1 cup semi-sweet chocolate chips (Now here you can get creative. Sometimes ½ cup semi ½ cup dark is good. But white chocolate messes up the taste.)

1. Preheat oven to 350°
2. Combine shortening, brown sugar, milk, and vanilla in a bowl and mix and beat on low or medium
3. Once that is mixed, add the egg and keep blending
4. In a separate bowl mix flour, salt, and baking soda and whisk or sift together lightly by hand
5. Slowly add flour mixture to the shortening mixture and keep beating on low (if you beat higher you are going to have a bunch of flour blow out in your face!)

6. While still beating on low, slowly add the chocolate chips.
7. Spoon dough onto a lightly oiled baking sheet. (Don't make cookies too big, or too small)
8. Bake 8–10 minutes
9. Let cool on counter 15 minutes before removing from sheet

CHAPTER FIFTEEN

Quilting Bee

Quilting Bees always seemed to Laurel to belong with other relics of a bygone era like butter churns or the ice wagon. When she received an invitation to join the next session of one, she was unsure what to expect.

Entering Bootsie Taylor's home she found a large canvas of sewn together scraps draped across the Taylor's round oak table. Around the perimeter sat Patience Daniels, Delva Hopkins, and Puddin Corder, each stationed like sentries at their corners, needles flashing in and out of fabric with the rhythm of women who'd done this their whole lives. Having no sewing ability, Laurel observed the women at their work, with each taking time to explain the precision put into every stitch. Their current endeavor was crafting a quilt for Puddin's baseball-obsessed grandson. Using cutouts of similarly colored cloth, the women recreated a grassy field, baseball mound, and a player in uniform with his raised bat aimed at the ball. Laurel was impressed at the detail achieved using nothing but random pieces of material. Despite the quilt only being half completed, their work was coalescing into an impressively accurate depiction.

"Years of practice," Puddin giggled in response to Laurel's praise of their skill. "We've been doing this a long time. The last quilt was for me. We made a different kind of fruit in every square."

Showing her novice experience with such crafts, Laurel remarked to the ladies, "The quilts Bessie had are thicker though."

"Oh, honey," Delva chuckled. "We ain't finished yet. Once we have the front all done, we start sewing the back. We stuff in cotton batting before we close each square section."

Laurel felt silly after the obvious explanation. "My grandmother's quilts are very beautiful. Was she part of your group?"

"Oh, my yes," Bootsie replied. "Bessie was quite skilled with a needle, till her poor fingers got stiff from arthritis. But that's why you don't make a quilt on your own. Other hands pick up the slack when your own start to fail." She went on to describe how years ago there were as many as three groups of four women gathered together working on multiple quilts.

"Your Aunt Flossie used to be part of the Bee," Puddin revealed. "But like Bessie, her hands are not what they used to be. She dropped out after Bessie had to. Those were the days though," she continued, enjoying the memories. "We'd have 10 or 12 of us together, all just talking away, enjoying our work and companionship."

"What happened to everyone else?" Laurel asked.

Bootsie answered with a mournful gaze, "Well, some died, like your grandmother...and a few others. Some took sick. Some, like Flossie, just couldn't manage the dexterity anymore."

"And some," Patience sighed. "Some just got busy with other things. A few got jobs—the younger girls—after their kids were grown. Some just plain got bored of it. I guess sitting around talking with a bunch of old women made them feel old. Seems a shame too. This is very relaxing. Keeps the blood pressure down. And you have something to feel proud about at the end of the day."

Though no one asked her to do it, Laurel began to scout out the next piece of fabric needed. When one lady laid her final stitch into a scrap, Laurel was ready with the next piece in a matching color. It was fun. It was also helpful, as no one had to pause their sewing to search for the next piece. After a moment of quiet, Puddin made a shallow gasp, as if suddenly remembering something important.

"I plumb forgot till just now. Do you girls know who I ran into at the drug store yesterday afternoon after we left Laurel's? Mary Peterson. And do you know what she was buying?" Puddin took a long, dramatic pause, leaving space for someone to shout out a guess. But no one did, they simply waited for her to continue.

"What, Puddin?" Delva finally howled impatiently. "A box of Ex-Lax? We don't know!"

Leaning across the quilt as if she were about to share highly classified government secrets, Puddin whispered, "One of those tests."

Rolling her eyes, Delva again chastised her friend. "What test? Pregnancy? Flu? Covid? Cholesterol? We weren't there Puddin!"

"One a'them AIDS tests."

Laurel stiffened suddenly. "Do you mean an HIV test?"

"That's the one!" Puddin answered. "I waited till she was gone before I asked the pharmacist assistant. She said she wasn't allowed to tell me. So, I waited till she got off work and I called her momma."

"Mrs. Peterson's mother?" Laurel asked.

"No, Sweety!" Puddin cried. "Debbie's mama. Debbie is the pharmacy assistant. I know'd she'd tell her mama about it. Her mama and I go way back. She told me that Debbie told her, it was for the Peterson boy."

Laurel's heart fluttered in her chest. "Are you saying they believe Cade may have HIV?"

"I don't know," Puddin replied. "Maybe. All I know is the Peterson boy got caught messing around with the Hinton boy. You know, he always did seem to me to be different. I guess he's one a'them gays."

"And they just assumed he has HIV because he is gay?" Laurel cried. "That is so offensive."

Delva exchanged looks with Laurel. "He works around your place, doesn't he?"

Laurel did not want to be drawn into local gossip, especially about someone she liked. She did her best to answer without betraying their confidence. "Cade cuts the grass around my grandmother's place and keeps the field behind the house pig trimmed."

"Bushhogged," Bootsie laughed. "Well, he always seemed like a nice boy. Don't guess it's any of our business."

"Now you know you'll be telling this to everybody that comes in The Fashion Statement, Boots!" Delva snickered.

"Only if someone asks if I've heard about it yet," Bootsie defended herself, as if that were much of a defense.

"Poor thing," Patience said, after remaining uncharacteristically silent. "His daddy is not a nice man. I hope he doesn't hurt that poor boy. But I suppose this explains why I heard the Hinton's were taking a trip unexpectedly. You know, the Hinton's live on our street. They asked one of our neighbors to collect their mail for a few days."

The talk upset Laurel. It wasn't that the ladies were being unkind, because they weren't. She was worried about Cade. What must be happening in his life right now? She hoped he would be by soon to cut the grass so she could check on him. The sewing went on and other conversations went around holding less shocking subject matters. Laurel was now at Bootsie's side handing her the next fabric scrap. She watched Bootsie's finger movements piercing in and out of the quilt, making carefully precise stitches.

Glancing up at her guest, Bootsie asked, "Laurel, would you like to try?"

Laurel threw her hands up in defeat before even trying. "Oh no! I have no skills at all when it comes to sewing."

"Well, neither does anybody else till they learn," Bootsie remarked. Rising from her chair and pushing the young newcomer into her place, she told Laurel, "I will guide your fingers for the first few, but you can do this Laurel. You're a smart accomplished woman."

"Yeah, if old buzzards like us can do this, you certainly can!" Delva cried. "And you have young eyes."

Laurel was about to say her eyes still needed readers, but before she could, Bootsie began directing her hands through the motions. Within a few seconds, she released Laurel's hands, allowing them to move freely with their newfound knowledge. "Look at that, Laurel! You are doing it. You are quilting!"

A girlish excitement overcame Laurel as she saw her very own fingers stitching the triangle cloth to its mate, rounding out the final piece of the baseball. The others noticed the smile of accomplishment on the young woman's face and the gleam in her eyes when Bootsie handed her another scrap of fabric.

"Go on," Bootsie urged. "You know how now."

As Laurel began sewing her very own piece of fabric from start to finish, the older women grinned to one another. There was something beautifully innocent and vulnerable about Laurel as she glanced up to Bootsie for approval after a few stitches. Bootsie patted her shoulder with a wink and nodded for her to keep sewing.

"You've never had anyone around to teach you things like this, have you Laurel?" Patience asked.

"No ma'am," Laurel answered. "I've never had any women in my life who did anything worth learning."

"I sure wish Bessie was here to see you," Bootsie offered. "Would make her smile for sure."

Puddin spoke up excitedly, "Laurel, you missed a lot not having a grandmother. Consider us three your grandmothers now. We done taught you about cooking. Now sewing. You stick with us, and we'll teach you a lot more."

Laurel smiled brightly at them, appreciative of the kindness she'd been shown from the moment she met them all. Bootsie handed her a new piece of blue fabric. "Keep going," she said. "You're doing fine."

"But where does it go?" Laurel asked, nervously.

"It's blue, Laurel!" Delva chirped. "Probably should go in the sky behind the baseball player, don't you think?"

Patience tilted the panel she was working on towards Laurel, showing her to just replicate what she was doing. Laurel took a breath and started patching the sky in place. She worked through the next hour, chatting away with the others about various things, from her travels to the preacher's sermon last Sunday. Bootsie had excused herself to begin prepping her pot roast for dinner. Laurel tried to give back her seat at the quilting table, but Bootsie refused. She assured Laurel it helped her more having her stand in for her for a little while because she'd forgotten about dinner.

Once the roast was in the oven, the girls were wrapping up this week's labor. Bootsie came to admire their combined work, praising Laurel for her efforts. "You can't tell where I stopped, and you started! You did great!"

Laurel wasn't sure that statement was totally true, she could certainly tell the difference from where she began, but she did have to admit to herself she had not ruined the blanket. Puddin folded the quilt over itself a few times until it was in a nice portable bundle to take home until the next meeting. As the tabletop became free again, Bootsie set out a stack of plates and forks before removing a pie from the refrigerator.

"Is this what I hope it is?" Patience squealed, slapping her soft hand onto Laurel's arm. "Bootsie makes the best Lemon Icebox Pie you'll ever taste. It should be in a---" she stopped short, giggling at her own words. "It can be in a book! Miss Laurel, you will definitely want to add this to your cookbook."

Laurel slid her fork into the light-yellow piece of pie. The wafer crust alone was worth the mouthful, but the tangy, sweet, yet tartness of the pie made her mouth water the moment it awakened her tastebuds. Laurel was relieved the pie was so good. Bootsie Taylor was not in her book so far, and after her kindness with the quilt, Laurel would hate to deny her a spot in the cookbook. But this pie was outstanding and would be a great addition because she had no other lemony desserts in the book yet.

"This really is fantastic pie," Laurel mumbled with her mouthful. "Would you be interested in me putting it in?"

"Into your book?" Bootsie exclaimed. "Honestly, I never considered it. I was going to show you my pot roast recipe and bring you a sampling of it tomorrow. I never thought about the pie."

"This pie has to go in," Laurel proclaimed. "If you have a good story with it, I would love to use it."

Bootsie, overwhelmed by the compliment, summoned her brain for anything she might connect to this pie. Only one memory really sprung to mind, but it wasn't quite like the tales others had submitted. She wasn't sure it counted.

"I don't have anything specific about when this was made. The only thing I have is a sad memory about a period of time when we never cooked this pie."

Intrigued, Laurel asked her to explain.

"Well, you see, my daddy loved this pie. It was his grandmother's recipe. That's why it's called Lettie's Lemon Icebox Pie. Cause back then they didn't have refrigerators in people's houses, just the ice box."

"Isn't that the same thing?" Laurel asked.

"Oh no, girl!" Delva cried. "An ice box didn't have no electric plug. Nobody had any electricity back then."

"We had electricity!" Patience argued.

"Okay then," Delva snapped. "Rich white people had electricity. But the rest of us just had an insulated cooler with a square box on top."

"That's where the chunk of ice went," Puddin explained. "You'd get a block of ice from the man who drove the ice truck through and put it at the top of the cooler. As it melted it ran down the sides and kept whatever was stored inside cooled off."

With the mystery of what an ice box was solved, Bootsie went about telling the story of her pie. "My Mama and Daddy had a sweet relationship back when I was growing up. Back then, most folks got married just to have babies to work the farm. Then some people got married cause their parents made them. I'm sure those people came to love each other over time. Seemed like they did to me. But my Mama and Daddy were different. They really did love each other. And they had a lot of kids to prove it."

"They sure did!" Puddin giggled. "Your mama and daddy had a heap of children."

"My brother Alvin was one of the oldest of my brothers and sisters," Bootsie went on. "He was a real cut up."

She laughed to herself a moment, lost perhaps in the memory of her brother's laugh. Laurel sensed she hadn't thought about him in some time and enjoyed being reminded.

Bootsie continued, "Alvin would come up to us and poke his fingers under our arms when we weren't suspecting. You know, tickling us. He was always laughing, that Alvin. And he loved it when Mama made Lemon Icebox Pie. Course, by then we did have a refrigerator. He could always trick Mama into making that a pie."

"Trick?" Laurel asked.

Bootsie nodded with a smile. "None of us ever really noticed it until Alvin made a joke one day about how she only ever made that pie when Daddy asked her to. Mama preferred cakes, cause they fed more of us. She had to make two or three pies for all of us to have a slice. Well, it became Alvin's running joke that every time we had Lemon Icebox, it was because Daddy wanted it, or as Alvin liked to tease, *her boyfriend*. He'd say 'Mama don't love us as much as she loves Daddy.'"

Feeling the need to clarify something which didn't need clarifying, Bootsie stopped her story to emphasize, "It was just joking you understand. Alvin didn't mean nothing over it. He just liked to pick on Mama, rile her up. Didn't really rile her, she enjoyed it. It was their way of kidding with each other."

"I understand," Laurel said.

"Well, Alvin took up with this girl. Her name was Gracie. Real pretty thing, she was. And Alvin decided he wanted to marry her. Daddy was against it. Said Gracie was only marrying cause her daddy had died and her mama wanted some young man to work their place. Daddy said we needed Alvin to stay on our farm. You see, my brothers weren't as old or strong as Alvin was."

"I was just a little girl," Puddin chimed in. "But I remember Alvin, and that poor girl."

"Well, I don't!" Delva exclaimed. "But now I'm not as bored as I was when you first started tellin' this story. Go on Boots!"

Smiling timidly, because she was aware it was taking far too long to tell a story which, had it been about other people, she'd have finished by now. But it was her brother. Her favorite brother. And she had not spoken of him in so long, she found herself taking her time. "Alvin and Gracie really did love each other. I truly believe that. Daddy was wrong, and that ain't something I say too often. But in this case, he was. He refused to let Alvin and Gracie get married."

Laurel interrupted momentarily to inject her own observation. "But wasn't Alvin grown? Surely, he didn't need your father's permission?"

"No, he didn't," Bootsie replied. "And he didn't wait for it neither. Alvin was gonna drive out to get Gracie and find the preacher, but Daddy wouldn't let him take the truck. He wrestled them keys away from Alvin, telling him it was his truck and if he was determined to go to that girl, he could walk!"

Bootsie took a breath, shivering slightly from the old emotions rushing back to her. "I'll never forget how Mama begged Daddy to let them get married and let him take the truck. It was pourin' rain, you see. And it was winter. But Daddy kept the keys and Alvin stormed out into the rain. He didn't make it to his girl's house. He got a few miles down the road and started feeling pretty sick. It was getting dark, but he saw our Granny's house further down the way. By the time he got to her door he collapsed."

More invested in the story than she thought she'd be, Laurel cried, "Oh no!"

"Granny doctored him as best she could. She called down to our house to tell Daddy that Alvin was real sick. Daddy wouldn't go. Too stubborn and mad to give in. Mama went. Took the truck and drove down to Granny's. I think that was the only time I ever knew my Mama to drive. She was gone all night into the next day. When she come back, she looked at Daddy, threw his keys at him, and said 'Alvin's dead."

Laurel gasped, as did Delva. Puddin, who still remembered that time in their shared history, picked up the story from her memory. "That Gracie girl had been waiting two days for Alvin to come and marry her. For two days she lived thinking she'd been jilted, and that Alvin gave in to his father. My oldest brother was a friend of Alvin. I remember him coming home and tellin' us what happened. He'd gone down to Gracie's place to tell her Alvin was dead. He said while he was standing there with her momma, Gracie went over to the fireplace, took down her daddy's shotgun, and shot herself in the chest. Shot herself right there in front of my brother and her mama."

Laurel could not fathom such a horrible scene. In her mind, rural life, especially a generation ago, was something she expected to be filled with nothing more than routine chores, backbreaking farm work, and menial events at best. Shakespearean love stories and Greek tragedies were not anything she would have expected in a place like Scroggins, Alabama.

Removing a book from a shelf, Bootsie flipped to the pie recipe. "Mama never forgave Daddy for Alvin's death. They went on together for the next 15 years, spoke some when they had to, but it wasn't ever the same. Mama never, ever, made this pie while my daddy was alive."

Bootsie pulled a dishtowel from where it was hanging over the handle of the oven. Dabbing the terrycloth to her cheek to catch a tear, raised her head in a triumphant manner. "When Daddy died from congestive heart failure, neighbors came over to pay their respects. All brought over some kind of dish. Mama was in the kitchen, making Lemon Ice Box Pie for the visitors to eat. She laid those pies down on the table and smiled so big. Said, 'I always did love this pie. So did Alvin."

Bootsie's Recipe known in real life as...

BIGMAMA'S LEMON ICEBOX PIE

Created by my grandmother Lettie Robertson,
who we often teased for only making it when our cousin
Randy came to visit from military duty.

Ingredients

3 eggs
4 lemons
1 can Eagle brand condensed milk
1 tbs sugar

1. Juice the lemons (don't cheat and use store bought lemon juice. That ain't right!)
2. Separate egg yolks and egg whites (hold on to those whites!)
3. Beat egg yolks
4. Add condensed milk to egg yolks
5. Add lemon juice to milk/egg mix
6. Beat together well (that means more than just stirring)
7. Pour into pie crust (this you can use store bought or make yourself)
8. Beat egg whites WELL (use a mixer if you have one), adding sugar little by little so it's even in the fluff
9. Spread egg white meringue over top of pie
10. Bake on 350° until top is brown (doesn't take long)
11. Refrigerate until it sets up the way it should (couple hours)

CHAPTER SIXTEEN

Lessons in Rural Life

Having gathered a few discarded boxes from The Community Store, ones Renzo Taylor had nearly tossed into the dumpster, Laurel spread them out on the bed and began sorting through her grandmother's clothes. All of Bessie's underthings, nightgowns, and shoes were neatly folded and packed away. She handled each item with a sense of nostalgia for a woman and memories of her which Laurel herself had never experienced. Although she'd never considered herself very sentimental, Laurel found herself setting aside a few dresses and blouses to hold onto. Why these items and not others, she didn't know. It was something about the patterns and colors in these few chosen articles that gave her a sense of what Bessie was like. She had a silly thought that she might want to make a quilt out of the fabrics. Like a little remembrance of her grandmother. Laurel felt sure the ladies at the quilting bee would be overjoyed to help her.

She left those items on the bed and carried the three boxes out to the back porch. Weeks ago, she planned to give these things to Leon Davis's mother and was ashamed she had not done it by now. Taking one of the boxes, she exited through the kitchen, balancing the box on her hip while she fumbled to open the door and then the screen door off the porch. Edging down the steps she heard the roar of a lawnmower starting. She hoped it was Cade.

When she got out to her car and saw that it was, she rested the box on the hood and rounded to the front of the house to follow him. His back was to her as he pushed the mower along the edge of the grass. Once he reached the end and turned around to cut the next strip, he saw her waiting. He seemed reluctant to stop, but once he finished the second pass, he switched off the motor.

He called out a sedated "Hello," but didn't leave the lawn mower and go to her. Laurel went to him, noticing as she drew closer, Cade had bruises across his face.

"He hit you!" she shrieked, reaching to touch his cheek.

He recoiled back a step, "It's fine," he assured her.

She ignored the protest, brushing back his bangs to get a better look at the damage. "This is what I was afraid of. I tried to text you."

"Guess you heard?" Cade replied, forcing a weak grin. "They took my phone away."

"I was worried."

"Don't be. I'm okay."

Looking around and not seeing the truck, she asked, "How did you get here?"

"My mom dropped me off. She'll be back in a while to pick me up, so I need to get back to the grass."

Without another word, he yanked the cord and restarted the mower. Something about his calm unsettled her. She wanted to ask more, to demand answers, but the fear of making things worse held her tongue. A part of her considered calling the police. But what if it made things harder for him at home? *Stay out of this*, her inner voice warned. *This isn't your world. It's not your place. None of this affects you.*

Returning to her car, she loaded the box, then went back for the other two. Hogg Road proved to be pretty much the same experience on the left of Bessie's driveway as it was on the right. She found the Davis house easily, especially since the name DAVIS was carved into a wall plaque over the front door. The place was in rough shape. Faded powder-blue paint peeled in long strips from the sun-bleached wood. The porch steps sagged with age, worn down by generations of feet. In some places the edges had broken off completely, the splinters smoothed by time.

As she placed the boxes on the porch, a dog yapped around her feet, tail wagging. Reaching down to pet him she realized he was not a stray. He was too well fed for that. He must be the Davis' dog, allowed to roam freely without a chain or fence to curtail his adventure. Leon Davis came to the door when she knocked, wearing a surprised smile once he recognized her. "Got another snake after you Miss Laurel?" he teased, opening the door to let her in.

Before she could reply, his wife Julia appeared, all energy and motion. She was small in stature and painfully thin. Her slightness, however, was not a sign of a lack of strength, her grip was strong. She had a lovely face, unadorned with makeup, but she didn't need anyway. Her hair was a soft light brown, straight, stopping at her chin. Though it was likely unintentionally cut into a pageboy style, it suited her and brought out her caring green eyes.

"Miss Laurel, I have been dying to meet you. You have got to forgive me for not coming to see you. I stay so busy around here in summer."

Laurel was about to ask what kept her so busy, but it wasn't necessary. The small room she entered faced the backyard where a half dozen children were running around at play. Laurel wondered how she had not heard them getting out of the car. "I see," Laurel commented, pointing to the window. "That is a large family you have."

Julia laughed exaggeratedly, "Oh no! Those aren't all ours. Two of 'em are. The others I watch through summer while their parents' work."

"Oh," Laurel replied. "You run a daycare."

Julia lowered her voice confidentially, "No daycare. I don't charge anybody. But with school out some folks don't have anywhere for their kids to go and not every mama can stay home. Anybody who needs a place for 'em to stay, just brings 'em here. What's a few more, anyway? Keeps my brood entertained, so it helps me too."

If Laurel did not already like the Davises, she certainly did now. This woman, poor in possessions, was rich in heart. Looking after other people's children all summer long for free! Before she could explain her visit, another woman entered from the kitchen, bringing with her the scent of something cooking. She moved slowly, her body thin and frail, her skin marked with age. She reached out a shaky, frail hand, introducing herself as Dean Davis.

"You, Mrs. Davis," Laurel smiled. "Are who I am here to see."

The elder Mrs. Davis brightened up to hear this, inviting Laurel to sit down. The moment Laurel's rear touched the chair cushion, she felt the spring poking through beneath the seat. She made sure not to react. She also observed a few places on the couch where strips of duct tape kept the stuffing held in. Leon, Julia, and Dean sat down as well. Laurel's quick inspective eye, noticed the rest of the room was similarly disheveled. The wooden coffee table was marred with years' old water stains and cigarette burn marks. The floor was scratched in so many spots it might have been a design. Under the television stand and tucked against the skirt of the reclining chair, looked to be bits of Goldfish crackers and potato chips.

Dean started things off by asking, "Now why in the world would you be down here to see an old woman like me for?"

With a nod to Leon, Laurel explained, "I hear you were friends with my late grandmother."

"Yes, yes we was real good friends," Dean grinned, showing a badly aged pair of dentures. "We were in school together when we was girls. 'Course Bessie was always smarter than me, but her people had books on their shelves in their house. I expect she read a lot. Real nice though, Bessie was."

Laurel stepped outside to retrieve one of the boxes and placed it on the coffee table. "I have this box and two more on your porch," she began. "I was cleaning out my grandmother's things and wondered perhaps you, being her neighbor and friend, might want any of them."

Dean's eyes widened like a child on Christmas Eve, anticipating what item she might have secretly admired of her friend, that might be inside the box.

"I would hate to throw these away," Laurel continued, hoping to frame her words less like charity and more as if Dean would be doing her the favor. "If I were in a larger city, I could donate these, but here I can only throw them away unless someone wants them. Someone who knew and loved my grandmother."

"I would be proud to have some of Miss Bessie's things, dear." Dean said thankfully. "I 'preciate you thinking about me. I am real touched."

Laurel turned to Julia. "There might be something for you too—especially if you wore the same shoe size."

When Laurel tried to make her exit, the ladies asked her to stay for supper. Laurel declined the offer graciously, making an excuse of prior plans. As charming as they were, she wasn't eager to eat anything prepared in a kitchen that matched the rest of the house. Walking out to her car, Leon followed her. Twisting his hat back and forth on his head, he told Laurel, "You are a fine woman, ma'am. I thank you."

"No need," she smiled. "Your mother really is helping me out, and you are the man who saved me from snakes and dirt hornets. I'll see you later...Neighbor."

"Neighbor." Leon tipped his hat and went back to the house, taking the boxes inside.

Deciding she did not want to think of herself as lying to the Davises about her plans, she made some. It helped assuage her guilt for her snobbery. She asked Janice to join her for dinner. While preparing the meal, she heard the lawnmower go silent. Half expecting Cade might come inside to cool off, when he didn't, she realized he must have finished and gone home without saying goodbye. It was probably too embarrassing for him. They could talk next time, when the events were not so fresh.

Janice could smell dinner from the moment she stepped onto the back porch. "Tell me that is Bessie's country fried steak!"

"It is!" Laurel shouted over the sound of the grease bubbling. "I had it too high I think, but I turned it down."

"Did you buy cubed steak or hamburger?"

"Neither," Laurel answered. "I found it in the freezer and thawed it out. It said country fried steak on her label."

"Then It's right, cubed steak." Janice investigated the skillet, adding, "I think it's done, honey. Time for the gravy."

"Gravy?" Laurel asked. "I used the flour mix she had written down, but it didn't say anything about gravy."

Laughing, Janice informed her naive friend, "Gravy is implied. Without steeping in gravy half an hour, it is only tough fried beef. Here I'll show you."

Laurel let Janice take charge, standing back and observing her at work. "Why didn't the recipe say it needed gravy?"

"It's implied," Janice snickered. Her hands went to work while Laurel made notes, but soon Laurel gave up on writing anything down. It was clear that there were too many factors involved that were impossible to dictate. "No one can tell you how to make gravy," Janice explained. "You feel how to make gravy."

"But why didn't you use a new pan instead of just pouring out the oil?" Laurel asked.

"It's a must to use the pan you fried the meet in," Janice pointed out. "The pan is already seasoned with the flavor. You pour out the excess oil, but keeping enough to brown the flour."

"How do you know how much?"

Janice simply shook her head, "It's one of those *eyeball it*, things. Same with how much flour. Too much becomes a paste, too little makes it greasy. And then you also have to consider how much gravy you need to make?" Glancing over her shoulder at her young, inexperienced friend, Janice smiled. "You will get the hang of it, I promise."

Once she was finished and the bubbling brown gravy was ready, Janice poured it in a dish and sat on the table with the rest of the meal. "There," she told Laurel. "Now you know how to make gravy."

"The hell I do!" Laurel cried. "I have no idea what you did. It was flurry of sprinkled flour, salt, pepper, water—I don't know what all!"

Over dinner, Laurel mentioned Cade's battered condition and what she heard during the quilting bee. She didn't think it was a betrayal of confidence any longer if Cade was allowing himself to be seen in a beaten condition.

"Is Cade safe at home, do you think?" she asked Janice.

Janice had come to serve as a cultural translator for Laurel, bridging the wide gulf between their different backgrounds and life experiences. Janice knew it would be hard for Laurel to understand that the customs Cade was held to in the rural South would not be the same as Laurel was familiar with.

"It isn't right," Janice remarked. "And if Cade were female, you could probably get the law involved. Unfortunately, an almost adult male like Cade...I doubt anything would come of it."

"It is assault!" Laurel declared outraged.

Janice agreed. "Listen, Laurel, I am in no way saying I think it's okay. All I am trying to explain to you is down here, any cop you told would probably have the same response. The boy is a man, not a little kid. He and his daddy got into it and his daddy straightened him out. If they caught their son in the same situation, the cop would do the same thing."

"I have never heard of anything more despicable," professed Laurel, with a scornful look on her face.

"Masculinity in the south, especially in the deep south, doesn't have a lot gray area. A man is a man and is supposed to act like a man."

Folding her arms in disgust, Laurel replied sharply, "Or everyone's idea of what a man should be!"

"Same thing," said Janice. "Every man here is just like the man standing beside them. If Cade can't fit that mold, nobody is going to take his side. That's just how it is."

"I don't believe that?" Laurel argued. "Just the other day I saw two other gay men in the diner. They weren't together, they were eating alone, but I could tell they were gay because they were wearing black eyeliner."

Janice hung her head, laughing to herself. "Laurel, those men work in the coal mine. That isn't eyeliner. That is years of coal dust that doesn't wash off."

"Oh."

Janice took her friend's hand and gave a light squeeze. "It's sweet that you care," she said. "But Laurel, I'm afraid you can't do anything to help that young man, except just be his friend. He may need one very badly."

CHAPTER SEVENTEEN

Church Social

Eyes subtly shifted. Conversations paused mid-sentence. A few heads turned discreetly, but not discreetly enough, when Linc Hopkins walked into the church Fellowship Hall with Laurel Holden. Perhaps a few people in Scroggins had seen them out together before, but any who did had kept it to themselves. The congregation at Christ's Love Baptist Church seemed genuinely surprised when they entered, clearly together.

Of course, merely entering the fellowship supper together might not have raised eyebrows on its own. Linc Hopkins, as many of the older folk would have described, was "raised right." He could have simply met Miss Holden in the parking lot and escorted her inside. But several other coinciding facts signaled to those pretending not to stare, that more was going on here under the surface.

The primary indicator was that this was an official church event. Not merely an event, it was a *church supper*. Further elevating the point, this was a 4th of July church supper—complete with fireworks after. Such an event in Scroggins was not generally something a man attended without a companion. The clincher though, was how they didn't part ways after coming in, in fact, prying eyes saw Laurel slip her hand into his once they were inside. This was a date and chaperoned at that. Laurel's Aunt Flossie with them.

Flossie's presence muddled the situation a bit. If anyone took offense by seeing Bessie Hogue's granddaughter on the arm of Delva Hopkins' grandson, the fact they had taken the time to bring Miss Flossie with them was a gracious gesture. Years had gone by since Flossie felt strong enough to attend an evening function. Her coming to the 4th of July celebration was not a small miracle. The pervasive eyes of the church were also evaluating how tenderly Laurel appeared to be treating her aunt. Any disapproval of her choice in date was lessened by the care she showed Flossie.

Laurel, too, was taking in the scene and making assumptions. It was not difficult to notice this church social was garnering more members of the congregation than any church service she had been to. By now, she knew the names and faces of most of the Sunday service members. Anyone else would require the assistance of her aunt, Linc, or Delva. Delva, upon seeing her grandson come in with Laurel, excused herself from the group she was talking to.

"Where's Janice?" Delva asked.

"She's stuck at work on some Fourth of July furniture sale," Laurel explained. "She said she'd try to make it by nine for the fireworks."

Delva glared playfully at her grandson, "Do I not get a kiss?"

"I just saw you this morning when I fixed your hot water heater," Linc teased.

"Does it still look like this morning to you?" Delva shot back, winning her the kiss.

The Fellowship Hall was a part of the church Laurel had not been in before. Her first observation was that it could have been decorated by whoever did Bessie's house. The same green and yellow linoleum in Bessie's kitchen and den ran through the entirety of the Hall. Flanking one end of the venue was an open kitchen while the opposite end boasted a wide brick fireplace. Dozens of people meandered around, visiting with their neighbors and fellow church members. Laurel noticed the Daniels sisters a few yards away. Patience appeared to be prattling on to two other women while Obedience shot her disapproving looks. The women, whom Laurel had never seen before, looked to share Obedience's wishes that Patience would stop rambling.

Linc stepped away to drop Laurel's chocolate brownies and his platter of smoked ribs on the food table while Laurel waited with Delva. Looking around the hall, Laurel remarked, "I didn't know the Daniels sisters went to our church?"

"*Our church?*" Delva repeated with a pointed smile and a sly wink to Flossie.

"*This* church," Laurel said, covering quickly. She'd been just as surprised to hear herself say it that way as her friend was. "You know what I mean Miss Delva?"

Laurel shocked herself again. *Miss Delva.* Somehow, she'd adopted this strange Southern quirk of applying *Miss* to any woman's name when addressing her. *When did I begin speaking this way?*

Delva leaned in closer to Laurel's ear to answer her question. "The Daniels sisters are Methodists, like their mother was. But their father's family built this church and he's buried in the churchyard out back. The Daniels sisters always come to our socials and Homecomings."

"Methodists don't cook as good as Baptists do," Flossie chuckled.

Still hung up on what Delva said, Laurel asked, "What are Homecomings?"

"She'll find out, won't she Flossie," Delva grinned. "We have ours in the Fall. You'll be here, don't worry."

Laurel grimaced. "Not if I can help it."

Delva and Flossie didn't look too convinced. Especially by the way Laurel seemed to perk up again when Linc returned. He was about to steer his little group to a table when Patience Daniels came hurrying over to say hello, her sister Obedience approaching more slowly behind, scolding her.

"Patience do not sprint off like a schoolgirl. We are in church."

"I only wanted to say hello to Miss Laurel," Patience said giddily. Grabbing Laurel's hand and squeezing it, she clamored, "You will never guess! I've been talking with Bootsie, and she suggested we invite you to be a regular part of our quilting club!"

Laurel shrank a little, muttering, "That is a terrible idea. I was only there for stories and recipes. If I joined regularly, I'm afraid I would ruin your quilts."

"No," Patience squealed. "You did just fine. And you'll get even better. We want you to join so much!"

Before Laurel could decline a second time, Delva gripped her shoulder in a very domineering, grandmotherly way and said, "She will be there." As Laurel turned to look at her, Delva simply nodded her head as if the matter was decided. Linc's words echoed in Laurel's brain, *don't get her riled.*

Linc took the subject in a different direction by addressing Obedience with a surprisingly warm tone of voice. "How are you, Miss Daniels?"

"I am well, Lincoln," she cordially replied. With a narrowing of the eye, she looked both Linc and Laurel over, adding, "I was not aware you two were friends."

"Yes," Laurel smiled defiantly. "Good friends."

"How nice." Obedience then turned solely to Linc, addressing school affairs. Laurel noticed that she spoke with authority and a clear understanding of matters regarding new school equipment and repairs. Linc then provided Obedience with an update on where things stood regarding both issues. Laurel tried her best to listen, but unfortunately Patience took the opportunity to commandeer Laurel as audience to whatever silly topic she'd bored the other women with earlier. Laurel only caught bits and pieces as she strained to hear Linc's conversation, but from what she could tell Patience was talking either about the rumored Winn Dixie said to be built soon, or how windy the days lately have been. Honestly, as far as Laurel knew, it could have gone either way.

Once the Daniels sisters left to choose a table, Laurel asked Linc, "What was that all about?"

"Obedience is on our school board. I was updating her on matters. I only have the summer to get everything in shape before the kids return."

"Oh, the school board," Laurel sneered. "I bet she gives you as much trouble as possible."

Astonishingly, Linc contradicted her. "Not at all, for all her conformity and propriety, Miss Daniels has been an ally to me. She is the main reason I was chosen principal."

"You're kidding?"

"Nope," he said. "There were a few families not exactly pleased with the idea of a black man presiding over their predominantly white school. Miss Obedience put an end to their talk and pushed forward my promotion."

"I never would have guessed that of her," Laurel replied, amazed. "Maybe I misjudged Obedience Daniels."

Snickering in her ear, Linc whispered. "No. She's still a bitch. Just not a racist bitch."

From across the room, the booming voice of Reverend Daws drew the crowd's attention. He stood atop the hearth, offering thanks, blessings, and appreciation before signaling the congregation to dig in. As the church members began making their way to the buffet, Laurel hung back from the line, allowing the real church people go ahead of her. But Delva nudged her forward.

"If you want the good stuff, you'd best get there first."

"Ain't that the truth," a familiar voice murmured behind them. Laurel turned to see Bootsie and Renzo Taylor. "You don't want to get stuck with nothing but Christine Blankenship's Chicken A' la King left."

Renzo scolded his wife with a playful grin, "Now Bootsie, you ought to not say things like that. Poor Christine does what she can."

Laurel smiled at the sweet man, only to almost laugh out loud when he whispered in her ear, "Everything she cooks tastes like the saltiest version of something her dog dug up in the yard. I ain't studyin' getting' stuck with that on my plate."

"Lordy, he ain't lying!" Flossie wheezed. "She brung that mess to my house when Norman died. Thought I'd be right behind him after I ate some of that buzzard she scraped off the road."

Ahead of them in line, the booming voice of Bud Rawlings started bellowing in his sports-call tone, "And WHAT will make it to the plate? Will it be FRIED CHICKEN, SWEET POTATO SALAD, or MRS. STANDISH's COUNTRY CLOVE HAM?"

Laurel giggled at the entertaining man as he volleyed his fork back and forth across the spread, mimicking a kind of anticipation as to what he would place on his paper plate. "And it's down to the wire with the line backing up behind me! What's it going to be? It's...it's... IT'S SWEET POTATOR SALAD, BREADED PORK CHOP, AND STEAMED COLLARD GREENS FOR THE WIN!!!"

Though Laurel had never met nor heard of Mrs. Standish before, she suspected the disappointed woman standing at a nearby table might be her. Cheering across the room came the voice of whoever made the breaded pork chops. Laurel evaluated that though Bud may be extremely loud, he was undeniably popular, bringing the fun with him wherever he went.

Once Laurel and Linc made it to the front of the line, she saw a selection of food laid out that embodied everything she ever thought about Southern cooking. Several platters of fried chicken, meatloaf, two crock pots of roast, pork chops, catfish, and three hams—and that was merely the meat section. The vegetable side was so full that some bowls and platters were edging off the sides of the table from lack of room. Corn on the cob, creamed corn, green beans, more different kinds of peas and beans than Laurel knew the names, carrots, potatoes, slaw, salads, beets, yams...and the fried okra. Despite the multitude of okra, it was going fast. Laurel ushered her aunt Flossie in front of her so that the old woman could get her dinner first. Most likely, Flossie understood the kind gesture, though she treated it as if Laurel wanted her to be her guide through the dishes like a front-line soldier in a landmine field.

As Laurel reached for a slice of ham, Flossie gently slapped her hand away. "Don't. Jane Standish uses way too many cloves, and they are probably still from the same bottle she used last year. I tell you, Laurel, honey, you won't get that clove taste outta your mouth for days. Wait till further down. Betsy Long always gets a Honeybaked Ham. Can't beat that."

Spying a bright golden platter of corn on the cob, Laurel licked her lips and said, "Oh, I want a piece of that corn."

"No, you don't!" Flossie said, like a mother scolding her child. "And don't even ask why. You'll never eat corn again."

Laurel turned around for clarification from Delva, who was following them in line. Delva offered no further explanation than Flossie had given, she merely nodded in agreement. It was only then that Laurel noticed what Delva was doing behind her. Linc Hopkins, an accomplished adult man, the leader of the high school, and seemingly one of the more sophisticated citizens of this town, was not filling his own plate. His grandmother was dishing up his selections as she did her own. Laurel shot him a disbelieving look.

Linc only shrugged, grinned, and said, "Hey, I'm not ashamed. She's been fixing my plate since I was two. She knows what I like and what I don't."

Three long rows of connecting folding tables stretched end to end across the length of the Fellowship Hall providing enough seating for all. Near the center-right of the second row, Linc pulled out three metal folding chairs for Laurel, her aunt, then his grandmother, before sitting down between Delva and Laurel.

Obedience and Patience Daniels took the seats across from them, joined by another woman Laurel had never met before, but it didn't take much to figure out who she was. Laurel had always seen the resemblance between Obedience and Patience, but the addition of the third woman proved to be the missing link between them. With the three of them sitting side by side, their shared characteristics left no doubt this was the third sister.

Patience immediately confirmed this with an introduction, "Miss Holden, this is other sister Prudence."

Prudence smiled graciously, reaching her hand over to shake with Laurel. Obedience quickly tapped it with her spoon. "Civilized people do not shake hands across a dinner table."

With a rebellious snort, Prudence answered, "I doubt civilized people beat dinner companions with spoons either." Returning her attention back to the newcomer in town, she said, "Laurel, please call me Prue. I have never felt as if the name Prudence suited me. I have heard a lot about you from Pati and Obie. Welcome...home, I suppose I should say."

Thanking the kind woman, Laurel was still a bit taken aback by the abbreviations Prue used regarding her sisters. Laurel could tell by Obedience's flinch, it was a liberty she loathed but had given up fighting a lifetime ago. With the sisters together, it was clear for Laurel to determine Prue was the more normal between them. She did not appear to share her elder sister's severity, or her younger sister's exuberance. Lost in her thoughts about the Daniels sisters, she must have unwittingly smiled, causing Obedience to ask, "Does something amuse you, Miss Holden?"

"Sorry," Laurel answered. "I am not meaning any disrespect, but having now met your sister, I am fascinated with your names. Obedience, Patience, and Prudence. I love it. The three graces."

Prue leaned forward, divulging, "We also have a sister named Harmony who lives in Texas, a brother named Worth, and our littlest sister lives in Kentucky with her husband. Her name is Babe."

Laurel could not stop herself from commenting. "Your names are

Obedience, Prudence, Patience, Harmony, Worth, and *Babe?*"

"Babe was the slut," Prue offered without pause. "Harmony tiptoed to the edge, but Babe jumped off the cliff."

Laurel, who had been putting a forkful of okra into her mouth, choked on it. Linc swiftly passed a glass of tea her way.

Obedience was aghast by her sister's remark. "Prudence Daniels!" she barked. "I find your candor both disparaging and distasteful!"

"But you didn't say untrue," Prue laughed, winking at Laurel and Linc. "Of course, she and Harmony are the only sisters who ever got married so maybe they knew something we didn't."

"From what I remember," Flossie remarked. "Babe got married a couple of times. Lord help the men. She was a wild one, that girl."

"The less said of Babe, the better." Obedience announced, calling an end to the talk.

Linc steered the conversation into neutral territory by explaining to Laurel that the sister's brother, Worth Daniels, was a retired State Senator living in Montgomery. Prue had a number of questions about Laurel's book project and even shared a few additional examples of how her mother helped teach her and her sisters many things. Laurel made a mental note to include them in Patience's recipe chapter.

Janice arrived just as most of the Fellowship Hall diners were finishing their meals and tossing their paper cups and plates into the trash. Laurel had made a plate for her, but Janice said she grabbed a taco on the way home. The fireworks would begin soon, and everyone started making their way outdoors to view from the parking lot. Laurel assisted Flossie to her feet, telling she and Delva to go ahead outside while she and Linc brought chairs outside for them to sit during the fireworks. As Delva led Flossie into the departing crowd, Linc and Laurel lagged behind for the chairs. Obedience hung back as well, ushering her sisters to go ahead without her.

"Would you like me to grab a chair for you as well, Miss Daniels?" Linc politely offered.

"No, that won't be necessary," she said flatly, adding, "I'm not that old yet, Lincoln." She took the chair Laurel was folding and handed it to Linc, silently implying he was to take both chairs outside alone, while she had a private moment with Laurel. Linc shot his date a protective look, checking to see if she was okay with it. Laurel nodded and watched him go through the door with each chair under an arm.

Alone in the Fellowship Hall with Laurel, Obedience folded her arms together with a stance of authority as she faced Laurel. The young writer prepared herself for whatever reprimand might be coming her way, judging from Obedience's demeanor. However, she was taken by surprise when the elder woman proclaimed, "I find it commendable of you, Miss Holden, forging a relationship with your aunt. Flossie has been quite alone since your grandmother left this earth. I have suspected she might follow Bessie quite soon."

Though the words sounded complementary, Obedience's posture still left it questionable. Laurel was not quite sure if she had been praised or condescended to. It was abundantly clear Obedience Daniels lived her life with a self-bestowed air of propriety to which anyone in her indomitable presence was measured by.

Laurel wasn't a person easily intimidated, nor did she want to be patronized, sparking her to say, "Should a person thank another person for complimenting them over caring about their own relative? I'm not clear on what I am supposed to say to your remark."

Obedience nearly broke her cool exterior with a smile, but only nearly. The hint of it told Laurel her remark was intended as praise. "There is nothing necessary you should say. I only wanted to convey how you have surprised me, Miss Holden. It isn't as if I expected you to be an inconsiderate person, family does mean something, after all. Doesn't it?"

"It is beginning to," Laurel said with a faint smile. "I have never been one who feels chained to anchors I didn't put there. But spending time with Flossie isn't something I see as a duty. I genuinely like her."

Obedience gave her an approving nod. "There are unfortunate people who find at the end of life, they have virtually no one left. Flossie seems more her old self since you arrived in Scroggins. If you aren't careful... Laurel...you may do something few others ever have."

Curious as to what was to follow, Laurel asked. "And what would that be?"

"Earning my respect."

Obedience left on that sentence to join her sisters outside, leaving Laurel alone with her thoughts. Laurel stood in the hall a moment, trying to make sense of that odd conversation, as well as the bevy of new and foreign feelings she'd found herself experiencing in this backwoods town. Never before had Laurel given a damn what anyone else thought of her—other than she was a good writer. Now as she felt a smile stretch across her face, Laurel almost resented it. Who was Obedience Daniels anyway? What a self-righteous old woman to believe her approval for someone even mattered! Yet, Laurel liked the way it made her feel and hated that she did.

Laurel joined the others outside in the church parking lot. Everyone was watching over the horizon of treetops waiting on the fireworks display soon to begin. Music streamed from open car windows where several radios tuned in to the local station providing a patriotic playlist to accompany the lightshow. Laurel found Linc standing behind Flossie and Delva's chairs. His parents, who skipped the supper, were standing a few feet aside, leaving room for Laurel. Laurel smiled at them as she stepped in and took Linc's hand. As the first rocket shot into the sky, exploding into a burst of red and gold, she placed her free hand onto her great aunt's shoulder. Flossie was staring upward with a brilliant smile, as if she were a child seeing something magnificent for the first time. Laurel wondered just how many years it had been since the elderly woman had seen this display. Without averting her eyes from the red, white, and blue splendor, Flossie reached up and patted her niece's hand, still resting on her shoulder. Linc gave a squeeze to the hand he was holding. Laurel looked over at him as he smiled at her. His brown eyes reflected the spectrum of colors overhead. Caught in the magic of the moment, he leaned over and kissed her cheek. In her periphery, Laurel saw Maple Hopkins nudging her husband, drawing his attention to them. Maple sent an approving smile her way.

Excited chatter from the crowd around the parking lot all seemed to be marveling at the sight above. After what seemed like only a few minutes, a deafening crescendo filled the air as the streaming music peaked into a raucous National Anthem. The sky exploded with dazzling colors all at once in a grand finale which held everyone breathless.

During her writing career canvassing the country, Laurel saw her share of firework shows from the East coast to the West coast and many in between. While the town of Scroggins' Independence Day show was modest in comparison to bigger cities, Laurel felt as if it were more magical. Maybe it was because the blackness of a country night skyline magnified the show. Or possibly it was that for the first time ever, Laurel wasn't among strangers. She knew the people beside her. Perhaps she had not known them very long, but she knew them as well, or better, than she had ever known anyone before. As the smoke dissipated in the air and the sulphury ash drifted down from the sky, Laurel knew this 4th of July would remain emblazoned in her mind forever, as the first she had ever truly experienced and shared with anyone else.

Those who had come only to see the fireworks climbed into their cars, already revved for the radio, and left for home. Church members who had prepared a dish for the supper, returned inside to retrieve their bowls, platters, and serving utensils. Amid the bustle of clearing up, Brother Daws caught Laurel's attention across the room, motioning her to join him by the fireplace. She maneuvered reluctantly through the exiting parishioners; certain he was going to ask her the question she'd been dreading. *When are you going to officially join our church?* She was well-rehearsed with a dodge to the question, but Brother

Daws took her off guard by asking something else entirely.

"May I have a private moment with you, Laurel. It's about your book." Daws sighed heavily, from either nervousness or having eaten far too much earlier. Laurel thought she heard him suppress a burp under his breath. "I know my wife tried to enter her cookies for selection in your book."

Feeling a little guilty for not having chosen a preacher's wife's cookie for inclusion in the book, Laurel blushed apologetically, replying, "I am very sorry Reverend. But Miss Patience—"

"Oh, I'm not here to chastise you Laurel," he informed. "My wife's cookies are not very good to be honest with you. Frankly, had you chosen them over the others I'd have been suspicious."

Laurel laughed. "They weren't that bad."

He gestured to the food table across the room where men and women were collecting their empty dishes. "I couldn't help but notice that you had three helpings of Lottie's macaroni and cheese."

Embarrassed by her own gluttony, and the fact an obese reverend was pointing it out, Laurel blushed. "I know I went back for seconds too many times. But it was so good."

"Good enough for your book?"

Smiling back at the preacher's devious suggestion, she admitted, "I already made a note in my phone to find out who made it. I was going to ask later. I didn't know it was your wife. Of course it'll need a story."

"It has one," Brother Daws confided. "One only I know about. If you would care to hear it."

Brother Daws glanced around before beginning his confidential story. "I've never told this to Mrs. Daws," he confided. "It is not something I am proud of, however, with your book focusing on this community, and she not having anything to include, I thought it might be a romantic surprise to her if she read, quite by chance, a story involving her in your book. I can see her face now, beaming and blushing at the same time."

Laurel grinned. "Now I must know it."

"Only use it if you think it goes with the theme of the others," Daws replied, stopping to shake hands with a departing parishioner before resuming. "I won't be offended if it doesn't get included."

"One way to find out," Laurel teased.

Brother Daws again reiterated this was not his finest moment as a person, as he began recounting a moment from the past. He'd been a young man then. Just out of Seminary school. A pal of his relentlessly badgered him about not being married, claiming no church would hire an unmarried preacher. However, young Galin Daws was not even close to thinking about marriage. His friend, through much cajoling, finally convinced Galin to go on a blind date with the best friend of his own girlfriend.

"I agreed to it," Brother Daws told Laurel. "My friend's girlfriend was rather pretty, you see. Naturally, I assumed her friend would be as nice and attractive as she."

"Understandable assumption."

Brother Daws paused once more, as Mrs. Standish said goodbye, carrying most of the clove-tainted ham she'd brought back home with her. "Delicious ham, as always, Mrs. Standish!" Laurel giggled at the little white lie. With a conspiratorial wink, Brother Daws continued. "I found out the next morning that my father had also arranged a blind date for me. The daughter of a man he worked with at the mill. And both dates were to be the same night."

"Oh, no!" Laurel gasped, politely.

"I told my father I wasn't interested in anyone he would be fixing me up with, and that I already had a date. But he said, 'Galin, you cancel that other date. This is the daughter of my supervisor, and you aren't backing out on it."

"So what did you do?" asked Laurel.

"This is the part I'm ashamed of, Miss Laurel," he said in nearly a whisper. "I paid my younger brother five dollars to go in my place to meet the girl my father wanted me to meet, then I went out to pick up the girl my buddy and his girlfriend had set me up with, then we were going to meet them at a movie."

"You paid your brother to be your substitute!"

Red-faced with remorse, he answered. "I did. And I felt real pleased with myself over coming up with that plan. My friend's girlfriend was so pretty and again, I expected her friend to be as well."

"But she wasn't?"

"Miss Laurel, when I knocked on the door to pick up my blind date," he took a dramatic pause, then continued. "It's not very nice of me to admit, but I was taken aback at the sight of her. She was plump, splotchy faced, and the only person I've ever seen whose face got worse when they smiled."

Laurel couldn't help but laugh, slapping his arm gently as she did. Brother Daws laughed too, but then quickly elbowed her as another parishioner came over to say goodbye. They straightened up like two kids who spotted the teacher coming by, then once alone again, fell back into snickering.

"What did you do?"

Brother Daws sighed, and confided, "Well, she immediately asked me if I was Galin Daws. And I flat out lied. I said I was collecting for The March of Dimes and then I high-tailed it out of there! Me! A young fella who just completed Devotional School, and I was lying like a rug to that girl!"

"You didn't!" Laurel gasped, covering her mouth with her hand.

Brother Daws hung his head in shame, "Yes ma'am, I did. Wasn't that just awful of me. But I tell you Laurel, I could have parked the church bus between that gap in her teeth."

Laurel accidentally laughed loudly, but everyone around was too busy with their parting conversations to notice.

"Well, I knew I had to get to my brother before he took that other date," Brother Daws revealed. "I ran all the way. Now, I know it doesn't look like I can do much running, but I assure you many years ago I was slim and slick and very fast."

"Did you stop your brother?"

"Got to him right before he rounded the corner to her house. Told him he could keep the five dollars, and I'd give him two more if he went back home. So, I went up to that other girl's house, the one my father set me up with, and knocked on the door. When I tell you the prettiest girl I'd ever seen in my life opened that door, I am telling you the Lord's Truth."

"Mrs. Daws." Laurel smiled.

"Indeed, only then she was Miss Fletcher. Well, what I did not know was that my father did cancel the date after all. He wasn't positive I would come and didn't want to be embarrassed. It was good my brother hadn't shown up."

"But you lost your five dollars, anyway."

"Seven actually. But I didn't care. I pretended I had no idea my father canceled and lied again saying he must have gotten confused. I said I did have a prior commitment but canceled it in order to meet her."

"You are quick on your feet," Laurel joked. "And surprisingly a really good liar."

"That's why people can't pull the wool over my eyes when I counsel them," he winked. "But back to that night. Since Lottie believed I was not coming over, she had not prepared a meal. I didn't care in the least. She was pretty enough to feast my eyes on, and my stomach could wait. But she insisted she make us dinner. She whipped up the quickest thing she knew to make, macaroni and cheese. I helped her prepare it. She used three kinds of cheeses all layered in separate stacks. And she crumbled crackers up really fine between each cheese layer. Then poured on more noodles and repeated the process. It was the best mac and cheese I ever ate. Over the years she's added pimento and other little touches to it, making it even better than it was then."

"And you have never told her the real story of that night?"

"Never. To this day she believes she was the only girl I saw that night. But if you want to use this recipe, I'll sneak it to you next Sunday. I think Lottie will get a kick out of it when she sees it in your book."

"I would love to use it. Thank you, Brother Daws."

"No thank you, young lady," he grinned. "When you get to be our age there aren't a good many ways left to surprise the person who knows you best, and it's a rare opportunity to do something romantic. She is going to love this."

Lottie Daw's Recipe known in real life as...

ROBERTSON FAMILY'S MAC AND CHEESE DELIGHT

Ingredients

Macaroni noodles

1 tsp sugar   Grated cheddar cheese
½ cup mayonnaise   Grated parmesan cheese
½ cup chopped yellow onion   Sliced provolone cheese
1/4/ cup chopped green pepper   Crackers
1 egg   1 tsp salt
½ cup chopped pimento   ½ stick melted butter

1. Boil noodles until done
2. Mix sugar, mayo, onion, pepper, salt, butter, egg, and pimento
3. In a casserole dish, layer a thin row of noodles
4. Drizzle 1/3 of the onion mixture over noodles
5. Sprinkle a light layer of crushed crackers over noodles
6. Sprinkle light coating of parmesan and cheddar over cracker layer
7. Lay a few slices of provolone over cheese layer
8. Repeat with another noodle layer
9. Repeat another layer of the onion mixture
10. Repeat crackers
11. Repeat cheeses
12. If have enough room, do it one more time.
13. Cover dish and bake on 350° for 30 minutes
14. Remove lid and bake 10 more minutes

CHAPTER EIGHTEEN

Three Isn't a Crowd

Whenever she dated in the past, Laurel would meet her companion somewhere. He almost never picked her up, although sometimes they may end up back at her place. Linc Hopkins already claimed the honor of being the first man to pick her up for a date and tonight he was about to stake another first. In her 33 years, she'd never once had a date take her to dinner at his grandmother's house. She couldn't recall even one time when she'd ever dined with a man's parents, let alone a grandparent. Then again, Laurel already knew Delva and liked her very much. As she and Linc came into Delva's house, Laurel could smell the meal through the door. Whatever she'd made was going to be scrumptious. They sat with Delva in the living room for a few minutes before dinner. This was apparently customary in the south, getting the preliminary meaningless chit chat out of the way before the meal, where the real talk took place. Laurel equivocated it to predinner cocktails.

Over the juiciest, most tender pot roast she ever tasted, Delva jumped right into her grandmotherly prerogative to ask anything she liked, however uncomfortable. "You ever dated a black man before?"

Linc choked on his sip of tea, sending Laurel an apologetic look before shifting it to one of curiosity. Grinning devilishly, he said, "Well, have you, Laurel?"

With not as much as a blush on her face, Laurel answered, "Yes. Twice before."

Rocking back in her chair, Delva slapped the table lightly, "Well, that's real liberal of you, child. Good for you Linc, you won't have to deal with so much nervousness."

The remark confusing her, Laurel asked, "Why should I be nervous?"

"Well, I guess you wouldn't be," Delva replied. "Even down here, it ain't so shocking anymore. Folks don't get up in arms the way they used to."

"Good to know," Laurel said.

Delva chuckled a bit to herself, "Gotta say, the two of you would make some pretty babies."

"Granny!" Linc cried.

"Oh, don't get embarrassed. Isn't that what dating is? Testing the water to see if they are the one you wanna pick to finish up your life with?"

Looking mildly uncomfortable, Linc commented, "Some people date simply because they enjoy the other's company."

"That is a load of diddly squat." Delva declared. "Everybody is looking for a person who will hold their hand at the end. People just say they like it casual. But they never do."

"I don't think so," Linc argued. "Some people have relationships without putting lasting expectations on it."

"Some people lie over the dinner table too," Delva quipped. She gave Laurel a nudge with the point of her toe under the table, "Miss Laurel, you better keep an eye out on him. Sounds like my grandson is using every argument to keep from being tied down. Don't you put too much of yourself in this if he can't do the same."

Laurel smiled at her warning, while also beginning to see her point. Linc was very quick to reject a future possibility. Was that a *him thing*, or just because it was her. "He is rather evasive isn't he Miss Delva?

Luckily, marriage is about the last thing on my mind right now as well."

Delva chuckled to herself, amusing herself by her own thought, "Now don't go sucking the sauce off the spaghetti and putting the noodles back in the bowl. Neither a you is a spring chicken."

Looking playfully across the table into Laurel's eyes, Linc clarified, "I wouldn't say marriage is the last thing on my mind. Just a bit soon."

Delva slapped her hands on the table again and yelped, "That's good to know, cause I'm not kidding about them babies. Ya'll make some pretty ones. Mulatto babies are always the prettiest. Just look at Beyonce. She grew up gorgeous."

Both Laurel and Linc shared a side eye to one another before Linc addressed, "Granny, I don't think anybody uses the word *mulatto* anymore. And Beyonce is not mulatto. Both of her parents are black."

"Naw she can't be." Delva said. "That pretty hair. That's white people hair if I ever saw any."

Laurel giggled, "Miss Delva those are hair extensions. That isn't her real hair." She turned to Linc and said, "And technically she African American and Creole."

Delva asked what the difference was and sat with interest as Laurel provided a short history lesson, which following, Delva remarked, "You sure know a lot about Beyonce."

"I've seen her a few times in concert."

The conversation immediately switched to how much Beyonce tickets cost and how well-fixed Laurel must be financially. Linc made apologies again for his grandmother prying into Laurel's personal business. Laurel graciously replied that it was all right, clarifying to Delva that though she once earned a reasonably good living as a writer, those days were long over.

"Good," Delva announced. "It ain't good for the woman to make more than the man. A man is a simple creature. There isn't a lot he can do in life compared to a woman. Let's let him keep believing he's the one who keeps his family going. It's about the only use in life he's got."

Linc was aghast at his grandmother's candor, candor Laurel was greatly enjoying. "You look at Miss Laurel's family," Delva added. "When your granddaddy got shot, who was it that kept the family going? Your Aunt Merle Hogue went to work, day and night, and Miss Bessie went to work at the school and took care of her husband till the day he died."

Laurel appreciated the respect her grandmother seemed to have in the community but was confused on something. "Did you say she went to work at the school?" She suddenly remembered something she had not really given any thought to. "I met a woman named Lorraine at the plant nursery. I didn't register what she meant at the time, but she told me my grandmother used to make sure she always had a school lunch, even if she couldn't pay for it."

Linc placed his hand over Laurel's, "You didn't know Miss Bessie was the school dietician? She was still there when I began teaching. I expect she fed a good many children who couldn't afford it."

"I wonder why Janice left that out when she told me about my grandfather's shooting."

Delva lifted a serving spoon from the platter, spooning more potatoes and carrots onto Laurel's plate. "Probably didn't think it mattered what work your grandma took," Delva remarked. "My point is its women who hold the men together and the men don't never even feel their hands holding them up by the shoulders."

Reminded of the forgotten memory, Linc spoke up, "You know, I had forgotten about your grandfather being shot. I remember Dad telling me the story once."

"Told you that so you'd quit picking on your sister." Delva chided, now delivering more roast and gravy to her grandson's plate. "You was a mean big brother for a spate of time."

Hanging his head, Linc simultaneously laughed and lamented. "I was pretty bad to Sandra. But she was so pesky. We get along great now," he shared to Laurel. "Gotta say, Dad telling me about what can happen if you bully someone too far helped me change my ways."

Laurel sighed to herself and confided, "I don't know how to process my grandfather's behavior. You'd like to think we all had amazing, wise, loving grandparents. Then when you find out you didn't..."

"Oh now, don't judge a man for trippin' over pipe that's poking outta the ground." Delva scolded.

Linc nodded along to his grandmother's sage advice—advice lost totally on Laurel. "I have no idea what you just said," Laurel admitted.

Chuckling at Laurel, Delva patted her hand, explaining, "Girl, all I'm sayin' is one blip in a man's life can't be all he gets judged on. That Jugger fella was plumb crazy. I remember him! I was younger than your grandmomma and granddaddy but I was old enough to see for myself that Jugger was a pest. Now, I ain't sayin he could help it none. He wasn't right in the head. And Ustus ought to let up on him some. But ever'body picked on Jugger a little. If it weren't your granddaddy, it'd a jus' been somebody else ole Jugger blew up on. Ustus wasn't a terrible man. He was right nice to most folks."

While Delva turned her attention to buttering a large hunk of cornbread before placing it on Linc's plate, she moved the conversation into other things ranging from Laurel's travels to her current progress on the cookbook. Laurel filled them in on a few of her endeavors before coming to Scroggins, all while watching Delva give her the same cornbread treatment. Laurel asked questions about Linc's childhood and while Delva was captivated in the retelling of Linc stories, Laurel discreetly scraped some of the excess butter from the bread before taking a bite. It was plain to see the topic of Lincoln Hopkins was a favorite and a true source of pride for the elderly woman. Laurel envied his grandmother's admiration of him. *This is how a grandmother is supposed to feel about her grandchild.* The hour was growing late—at least for the older generation.

The time to go was signaled by Delva's strange invitation, "Why don't ya'll stay the night now? No sense in gettin' out again."

Linc thanked her for the offer but declined, rising from his chair and kissing his grandmother on the cheek. Laurel stood as well, offering to help clean up—and genuinely meaning it. Delva refused, but made them wait while she filled two paper plates with leftover roast and vegetables. Pulling a roll of foil from a drawer, she stretched a sheet over each plate, tucking the ends under. Presenting them to her guests, she told them it would make a good lunch tomorrow.

"I'd give you the cornbread, but Imma gone crumble the rest up in some buttermilk in a minute before I go to bed."

Once Laurel and Linc were in the car and Delva had turned out the porchlight, Laurel commented on how odd it was for his grandmother to invite them to spend the night with her. This garnered a chuckle from Linc. "Laurel, you are the cutest thing. You don't speak Alabama yet. Granny was not asking us to stay. She was telling us to go."

"What?"

Linc nodded, still grinning. "Down here, when someone asks you to stay the night, they are telling you it is late, and they are ready to go to bed."

With her mouth open, and more than a little embarrassed to have overstayed their welcome, she asked Linc, "Why didn't she simply say she was tired?"

"It would be rude!" Linc answered, as if the question itself was absurd. "No one would say that to a someone they care about. It would hurt their feelings."

She twisted in the seat to face him, the moonlight streaming through the window highlighting her bewilderment. Laurel still couldn't grasp the choreography of words these Southerners used to imply their veiled meanings.

"If you already know what she means by it, why would anyone be less offended than being told directly it is time to go?"

Linc patted her leg. "It's just nicer, that's all. Jeez," he added, with a teasing grin. "No wonder you moved down here. You alienated all your friends with truth."

Pulling up into the driveway, Linc turned to his date with a guileful smirk. "You all right walking into that dark house alone?"

With a playful gleam in her eye, Laurel replied, "Maybe I am beginning to pick up on Alabama-speak, after all. Is that your indirect way of asking me if you can come inside?"

Switching off the engine was his answer. Taking Laurel by hand, they walked towards the back porch. Laurel stopped at the screen door. Standing one step higher than Linc, she turned around so she could rest her arms over his shoulders. "I am not from Alabama. I will say what I mean." Using Delva's words to her benefit, Laurel grinned and said, "Why don't you stay the night. No sense in getting out again?"

Linc liked her boldness. With the porchlight glowing behind her, illuminating the edges of her blonde hair, gave a golden aura around her. Her face, shadowed with the light on her back, was not necessary to see. He could feel her eyes on him, and her lips parted, waiting for his kiss. They went inside, turning off the porch light as the screen door slammed behind them.

Delva's Recipe...known in real life as...

MICAH'S POT ROAST

Ingredients

3 tbsp Olive oil (divided into 1 tbsp, and 2 tbsp)
Kosher salt
3-5 lb. chuck roast
2 yellow onions peeled and diced
6 carrots chopped
4-5 Yukon Gold potatoes cut into squares (I prefer to peel them, but you don't have to)
Pepper
4 ½ cups Beef stock divided into two 2 ½ parts
3 Rosemary sprigs
3 thyme sprigs
Dutch Oven pot

1. Preheat oven to 350°
2. On stove, heat 2 tbsp olive oil on medium high in Dutch Oven
3. Generously salt and pepper roast on all sides while oil heats
4. Put onions and carrots into pot, cooking quickly in oil, stirring constantly, until glazed brown
5. Remove onions and carrots to a plate
6. Add remaining olive oil to what is still in pot and sear all sides of salted roast until brown, sealing in juices
7. Remove roast to plate, then pour 2 ½ cups beef broth in, stirring quickly with wooden spoon to deglaze bottom of pot, and loosen any burned bits of salt, onion or carrot, in the bottom
8. Return roast, onions, and carrots to pot and add potato slices

9. Pour the remaining beef stock into pot, and tuck rosemary and thyme into the broth on each side
10. Cover and bake in oven for 4–5 hours. Do not check until 3rd hour, just to see if you need to add any more broth. (You probably won't, it is supposed to reduce to a little for drizzling on meat when served)
9. Pour the remaining beef stock into pot, and tuck rosemary and thyme into the broth on each side.
10. Cover and bake in oven for 4–5 hours. Do not check until 3rd hour, just to see if you need to add any more broth. (You probably won't, it is supposed to reduce to a little for drizzling on meat when served)

CHAPTER NINETEEN

Sound the Alarm

The Community Store was busier than Laurel had seen before with a total of four customers present at the same time. Renzo Taylor shouted a cheery "Good Morning," as she came in. He was at his one register, totaling and bagging the groceries of a woman she did not know. However, peering over the top of the can good aisle, Patience Daniels was waving to Laurel in her friendly manner. Lottie Daws was beside her, sending a less animated, but still warm wave of her own. Laurel, needing canned green beans anyway, steered her cart their way. A few rows behind them, meandering through the meat cooler, was Sheila Bevins. She smiled at Laurel, who smiled politely back as she turned into the canned good section.

Patience caught Laurel by surprise when she asked enthusiastically, "Did you hear the latest on the Peterson boy and the Hinton boy?"

"Patience Daniels!" Lottie exclaimed. "Shame on you, spreading gossip about other people's troubles."

Laurel felt her stomach turn. Had something happened to Cade? An accident? "I haven't heard," she told Patience, her stomach knotting. "What about them?"

Patience blushed slightly, then gave a disclaimer. "I'm not saying it's true, you understand. But rumor is the Peterson and Hinton boys got caught together, kissing. Each other! If you know what I mean?"

Laurel rolled her eyes, "Yes, Patience. I understand. But what happened?"

Patience pulled Laurel by the arm, confidentially close. "The Hinton's go to our church. I overheard our minister telling Obedience that the Hinton's have taken their boy to one of those conversation camps."

"Do you mean, conversion camps?" Laurel replied. "As in *Pray the Gay Away* kind of thing?"

"I suppose."

Mrs. Daws seemed very uncomfortable with the conversation. "Ladies, we should respect the two families involved to settle their private matters. I don't believe it's very kind to be discussing it like this."

"But what about the Peterson boy?" Laurel pressed, ignoring the preacher's wife's protests. "What happened to him?"

"Nobody knows," Patience frowned. "Nobody has seen him."

Laurel looked at Lottie now, a sincere and worried look on her face. "Mrs. Daws, Cade Peterson does some work for me around Bessie's place. We are...sort of friends. If he's in trouble, I'd like to help."

Lottie understood now and decided to share what little she knew about the situation. "Seems like his parents either threw him out or he left on his own. His sister Angela spoke to Galin. She is very worried about her brother. Angela said he left home with only a few clothes and a camping tent."

The Community Store, being a small establishment with low shelves and high ceilings, was not a space where conversation was easily muffled. Sheila heard the women talking and pushed her shopping cart to their aisle. "I couldn't help but overhear," she began. "Several days ago, while I was on my way to babysit my grandson in Tuscaloosa, I saw the Peterson boy walking on the shoulder of the highway carrying a big backpack. He was about a mile or two from the interstate. I bet he was heading out of town. Trying to hitchhike maybe. Guess he's long gone by now"

"No," Laurel said, mostly to herself. "I don't think so."

Laurel moved quickly through the store, grabbing only what she needed, forgetting the rest for later. Cade had overtaken her thoughts. As soon as she got home, she put everything away quickly, then rushed out of her back door. Briefly, the thought of the black snake crept into her mind, but she didn't care. She took the trail adjacent to the field behind the house. Moving past the abandoned chicken houses, Laurel retraced the steps she'd walked with Linc until she came to the trail going into the woods. Sheila Bevins may have seen Cade walking in the direction of the interstate, but when Mrs. Daws mentioned he had left home with a camping tent, Laurel knew he'd been walking towards Hogg Road, not Interstate 59.

* * *

Sunlight weaved through the branches where it could manage to break between leaves and pine needles. This trail had been here for generations, permanently worn into hardened, almost glassy dirt. A carpet of dry, brittle pine needles blanketed the way, marking the passage of years. Laurel listened closely for any suspicious sounds, but all sounds seemed suspicious. Chirping birds above, stopped and started again with her footsteps. Crackling sounds from distant reaches of the thick woods echoed around her. It could have been someone walking. Or it might have been limbs shifting in the breeze or under a squirrel's leap. She wasn't well acquainted with all the noises a forest makes on its own, without human interference. Branches snapping, pinecones falling, and even bark shedding from tree trunks.

Summer was half over now, which meant it was at its hottest peak. Even the canopy of tall trees only mildly lowered the humidity in the woods. She remembered Linc telling her that snakes were more likely to crawl between the mazes of trees, where undergrowth and last winter's fallen leaves kept the ground cool. He said that Fall and Winter are the only times venturing off the trail was safe. Laurel kept to the path assuming if Cade were out here, she would find him along it or in one of the small grassy clearings it occasionally broke off into. She followed the trail to its ultimate end, bringing her out into Bessie's backyard. She hadn't seen a trace of Cade during the entire hour she searched.

Heavy-hearted, she walked towards the back porch. Something in her shoe was pressing her ankle. Pausing to grab hold of one of the iron posts by the door for balance, she pulled the crown of an acorn from her sock. *How did that get in there?* Lifting her hand from its resting position on the post, she felt the prickly residue of iron rust in her palm. She really did need to have these random posts removed. They were just in the way. Perhaps they'd been useful to a blind man back in the day when rope was attached, but now...

A blind man. Why hadn't she thought of that before?

Laurel jumped up the back steps in two strides, flinging open the door and rushing to the light switch Janice had cautioned her on her first day to avoid. Bracing for whatever sounds were about to explode, she flipped it. As if Gabriel himself were descending from the skies, the body-shaking eruption of an air horn pierced the tranquility of the afternoon, racing across the property, as well as up and down the dirt road.

Immediately, the phone began ringing. Neighbors—some she hadn't even met yet—called in succession to see if she was alright. She apologized profusely to her callers, lying that she did not know what the switch was operating. Of course, everyone explained its past purpose to her. She thanked them all and asked them to visit sometime so she could meet them. The moment she hung up with the last caller, Julia Davis burst into her kitchen with Jancie directly behind her.

"Are you okay, Miss Laurel?" Julia cried, out of breath. "I ran the second I heard it."

Glaring at her across Julia's shoulder, Janice folded her arms with a sharp look of condemnation on her face.

"Julia, I am so sorry!" Laurel explained. "I had no idea that switch was an alarm. Please forgive me for frightening you."

Smiling sweetly, Julia Davis replied, "No worries, Miss Laurel. I'm just glad you ain't hurt or nothing. But if you ever do get in some trouble, just hit that thing and somebody'll come running."

Excusing herself back to her house before all the children drove Dean to distraction, Julia left to walk back home. Janice was still standing with her arms crossed, scowling at her young friend. "You know exactly what that switch does. What's going on, Laurel?"

"It's Cade," Laurel told Janice. "He left home a few days ago and was spotted walking this way. Lottie Daws claims her took a tent with him."

Janice began to nod, relaxing her arms now. "I see. You think he may be hiding out in your woods. But that's a bit farfetched, don't you—"

Cade burst through the kitchen door, cutting off Janice at the most ironic time, his chest heaving as he gasped for air. "Laurel? You alright?"

Janice simply grinned, tossing her hand up to wave goodbye as she left them alone. Laurel looked at Cade, seeing an entirely new set of bruises on his face and arms. "I am fine," she snapped. "You are not." She went to him, lifting her fingers to his blackened cheek and swollen eye. "Your father did it to you again?"

Cade didn't reply. He didn't have to.

"And you've been sleeping in a tent in my woods."

It wasn't a question. Cade simply looked at her guiltily.

"Why didn't you just come here to me?" she asked. "You don't have to sleep out there scared in the dark."

"I didn't want you to get involved," he said. "But I didn't know where else I could hide where nobody would find me. You never go in those woods."

Grabbing a dishtowel and a bottle of peroxide from her cabinet, she said, "I did today. Sit down. Your father broke the skin when he punched you and this wound is not clean."

Cade pulled a chair from the table to sit while she stood over him,

225

sterilizing a deep gash where his father's knuckles punctured his cheek. "My friend's parents caught us hooking up. They called my dad. They blamed me for corrupting their *decent boy*. His parents sent him off to one of those Pray the Gay Away, conversion camps. Mine made me take an HIV test."

"I heard about that."

"They told me I had to choose whether I was normal or a queer," Cade said. "I told them I can't help how I feel. So they tossed me out. They said if I was gonna be a faggot, I could get out of their family."

"I am so sorry, Cade."

"It's fine. I never thought they'd understand or accept me, anyway. It's not a big surprise." He was being brave, stripping all emotion from his heart just the way Laurel used to do when she was his age. "I just need to figure out what I'm going to do."

Giving him a reproachful look she said, "What you are going to do is go get your stuff out of that tent and move into one of my spare bedrooms. And you are going to finish up your senior year in school."

Cade waved his hands, vehemently declined her offer. "No, no. I am not putting you in the middle of this. It's my problem. I'll get a job somewhere...Tuscaloosa maybe. I'll be fine."

Frustration rising within her, Laurel jerked a chair from the table and sat down beside him. "Do you know how stupid that sounds? You are going to finish high school when it starts back in a couple of weeks. And you will live here as long as you need to."

"I can't let you do that."

"Nobody lets me do anything, Cade." Laurel grinned. "We are pals, right?"

He nodded, holding back tears.

"Friends do not let other friends live in tents in their snake ridden woods. Besides," she added with a grin. "I still need somebody to do my yardwork and bushhog those fields. Do you expect me to drive that tractor?"

He laughed. Then just as quickly apologized.

Taking both of his hands into hers, Laurel told him, "You have done nothing wrong but ask to be respected for who you are. Your asshole father is the one who should be apologizing."

Frowning, Cade replied, "He's not going to let me stay here."

"How is he going to stop you?" Laurel asked. "At age 16 you are legally free to choose where you want to live. They can't stop you."

"How do you know that?"

"I used to be a lot like you, Cade," she confided. "Not gay, obviously, but I had a home life I had to escape from too. And now you have escaped. You're free Cade. You can be who you are, and nobody can force you into being who they want you to be. Now, go get your stuff. The pink room is mine, but you take whichever other you want. I'll start dinner. And when you get back, take a shower. You smell like you've been living in the woods."

He let out a little laugh. The expression of gratitude on his face, in his eyes, was the most genuine look she had ever received. She found herself startled at not only how good it felt, but how it felt almost natural.

CHAPTER TWENTY

The Petersons

Cade had been living with Laurel for a couple of weeks without incident, perhaps lulling the two of them into a false sense of security. The school term had begun a couple of days ago, Cade's senior year, and perhaps someone had seen her driving him to school and reported it to his parents. The last thing Laurel expected on this bright late summer morning was to be accosted in her driveway by the Petersons. Laurel and Cade walked out to the car as they had the last two mornings, she would drop him at school and then had plans to take her aunt Flossie into Tuscaloosa. Just as she unlocked her car, Hank and Ruby Peterson pulled their truck into the driveway, blocking them in.

The scene erupted into immediate chaos as Cade's mother, came rushing forward, her accusatory finger pointed at Laurel. Ruby Peterson was already mid-shout, with a sentence she must have begun before leaving the truck, "...messin' in folks' family business! You ain't got no right getting' our boy here to shack up with you! I bet you're who started him down this devil's road?"

Laurel squared her shoulders in the face of Ruby's aggression. If this was going to be a physical confrontation, the woman would get what she came for. But Cade, jarred by his parents' arrival and behavior, jumped to Laurel's defense.

"Mama, leave her alone! She hasn't done anything to anyone!"

Cade's father stepped menacingly from the truck, his eyes seething with repulsion, aimed directly at his son. He loomed by the truck as if daring his son to action.

Ruby's verbal assault didn't let up as she stalked closer Laurel's way. "She done made you some kind of sissy, Cade! Like her high and mighty city friends, I bet! Brought you into this house so she can keep you livin' wrong with the Lord."

Not an easily insulted or intimidated woman, Laurel slammed her own car door shut, pacing straight towards Ruby Peterson. "Have you always been the stupidest person you've ever known or did marrying Hank act as the catalyst."

Ruby, possibly not even understanding the insult, continued ranting as she charged at Laurel. Though Laurel did not appear apprehensive in any way, Cade instinctually headed his mother off, grabbing her at the hips moments before she reached Laurel. "Stop it Mama! She didn't do anything."

Hank darted forward, yelling out, "Boy, you let go of your mama!"

Twice Cade's size, Hank jerked Cade from away his mother, freeing Ruby. Hank's swing was much too rapid for Cade to register until the impact of it reopened the existing gash on his cheek, sending Cade toppling backward to the ground. Towering over his son, Hank gave him a punishing kick to the stomach as he shouted, "Grabbin' your mother like that after she's tryin to defend you! You ain't got the right to lay your filthy faggot hands on her for any reason!"

Both Laurel and Ruby, distracted by Hank's attack on Cade, stood frozen in place watching Hank loom over Cade, who lay clutching his stomach, gasping for breath. Cade attempted to back away on his hands and feet, not having time to stand before Hank was on him again. Snatching Cade up by the shirt, Hank lifted him from the ground, ramming him into the grill of his truck. "Never thought I'd have me a dick sucker for a son. You make me disgusted."

Caught in a fit of rage, Laurel ran at Hank Peterson, pounding her fists into his back, demanding he release Cade. With her back towards Ruby, Hank's wife seized the opportunity, snatching Laurel by her hair, dragging her off her husband.

Cade struggled against his father's grip, screaming for his mother to leave Laurel alone. Hank plunged his fist into Cade's chest, the brutal blow knocking the boy flat against the truck, then sinking to the ground.

No stranger to self-preservation, Laurel drew from past experiences with a self-defense class. *Change the balance of power*, she reminded herself. Assessing her situation, Laurel swept her leg back, catching Ruby's ankles, brushing Ruby's feet from under her. As Ruby toppled backwards, she released Laurel's hair so her hands could brace for the fall.

Once she hit the ground, Ruby jumped back up again, taking an unladylike swing at Laurel. But Laurel remembered her tuck and weave maneuver from self-defense class and evaded the punch. Then Laurel swept up, fist clinched, for the perfect upper cut. Ruby barely had time to register the blow to her jaw, before Laurel's left jab caught the side of her face, sending Ruby crashing down to the ground. However, Ruby did not quite make it to the ground, as Laurel's knee was ready, meeting Ruby's face midway to the dusty driveway. Ruby Peterson now lay swelling and bleeding on the gravel, possibly missing more teeth than she arrived with. But that was only something her dentist could decide.

Infuriated by what she'd done to his wife, Hank raced at Laurel with enraged eyes. Laurel prepared for engagement with Hank—although this time she was a little afraid. Cade leapt onto his father's back, doing his best to stop him. But suddenly a piercing sound erupted through the air, causing everyone to pause in place. None of them had seen the truck stop in the road and Leon Davis step out. The barrel of his rifle was still smoking from the shot he just released into the air. Cocking it for another, he nodded to Laurel, "You okay, Miss Holden?"

Bending over with her hands on her knees, sucking in oxygen, Laurel nodded. Cade let go of his father and moved around the car to Laurel. Hank Peterson moved towards Leon. "Ain't none a this concerns you, Leon. I'm dealin' with my wayward boy, and this bitch woman what took him in. I don't have any beef with you, yet."

Staring unblinkingly at Hank, Leon's eye tilted into the site of his rifle, ready to fire. "This lady is my neighbor, so that gives me a beef with you, Hank." he announced. "She's a good woman too. I expect you got some stuff to sort out in your family, but you're gonna leave Miss Holden out of it."

For a moment it looked to be quite an intense standoff, both men locked in stares and ready to strike. Then Hank blinked. He wiped his brow with his sleeve, then challenged Leon by taking another step towards him. "That's fine by me. But I'm takin my boy and I'm—"

Leon fired again, his bullet piercing the dirt only two feet from Hank's shoes. Hank jumped back a few feet, shocked by the move. Leon was ready with his next shot, if needed. "From what I heard, Hank, you threw the boy out." Leon's firm voice matched Hank's, like two lions ready to fight to the death. Leon then added, "Don't seem to me that you like him much." Glancing at Cade, Leon asked, "Boy, you wanna go back with them or stay here?"

The boy looked both defiant and scared beyond belief, but he managed to stammer, "Here, Mr. Davis."

Looking again at the Petersons, Leon said, "Guess that settles that. If the boy changes his mind, he knows how to get home. In the meantime, if I see either a you on Miss Holden's property again, I won't be firing warning shots. See, this is her place. She can take anybody in she thinks needs it. As for your boy, from all I hear, he knows his own mind. Knows who he is. He don't need you tearing his face up just cause you don't like it."

A long deliberating silence followed until Hank, admitting defeat, crawled back into his truck. Offering no assistance to Ruby, she staggered herself to the passenger side. Her mouth, nose, and the gash in her cheek smeared with blood. Once the Peterson truck was out of sight, Laurel dashed to Leon.

"Thank you so much, Mr. Davis! I don't know what they might have done had you not come along."

Shrinking from the gratitude, Leon shifted his hat and simply said, "Not right to attack a woman." Then a slick grin crossed his face as he let out a throaty chuckle. "Even if that woman appears to know how to handle herself pretty damn good." Leon turned to Cade.

Laurel laughed. "Still, I thank you."

Leon went back to his truck and wracked his gun on the back window, then he turned back to look at Cade. "Son, not everybody is like they have you believing."

Cade swallowed the lump in his throat and nodded, nearing tears.

"I admit, I don't understand it, son. But then again, I ain't got to. You got every right that I do to live the way that is right for you."

Laurel and Cade watched as Leon Davis drove off into the morning, heading to work. Then in her unintentional maternal tone, she told Cade, "Go change your clothes before we go to school. You have a Geometry test today."

* * *

The half hour drive into Tuscaloosa provided Laurel enough time to relay the events of the morning to her aunt Flossie. Flossie listened intently with only a few elongated enunciations of "No's" and "Well, I'll be's." When Laurel was finished summarizing her eventful morning, Flossie held her head down, sighing to herself. "That family ain't never been nothing but white trash anyways. I know'd Hank's Daddy. He was a shithead too. Got it honest."

Always entertained by the elderly woman's candor, Laurel laughed before saying, "Cade is a good kid though. I am most worried about his mental wellbeing."

"Well, honey, alls I can tell you is keep doin' for him. If things had been different, he may have had it some better, but maybe not."

Driving down the interstate into town, Laurel found herself having a real moment of introspection. Never once had she imagined that she would having any kind of conversation with someone she was related to, especially a rural elderly woman as grammatically challenged as Flossie. Yet somehow, she felt warmed by it. As if some blank place in her heart had been filled in with authentic connection to someone sharing her blood. Furthermore, there was a wisdom within Aunt Flossie that Laurel would have never expected to find in a person she once would have deemed "backward". She even now found herself about to seek her aunt's guidance.

"Aunt Flossie, I have never really been close to anyone. Never felt invested in other people enough to delve too deeply into their problems. But with Cade, I don't know…maybe it's because he's young. He still has a chance to shed his demons before they change him. I can relate to some of what he's been through."

"Now, honey what demons have you had time to pick up in your short life?"

Appreciating how Flossie viewed it as a short life so far, Laurel confided a small insight into her chaotic childhood. The loneliness she felt. The unworthiness she felt every time her mother chose a man over her, compounded with her already fragile self-worth over her father abandoning her and his family never reaching out.

"I have literally been alone my entire life," Laurel said. "I wonder if I am trying to fix the broken part of me by trying to repair what is broken in Cade. I also wonder how long before I will ruin this relationship with Linc, just like I always do. Things are simpler when you keep to yourself."

Flossie let out one of her signature caws of laughter, slapping her niece's knee. "Honey, there's an old saying. *People who keep to themselves get left to themselves.* Let's say you do end up gettin' hurt. At least you finally let yourself feel something at all. Hurt heals up. But loneliness always feels the same."

"I can't tell you how many hours I have spent in therapy through my life," Laurel grinned. "And they didn't possess half the insight you do. I only wish I could be sure about things before I get too far involved."

"Laurel!" Flossie shouted. "You are already involved or else you wouldn't be frettin' over none of this. You like that good looking black man, and you care about this struggling boy. Far as the black man goes, I can't help you much there 'cept tell you to take a chance. But when it comes to the Peterson boy, it's only natural you'd feel close to him. Even if you don't know why."

"Because we have had similar childhoods?"

"Naw," Flossie replied, her tone changing to a more serious one. "Cause you and he got the same blood pushing through your veins."

CHAPTER TWENTY-ONE

Marriage is Forever

Blindsided by Flossie's obscure statement, Laurel stared at her elderly aunt, forgetting momentarily about the road. Flossie yelled at her to slow down. Looking back towards traffic, Laurel saw the braking cars ahead and slammed the brakes. Flossie told her she would explain the story over lunch, providing Laurel could get them to town alive. Laurel got them safely to the restaurant where they ordered lunch before launching into whatever Flossie had meant by her earlier statement.

"It's true, honey." Flossie confirmed. "But I 'spect I am the only soul left who knows about it. And don't you go saying nothing 'bout it either. Your Grandmaw did her best to keep that shame shut down all the rest of her years."

"What shame?" Laurel asked. "How is Cade related to us?"

Stirring the lemon wedge into her tea, Flossie quickly made the distinction. "Not us, darlin', just you."

Laurel sat at full attention listening to the long-buried secret exhumed by her grandmother's sister. Flossie, balancing the tightrope between her love for gossip and her loyalty to her sister's memory, began.

"It was a long time ago. Even before Ustus got shot and blinded. We knew he was runnin' around on Bessie. You hear tales, but nothing anybody was sure enough about to go to her."

"My grandfather cheated on her?"

Cackling in her amused way, Flossie said, "Honey, most fellas messed around once or twice. Not my Norman, you understand. That man was tried and true decent. But a lot of men ran around some. Ustus was no different. I heard tell he even carried on with Babe Daniels a little, but that was just talk."

"The Daniels sisters' sister?"

"She weren't nothing but a trollop, anyway." Flossie remarked. "But she ain't in this story. There was this gal named Chippy Rose..." adding, with another of her trademark cackles, "Ain't that a stupid name? Anyway, some folks saw Ustus' truck parked over at Chippy's place once or twice a week. Her husband died in the war." Laurel was curious which war she meant, then judged from the timeline of her grandfather's age she must have meant World War II. Flossie continued, "We all knew about it. I asked Norman to tell me flat out once, and he said, 'Yeah, I think he is." Flossie's broken way of speaking was sometimes hard to follow, but having spent enough time with her by now, Laurel could understand Flossie-speak.

"Norman told you he believed Ustus was in love with someone else?"

Flossie chuckled again. "Lordy, you young folks and your labels on everything. I don't know if I'd say *in love*. Ustus just laid with her sometimes."

Laurel was about to ask what she meant but stopped. 'Laid with' meant sex. *Is that where we got the term I got laid?*

"Well," Flossie went on. "My sisters and me—my sisters Laudie and Notie. You don't know them, and they're dead now, which for you is one of God's mercies because they was the most persnickety two women you'd ever have the misfortune of meeting. Anyway, the three of us went to Mama and asked her if we should tell Bessie what we been hearing. Mama told us right off to stay out of it."

Laurel was stunned by the statement. "Her own mother didn't want you to tell her that her husband was cheating on her!"

"Mama said, 'she ain't gone believe it unless she sees it. Nothin' to gain gettin' between married people. They'll handle their own marriage woes themselves. And if Bessie don't never find out, she won't be upset."

"That is horrible advice!" Laurel declared.

Flossie couldn't say whether it was, or it wasn't, but it was the advice they took. None of the sisters said anything to Bessie. Months went by, until one day while Flossie was shopping in The Community Store, Midge Taylor...

"Who?" Laurel asked.

"Ole Renzo's mama," Flossie answered. "Renzo hadn't taken the store over yet."

Midge Taylor had waved Flossie over to the counter and whispered in her ear, "Bessie's done found out!"

Rushing from the store without anything she came for, Flossie hopped in her car and made her way to Bessie's house. "When I pulled up, I seen Bessie a'sittin on the porch swing looking at her feet," Flossie described. "I went to her, and she told me. She'd been taking some stew out to the Dobbs place cause Old Lady Dobbs was recovering from a broken hip. She fell sloppin' pigs. Well, Chippy Rose lived right down from the Dobbs' place. Bessie saw the back end of Ustus' truck sticking out from the side of the house. She pulled in there and went up to the door."

The recounting of the event was interrupted by lunch being delivered to the table. Once the waitress was gone, Flossie picked back up where she left off. According to what Bessie had told her, the moment she stepped on the porch she could see Ustus quite casually seated on a sofa reading the newspaper. It looked as if he were just as at home there as in his own house. Bessie, being the honest and fearless woman she was, opened the screen door and went inside.

"What are you doing here?" she asked her husband.

Ustus was startled and speechless. Bessie had taken him by surprise, but he recovered quickly, staring at her as if she were the one with the gall. She asked again why he was in Chippy Rose's front room. At that point, Chippy entered from a back room, demanding to know what was going on.

"Just what I am trying to find out," Bessie declared. "I would like to know why my husband is here in the middle of the day, reading a paper on your couch like he's the man of the house?"

"Now any other woman would been shakin' in her boots," Flossie told Laurel. "But Chippy was a bold and cussed thing. She put her hands on her hips and declared Ustus *was* the man of that house."

"She said that?" Laurel gasped.

Flossie continued, saying how Chippy bragged to Bessie that she had as much right to Ustus as Bessie did. "Bessie being a Godfearing, Christian woman," Flossie explained to her young niece. "Resisted the urge to beat that whore of a woman to a bloody pulp."

Instead, Bessie had asked Ustus what Chippy meant by the remark. Ustus made no apologies. He portrayed no noticeable guilt. In fact, in all his smugness, he seemed to be more annoyed at having to explain, than feeling remorse. He rose from the couch and walked to the door Chippy had entered from.

He told Bessie, "Come see."

His wife joined him in the doorway where upon she saw a small wooden baby bed and what looked to be around a six-month-old baby asleep for his afternoon nap.

"Ustus had a baby with Chippy?" Laurel gasped.

"More than one, some say," Flossie admitted. "But I only know for sure about the boy. It was Ustus' all right."

Laurel felt a wave of empathy for Bessie. To have her husband's betrayal thrown so callously in her face must have been mortifying. The irony was also not lost on her now as to why her grandmother had never tried to know Laurel's mother. It could only have revived her own pain and humiliation.

"What did Bessie do?"

Flossie went on with her story, saying how Bessie kept her composure despite the shock. "Your Grandmaw wasn't the kind to let nothing break her. She just looked at the boy, then back to Ustus and told him, 'It is probably best you come on home in a little bit, Ustus. It'll be suppertime soon and your real family will be at the table waiting for you.'"

Laurel slapped the lunch table in outrage, causing the silverware to bounce. "You mean she didn't punch Chippy? Or bash her husband's head in!"

Bessie was a lady, Flossie explained. Lowering herself to such a tantrum would have only shown Chippy and Ustus how much hurt they had caused her. She might be able to forgive Ustus one day, but if she had broken down in front of them, she would have never forgiven herself. "I sat on the swing with her when I found her back at her house. Same swing you got now." Flossie said.

"Sixteen years," Bessie had told her. "Sixteen years with that man and he's got a kid with her. He has a son that isn't my son."

Flossie had then asked her sister the glaring question before them, "Bess, you figuring on leavin' him?"

"No, I'm not going anywhere," Bessie had shot back at Flossie, with a look of disbelief, as if the very question was offensive. "Where would I go? Back to Mama's? With all my kids? How'd we survive? And I don't go anywhere without my kids. No, this is their home. They are Hogues and this is Hogue land. This is where they belong. And I am a Hogue too."

"I just wondered if you was thinking about divorce," Flossie asked her sister. "People do it sometimes, I hear."

"Divorce is a sin against the Lord," Bessie pronounced. "I married that son of a bitch for better or worse. I promised God I'd stand by him, and I don't break promises. I especially don't break God-promises. Ustus is the one who lied to God and to me. He's the one who's gotta pay for that. He and that woman will answer to God for what they've done. Him for betraying his family and her for being low-down nasty enough to lay with another woman's husband. They are the ones with stained souls. My soul is clean."

Laurel was watching her elderly aunt's eyes as she recounted the story. They were misty now, wet with the tears of anguish perhaps Flossie carried for her sister since Bessie had been too strong, or afraid, to carry herself. "So, she stayed with him."

"Yep," Flossie nodded. "He come home at supper time. She asked him if he'd called off that situation they'd discussed earlier. Ustus said he did, and it wasn't gonna be a problem no more. And that was that."

"And she just went back to the way things were before she found out?" Laurel gasped.

Cackling again, possibly grateful to now recall the more pleasant animosity her sister could muster, Flossie laughed. "Naw, I wouldn't say that, Laurel. Your grandmaw could be an ice-cold thing when she needed to be. I expect not a day went by again when Ustus wasn't reminded of what he did. Not that Bessie woulda ever said another word on it. But she was cool as a cucumber with him the rest of his days. I bet Ustus got to missin' the old Bessie after a while. But he killed off that part of her. That bedroom off the den, that was Ustus' room from then on to when he died."

Laurel couldn't decide if Bessie's brand of revenge was the best way to have gotten even with Ustus, but it was not anything she could change. She asked her aunt if Ustus kept his word after that and never saw Chippy again.

"He left her alone. She did come by once. Norman told me. But I never said nothing to Bessie about it. It was years later when Bessie was working in the school cafeteria. Ustus was blind by then, you see. I guess Chippy came by to get a look for herself at what happened to him. She said she was married to somebody and her husband was raising the boy as his own. Chippy said goodbye to him and went back home. Ustus just sat in the house alone again until Bessie or the kids got home in the afternoon. Him just sittin' in his darkness day after day."

"I want to feel sorry for him," Laurel admitted. "But I don't think I can." She had been so engrossed in Flossie's history lesson that she completely forgot the original purpose for it. Then the thought sprang back to mind as she exclaimed, "How is Cade related to me?"

Flossie grinned, shaking her head at the lunacy of it all. "Chippy Rose married Daniel Peterson. That boy in that bed Bessie seen, was Hank."

Leaning back in her chair with her hands gripping the sides of her head in shock and frustration, Laurel stared at the ceiling of the restaurant for a moment, collecting herself. When she finally processed this new development, she looked back across the table at Flossie, who had a bit of cole slaw stuck to her chin. Laurel took her napkin and reached across to wipe her aunt's face. Then almost laughing at the absurdity of it all, asked, "Aunt Flossie, are there anymore bombshells you'd like to drop on me? Anything else I don't know yet?"

The old woman cackled in her sweet way and replied, "None I can recollect at the moment, honey. But Laurel, you been gone from this family a long time. You was bound to come back and get a few surprises."

CHAPTER TWENTY-TWO

Sins of the Father

When Laurel picked Cade up from school that afternoon, she was pleased to hear his day had been less eventful than the way it began. The fight with his parents that morning couldn't have made his day any easier. She considered telling him what she'd learned from Flossie, but decided against it. For now, at least. He was struggling emotionally, and any new bombshells would only convolute things. When he had homework to do, she left him at the kitchen table and went outside to sit on the porch. Her mind still had not completely processed everything that happened that day.

The hanging baskets around the front porch which she planted a few weeks ago, now brimmed over with flowers. Petunias of red, deep purple, and white intermingled with orange and white zinnias. She understood what Janice and Flossie meant when they said Bessie's porch was always a place of respite and peace. The addition of the flowers, along with the fresh coat of light green paint Cade put on the floorboards, cheered the front of the house up a great deal. Laurel sat on the porch swing, breathing in the fresh air, allowing her mind time to let everything sink in. She was glad the day was nearly over. Beginning with the fight with Cade's parents in the driveway, then moving into the discovery that her grandfather had another set of children on the side, was a lot to think about. It was still hard to believe that Hank Peterson was her uncle. She wondered if he would have come at her so furiously that morning if he'd known. Probably so. If he had no qualms beating up his son, why should a niece matter?

Cade came out on the porch after half an hour.

"Finished already?" she asked, surprising herself with the motherly tone.

"Got it all done," he answered. "And I think most of its right."

"You can always Google it to see," she suggested.

With a devious grin, he admitted, "I did. How else do you think I got most of them right?"

She rocked the swing back and forth as he settled down beside her, nestling into one of the pillows. The quiet creak of the swing seemed in sync with the afternoon chirp of crickets.

"You seem like you have something on your mind," she said. "Is it about this morning?"

With a short nod, he said softly, "I just feel bad about what happened before school. I'm really sorry—"

Laurel stiffened her back a bit, "I told you this morning you have nothing to apologize for. You are not responsible for your parents' behavior."

"But aren't I?" Cade frowned. "All this trouble because of me. Because I'm gay. Because, according to them, I am dirty and sinful. I've tried not to be this way, over and over."

"Cade, being gay isn't something you can change with a little willpower! It's part of you. You can't change it anymore than you can change your height or the color of your eyes."

"Not according to them," he replied. "They say I'm not how I'm supposed to be. That I'm just made wrong. Or damaged."

Laurel, now fully upright, feet no longer rocking but planted firmly on the floor under the swing, stared directly into Cade's eyes. "Nothing is wrong with you, Cade. Parents are supposed to love their children as they are. Not as they wish them to be. If anyone is damaged, it's them, for being cruel and unfeeling when it is so obvious you're hurting."

"But God," Cade whispered. "If I am disappointing God..."

Frustration simmered inside her. She had heard this argument too many times. People living in turmoil merely because of the ideological burdens placed on them by simplistic and unyielding minds. "Cade, do you even believe in God? Or are you afraid not to because it is all anyone has ever taught you?"

He appeared to be caught off guard by the question. "It's a given, isn't it? I've never heard anybody who didn't believe in God."

"It doesn't have to be mandatory, Cade. Do you truly believe? Because it is okay if you don't."

He thought a moment, then answered. "I do, Laurel. I really do. I know it doesn't fit with being gay. I just don't know how to not be who I am and stay right with the Lord."

Pushing her hands through her hair, Laurel counted mentally to three, forcing herself to be the kind of person who helps someone rather than lambast them for beliefs she found childish. "Okay," she sighed, resigning herself to meet him where he was, not where she would prefer him to be. That would be doing exactly what his parents were guilty of. "How can you be so certain that living your truth is offensive to Him?"

"It says so in the Bible!" Cade cried. "Everybody knows homosexuality is a sin. It's all my family ever says."

Stifling a laugh, Laurel quipped, "Forgive me Cade, but I do not look to your parents as a bastion of intelligence."

He grinned.

"As for the Bible," she continued. "You shouldn't lose sight of the fact the Bible was written by men. Human men. Man always adds his own spin to everything. When you examine that period in history, most of what was written had political undertones. Look at how women are treated in the Bible. Did you know that in the original text, there is no mention of Mary Magdeline being a prostitute. That's a label men gave her when they rewrote it because they couldn't stomach the idea Jesus might have respected and trusted a woman."

"Seriously?" Cade asked. "How do you know that? I've never heard that before."

"I studied Latin in college, and we had to translate the New Testament from the original known text. Many things were misinterpreted when the King James Bible was written. And some of them on purpose. I have traveled across the world. I have spoken to scholars far smarter than you and I will ever be. There is so much history people decided to ignore. Like how ancient Egyptians just erased certain Pharaohs from their records."

"I didn't know that either."

"And as for the mention of homosexuality in the Bible," she informed him. "It is a rather well-known mistranslation which had nothing to do with same-sex coupling. In fact, once the translation was corrected, the mistaken text was never printed again. But evangelicals latched onto the incorrect version and the King James Bible is the version most Christians own and live by."

"That's not right!" Cade exclaimed. "If they know it's a mistake in the translation—"

Laurel nodded. "But it fits the narrative they want others to believe. Think about all the hatred and damage done to people over *that one* mistaken translation. And not only the gay people the mistranslation is used against, but the misguided animosity instilled in *faithful people* who only wanted to live as God wants them to live. Those people have been harmed too because they've been *intentionally lied to* and led to believe something that *never was* scripture."

She could see Cade's mind was blown. She took a deep breath, adding, "So Cade, don't stake your faith or your self-esteem on the opinions of others. If you love God, and you try to live with a kind heart, you shouldn't allow anyone to tell you that you are damaged."

"I guess you're right." He seemed more at peace now. At peace in himself.

"Honestly, Cade. I'm stunned no one ever calls out the sheer audacity against God from these judgmental people claiming to be Christians."

"Audacity?" Cade replied. "What do you mean?"

"*Audacity*, means--"

"Laurel, I know what the word audacity means. I am not an idiot," said Cade. "I just don't understand what you mean by Christians showing audacity towards God."

"It is very simple," Laurel explained. "Where do your parents, or churches, or anyone who claims they believe in God, get off by assuming they know what God intended or didn't intend to create?"

"Huh?"

"Cade, do you believe that God knows everything? That He designed everything on earth to be just the way He wanted it to be? Fish, animals, birds, humans?"

Tucking his feet back under the swing so that the toes of his shoes dragged a little when the swing moved, he said, "Yes."

"Then it is far more likely God designed you and millions like you for His own specific reason. The fact that a bunch of close-minded people cannot wrap their tiny brains around the reason doesn't mean there isn't one. In my opinion, the real sinner is the one who tells a gay person they are not what God planned. That's what I mean by audacity. As if they are so important that God should have run His plans by them first."

Cade felt lighter from their talk, as if a few invisible chains melted from his body. She assured him again—his sexuality wasn't shameful. That beyond Scroggins, the world held millions of people who didn't think like his parents. She told him about the Episcopalian pastor from her yoga class—a lesbian with a wife and two sons. About James and Scott, the gay couple next door in her old apartment who adopted two Nigerian children while on a mission trip. She wanted him to understand there were broader minds out there living beyond this narrow sliver of society he inhabited.

He went back inside, feeling much better and wanting to cook dinner himself. He'd been doing a lot of that lately, which Laurel greatly appreciated. Everything the boy made was delicious. Of course, her bathroom scale told her every morning it was a little too delicious. She remained on the front porch a while longer, mulling over the things she said to Cade, as well as all she learned earlier in the day from Flossie.

Laurel wished she could have said the same things to her grandmother as she had to Cade. Although the situations were vastly different, Bessie too had lived in a prison of propriety dictated to her by social and religious beliefs. Had Bessie made other choices, if she'd left the man she no longer loved or respected, what might the rest of her life been like? What might Laurel's life have been like?

It was a lot to think about and probably best left undisturbed. However, Laurel was grateful to Flossie for sharing the big secret with her. It helped her understand her grandmother better and possibly helped her work towards forgiving her for the neglect in Laurel's life. Laurel tried to put herself into Bessie's shoes. To be raised with the belief that divorcing an unfaithful husband was a worse sin than what Ustus had done to her, must have been quite a cross to carry. Blaming herself for marrying the wrong kind of man and choosing to live with the consequences rather than risk offending God, seemed so pointless to Laurel. But it explained so much. Bessie's loyalty to Janice as the only true wife was understandable when Laurel considered Ustus' betrayal.

There was another side to it too, one implied but not spoken. Janice, on some level, must share Bessie's idea of marriage. Why else could she not bring herself to move on after Charlie left her for Laurel's mother? Why else would Janice live the remainder of her life living beside her in-laws? If Bessie had considered Janice to perpetually be Charlie's wife, then didn't that make Janice now his widow?

All of Bessie's decisions explained why she never endorsed or acknowledged Charlie's marriage to Laurel's mother. In Bessie's mind it was not a valid marriage, and Laurel not a legitimate extension of her family. Janice was Charlie's wife and by those terms, now his widow. By proxy, Laurel was an extension of Charlie. Therefore, Janice might consciously, or unconsciously, feel a duty to Laurel. She was Janice's husband's daughter after all. There was no doubt about Janice's genuine affection for her. Laurel felt it and knew it was real. And though she may not care to admit it, Laurel reciprocated that affection.

It was all such a clusterfuck of twisted obligations, loyalties, and tainted moral ideals. Laurel found herself completely bewildered by such a mindset, and yet, completely understanding it. *I think I've been here too long. This shit is starting to make sense to me.*

CHAPTER TWENTY-THREE

Syrup Day Reunion

A s much as she may have wanted to get out of being drafted into the quilting circle, Laurel found herself greatly enjoying spending time with these ladies. It was now her third time participating, and this gathering was proving as educational as the others. Puddin's grandson's baseball quilt would be finished today, with only the sewing of the back and filling it with cotton left to complete. Laurel found this a much easier technique to follow. The back of the quilt was one solid piece of off-white fabric, and she only had to follow the lines of the squares on the front, leaving the last side open to stuff before closing it.

The women chatted away while they worked, covering the Scroggins grapevine in every direction. Mrs. Glover bought a new car, splurging to get an electric one. "Now there ain't one a'those charging stations within 20 miles of here!" Delva balked.

"No, Delva," Patience explained. "She says they put a plug in her garage, so she can charge it at home every night."

Thumbing her nose at the idea, Bootsie declared, "And her electric bill is gonna shoot sky high, what do you bet!"

"Laurel," Puddin asked. "You ever drove one of those electric things?"

Laurel said she had never driven one personally but had ridden in several electric Ubers. Her detailed description of how quiet and safe they were, did not impress the others.

"My sweet Hershall would not have liked it at all." Puddin announced. "Automobiles should run on gasoline the way the good Lord planned them to."

Laurel let that comment go by without saying anything. The topic switched to how Miss Ellie Dorran's son was planning to come home for a few days. According to the ladies, he was a "big wig" of finance in Chicago.

"I am supposed to visit Ellie Dorran," Laurel shared. "She has something she wants me to include in the cookbook."

"Well, good luck with that!" Delva snickered. "The Dorrans have always been uppity. I can't believe her son is even comin' home. He hasn't seen his mother in three years."

"He's coming back for their Homecoming," Bootsie informed them. "Their church's Homecoming is this weekend."

"I still do not really understand what Homecoming is supposed to be?" Laurel admitted.

Delva added to her confusion with, "In my time we called it Decoration Day."

"We still call it that," Bootsie replied. "Laurel, it is when members of the church have a big communal lunch outside after services. Then we all decorate the graves of our loved ones who are buried in the churchyard. Ours comes at the end of this month. It used to be in June, but it was too hot. September is better."

"Lots of people who move off come back for Homecoming," Puddin said. "And now you're here to look after Bessie and Ustus."

Laurel made a mental note to ask Janice what this was going to entail. Before she could ask more about the event, Delva moved to another subject, taking Laurel off guard. "You gettin' much flack over taking the Peterson boy in?"

Laurel, now unembarrassed to wear her readers in front of the ladies, shifted them back on her head to hold her bangs out of her eyes while she fought the crooked stitch she kept making. "Only from his parents," she answered. "They continue running their mouths. But I think Linc is getting some pushback. Honestly, I would have assumed there would be more animosity down here over his and my dating than over Cade being gay."

Delva snickered again as she stitched her square closed. "Oh, there is. But folks know better than to say it out loud. Prejudice don't ever go away. It's learning to keep it inside your head and not let it spill out your mouth that makes progress. But not a lotta folks have come that far with gays yet. Getting there, but not there yet."

"And it isn't only his being...that way...bothering people." Puddin explained. "Sweety, you are a fine looking, older woman."

"Older!"

"Compared to him, yes older." Puddin emphasized. "It doesn't look right to some for a seventeen-year-old boy to take up living with a woman in her thirties."

Flummoxed by the logic of the argument, Laurel argued the rationale of whoever the gossips were Puddin referred to. "The implication alone discredits anyone's reason for outrage. What could be improper about a gay young man living with a woman of any age? Surely, no one would believe we have a sexual relationship?"

"People do talk." Bootsie commented.

Incensed by it all, Laurel cried, "If Cade and I were having an illicit affair, wouldn't that completely contradict his being gay? Obviously, we have a platonic friendship."

Patience sat a little higher in her chair as though she had something of great importance to contribute. For a second, she looked a little like her oldest sister. "You just keep doing for that boy, Miss Laurel. It isn't right for parents to turn their kids out on the street."

"Well, I had to once." Bootsie piped up. "Renzo and I had enough and put our boy Gillis out of the house for good."

"Yeah, but that was different," Puddin declared. "Your boy Gillis was on dope and stole from The Community Store register. You had no choice."

Laurel was hearing this little bit of dirt for the very first time. "What happened after you threw him out?"

With a touch of pride in her eyes from knowing she had been right, Bootsie told her, "He straightened up. Took a minute, but he did. Got off the drugs. Found a job in Decatur, and now he is the district manager of the Step Tread shoe store chain. His region stretches from Birmingham to Nashville. He and his wife have 3 adorable kids. And..." she said triumphantly, "Not only did he get himself right with us and God, that boy actually paid back every cent he stole from us once he started working."

Laurel noted to Bootsie how remarkably rare something like that was, adding, "Happen to have a recipe to go along with the story of Gillis' fall and rise?"

The kind lady shook her head with an amused smile, "Sorry to disappoint you, Laurel. Afraid I don't."

"Oh, that reminds me!" Puddin exclaimed. "I have another story to pitch you, myself. I didn't think a thing about it till the other night when I was talking to my neighbor. They adopted a new dog. It made me think of it."

"Is it about a dog?" Bootsie asked.

"No, about my mama," Puddin cried. "It's a real good story, Laurel. I believe you'll like it for your book."

Puddin started telling the women the story of her mother. To everyone's surprise it was not something they'd heard before. "My Mama's name was Thursee," Puddin began. "When Mama was about six years old her Poppa died. Her Momma was part Indian."

"Native American," Patience corrected.

"Same thing," Puddin scoffed. "Anyway, Thursee's mother had no way to take care of her children with her husband dead. And because she was Indian—Native American—her kids wouldn't be accepted by her own people if she was to go back to them, wherever that was. She had to find a place for her kids to live, since she wasn't able to keep them fed on her own."

Puddin had Laurel's attention from the start. Her fingers stopped their work on the quilt, as did everyone else's, and they all listened with piqued interest. Thursee and her siblings were brought to their community's church one Sunday after preaching. Their mother stood before the congregation and asked who might be willing to take her children into their homes to care for.

Puddin added, "My grandmother was apparently a dark woman, and not a lot of people trusted her. They called her 'the red woman.'" However, Puddin explained how the preacher of their church implored his members to take pity on the children, who—Puddin insisted, "all looked white."

Being a little girl, Thursee didn't understand what was going on, and she began to cry. However, her mother snapped her out of it by telling her, "We ain't got time to cry. We only have time to plan." Thursee's two brothers were the first to find homes when a farmer, possessing no sons, agreed to take them in to help on his farm. Thursee watched her brothers walk from the church with the stranger and his wife. Thursee did her best to stay still and not cry, focusing instead on the little cardboard fans the women sitting in the pews were waving across their faces to combat the afternoon heat rising inside the church.

Thursee's baby sister, Sertsie, only 3 years old, was squirming, trying to get out of her mother's arms. Their mother passed Sertsie off to her eldest daughter Jaylee. With only the three girls left needing homes, the preacher had to speak out again to his flock using words like "Christian heart" and "Generous". Finally, a couple stood up, agreeing to take the little one, and Sertsie was carried off by the two strangers. Thursee and Jaylee were all that were left. It was beginning to look like no one else was going to come forward to give them a home, until a man and his wife agreed they would take Thursee home with them. The man's name was Bide Collier, and he owned a farm a few miles away. When the Collier's took Thursee by the hand to leave, Thursee's momma told her "Grow up to be a good girl and help Mrs. Collier all you can."

"That was the last time my Mama ever saw her mama." Puddin said.

"What happened next?" urged Laurel.

Puddin continued with her tale, telling them that the Colliers took Thursee to a lovely farm. The house was unlike any the child had seen, two stories, painted, and had flowers in window boxes. Since the Colliers had never been blessed with children of their own, Thursee had a bedroom all to herself.

"Are you rich?" Thursee asked Mrs. Collier.

"No, Thursee, we aren't rich."

"But you got so many things," the little girl replied.

Mrs. Collier put her arm around the child and gave her a sort of hug. "We're not rich. I think you have just seen one way of living. You'll get used to things."

Mrs. Collier was right. It didn't take her very long to get used to how things were on the Collier farm. It was a beautiful place, Thursee thought, but it did take a lot of work to keep it that way. There was much to be done and Thursee was expected to do her share, but somehow, she didn't mind it. She never really understood what the word plenty meant until she spent a few weeks with the Colliers. Whenever Thursee went out into the garden to pick something for Mrs. Collier to cook, she had trouble deciding what to bring in. It wasn't the same scramble to find something—anything—that could feed six people like it had been at home. The Collier garden was what Thursee imagined Eden to look like. In fact, once when Mrs. Collier was with her in the garden, Thursee forgot herself and in a pang of midday hunger reached down and picked a tomato off the vine, taking a bite. Mrs. Collier saw her and smiled. She didn't slap her hand or scream at her. She didn't tell her she was being selfish and how there wouldn't be enough for everyone now. She only smiled and picked one to eat as well. Thursee liked living there and the pain of her lost loved ones was slowly being replaced by her affection for the Colliers. Thursee did not allow herself to think about her family much. It was mostly at night, all alone in her room, when she missed her brothers and sisters. The Collier's gave her an easier life, but it could be lonely at times.

One day Thursee saw Mrs. Collier bringing out a bunch of glass jars in crates. She asked what they were for, and Mrs. Collier replied, "Tomorrow is syrup day!" Thursee had never heard of syrup day. As she helped wash the jars that evening, Mrs. Collier explained, "The cane is ready and we're going to make syrup out of it." When the child asked how, Mrs. Collier replied, "The men will bring the cane in on wagons, and they'll bend the cane with rods to get all of the juice out. Us women will boil that juice till it turns into syrup. Then we'll all have delicious sugary syrup to eat with our biscuits and pancakes."

"Does it make enough?" Thursee asked.

"Enough for everybody to have plenty to last till we do it again next year! But we need to sleep good tonight because it takes all day to make. There'll be a lot of people coming over. I think even your little sister may come."

Thursee was jolted back into reality, "Sertsie?"

After that, Thursee could think of nothing else. It had been months since she'd seen her baby sister. She wondered if Sertsie would remember her. The following morning the yard was filled with people and the meadow just beyond the house was covered with parked wagons and one or two motor cars.

Men began hauling sticks of cane to a worktable whereupon they proceeded to bend the cane with the metal rod. Thursee watched in fascination as this appeared to allow juice from within the cane to drip out into pales. The collective juices were then poured into a large pot hanging over a roaring fire pit. She had never seen a liquid boil so furiously. Mrs. Collier kept the pot stirred with a giant wooden spoon.

Thursee had never seen such a large spoon and Mrs. Collier was having a hard time with it. Her arms were growing tired, making her often switch which shoulder the end of the spoon rested on.

Thursee was just about to turn to go look for her sister when one of the women said to her, "You there, you're that orphan girl the Colliers took in, aren't you? Why don't you come over here and let Livia rest a spell."

Thursee didn't know who Livia was, but figured she meant Mrs. Collier. Thursee was only too happy to help and had the woman just asked her she would have obliged. She didn't have to be unkind about it. She went to the pot and reached to take the spoon away.

"It's very hot Thursee," Mrs. Collier said. "And this spoon is too heavy for you to handle. I think I'd rather do it myself. Besides, I don't want the water to pop on you."

"Oh, let her do it Livia," the mean woman said again. "What's she here for if it ain't to help you with the work 'round this place?"

Mrs. Collier smiled to Thursee, saying, "You're just a little too young for this job. If you like, you may watch me and then maybe next year you'll be big enough to help."

Thursee stood beside her watching the liquid of the cane water pop and boil. Things were floating to the surface of the water. Bits of the cane were boiling up. Mrs. Collier called them dregs, and she removed them with the spoon and tossed them to the ground. It was clear to Thursee that Mrs. Collier was getting tired. She could tell that her arms were giving out because she kept grabbing them and massaging them to get the feeling back in. Thursee wished she was big enough to help. However, there were plenty of other women there and any one of them could have taken over. Mrs. Collier just liked to do things herself.

The fire started to get smaller and Thursee asked if she should gather more wood. A woman standing near her explained that it was all right. They wanted the fire to die down some so that the thickening syrup would not scorch now that much of the water had boiled away. A few women even came over with water pails and drizzled some on the fire to lower the temperature. Finally, Mrs. Collier's arm gave completely out, stirring the viscous liquid. She handed the spoon over to another woman. Mrs. Collier took a rest under a tree with a cold damp towel to wipe her face. Thursee stuck close to her side.

"Can I get you a drink of water?" she asked Mrs. Collier.

"I'm all right, Thursee," Mrs. Collier answered. "I'm just tuckered out is all. I'm not as young as I used to be. I used to be able to do that all day. Can't now. My arm's numb and my back aches. It's no fun getting old Thursee. But it'll all be worth it when that syrup is done."

"Can we taste it to see how it's coming?"

"Oh, not for a while now." Mrs. Collier advised. "You see that syrup has to sit there and boil all day. We just don't want it boiling so hot that it burns. Later on today when most of the water's gone and the cane water has cooked into a thick syrup, we'll put the fire out and let it cool. Then we can fill cans and bottles, and everyone will have delicious syrup to take home."

"Can we have some tonight?" Thursee exclaimed.

"Of course, we can." Mrs. Collier smiled rubbing the feeling back into her arm. "Now you go have a good time with the other children."

This was her chance. Thursee could finally find her sister Sertsie. She ran off excitedly, searching the faces of every little girl she passed. Not finding Sertsie in the yard, she checked the barn. Opening the barn door, Thursee saw a bunch of children had formed a line and were taking turns climbing up on bales of stacked hay. This hay was what Mr. Collier used to spread out on the floor of the barn, so it was unlikely that he'd mind the kids doing this. It wasn't special hay.

As the children all turned to stare at Thursee, Thursee saw her! Sertsie! She was climbing up on the rail of the goat pen, trying to pet the goat. Thursee rushed to her baby sister and picked her up. Tears flowing from Thursee's eyes. She had dreamed of this moment and here she was holding Sertsie again! Her baby sister—the only family she had left in her world.

"Sertsie, Sertsie," she cried. "I have missed you so much. Have you missed me?"

"Let go of my sister!" a boy yelled from the top of the haystack. Jumping down, he sprinted over to them. "Let go of her!"

Thursee was shocked. She didn't know what was happening or what to say. "She's my sister, my baby sister Sertsie."

"Her name is Mary Beth, and she's not your sister, she's mine!" the boy said firmly.

Thursee looked down into the face of the little girl in her arms. It was Sertsie. There was no doubt about that. She knew her own sister's face. Yet, that face looking up at Thursee had a strange look of fear in her eye. Then Sertsie began to cry, reaching for her brother to protect her. Sertsie did not know Thursee any longer.

"It's all right Mary Beth," he told the little girl, "Brother's got you." Sertsie seemed to stop crying and gave the boy a smile.

"That's my sister." Thursee muttered again, not sure what to say or do. She needed this boy to understand and to believe her. Sertsie was the only thread of family she had to cling to, and he was stealing her. "Sertsie?" Thursee mumbled dumbstruck. "Sertsie, it's Thursee? Don't you remember me at all?"

Mary Beth Kearny turned her head away quickly and squeezed her brother's neck. He carried her out of the barn. Thursee stumbled out from the barn door, feeling as if her very soul was ripped away. Or maybe it had only been her past. Her past stripped away inside that barn. She said goodbye in her heart to Sertsie and Jaylee and their brothers. Her future was with the Colliers now. She stumbled back towards the house, deeply in need of one of Mrs. Collier's lovely smiles. Approaching the house, she saw everyone gathered around something. She realized the syrup must be ready! Excitedly Thursee wedged her way through the circle of men and women. As she eased forward, expecting to see jars being filled with delicious thick syrup,

Thursee's eyes caught a different sight. The men and women were not watching syrup being poured. It was Mrs. Collier everyone had surrounded. Mrs. Collier, laying on the ground, her head rested in Mr. Colliers' lap. She was dead. Thursee was truly alone now.

No one said anything for a full minute as Puddin sat beaming with pride at her captivating story. "Do you like it, Laurel? Can it go in your book? I got that syrup recipe written down at home."

Laurel didn't respond. She could only sit there. Delva was the one who spoke out first, bellowing, "Puddin Corder, that is the most depressing story I done ever heard in my 78 years on this earth! Ain't nobody wanna read that!"

Puddin looked hurt, and deeply disappointed. "Miss Laurel, you don't like it?"

Finding her words after having been emotionally rendered speechless, Laurel answered, "No, I think it's a good story. It is just so damn sad. That poor girl. Poor Thursee! And she was your mother?"

"Yes," Puddin answered. "But she grew up and got married and had children. Her life didn't stay sad."

"Still," Bootsie commented. "The poor child. Did she ever meet up with any of her family again? What about her brothers or Jaylee?"

"Well, nobody adopted Jaylee cause she was too old." Puddin informed them. "Mama said she moved to Birmingham and got work in a saloon boarding house. My Daddy always said to us, she became a prostitute. My Mama would get mad at that, but I think it was true. But no, she never saw any of them again."

Laurel shook her head, returning to her sewing. "I thought you people down here were supposed to have these down-home idyllic lives. But my God, I keep hearing the most gut-wrenching stories!"

Delva snorted into the air. "Girl, wasn't nothing down here what ya'll painted it out to be up north. You haven't seen a mess of troubles till you walked a generation or two down these bumpy, twisty dirt roads."

CHAPTER TWENTY-FOUR

A Stewless Dinner

The change in Flossie's agility and health had become noticeably improved over the months since Laurel first met her. So much so that Flossie was insistent both Laurel and Janice come over for dinner.

"It'll be an early dinner though, cause ya'll got to be gone by Wheel of Fortune," she asserted. "Or ya'll can stay and watch it with me, if you be quiet till it's over."

Laurel protested her aunt going to the trouble and work of preparing a meal for them, suggesting she pick something up from the diner. However, Flossie was not open to debate. She felt like cooking a large meal and was going to. She even called back later in the morning to say, "I done plumb forgot my manners. If you want to bring your colored boyfriend tonight too, he is more than welcome. And that boy you took in. But don't let him bring anybody, I ain't ready for that yet."

Laurel did not know what to reply. The thoughtful inclusion was sweet, although the wording of it gave her pause. However, to her surprise Linc found Flossie's invitation thoughtful, not at all offended by its phrasing.

"If your aunt has the decency to invite me to her home for dinner," Linc told Laurel over the phone. "I am not going to offend her by declining. Now if you'll let me go, I have a student in my office who doesn't seem to understand he can't listen to Spotify in class."

She could hear the smile in his voice and knew him well enough by now to know the student was not in real trouble. It would be just another of Mr. Hopkins' fatherly lectures. Before Linc hung up the phone, she shouted, "Tell Cade about tonight!"

Laurel hoped he had heard her. She would have simply texted Cade, but she had been on the receiving end of one of the principal's lectures as well recently for texting with Cade during class time. As the screen on her cell phone flashed CALL ENDED, Laurel found herself smiling at her own disappointment that Linc hadn't been able to talk very long. *Is this what attachment is?* She didn't allow her mind to entertain the thought for long. It was a little more than she was comfortable thinking about right now.

The foursome arrived at Flossie's house promptly at 4:30 and could smell the pork tenderloin wafting through the open windows from the yard. Flossie was overjoyed to be entertaining, greeting all her guests with a hug before directing them where to sit in her living room.

"Now Linc, you are a big, tall man and that couch is real low to the ground. I had my son-in-law Ernest cut the legs off so I can get up and down better." She escorted him to a taller reclining chair. "This was Norman's chair," she explained. "He had them long legs like you got."

Next, she showed Janice to a padded rocker and matching stool. "You sit here hun, cause that's where Bessie liked to be, and you are so much like her."

As for Laurel and Cade, Flossie declared, "You two can sit anywhere you like. On the couch with me, or Laurel if you wanna be close to your man, there's room on the arm of that recliner." Linc and Laurel shared a discreet wink as Laurel and Cade both sat on the couch with Flossie. "I'm tellin you," Flossie motioned to Laurel, "It ain't gone bother me none if you sit on that arm. It'll hold you. Norman used to grab me by the arm sometimes when I'd go by and pull me onto that chair with him." Suddenly she blushed, stopped herself, and quickly said, "Well, ya'll don't need to know about all that stuff."

The usual pre-dinner conversation went around the room with everyone briefly mentioning their day. Cade took a test he was nervous about until Linc relayed that his teacher reported Cade scored 85. Janice shared how it must be that time of year once again, because Puddin Corder came into the store considering new furniture.

"Is she redecorating already?" Laurel asked. "I thought all of her things were new when I came to town this summer."

"They were and still are," Janice chuckled. "Remember, she changes that room twice a year."

Laurel mused softly, mostly to herself, "Have I been here that long?"

Ignoring Laurel's murmurings, Flossie shouted out with great amusement, "Dear Lord, I hope Puddin ain't fixin' to make it plaid again! The last time I was there she had plaid stripes ever'where. I 'bout fell outta the chair just from dizziness."

Sharing a laugh with everyone, Janice confided the secret planned design, "It is God-awful, but Puddin says she wants everything done in chartreuse this time."

"I like chartreuse." Cade defended.

"Yes, but everything?" Janice gasped. "Puddin's living room is gonna look like a highlighter exploded."

Cade wondered aloud why Mrs. Corder changed everything so often. It was Flossie who answered, "Boy when you get old you'll find yourself doing a lot a things that seemed strange to you while you was young. I always reckon it's her way of passing time till she meets her maker."

Janice voiced a different opinion. "I believe she misses her husband so much that keeping the room everchanging makes it harder to notice he isn't there."

"That is sad." Laurel frowned.

Linc disagreed, "I think it is beautiful. To love someone so much it pains you to be reminded of their absence. It takes quite a love to produce such a reaction."

Flossie soon hopped up from the sofa with a spryness Janice had not witnessed her show in years. She was off to get the food on the table and quick to dismiss anyone's offer to help. Once they were all seated around the table, Flossie handed Linc the fork and knife to portion out the meat for the table. The golden-brown pork, infused with flavors or carrot, onion, and thyme awakened all the correct senses as helpings made it to each plate. Along with the pork, Flossie had a skillet of fried potatoes chopped into squares glimmering a golden brown. Cornbread, purple hull peas, and corn on the cob trimmed out the remaining room on the plates.

"Mrs. Jordon," Cade moaned. "These potatoes are out of this world! How did you make them?"

"Oh, that ain't nothing to fuss over. Instead of salt, I crush up beef bouillon cubes. Sprinkle some of that with black pepper while their frying in the oil and that's all you need."

Cade was impressed, making quick notes into his phone so he could replicate them later. The meat tasted professionally prepared. Laurel was harkened back to a few restaurants she's critiqued back in the day who could have stood to learn a lesson on tenderloin from Flossie Jordan.

"We almost had some radish stew with it tonight," Flossie revealed. "But that didn't work out too good."

Laurel was rather thankful for whatever went wrong with the radish stew because it sounded dreadful. However, politeness required her to ask about it.

Smacking on a piece of bread, Flossie pointed to a side window. "I got a garden out in the side yard. It's where I growed these peas and corn. Well, this spring we had us a mess of baby bunnies out there." Reflecting on the little bunnies caused her to giggle to herself. "Cutest blame things you ever see'd in your life. I'd just sit out there in my lawn chair under that sweetgum, and watch those critters chase around after their momma.

But then they got grown and started messin' with my garden."

Dabbing her mouth with a napkin after swallowing a bite of juicy pork, Janice remarked, "Rabbits will tear up a garden, that's for sure. Did they get many of your vegetables?"

"Hell, I don't know," Flossie answered, downing a spoonful of peas.

Her reply caused a little confusion among the others. Her previous statement about radish stew hinted that the rabbits had been the reason there wasn't any. Flossie picked up with her story without concern. "The other day I was sittin out there under that sweetgum just a'watching those little buggers jumping around in the garden. Ernest was over here fixing my washing machine, and he come outside, and I told him, 'Look there Ernest, ain't that the cutest thing? But while you're up, go get me that gun."

In one instant, all the varying levels of attention anyone was paying to her story shifted into one focus, drawing everyone back to Flossie as their minds shuddered to think why she'd asked Ernest to bring her the gun.

"Gun?" Cade repeated.

"Yeah," Flossie answered. "Norman's old pistol in the drawer over there in the China cabinet. Well, Ernest brung it out to me and I lined up my eye with the dohickey on top that shows you where to aim."

"You didn't?" Laurel stammered.

"I shot at the rascal but missed. Then Ernest tried to get him for me, but it was long took off by then."

"You were trying to shoot the bunnies!" Laurel cried out.

"Lordy girl no!" Flossie laughed. "Why'd you think that?"

"You said they were eating your radishes!"

Flossie appeared confused. "I ain't even got radishes out in that garden!"

Cade gulped, "Then why were you shooting at the rabbits?"

"I wasn't shootin' at the rabbits," Flossie declared. "I was shooting at that old rattlesnake out there raisin' his head up, about to strike at my rabbit."

With a collective sigh of relief, Laurel remarked, "You said nothing about a rattlesnake Aunt Flossie. We thought you were about to say you shot the rabbits."

"Then where did radishes come in?" Janice laughed. "At the start of your story you said we almost had radish stew."

"Naw, I said rattler stew." Suddenly Flossie let out a raucous howl. "Oh, I see now! My dentures slipped a little when I said it earlier. Guess you didn't hear me good."

Everyone exchanged puzzled glances, except for Linc, who was happily eating and undisturbed by the story. When Laurel raised a brow his way, he said, "What? I heard her say 'rattler' when she said it the first time. Sounded quite clear to me."

Flossie laughed, then spooned more meat and peas onto Linc's plate. With dinner finished, Laurel and Janice insisted they wash the dishes for Flossie in repayment of the fine meal. Flossie did not fight them on the offer, being that it was time for Wheel of Fortune. When Linc offered to assist them with the dishes, Flossie made a different proposition. "I'm real good at these puzzles, Mr. School Man," she teased. "Let's you and me make a bet. I'll bet you another home cooked meal and you bet me you can get that niece of mine to start coming to Sunday School."

"Now, Mrs. Jordan, you know as well as I do no one can make Laurel do anything."

With a coy wink, Flossie grinned, "Oh, I bet you could."

Cade offered to help in the kitchen, but Flossie declared him the judge between she and Linc and their bet. While the three of them watched Wheel of Fortune, Janice and Laurel cleaned the kitchen.

"You seem to be fitting in rather well lately," Janice observed. "Yard all tidy. Flowers planted around the house—and not just in the porch baskets. Joined a quilting bee." Janice was having fun teasing Laurel over her newfound provincial life. "Now you have a relationship with your aunt. And she really loves you, you know?"

"I know."

Janice continued her assessment of Laurel's new life. "Now Cade is living with you while he finishes school. All this, and you have a boyfriend."

"I would not go as far to say boyfriend," Laurel commented.

"Are you dating anyone else?" asked Janice.

"No."

"Is he?"

"No," Laurel blushed.

"You have a boyfriend," Janice challenged. "And your cookbook is half written from what you tell me. Have you given thought about what you'll do once it sells and is a success?"

Laurel wiped her brow with the soapy back of her hand. Janice took the dishtowel and wiped the suds away while Laurel struggled to come up with an answer. "You are stretching the possibilities a bit to describe the cookbook as a potential hit. I do not even know if a pub house will want it. It's just something to occupy myself with while I am staring at this fork in the road."

Janice took the plate Laurel finished washing, giving it a rinse under the tap before drying it and putting it in the cabinet. "You know Laurel, there is a funny thing about forks in the road. Everyone always assumes we are supposed to choose a path."

"Isn't that the point?" Laurel asked, handing Janice the last freshly washed plate, then started on the utensils. "You come to the fork in the road, and you either go one way or the other."

Laurel wasn't paying attention to what she'd been washing under the sudsy water until she lifted it out to hand to Janice. Holding the large chrome serving fork out before them, Janice grinned. "You know Laurel, most people do go one way or the other. But sometimes, for some people, they find what they're looking for along the way. They don't even need to choose a new path. For those people...the journey ends with the fork."

Flossie's Recipe...known in real life as...

FANCY PORK

(Need 2 days)

Ingredients

Dutch oven pot
Loin of pork
¾ cup kosher salt
¼ cup sugar
2 tbsp vegetable oil

1 quart no sodium chicken broth
4 sprigs of thyme
1 chopped yellow onion
1 chopped carrot

DAY ONE
1. Mix salt and sugar, then rub all over pork loin
2. Refrigerate over night

DAY TWO
3. Preheat oven to 300°
4. In Dutch oven, heat oil on medium high
5. Slice loin and belly into squares
6. Brown pork squares on all sides (you aren't cooking it yet, just sealing in the juices)
7. Once all pieces are seared, remove to a plate for a minute while you glaze the carrot and onion in the pot
8. Once they are a little brown, golden but not brown, add thyme and broth
9. Put the pork back in and cover
10. Place in the oven for 2 hours
11. After pork is cooked, you can reduce the remaining broth by boiling it on the stove for 10 minutes

12. Pour over the pork and serve

    NOTE: If you can find an unsliced side of bacon, you can cut it up in squares like pork and cook with the loin and it is even more delicious. Not healthy, but SO GOOD!

CHAPTER TWENTY-FIVE

Pound Cake and Shattered Pride

Miss Ellie Dorran was not a name Laurel had heard until recently, when the name came up at the quilting bee. The Dorran's, Laurel was told by Delva, were Presbyterians. This was Delva's shorthand for there being no reason Laurel would have crossed their path. She hadn't realized until Delva's remark, that the only people Laurel had associated with in Scroggins were Baptists. *Well, the Daniels sisters are Methodist,* she thought to herself as she drove to the Dorran home. *But their father's family founded the Christ's Love Baptist Church, so technically, they count. Besides, Methodists just Baptists that drinks wine.* Hearing her own words echo in her head, Laurel couldn't believe these thoughts were running through her brain. As she shut off the car in front of the Dorran house, she thought, *Oh shit! I am becoming one of them. I am even beginning to think like they do.*

Ellie Dorran, or more properly, Miss Ellie, as she had been called all her life, had a private nurse attending to her needs during the day. The nurse introduced herself as Maggie while showing Laurel into the formal living room. The room was decorated with enough antique copies of furniture to film a period drama, although the 1960's walnut veneer paneling on the wall ruined the effect. Miss Ellie was waiting for Laurel on the pale blue faux satin couch. The frame of the couch was of dark wood dented around the legs from years of vacuuming. The couch's high back was also framed in wood with two round fabric sections flanking a higher oval center. The carpet nearly matched the furniture fabric, and Laurel noticed the linear shade changes in the grain revealing it had been freshly vacuumed before her arrival.

Miss Ellie herself was a woman of 92 but one would not know it by her personality. Graceful, charming, and fully coherent in every way, Laurel was impressed by the lady upon first sight. Her hair was silky white and chin length. Her stylish crème dress, no doubt, came from the more elegant rack of a higher-end chain store. She was quite different from most of the other women she'd met in Scroggins.

"I understand you have a recipe you would like to share with me, Mrs. Dorran."

"Call me Miss Ellie, sugar. Everyone always has."

Maggie, as if on cue, brought over a well written recipe, on scented paper no less. Laurel looked it over, finding it to be for a pound cake with something described as Praline drizzle. The ingredients were many, making it greatly differ from the pound cake recipe Laurel knew from her grandmother's files. This one required more eggs than she would have expected, not that Laurel was in any way a cake baking expert, but she had seen enough over these last months to know a little about the subject.

"It is my sincere hope you might consider me for this book." Miss Ellie started with a gentle hint of guile in her eyes. Laurel asked if she had more recipes for consideration other than the Pound Cake, to which Miss Ellie dismissively answered, "Oh you will not think it so simple once you taste it."

Maggie was like a shadow popping up when least expected. Surprising Laurel from the right, she stood holding a covered plate, revealing a slice of the dessert in question. The glimmering brown drizzle twinkled under the overhead light. Before Laurel could even ask, Maggie withdrew a fork from her apron pocket, handing it to the writer.

For a moment it all seemed like something from a film noir with Laurel as the intended victim of whatever poison the cake was laced with. She sat down on a settee near Miss Ellie and slid the fork through the cake with the ease of softened butter. "Here goes," Laurel said whimsically as she pushed the forkful of yellowish tan cake into her mouth.

If ecstasy was a food, it would have been this cake. Laurel's eyes closed with delight, imbuing only her sense of taste the full enjoyment. She did not remember even needing to chew. The moist bite practically dissolved on her tongue, melting its creamy buttery goodness down the back of her throat like a butter rum shot at Christmas.

"Okay," Laurel mumbled, shoving another, larger bite into her mouth. "I hope you have a good story with this cake, or I may be forced to shed my writing integrity and make one up to make this recipe qualify. This is phenomenal, Miss Ellie."

Pleased by the writer's reaction, although not in any way surprised by it, the genteel old woman boasted a devious smile and made a confession. "I was certain you'd want to include it and frankly it is the only recipe I care to contribute because it is *the story* which holds the most importance to me."

"I am all ears," Laurel replied, adding, "Do you mind if I finish this piece of cake while you tell it to me?"

Delighted by the question, Miss Ellie laughed, "Not at all. Would you like a glass of milk or tea or coffee to wash it down?"

Beaming with continued pleasure, Laurel cried, "It doesn't need anything to wash it down. I have no idea how a cake can be this smooth."

Laurel's hostess asked if she wanted a moment to switch on a recorder or perhaps to finish the cake so her hands would be free to jot down notes. Laurel assured her it would not be necessary. "I have a great memory. Besides, it is a loosely fictional book. I will make a few enhancements here and there to punch the stories up enough to hold readers attention."

Miss Ellie seemed slightly disappointed to hear this, but let it slide, saying "As long as the prime points of the story remain unchanged. That will be important to me."

Ellie Dorran began her story by noting she was a great beauty in her younger days, a self-imposed compliment which Laurel did not doubt for a minute. Even now at 92, she was slender, poised, impeccable—if not slightly wrinkled—complexion. Her eyes still sparkled with the crystal blue of youth and her hair, though white, was lustrous. She was a beautiful woman even now, so Laurel could only imagine what she must have looked like back then.

As Miss Ellie continued reflecting on her past, she confided how she had come from modest means. Although she never lacked for male suitors when young, at the age of 18 she began devoting most of her free time to the company of Harland Winfield. "Harland had a fine job at the textile factory in Clanton, Alabama. He was a supervisor of sorts, if I remember correctly. Considered quite a catch," she bragged.

Ellie and Harland went out quite often, venturing away from Scroggins for more bustling areas such as Tuscaloosa or Birmingham. "We liked to go where streets were paved and sidewalks had streetlamps. Harland took me to restaurants, movie shows, and even once to a play at the Alabama Theater." Pausing a moment to think back, she continued. "I believe the play was *Grand Hotel*. I found a movie version once on television."

"Did you date very long?" Laurel asked gently. Laurel's time in Scroggins had taught her not only about cooking, but about storytelling. Through her many interviews so far, she was learning to recognize a tragedy before it revealed itself as one. Miss Ellie's married name was Dorrans. Harland's name was Winfield. Laurel already understood things were not going to bode well for poor Harland in this story.

Answering Laurel's question, Miss Ellie answered, "We did not date long by today's standard, a few months." Miss Ellie continued, "One night we were on our way out of town to meet Harland's friends in Bessemer at the Bright Star restaurant. Do you know the place, dear?"

"I do not," Laurel admitted.

"You must go sometime. It isn't very far from here and open to this day. Have the Greek steak, it is wonderful." Laurel nodded at the suggestion and Miss Ellie returned to her memories. "We were driving somewhere along Highway 59 when Harland began telling me about the many pieces of furniture he had been buying and storing in one of the mill's storage facilities. I asked him why in the world he was buying so much furniture, and he said to me 'so we have everything we need to set up housekeeping after we are married." On the verge of commenting on how beautifully sweet that was, Laurel stopped herself after she noticed a look of repulsion on Miss Ellie's face. "Can you believe his nerve?" she asked Laurel, who could only stare blankly back. "I immediately corrected Harland, telling him I had no intentions of marrying him!"

Well, that was not at all where I thought this story was going! Laurel strained to keep her confusion concealed. Mustering her best, reporter-mode dispassion, she asked, "How did Harland take the rejection?"

"He slammed the breaks down and we skidded across the road. We barely stopped before hitting the trees. He turned to me with his hands pressing the steering wheel so hard I thought it might bend. 'What do mean you are not going to marry me, Ellie?"

Placing her delicate white hand to her chest as if she had been the affronted party, Miss Ellie explained, "I told him, I did not feel that way about him. He asked me if that was true, why did I keep going out with him then." Then, with not a hint of remorse in her crystal eyes, the elderly woman said, "I told him, 'Because you have a car.'"

Laurel choked on her own held breath, coughing into her hand,

"What?"

As if she were absolving any stain of heartlessness with her explanation, the woman replied, "No man had a car around here, you see. Costed too much. Besides, most of the roads were nothing but ruts in the dried mud made from years of wagons. Why, even Harland's car got caught in those ruts sometimes and we'd have to ride it out until the ground evened enough to pull loose."

"So, you only dated him because he had a car?" Laurel repeated, having to remind herself this was a very old woman. Even though cars were not a new invention when Miss Ellie was of dating age, they probably were rare around Scroggins back then. Still, the audaciousness of it had Laurel floored.

Unabashed by her youthful behavior, Miss Ellie reiterated, "How else was I going to be able to see the inside of a real restaurant or a genuine theater? He asked me out, and I said yes. If he implied a lifelong commitment from that, it was no fault of mine."

Hating to see the logic in this, Laurel had to concede the woman wasn't wrong. Thoughtless, apathetic maybe, but not exactly wrong. If anything, Laurel had to admit to herself she would have reacted the same today, so maybe Miss Ellie was a woman before her time.

"What did Harland say?"

"He pulled a diamond ring out of his pocket!" Miss Ellie exclaimed. "Said he had just finished paying it off and how he already told his mother, as well as his friends and coworkers at the mill, that we were to be married."

"Wow," Laurel gulped. "What happened next?"

"I told him that was a foolish thing to assume without asking me about it first." Miss Ellie then lowered her voice somewhat before adding the one hint of regret she had, "Then I said something I probably shouldn't. I told him I wasn't interested in him at all. Never had been. If anything, I liked his better-looking cousin."

Laurel's eyes bulged at the admission.

"Well, you can imagine how that wounded his ego," the old lady sighed. "He threw that diamond ring all the way into the woods and took off like a mad man down the road, with me scared to death beside him. I yelled for him to stop, and he finally did. I suppose he hoped I had rethought my answer, because he looked rather hopeful when he brought the car to a halt. But I just wished him well and got out. I said, I would find my own way back home."

"He left you there on the side of a road?"

"Yes, he did, Miss Ellie replied. "Can't say that I blame him much. I have always wondered if he went back to search for the ring. As for me, I began walking. Eventually I came to a house with the lights on. I knocked and explained to the family what happened to me."

Oh, here it is, Laurel thought to herself again. *It was the home of the Dorrans. This is the story of how she met her husband.*

"I hadn't had anything to eat," Miss Ellie said wrapping up. "They'd finished their supper but had some pound cake left. The wife fed it to me before her husband and she drove me back to Scroggins. Best cake I ever ate. She gave me the recipe."

At a loss for words as to what to say, and completely lost in the meaning of the story, Laurel stared at Miss Ellie, who only stared innocently back. She reached over to where Laurel had unknowingly dropped the recipe onto the settee beside her. The elderly lady placed it back into Laurel's open hand, jarring her into a response. "Well...this is quite a departure from the other stories I have collected. But it is reasonably funny, and the cake is much too good to omit. But may I ask you, Miss Ellie just why you want this particular life event depicted with your name and recipe?"

Smiling proudly, the old woman revealed, "My sister Ulma was always so full of herself because she thought she was better than the rest of us simply because she had a larger house and expensive things. She's still alive now. And before I leave this world, I just think it would be nice for her to find out, and see it printed for the world to see, that her husband and her beautiful house full of furniture, were originally mine and I turned them down."

Aghast at the vindictiveness, while highly impressed with the level of retribution, Laurel asked her final question. "What if she never reads the book?"

"Oh, I'll be sending her a copy of the book. Don't you worry about that."

Miss Ellie's Recipe...known in real life as...

MISS NORMA'S POUND CAKE

Created and given to me by a wonderful lady I used to know named
Norma Harmon

Ingredients

½ L.B. softened butter
3 cups sugar
6 eggs at room temperature (No lie! Don't use cold eggs!)
½ pint whipping cream
3 cups sifted flour (Sifted!!!)
1 ½ tsp vanilla extract

1. In mixer, cream the butter and sugar together for 1 minute
2. Add eggs one at a time and beat well after each
3. Add flour and cream alternately, beginning and ending with flour
4. Pour batter in lightly greased and floured bundt pan
5. Place pan in a COLD oven and cook for 1 hour at 325° (it is gonna take longer, but keep checking it after the first hour because it doesn't take too long after)
6. Let cool a few minutes, but only a few otherwise it will not loosen from pan when you flip it over onto cake plate.

It does not need any icing drizzle (BUT Pound Cake isn't Pound Cake without one, so here is a drizzle recipe...)

PRALINE DRIZZLE

Recipe given to me by my mother, Barbara Walker

Ingredients

½ cup sugar
1/3 cup packed brown sugar (light or dark, I prefer light)
2 tbsp dark corn syrup
½ cup whipping cream

1. In saucepan combine sugar, brown sugar, and corn syrup
2. Stir in whipping cream as you cook over medium heat
3. Once sauce starts boiling, stir constantly till sugar dissolves
4. Reduce heat uncovered for 10 minutes or till thick
5. Makes about 1 cup drizzle sauce

CHAPTER TWENTY-SIX

Town Scandal

Laurel wasn't completely sure what the urgency was for her in coming directly to Puddin Corder's house. She had been consumed with the Muse, writing in touching detail the story of Brenda Rawling's grandson being born and the stray cat who (with some artistic license) orchestrated it. *How do these people expect me to write their stories if they keep interrupting me every other day?*

Pulling into Puddin's driveway, she was met immediately by Puddin where she ushered Laurel inside almost as if paparazzi might be hiding in the bushes. Seated in the half-painted disarray that was once Puddin's living room, Laurel saw Prue Daniels waiting on the newly delivered, still sheathed in plastic wrap, chartreuse sofa.

"Miss Laurel," Puddin said with an excited pace in her tone. "Prue and I are good friends, and she knows you and I are good friends—"

We are? Laurel thought to herself, smiling a hello to Prue. *I suppose we are.*

"Puddin, allow me to tell it," Prue requested of her friend, before averting her face to Laurel with the eye roll she didn't want Puddin to observe. "It will go quicker if I tell it."

"Tell me what?" Laurel asked, sitting beside Prue, and nearly sliding off the slick plastic.

"Sorry about that," Puddin blushed after Laurel's descent off the cushion. "They delivered it today. I want to keep the plastic on until the painters finish."

Prue took control of the conversation, facing Laurel directly with distress in her eyes. "We do not know one another well, Laurel," she began. "But when I met you at the Church Supper I felt as if we were likeminded in many ways. I felt compelled to warn you preemptively about something."

"You have my full attention."

"I keep myself busy with a few clubs and charities, mostly in Tuscaloosa. This keeps me away from home a lot of days. My sisters and I have never had a need to work because we inherited our father's sawmill money. I do what I can to stay busy to keep from being driven crazy by Obedience's oppressive personality and Patience's prattling on about absolutely everything of unimportance..."

At this point, Laurel was thinking to herself, *is it faster with you telling it, Prue? Even Puddin doesn't give this much lead in to gossip.*

"I was at a planning session regarding an event hosted by the Teacher's Credit Union for this coming Christmas," Prue continued, hopefully drawing nearer to the point of Laurel's summons there. "After the meeting, a friend of mine who serves on the committee with me asked about the controversy happening here in Scroggins involving the high school principal."

Laurel's heart began beating at three times the normal rate. Her natural inclination to let her thoughts run to the worst of possibilities seized her mind. *Shit, he's married. He got arrested for drugs. He solicited a minor. He used to be a woman.* "What has Linc been accused of doing?"

"Truthfully, nothing," Prue admitted. "Except being romantically entangled with a woman who is housing a runaway."

"What?" Laurel shouted. "You must be joking!"

"I wish I were," Prue sighed. "The way the Petersons are telling this is that you have corrupted their son, convinced him he is gay, and urged him to flee his home to move in with you. And Linc, being the boy's principal, is implicated by association. Not to mention he is frequently seen at your house."

Laurel's mind was blown by the accusations. "The Petersons are ridiculous, Prue! Nothing even close to what they are claiming has happened."

Prue assured her she knew this already. "I do not believe any of the exaggerated claims Cade's parents are screaming. However, they have now caught the attention of the County Board of Education.

My sister Obedience sits on the Scroggins school board, but she has not breathed a word to me about this, and wouldn't even if I asked her. She takes her responsibilities seriously. But even her influence is minimal. She is on the Scroggins High School board, not the County Board of Education."

"Could Linc lose his job over this?"

"I think he could. You need to prepare him. I don't think he knows yet."

* * *

Linc arrived at the house directly following work on Laurel's request. However, it was plainly evident he had already heard about the trouble during the interim. Thankfully, to give them time alone, Janice invited Cade to dinner at her house. The last thing Laurel wanted was for Cade to feel responsible for Linc's trouble. Linc was livid over the situation facing him, voicing sincere fear he might lose everything he had worked for over the scandal.

"I do not see what the big deal is here, Linc!" Laurel asserted. "These people are making something out of nothing and adding lies on top of it. Surely that can be explained to the Board. Besides, it has nothing to do with you."

"Regardless, it has blown up all over me!" Linc exclaimed. "That boy's parents are whipping the whole community into a frenzy."

He began walking back and forth through Laurel's kitchen into the den, then back. His quick, even steps shook the floor beneath his feet. Made only of boards, joists, and linoleum, there wasn't much impact it could sustain without feeling like an earthquake. The drinking glasses in the kitchen cabinets rattled together as he paced like a caged animal looking for an escape.

"Do you blame me for this?" she asked, expecting an immediate 'No' to follow. Linc's lack of response triggered her into frustration. "You do, don't you?"

His normally composed behavior, now replaced with intensifying anxiety, did not leave Linc much room for measured, careful responses. "I don't blame you necessarily, Laurel. I just do not know why this all fell at my feet."

He could tell from her intensifying eyes and reddening cheeks she was about to take the defensive route. A more experienced girlfriend might have stood a better chance at recognizing this was a time for rallying around her man and showing him he was not alone in his trouble. Unfortunately, Linc knew Laurel was not an experienced anything when it came to relationships.

"What was I supposed to do, Linc?" she howled. "Leave that boy in the woods living in a tent?"

"I don't know, Laurel!" Linc fired back. "He may have gone back home after a few days in the woods. We will never know now."

"To go home to more shame and ridicule? Not to mention the beatings!" she screamed. "To live with parents who despise him. Cade would become another street kid roaming city after city, selling drugs, or stealing—or worse, selling himself to survive!"

Laurel could feel herself slipping into a tunnel vision of what horrors await a homeless teen Cade's age. Having lived a few of them herself, she could not change course in her mind to consider anything else. This newfound maternal streak within her was woefully unfamiliar, but its power kept her from noticing it was Linc who needed her support now. She was unable to see that as strong of a man as Linc may be, this was when he required her ferocity in his corner, not someone else's. As for Linc, he was equally distracted by his own desperation amid the looming threat of losing everything he had worked for. It made it impossible for him to recognize that Laurel's tirade over Cade was only a masquerade to conceal her fear that Linc held her responsible.

"I have lived in cities plagued with homeless, Linc." Laurel was doubling down now on making this issue about Cade's well-being, rather than Linc's predicament. "Those people started out like Cade. They once had families. Places to live, before something put them there. It doesn't take long before any hope of redeeming their lives is gone."

"I don't need some moral lesson on the genesis of a fallen life right now, Laurel! I am fighting for my own." Linc's scalding reply took her by surprise.

"So, I am supposed to toss a helpless kid out on the street to make these uneducated morons feel better! They have no idea what they are even talking about!"

"Oh, I'm sorry," he bit back sarcastically. "*Big City Laurel* knows everything we dumbass hicks wouldn't understand."

Her hands pulled at her hair. She did not know how to release the aggression pounding throughout her entire body. She grabbed the tea pitcher sitting on the table and smashed it into the sink. It didn't make her feel better. She counted to five, releasing a deep breath after, then said more calmly, "That's not what I mean. But yes, Linc, I do know things you don't. I have seen people forced onto the street, believing it temporary until they can find shelter, then a job. But Linc, that almost never happens. Weeks of rain, wind, ice, heat, sweat—their clothes smelly, their bodies filthy. Some get sick. Some dull the humiliation with drugs. In two years' time even the brightest and most ambitious man goes to ruin. I am not going to let someone as remarkable as Cade Peterson fall into that hell."

Scoffing at her dramatic example, Linc said, "His parents would not let that happen to him."

"They threw him to the street because he wouldn't lie about who he is inside, just so they won't feel embarrassed. REAL parents love their children the way they are. Parents who try to change their kid only love themselves."

Looking her in the eye, Linc replied, "You aren't this boy's mother."

"I know," Laurel said boldly. "I am better than she is."

Linc took a moment to dial down his fury by taking a seat on the couch, his hands folded together between his knees. He felt defeated, and he needed her to comprehend why. "Laurel. I am a black man in a town with a low black population. I have worked my ass off to prove I am dedicated to this place and its children. Do you know how hard it is for a black man to become principal of a predominantly white school? Because *I do*. I am in the 1 percentile of black male educators in this country. And they made me principal! I only got the job because I am doubly educated in comparison to my white counterparts, and I still just barely got the job."

Laurel Holden, caught in her ideals, could not see the relevance in Linc's situation when compared to Cade's overall survival. "Your job is not in jeopardy," she told him. "Once the Board of Education is given the full picture..."

"It won't alter a thing," Linc interjected. "You just don't understand Laurel. And you can't! There is no way someone such as yourself can possibly fathom how fragile my standing in the community can be." He snapped his fingers sharply towards her face. "And just like that! All the trust, all the respect, all the surface level camaraderie these people show me can disappear."

Refusing to see his point, believing it to be based in hysteria, Laurel assured Linc, "You are inflating your fears. People know you and like you. No one is going to listen to Cade's stupid, racist, homophobic, uneducated parents."

Linc's temper began swelling again, astounded by her inability to see things as they really are. She was dug in, leaving him feeling unseen and unheard. "This is Alabama, Laurel!" he shouted. "Book bans. Abortion bans. Anti-LGBTQ+ laws! What does an uppity northern white woman know about what life in the south is like for a black man living in a community centuries-bred to hold him down as unequal? Do not tell me my concern for my future is ridiculous." Pulse racing and heart pumping, Lincoln Hopkins had even more to unload upon her, "And just because you believe the Petersons are neanderthals does not mean their beliefs are not as deep or as real to them as yours are to you. You are not in Oz, Dorothy. You are smack dab in the middle of black and white Alabama and things aren't as pretty as you'd like to believe."

Unable to control his composure any longer, and fearing he might say something to cross the line of what could be forgiven—if he hadn't already—Linc went out the door. She did not go after him. She remained arms folded, defiantly in place. *I do not chase after people.*

* * *

Though Linc had been gone twenty minutes or more, Janice still made exaggerated sounds coming into the house, warning Laurel of her return with Cade. "How was dinner?" Laurel exclaimed with a cheeriness she did not feel. Not waiting for the answer, she informed them, "I am sorry I couldn't join you, but I had to finish up a few chapters. Transitioning these stories from their voices to my voice as a writer, is more difficult than I thought it would be."

Moving to the fridge to grab a can of Coca-Cola, Cade said, "Dinner was great. I had no idea people knew how to make their own homemade pizza! Janice should put that in the book."

Janice offered a thankful smile as her eyes inspected Laurel for emotional damage. Cade, oblivious to everything, thanked Janice again, said goodnight to Laurel, and went to his room at the front of the house, out of ear shot.

"You okay?"

"No." Laurel said. "I am the furthest from okay."

Janice lovingly pushed her friend towards the den couch and sat by her, placing a supportive arm around her shoulders. "Do you wanna have a good cry?"

A cynical laugh escaped Laurel's throat, "I do not cry. If I've ever cried it would be classified information." She laid her head onto Janice's shoulder, "Linc is wrong, Janice. You agree with me, right?"

Tucking Laurel's rogue tuft of hair behind the ear, Janice offered an almost motherly caress with her knuckles to Laurel's cheek. "Nothing is that simple. Our beliefs are ours. Just because we believe something doesn't make it correct, and it doesn't mean it's wrong. Just ours."

"He blames me. He thinks he may lose his job."

"He could," confirmed Janice. "And that started by you supporting Cade, but it doesn't mean you shouldn't have done it. And Linc's issue isn't just Cade. Lots of things caused this. If Cade had different kinds of parents. If Linc had chosen a more diverse town for his career. If the two of you never started a relationship. And that ugly little word called *racism*...its imbedded in all of us one way or another—black and white alike—try as we might to get rid of it."

"Are you saying Linc shouldn't have tried to be a success in his own town or date a white woman?"

"I'm not saying anything like that. All I'm saying is our choices come with benefits and consequences. Someone like Linc must balance his choices way more carefully than you or I have to. His set of struggles are something we can't understand, even if we think we do. Even Cade's chance of building a future for himself is more in reach than it was for Linc, especially here. So instead of being angry at him, maybe understand that man is scared. He has achieved a level of respect and authority none of his ancestors had. That's quite a burden to carry without fear of losing it. Cade only has a few years of oppression to face. Linc will never be free from his."

Defeated and bereft of responses, Laurel knew Janice was right. Everyone's life is full of complex and delicate situations, constrained by some part of society, and subject to drastic change without notice. Her own life was a perfect example. She just wished things in this simple community were less complicated. But humans are the same everywhere, and so are their struggles. Depressed inside her revelations, Laurel said the first thing that came to mind.

"Cade is my cousin."

"Well, that is new," Janice replied.

Laurel sat upright pressing her hands to her head, "I promised to not tell that."

"I didn't hear anything," Janice smiled.

"Cade doesn't know. His parents don't know. I just found out myself."

"Did you know before you took him in?" Janice asked.

"No," Laurel answered. "I only found out two days ago."

Laurel felt herself being pulled again into Janice's arms, only this time it was a full and deeply felt embrace. Laurel felt such comfort from it. It was an unfamiliar sensation, but somehow, she felt better.

"What was that for?" she asked.

"That, my friend," Janice smiled. "Is for being the kind and compassionate soul you are. You did not get that from your father or your mother. You, my girl, earned and worked for it yourself."

CHAPTER TWENTY-SEVEN

A Dose of Reality

In her own intuitive way, Delva Hopkins knew how to stick her fingers into other people's messes and without their knowing, clean it up for them. With all the back and forth in town about the Peterson boy living at Laurel's, as well as the potentially disastrous blowback it might have on her grandson's career, Delva moved her little chess piece across the board understanding what subsequent moves would follow from it. With the holidays approaching, The Bake Shop would need extra help. She hired Cade Peterson after school and weekends to assist with the baking and general store upkeep. This provided several advantages. It gave the boy an opportunity to earn some money. It allowed reliable hours of privacy at home for Laurel to reach out to Linc, or vice versa. Above all, it would allow Scroggins' customers a chance to meet, speak with, and shed their fear of, the gay Peterson boy.

Wiser than some gave her credit for, Delva understood the best way to overcome prejudice is proximity. Fear, hate, and condescension are so much harder to maintain once you get to know the person you harbor it for. Delva and her family were proof of this. Had her mother not been the paid caregiver of that old white Baptist woman decades ago, Christ's Love Baptist Church members wouldn't be associating with the likes of Delva Hopkins. But Delva grew up in that church, sitting beside her mama and her mama's employer. Once that white woman died, Delva and her mother were already excepted by and imbedded into these white people's church. Now, no one thought a thing about Delva, her children, her grandchildren, or anyone else of color taking a seat in the pews. Proximity ends prejudice.

Knowing how his grandmother's mind operated, Linc quickly figured out Delva's scheme, recognizing her hiring Cade was primarily done for his benefit. He could not let her gesture go without at least trying to test the theory. On the next Saturday afternoon, after not hearing from Laurel all week, Linc showed up at her door when he knew Cade was at work.

His unexpected visit threw Laurel off guard the moment she went to the door. The sight of Linc through the door window immediately brought her anxiety and animosity to a rise. A rise which would quickly spiral. She was not a woman who enjoyed ambushes, nor did she like being presented with a heavy conversation before she had prepared for it. Understanding her mind more than she allowed herself to believe anyone could, Linc did not enter the house to challenge. Instead, he only asked if she would sit with him for a chat.

Laurel led him to the couch where they sat together, but with a wide gap between them. His eyes were intense, but not threateningly so, as he folded his hands together across his knees and asked, "Laurel, what led you to choose the career you chose?"

It was an odd and random question, especially considering the root of their spat had nothing whatsoever to do with her career path. Defensively, she replied, "What do you mean?"

"What spurred you to become a travel and food writer?"

He observed her tense reaction. Linc knew that his simple question would not only bewilder her, but push her defenses up. Although she couldn't yet decipher how he was going to do it, Laurel knew he was about to backdoor her into a trap. Holding her cool as best she could, she shrugged. "I don't know. Why do most people end up doing what they do?"

"I knew I wanted to teach," he answered. "I always knew. And if ever it were possible, I wanted to one day become a school principal."

She seemed surprised by such a mundane ambition. "Why? Why would that be your dream when other boys want to be doctors, or firemen, or football stars."

Linc smirked. "Most young black men fantasize about sports fame as their way out of the background and into the spotlight. But I wasn't one of them. That's the first thing people down here think when they hear about a black man reaching success. 'He went pro and got a lucrative contract." Linc rubbed the back of his neck as he leaned back into the vinyl couch cushion. It made a cheap, crinkly sound against his back. "Basketball, football, baseball," he continued. "If a black man achieves wealth, it's because he's an athlete or a rapper. That's the assumption. But I wanted to be someone who shaped minds. I wanted to show other kids like me that their brain is their way out. Being a teacher didn't pay well. Neither does being a principal. But I believed I could make a difference."

"Have you?" she asked, realizing the way she said it sounded more critical than she intended.

"I think so," Linc smiled. "Kids who come from nothing, white and black, but especially black, see me encouraging them, guiding them, and sometimes helping them correct a bad path they are choosing. In rural places, you either stay as simple as your parents were, usually falling into drugs or alcohol to numb your lost dreams. Or you raise yourself up to a place where you feel you have achieved something those who came before you didn't. It doesn't have to be big, just better than you were."

Laurel nodded in understanding. "I think I have done that with my life. I've traveled to places I'd never have gone. Met people from all walks of life along the way. I believe my experiences enlightened, and possibly encouraged, other people who read about them."

Satisfied with her answer, and knowing it was the truth, she waited for his validation. But the glance he gave her did not feel especially validating. "Forgive my interpretation, Laurel, but that was a trite and wholly unconvincing answer. I don't believe you."

"You believe I am lying to you about my job?"

"No," Linc frowned. "You are lying to yourself. You gave me a flat, insincere reason for the path you chose. It sounds quite noble, but of course, we both know it isn't."

Laurel was astounded by his inference, and by his judgmental tone. Her fists clinched at her sides. With irritation in her tone, she reiterated what she said before but with a touch more introspection, to give it the appearance of sincerity. "Maybe I chose my path because I spent my life dreaming of other places...any places...other than where I was."

Her admission awakened a vulnerability in her eyes, one Linc had not yet seen. The brief show of it caused her to squeeze her fists harder. Had Bessie's couch not been made of such cheap faux vinyl, her knuckles pressing into the seat cushion probably wouldn't have made any noise. But this couch did and she noticed him looking down at her hands.

"Okay," she admitted. "Maybe I wanted to see anything other than the same four walls I spent my entire childhood behind. Alone most of the time. There is nothing wrong with that."

"Nothing at all." Linc agreed, lifting her nearest hand to place in his own. Gently he loosened her fingers until they relaxed into his palm. "Tell me more," he asked.

Laurel emitted a sarcastic laugh, "And honestly, I liked other people cooking for me. Dining in all those restaurants, on the magazine's expense account, felt great. The way hotel staff, or restaurant management treated me...as if I were someone. Someone they had to impress. I enjoyed it."

"You felt special."

"Yes," Laurel said. "Certainly more important than my mother ever made me feel. You had your mother and Delva. Hell, Delva still makes your plate for you! I had to fill my own plate, but there was rarely any food in the apartment to put on it."

"That must have been really hard." Linc whispered, stroking her fingers as the blood rushed back into her hands. "Did you have friends who ever let you stay at their homes or join their family for meals?"

Laurel's icy face stared forward at the opposite wall, unwilling to let him see her eyes. "I did not have friends." Then with an almost a triumphant raise of the head, added, "I had nothing in common with other children. They walked around so naive, so carefree. Not one of them knew what really existed out there."

"But you did."

She turned her frozen glare towards him this time. "Yes. I did. And I am stronger for it."

"And now?" Linc asked. "As an adult in her 30s, how many friends are in your life?"

Once again, his random questions didn't seem to hold a point, and it was grating on her. With sarcasm, Laurel answered, "Friends I have now? You! I assume. Your grandmother. Janice—"

"Not in Scroggins, Laurel," he challenged. "Before you came here. Name me three close friends you have."

"Daniel Threston," she answered proudly. "He is a restaurateur in Boston..."

"Besides someone you met over work and have a slight acquaintanceship with. Name *a friend*."

Growing restless with whatever angle he was working towards and becoming angrier by the minute from his air of superiority, she shrieked, "What are you getting at Linc! Why are you attacking me?"

Linc didn't bite the bait. Retaining his collected demeanor, which was seriously pissing her off, he asked, "How is asking simple questions that most anyone could easily answer, be attacking you?" Then he asked it again. "Do you have one single friend in your life who has always known you?"

An unexpected fury rose inside her, magnified by long-locked away emotions he'd managed to dredge up. She was not about to let this backwoods school monitor interrogate her any longer. "Who the hell do you think you are to make assumptions about me? You barely even know me at all!"

Linc faced her now, meeting her rage with reason. "Does anyone?"

Red-faced and panting with adrenaline, Laurel felt the familiar panic come over her. She'd always avoided conflict, when possible, but when met with it her only two responses were fight or flight. She wanted to fight, wanted to lash back with something good to pick apart his character. But she had nothing in her arsenal. *I don't know him that well.* And she didn't. It takes real intimate engagement and genuine vulnerability to connect enough with someone else to know how to truly, and deeply, hurt them with your words. Laurel never allowed herself to reach that level with anyone. To become that close with another implied a mutual reliance on each other. A *'you hold my baggage, and I'll hold yours'* kind of relationship. But Laurel was never interested in hearing about other men's baggage and she wasn't about to let them peek inside her own.

"Does anyone know you, Laurel?" he asked again.

Suddenly his words rang true—and she didn't like it. Linc had proven he could dish it out the judgement, but could he take it in return? She wanted to see. She wanted to bash in his self-worth and see how he enjoyed it! But it's hard to throw stones when your hands are tied, and Linc had tied hers with the truth about herself.

With *fight* unattainable, she chose the other option, *flight.* "I think it is time you left, Lincoln." Her voice was cold, her glare devoid of any feeling. This is not the way I expected this relationship to go."

Unshaken by her dismissal, Linc asked, "Can it be a relationship when one party hides behind walls?" He gripped her hands, forcing her to look into his interrogating eyes. "How are those walls serving you, Laurel?"

"Get out!" she demanded, jerking her hands from him. "This is over. And I'll have you know I have led a fantastic life! I have traveled the world. I have met interesting people. Considering how my life began, I think it turned out magnificently. Yeah, maybe I don't have family the way you do. Maybe I didn't make friends with every single person I ever met! But my choices served me well. They kept me safe."

Shaking his head as he rose to leave, he had one final thought to impart. "Not safe, Laurel. Your choices have kept you stuck. You were unconscious until you came here. Maybe that's why your career fell apart. Maybe God had to jolt you out of your coma to get you here, so you might find out who you are."

Laurel released a loud, angry laugh. "I seriously doubt your magic fairy in the sky killed off the magazine industry just so I would come to Scroggins and meet my great aunt and my father's first wife."

"I don't mean find your family," Linc frowned. "I mean find YOU. You've spent the last ten years writing about other places and other people. You're still doing it even now. Why don't you write *your story* for a change? You might just find out if you like yourself or not."

Following him to the door to make certain she got the last word, she smirked, "It is pretty clear you don't think very much of me!"

Linc turned around in the doorway, one hand on the doorknob while the other lifted to her cheek. She flinched but did not swipe it away. The tears were there, though she stubbornly refused to release them. Linc, not ashamed of his own, let his drip across his cheek.

"I already think the world of you, Laurel Holden," he said through the glass. "And I've only ever seen a fraction of you. One day, I hope you'll let me see behind the scars. I bet she's more beautiful than I imagine."

CHAPTER TWENTY-EIGHT

The Boundaries of Love

S lumped over the couch watching television with the volume turned loud enough to hear over the hum of the air conditioner behind him, Cade barely heard the knock at the front door. Laurel, sitting at her laptop in the kitchen, didn't hear it at all. Cade turned the volume down to double check he'd heard correctly. When he faintly heard another rap at the other end of the house, he called through into the archway to Laurel, "Nobody comes to the front door. I'll get it, though. You keep writing."

Cade moved into the white bedroom, through Laurel's pink one, and into the front parlor. He could see through the sheer covered window the outline of their visitor. He would never have expected it to be her. When he escorted her through the house to the kitchen, Laurel was equally surprised. Obedience Daniels gestured to Cade to withdraw a chair for her at the table. He followed her direction, holding it out until she sat down. Laurel joined her, still not saying anything, as if taking her cues from Obedience. Cade excused himself to give them privacy, but Obedience reached for his arm, clutching it boldly, and directed her finger to another chair for him to join them.

Both Laurel and Cade exchanged puzzled looks, still not saying a word. Each so caught off guard by not only the visitor, but the authoritative manner in which she was conducting the room. The young woman and the younger man were not people who complied so easily to another's authority, but Obedience had put them off their game by her very visit.

"I know you think me a harsh woman," she said, not clearly addressing to whom her remark was intended. Perhaps both. "And I am. Someone had to be. My brother Worth had little time for anything other than politics. Our father died, and I was left with the responsibility. I have had to be what I am because I had sisters to look after." Obedience touched the tips of her long spiney fingers together as if in prayer or consideration. Then she returned to her point. "I won't say I have not made mistakes. My sister Harmony sought asylum from me by marrying the first man who asked."

"And Babe?" Laurel asked, hinting at a grin.

Shaking her head as she closed her eyes, Obedience almost smiled herself. "The less said about that one, the better."

The ceremonious way their unexpected guest entered, and the almost-amused break in her personality left Laurel feeling a bit perplexed, provoking her to finally ask rather bluntly, "And why are you here exactly?" Immediately realizing how rude that sounded, Laurel corrected with, "Not that you aren't welcome. It is just that you've never visited me before without Patience."

Obedience turned her attention to Cade. "I am here because of the growing animosity in the community over your circumstances, young man." She then regarded Laurel with her next remark. "And your romance with Mr. Hopkins."

Laurel felt a shiver of anger crawl up her spine, and was the verge of lashing out to her uninvited visitor that she'd had enough of uncharitable townspeople weighing in on their private affairs. But before she could get the words out, Obedience spoke again, rendering Laurel silent for the moment.

"I would like to share a story of my own with the two of you...and only the two of you." Staring directly at Laurel, Obedience smirked playfully, "This is not to be in your book."

"No ma'am."

Obedience gave a nod of gratitude. "I rely on a mutual trust and respect among the three of us that what I have to say will never go further than this one moment in our lives."

Laurel smiled at their guest, as did Cade, then she assured Obedience, "We do not tell other people's confidences."

"Thank you." Obedience took a deep breath, about to begin her speech, observing the intensely serious way both Laurel and Cade sat staring at her, anticipating her next words. Obedience gave an impish glance at Laurel and quipped, "Am I not to be offered a glass of tea or cup of coffee?"

Cade and Laurel's all-encompassed attention broke, and Laurel flushed with embarrassment. "I am so sorry," she apologized. "We have completely forgotten our manners. Cade pour Mrs. Daniels a glass of iced tea please."

Cade hurried to the dish cabinet and brought out the nicest glass on the shelf, filled it with ice, then tea, and placed it before Obedience. Half expecting her to next ask, "What no lemon?" He braced himself for repudiation, but none came. So he returned to his seat.

"You have collected many tales and recipes in Scroggins," Obedience began. "I have come with no recipe for my story. However, I have told you I do not wish it printed either, so I only ask you both to listen. It is not a small act, my sharing it with you." Obedience was once again, gently reminding them of their vow of secrecy. "I, as you undoubtedly know, never married." Then with a gentle grin of acknowledgement, admitted, "I am aware we are something of a joke in the community. The three spinster Daniels sisters: Obedience, Prudence, and Patience. And I admit my sisters have more of a childlike composite to their personalities, which explains to anyone who has met them why they never had offers of marriage. However, unlike Prudence and Patience,

I have had opportunities for marriage. Not many, but a few."

Laurel and Cade eyed each other quickly. Having only been in town for a few months, Laurel knew it was possible for Obedience to have had a few great romances in her youth that no one had yet mentioned to Laurel. But when she saw Cade's face appear just as flummoxed by the revelation as she felt, Laurel understood that no one in town had ever been privy to Obedience Daniels having ever been in love.

Their visitor continued telling her story. "I declined proposals when they came," she informed them. "And I find it important at this time to share with the two of you—and only the two of you—just why I turned them down."

Obedience had her audience hanging on her every word, and she was enjoying the attention. But something in her eyes, as well as her tone, which quivered a little now, hinted that it wasn't the spotlight she craved. She was a woman who had lived a life knowing something no one else knew. Something she'd never shared. And sharing it now made her feel things she'd long kept buried.

"I was in love once. And only once." She stressed the last part emphatically, as either an illustration of her resilience, or a tribute to the depth of the one love itself. "If you were to ask my sisters, they would hold no recollections of my romance. No one would. No one ever knew. In fact, I am sure the two of you find it difficult to believe even now."

"I don't," Cade said. "I don't find it hard to believe at all."

Obedience smiled, then forced her face back to its normal seriousness. "I admit I was shocked by my own brazenness at the time. By my capability to develop feelings so quickly for one not merely below my station, but out of the realm of possibility." She paused again. Another deep breath. Then said, "His name was Gerald. He worked for my father...as a farm hand. A sharecropper more precisely." Obedience turned to Laurel, "He was a colored man."

It was now clear to Laurel what compelled this domineering, repressive woman to come today. She'd lived through a similar situation as both Laurel and Cade were going through, only for Obedience, there had been no choices afforded her.

Her eyes changed as she continued speaking of Gerald. They lost their intensity. It was then Laurel could see why Obedience Daniels' personality was the way it was, because it was powered by an internal rage she could never shake. A fury over an unfairness Fate dealt her. Yet now as she spoke of Gerald, that rage relaxed, giving way to an almost jubilant gleam in her eyes.

"I loved him with everything I had inside of me. And he truly loved me. Of that I am unshakably certain."

Laurel slid her hand across the table and squeezed Obedience's. "Of course he did."

Obedience smiled once more as she continued. "He was a gentle man, but strong. His arms and legs were stronger than four men put together. And he had the deepest, most tender eyes I have ever looked upon in my life. They were the color of honey."

Cade, stirred by something inside himself, reached and placed his hand over hers and Laurel's. A lone tear escaping her eye, Obedience placed her free hand atop his and sat there a moment her trembling hands clasped with theirs. Then she withdrew her hands to her lap, and moved on. "You cannot know the agony of loving someone so greatly while knowing you have absolutely no path together." Her eyes flashed toward Cade, "Perhaps you can more than most. But even in this day, you have options. I had none." She paused again, as if contemplating the truth in her statement. "Perhaps we did, but we were both too afraid to test the limits of society. Others in the country were boldly chartering the territory, but we...mostly I...lacked the courage." The tears swelling in her eyes made her appear surprisingly younger, even beautiful.

"What happened to Gerald?" Cade asked.

"I made him leave," she explained. "Begged him to leave. Of course, he fought me on it, but it did not take long to conclude it was the inevitable ending. I could not possibly live in a town where we would both reside, me on my end and he on his, and never see one another. Or worse, be unable to resist the 10 miles separating us and eventually be caught. Back then Gerald could have been hung from the nearest tree limb, and no white person in town would object. There was no other way but for him to leave. Gerald found work in Georgia."

Cade was moved by her story, but his youth was grounded in modern times. He was not yet capable of understanding the constraints were vastly different than his own. "But you've heard from him over the years? Surely, there was a time when you realized the world has changed enough—"

"It did not change in time for me," Obedience whispered. "Gerald eventually married, had children, probably grandchildren. When technology entered my life and I consented to having the internet in our home, I looked him up once on Prudence's computer. My Gerald had died a number of years ago. From all accounts he had a full life, without me."

Laurel tossed propriety to the wind, reaching under the table and grabbing Obedience's hand again. Gently she caressed the back of it while her tears rolled down her cheek to match Obedience's own. "It must have hurt a great deal when he married someone else."

"Perhaps," Obedience replied. "In the girlish part of my heart. But the rest of me was elated. I loved him that much, you see. The last thing I ever wanted for him was to suffer as I suffered. Perhaps it is easier for men. Maybe he never loved his wife as he loved me. I used to find myself hoping so. It matters very little really. Gerald was able to have a full life. And that was enough for me."

"But why didn't you?" Cade asked. "Why could you not allow yourself the same thing?"

Obedience sat straighter in her chair, returning slightly to her usual stern self, "Young man, if it were possible for you to forget your heart and submit to your father's demands to court and marry some female, you wouldn't be living here with Laurel. We cannot erase who we love or why we love them."

"But I'm gay," Cade said. "Being open to finding another guy I could love is very different than forcing myself to live my life with a woman I'll never be attracted to. You might have met someone else after Gerald."

"I wasn't interested in anyone else. To have done so would have only diminished what I'd already had." Obedience knew he was far too young to understand what she was saying. Perhaps Laurel was as well. Sometimes only the very old have lived long enough to comprehend the very deepest of emotions. "I have cherished my anguish through all these years," she admitted. "Even my agony was beautiful because it kept me continuously connected me to him."

"I think I understand," Laurel smiled. "You always belong to him and that was enough."

Obedience nodded her head, then wiped her tears.

"I appreciate you sharing your story with us," Laurel told her. "And it is safe with us."

Obedience stood from her chair, ready to make her departure. But she had one final plea to make to these young people. Turning to Cade, she offered, "Young man, do not give in to your parents or to the cage society tries to lock you within. Get out of here as soon as you can. Build a fine and beautiful life for yourself with someone you truly love. Let no one dictate what your heart ought to feel." Then to Laurel, she advised, "Laurel, you must step beyond yourself to understand that Linc's fears are well founded. Alabama has changed since my time, but not that much. If you love him, stand with him, even if you don't understand his concerns or his devotion to remain in this community. If you don't truly love him, don't add to his troubles by wasting his time."

* * *

Obedience had been gone well over an hour when Cade disappeared

SOMETIMES IT'S THE FORK

to his room, leaving Laurel alone in the kitchen with her thoughts. Her thoughts were not something she especially wanted alone time with; she opened her laptop to work on the book. But her mind kept racing between her fight with Linc and the words Obedience parted on. It was all much too much to think about, once again kicking on her fight or flight tendency, though to a more minor degree. She decided to check on Cade, ignoring her own struggles at hand. He wasn't in his room, but the front door of the yellow room was ajar. She stepped out onto the porch to find him rocking gently in the swing, his legs propped up on the arm.

"Room for me?"

He swung his legs down and patted the space beside him. She was about to ask how he was doing when he blurted out, "I think I'm going to get out of here."

With a raised brow she asked what he meant.

"Out of Scroggins," he said. "Out of your hair. Out of Mr. Hopkins' hair. If I weren't here, nobody would be saying shit about you or judging him for being involved with you."

Antagonized by the statement, Laurel jumped to her feet pacing the porch like a defense attorney pleading to a jury. "That is exactly what not to do!" she bellowed. "We are not giving in to these idiots! Besides your parents, how many of them are there anyway? I know a lot of people in Scroggins now. I can't believe they would be siding with your mother and father."

Cade almost laughed at her naivety. "You'd be shocked how people can turn on you when *gay* gets thrown in the mix. Mr. Hopkins shouldn't lose his job over me. And you can't end your relationship over me either. I am the fly in the ointment. I'll go somewhere else and be all right."

Running her hands through her hair, she let out a little shriek of exasperation with the situation. "Cade, you just started your senior year in high school. You are not an adult yet. Do you know what could happen to you if you went out on your own?"

"I don't care, Laurel! It's better than ruining your life and Mr. Hopkins. And I shouldn't be here anyway. You feeding me and clothing me and driving me to school. I am a mooch draining your money, and you don't have that much to play around with."

"You are working at Delva's now," Laurel reminded him, although he shot her a snarky look. They both knew the tiny bit of money he made at the new job didn't come near to paying his keep.

"I'm going to go," he insisted. "I can get a job somewhere. Or hell, go home and live by their rules another few years till I can figure something else out. Either way, you and Linc can be free of the problem."

Laurel's anger got the better of her. She slapped the nearest post holding the roof, lodging a splinter into her palm. Cade pulled her back to the swing and used his fingernails to pull it free. Then, suddenly they both started to laugh.

"We are quite a pair, aren't we?" he smiled.

"We are." Laurel said. "We truly, actually are, Cade." She took his hands into her own, flinching at the sting around the tender splinter wound. "I need to tell you something I just found out a couple of days ago. We are a pair, Cade. Because we are cousins."

His eyes looked at her with total confusion. "What are you talking about?"

"My grandmother left me this house and her savings. But Cade, this house and that money is just as much yours as mine. My grandfather was your grandfather. You are my cousin."

He sat on the edge of the porch as she told him everything Flossie had shared with her. The revelation blew his mind. And the irony was not lost on Cade that his self-righteous, judgmental father was the bastard son of the town whore and a blinded bully.

They sat together, legs dangling off the porch just over the bed of delphiniums Laurel had recently planted, as the sun began its descent behind the trees. He wasn't sure how to handle the information. "Ustus Hogue..."

"Was your grandfather too," she nodded. "My philandering absentee father and your horrible bigot of a father were brothers."

"What a family!" he chuckled.

"This house and that money are ours Cade. You belong here just as much as I do. We are both a pair of Hogue bastards, discarded and forgotten, yet somehow brought back together. You and I are the last of this family." Then with a tender, vulnerable look in her eyes, she said, "I have never had a family, Cade. Stay with me. Be my family. Please don't leave. I'll take care of you, and you'll take care of me. We will see this out together."

CHAPTER TWENTY-NINE

I Will Not Love

The hallways were filled with bustling students midway to their next class before the ever-nagging bell sounded from the corners of every corridor. A fair share of stragglers, unphased by the countdown, leaned against metal lockers sharing the confidences, running jokes, and grapevine gossip of the school day. Cade was making a quick pass through the halls trying to avoid the snide remarks, jeers, or screams of "faggot" from the boys who were either as unevolved as their parents or had something of their own to hide which forced them to cloak themselves in harassment.

Out of his periphery, he thought he spied Laurel rounding the hall. After a second look he confirmed it was. She appeared lost and meandering, looking at door plates and room numbers hurriedly. She saw Cade watching her. Shrugging her shoulders towards him, he could tell from her manic energy why she was there. He pointed down a connecting corridor and flashed the numbers 23 with his fingers. Laurel chartered her new course, and Cade made his way to class.

Linc Hopkins was at his desk hovering over student files and county reports, but he wasn't paying attention to any of them, his mind elsewhere. Suddenly his door swung open and *elsewhere* barged into his office.

"I don't love!" Laurel pronounced emphatically. "I didn't love my mother. I never had friends I felt especially close to. As for men, I never got any closer than *mildly liking them* before things ended."

"I understand," Linc said, repressing a grin. She was a mess, showing more passion and animation than he'd ever seen her display. And it was fairly amusing to see.

Laurel came closer to his desk. "I am not going to love you, Lincoln Hopkins!"

The moment he heard her say his full name he was reasonably certain he had her. Folding his arms and trying his best to hold his face expressionless, he said, "Understood."

"You wouldn't want me to love you anyway!" she continued. "I am impulsive, selfish, temperamental, and I cause problems every time I get involved with anyone. Like right now, look at the chaos I have caused you just by being me. You are much better off without me in your life, Lincoln."

Rising from his chair, he walked around to the other side of the desk, closer to where she stood, and leaned again, arms folded once more. Only this time he wasn't suppressing his smile. "I agree with you, Laurel. You are a mess. I don't have time to sort you out. And my career is very important to me. These students are very important to me."

His concession registered in her eyes. Linc saw that one fleeting second of disappointed flash before she continued her act. "Good, then we are on the same page. We are better off not continuing to see each other."

She released a long breath of resignation, then turned to leave. But Lincoln grabbed her hand before she stepped out of reach, then he held her in place by stretching his arms across her delicate shoulders. Looking her directly in the eyes, he said, "The problem with it all Laurel, is that you are more important to me than any of it."

"What?" she stammered.

But it was too late. He saw the flash of relief in her eye, eradicating every ounce of bluster and pretend isolationism she so desperately lived by. Still, she did her best to keep up the act. "Linc, I don't think we would ever work as a couple. I'm too...you're too...We can't risk—"

"Oh, this is definitely not going to work," he laughed. "It is going to blow up *royally* in our faces. You are a ridiculously lost woman possessing zero self-awareness. While I am a an arrogantly stubborn and unyielding man. But God in Heaven, please help me, because I want to see this thing out."

Her shoulders relaxed under his arms, despite her desire to cling to her patented standoffishness. "You just said this would blow up in our faces."

"Remember the fireworks?" he replied. "Some explosions are glorious and mustn't be missed."

In all her life, no one had ever said anything more perfect to her. It would have been much too easy to tell her he loved her. Easy and cliché. Could he really know her so well as to know the way to lock her down and reel her in was to admit it was going to be a glorious catastrophe? She thrust her hands to his face, pulling herself into him for the longest most passionate kiss she ever recalled having in her life.

They sat together a while in his office, talking. Really talking this time. No pretense. No walls. No armor. Laurel admitted she couldn't fully comprehend all he'd had to overcome to get where he was now. She even apologized for being dismissive of his problems and flippant regarding his genuine fears.

Linc did his own share of acquiescing, telling Laurel that contrary to her own earlier statement about not becoming involved with people, or loving them, what she had done for Cade was a glowing example of compassion. He described her caring heart to her in ways that made her think he must be speaking of someone else. But as he counted off the examples of kindness she'd shown and people she'd touched since coming to Scroggins, she began to see herself not as she'd been before, but the way he thought her to be.

Their problems were certainly not over. Not with Cade's parents stirring up bitterness and controversy in town and with the Department of Education, but Linc and Laurel decided to face things head on together. Although they weren't quite sure how yet, they would take it all on as a united front.

"I have been called in to meet with my supervisors on Monday," Linc revealed. "I believe I can convince them nothing tawdry is going on at your house with this kid. I will also explain the abusive nature of his parents."

"Do you think they'll take your word on it?"

Linc smiled, ready to reveal the one ace up his sleeve. "You'll be happy to know that with all this talk spreading around town, your neighbor Leon Davis called me up to tell me he was a firsthand witness to the Peterson's abuse. He has offered to speak to the Board of Education for me."

"What a lovely man!" Laurel replied.

Linc then added, "I also think we should say something at church on Sunday, if Brother Daws will allow us."

"I'm not going to church!" Laurel exclaimed. "After half of those people started badmouthing us over nothing, I am not going back there again. I don't care how bored I get or how many recipes I miss out on."

Squeezing her hands, Linc gave her a stern eye. "That is just what those people expect you to do. Avoid the stares and whispers so their lies can fill the empty spaces. No Laurel. You are not a quitter, and I am not a coward. We will be in church this Sunday. Besides, my granny and your aunt would never forgive us if we missed. It's Homecoming."

CHAPTER THIRTY

Homecoming

Having spent months now in Scroggins, Laurel had learned here and there what Homecoming, also called Decoration Day, was all about. However, experiencing it was going to be something else entirely. The day held a semblance of pride for the members of the church. It was a day when former church members, or descendants of members, returned home again for a church wide picnic before adorning the graves of their loved ones. This adornment usually was with new flowers in the urns of across the headstones, but sometimes it went further. Some of the older headstones might need polishing, to scrub away the year's pollen and fallen tree sap. Some more dedicated descendants were even known to lay new layers of cut sod to a grave if the grass looked a little sporadic.

In the days leading up to Sunday's Homecoming, Janice texted Laurel several reminders to make a dish for the picnic. She'd also assured Laurel that she would take care of the flowers for Bessie and Ustus' graves since she knew what sort of colors Bessie had liked best. Flossie also blew up Laurel's phone that week, with her own reminders about the food and flowers. Topping it all off, Delva sent word home through Cade about the same things. Finally, when Linc mentioned it Friday night, Laurel exclaimed, "Does no one have faith that I won't forget to make a dish?"

Laurel's natural inclination was to skip this event entirely. Still angry over the stir her taking Cade in and her relationship with Linc was causing, she wanted to avoid Christ's Love Baptist Church and never go back. But Linc continued arguing how that would only give credence to the rumors, hinting that Laurel had something to feel guilty about. Although Linc assumed he'd been the one to convince Laurel to attend Homecoming services, the real reason was a little larger than his persuasive mind. More calls had come in nearer the end of the week, from various Scroggins' citizens, adding their gentle reminders to Laurel not to forget a dish and flowers on Sunday. Laurel got the hint. These people were not doubting her memory or devotion to her family's graves; they were providing subtle subtext letting her know she belonged there and they hoped to see her.

Laurel stayed up late Thursday night pouring through Bessie's recipe books for the right offering. Cade had already begun his grandmother's Chicken and Dressing so that it would be perfect by Sunday morning. Once Laurel chose her dish, she canceled her plans with Linc Saturday night, explaining she had to make her dessert. He understood and took no offense at the cancellation of plans, however, was disappointed when she would not share with him what she would be making. He also wasn't too happy that she'd already mentioned to Delva that she'd be canceling her date and cooking all night and suggested to Linc, "Since we can't go out tonight, it's a perfect time for you to fix that broken caster on your grandmother's bedframe. She's been sleep at a tilt for days."

As Laurel toiled in the kitchen that Saturday night, Cade watched TV in the next room but couldn't help but look back through the archway between the den and kitchen, trying to determine what exactly Laurel was doing. He got up from the couch and propped his arm against the arch, staring with unbreakable interest. Laurel was at the table with a screwdriver in one hand and a hammer in the other, chiseling away on the shell of a coconut. The nut was a hostile little thing, rolling across the table away from her with every tap of the hammer. He thought about interrupting her, having a reasonably accurate idea of what she was trying to do, but it was too funny to stop. He simply stood there watching the scene play out.

Laurel made several other attempts to open the coconut by hitting the screwdriver with the hammer, sending the impenetrable ball rolling off to the floor with a thud. Still unaware Cade was watching, Laurel put down the tools and rifled through a metal toolbox in one of the chairs until she found a better option. Withdrawing a hacksaw, she began sawing at the coconut shell. The effect was no different from the hammer and screwdriver. The coconut just rolled back and forth with the blade.

Beginning to think she might seriously hurt herself as she began hacking at the coconut shell, Cade cleared his throat from the archway. "Laurel, I won't ask what you are doing because I think I know. Are you by chance making Coconut Cake for tomorrow?"

Exasperated, she slammed the saw on the tabletop and pushed the hair out of her eyes. "I sure as hell was trying to, but this thing is like a cannonball."

"They make coconut milk and coconut shreds you can buy in stores," Cade told her.

"They do?"

Taking the rare opportunity to poke fun at her ignorance, he added smartly, "Yeah, I don't think even Polynesian people go through all that shit with real coconuts. They buy it at the store too."

Looking baffled, Laurel cried, "Then why didn't my grandmother say that in her list of ingredients?"

Cade rolled his eyes playfully, "Because I'm pretty sure she assumed anyone would know that." He pulled out his cell and made a quick call to ask permission, then hung up and grabbed Laurel's keys off the wall hook. "Mrs. Hopkins said I can run out to The Bake Shop and pull some coconut milk and shreds out of inventory for you. I'll be back in a few."

Once Laurel had ingredients she could work with and didn't require a set of tools she'd borrowed from Leon, she made her grandmother's cherished coconut cake. A few hours later when it was covered in frosting and coconut shavings, Laurel and Cade stood together admiring it.

"Looks good," he praised. "Now I wish you'd made two so we could have one at home to eat tonight."

* * *

A gripping tension had her stomach in knots that morning as she dressed for church. Though she'd been a dozen times before, somehow today felt different. Like walking into a lion's den. Cade felt it too. Although he'd gone to church with Janice and Laurel a few times since moving in, today would be different. His parents would probably be there. Though Christ's Love wasn't their regular church, it their home church—the place they'd attended as children with their parents. It being Homecoming, they were sure to be there and if for nothing else, to cause tension and trouble.

Linc texted a little before nine that he was on his way to pick them up. When they heard his car pull into the gravel driveway, Laurel and Cade exchanged anxious glances knowing it was time to leave. Cade took his chicken and dressing from the oven to carry to the car, with Laurel behind him holding her coconut cake. As the screen door of the back porch slammed shut behind them, both Laurel and Cade froze for a moment in surprise.

In all the other times Laurel had gone to church in Scroggins, she'd either driven or ridden with Janice or Linc. This was the first time she would be arriving at church via a convoy. Linc, dressed in a crisp navy suit and yellow tie, stood by the car waiting to drive them, a wide grin across his face. Laurel moved slowly towards him, profoundly moved by what she saw beyond his car. The dirt road in front of the house was filled with vehicles, engines running, windows down, with smiling faces staring back at Laurel. Linc's parents, Owen and Maple, were in their car with the engine running and Delva in the back seat. Just ahead of the Hopkin's sedan, a familiar pickup truck idled, ready to depart. Leon Davis, his wife Julia, and his mother Dean were dressed in their finest waving from the windows. Ahead of them, honking the horn hello, sat Janice and Flossie. The fact Janice had picked Flossie up, when she lived across the street from the church, and brought her back here, hinted that someone had planned that they should all arrive at church in a united front. Then Laurel's eyes noticed another car pulling up directly behind the Hopkins's. Waving from the passenger window sat Bootsie Taylor, with Renzo smiling behind the wheel.

Speechless, Laurel and Cade got into Linc's car. Filled with humility and gratitude, Laurel processed this gesture of solidarity these incredible people were showing her. Unable to suppress her smile, she and her entourage departed for church.

The parking lot of Christ's Love Baptist was at capacity, with cars even lined up parked on the banks of the highway. Laurel expressed her surprise, to which Linc explained it was this way every year. "That's why it is called Homecoming!"

Flossie, Dean, and Delva were let out by the church door while the others parked, but neither woman entered until the rest of their party returned from parking. Linc took the helm, with Laurel at his side, opening the door of the church to dozens of faces turning to look at them. He walked hand in hand with Laurel. Just behind them came Flossie, Janice, and Cade, with the Davises, the Hopkins, and Taylors after. Everyone splintered off to their usual seats, which were still sitting empty awaiting them. Despite the numerous strangers in town, people knew the custom, and those who didn't were quickly alerted by someone nearby telling them, "That seat is taken."

Brother Daws looked especially dapper in a brand-new baby blue suit. The snappy outfit and his gleaning white hair made him look a little like a cloud floating through the clear horizon. Mrs. Daws was seated up front, with what looked to Laurel to be her adult children, home for Decoration Day. Laurel grinned as she saw the familiar sight of Lottie's hand removing a pesky hairpin from her updo. With so many people still coming in, delaying the start of services, Laurel wondered how many hairpins she'd pulled out so far before services even started. Lottie saw her watching and chuckled into her hand. Laurel mouthed, *how many?* Lottie held up 4 fingers. They shared an amused smile.

That one exchange somehow changed the world.

It changed Laurel's world at least. Something as simple as a shared laugh with the preacher's wife over something as silly as hairpins, aligned everything in Laurel's life. It was as if a light clicked on inside her. Laurel felt almost dizzy. Her arms and legs began tingling from within, running down her body into her toes. Her mind translated the sensation strangely. Laurel felt as if tiny invisible roots were sprouting from her veins, intertwining downward until they reached the ground, then squeezing between the floorboards, winding through whatever pipe and wiring lay beneath the foundation, before anchoring her to the land holding it all in place. She could feel her roots tunneling deeper and deeper underground until they came to a stop, binding her to this place. Something as simple as a private joke and smile shared with Lottie Daws gave Laurel the roots she'd never known. *This is my home. This is my community.*

Somehow services were continuing without Laurel's awareness. How long she'd been distracted by the strange sensation coursing through her, she didn't know. But now the choir was singing. They sang their hearts out along with many members of the congregation. Laurel's mind continued spinning. An empty life flashing before her eyes. One filled with anger and resentment...and hurt. So much hurt. But all of that felt as if it were melting away, running down the roots of her feet into the cleansing hallowed ground.

Brother Daws was now preaching a sermon Laurel only caught in random snippets. It was about community. Home. Brotherly love for one another. Only when she felt a hundred pressing eyes on her, and on Linc, did she finally hear some of what the reverend was saying. "We are called to be of service to one another," Daws told the church members. "WE DON'T KNOW what travails our brothers and sisters may be experiencing. What burdens are weighing them down. But the Lord smiles upon us when HE SEES us lift that weight from them and raise our troubled brethren off the ground."

The crowd filling the church pews were nodding now, shouting several "Amens" across the room. Brother Daws continued with his message. "We should strive to raise these burdened brothers and sisters high into the air. Raising them ABOVE US to be closer to Him. When we put others before ourselves and we lift them higher than ourselves, pushing them above us so THEY may be healed first...that is when **GOD KNOWS** you love HIM."

Brother Daws was looking directly at Laurel now and everyone in the congregation knew it. "Some among us who have never known God's love for them, never known God's peace, are still STEEPED in enough GRACE, to offer love and peace to someone else weighted with worldly burdens."

She heard Cade catch his breath beside Flossie, and saw her aunt take Cade's hand. As Laurel looked back at the pulpit, Brother Daws had not shifted his gaze from her and he wanted everyone to understand who he was referring to.

"Now I ask you brothers and sisters, isn't that what it's all about?" A collective hush filled the sanctuary as a sea of heads nodded in the spirit of realization. His flock was listening, fully comprehending the message as he continued. "When we encounter someone hurt, someone lost, someone *abandoned*, that is our BROTHER or our SISTER. A member of a family WE ARE ALL a part of. He is me. I am her. She is him. THEY are YOU! And God is watching. GOD IS WATCHING how we treat HIS children."

Linc was the one to release a sigh now and it was noteworthy because it was not an ordinary escape of breath. It was a release from his troubles. The energy in the air had palpably shifted inside the church. Brother Daws, in one inspiring Homecoming sermon, had just discreetly absolved Laurel from any wrongdoing. He had quietly confirmed Cade's place in God's Kingdom and declared Linc innocent of all the manufactured controversy.

Somehow, the preacher's subtle absolution reignited the root system sprouting from Laurel. The tendrils of unseen vines rooting her to the soil, pushed further through the ground, stretching beyond the church into the graveyard. Her roots charging towards the roots of her family, intertwining, merging, synergizing into one collective thread. The walls around her heart crumbled. Once again, the life she'd lived before coming to Scroggins played swiftly in her mind. Like having a failed test returned with the

correct answers written in red, Laurel saw her mistakes vividly. And she knew now how to not repeat them.

She remembered that day, months ago when she couldn't find the turnoff to Bessie's house from the highway, even with her GPS. It suddenly became clear in her mind that she hadn't found Hogg Road until she'd stopped moving and stepped from her car. *She had stopped moving* and seen the path she couldn't see before. From that moment Laurel had begun shedding her armor little by little. She'd waved at a stranger, who turned out to be Janice. She met the Taylors, then Delva, then Puddin. She met the Daniels sisters and the Davises. The Bevins, the Rawlings, so many people. Laurel had come to Scroggins starving for something she never knew she was hungry for, and Scroggins literally and figuratively fed her.

Laurel, again unaware, lost within herself, jolted back to the present the moment she felt Delva's gentle hands pressing into her shoulders. Looking up, Laurel heard the music ringing from the organ and the church members softly singing a hymn. Delva's cool dark hands wiped

Laurel's cheeks. She wasn't even aware she'd been crying.

Staring up into Delva's tender eyes, Laurel asked, "What's happening?"

Smiling proudly as she shook her head, Delva answered, "Baby, I think you are being Saved."

Laurel found Linc crouching beside his grandmother, her eyes searching his with confusion. Linc simply shrugged and said, "Only you know."

"But I don't believe in anything," she whispered to Delva.

"It don't matter, baby," she replied. "It believes in you. Come on."

Laurel wasn't sure what was happening. Delva led her by the hand from the pew down the aisle to the front of the church where Brother Daws waited. Two others were already there, each overcome by something themselves, stirring them also to tears. Linc's mother and Janice followed after Delva and Laurel. Delva directed Laurel down on a knee, and bent to the floor with her, sliding her loving arm around Laurel's waist. Delva began praying. Janice joined on Laurel's other side while Linc's mother gently swept Laurel's hair from her tearstained face and tucked behind her ears.

"This is salvation," Delva whispered to Laurel while Brother Daws came to her, placing his hand on her head and told her how protected in love she would always be from now forward.

Laurel felt like a charlatan. Like she was dishonoring the faith of these good people by joining into this. Quickly she tugged at Brother Daws sleeve and whispered. "I think this is a mistake. This isn't me. This isn't who I've ever been."

For the first time in her life, Laurel saw a father's eyes look sweetly down onto her as Daws replied with a grin, "Sister Laurel, I think that's the point."

Laurel felt like she should stop them. It was a mistake. They were wasting their time. She was not Saved. She was not overcome by salvation. She was only emotional because she'd just had a breakthrough,

317

Laurel had finally figured out where she had gone wrong in every misstep of her life. God hadn't imbued her with Glory. She'd simply dropped her armor and allowed herself to feel, to connect. All those interactions she had with people in Scroggins, which she kept telling herself were only for the book, were actual *friendships*. Real friendships. She discovered that she genuinely loved these people. But nothing spiritual had taken place. It was only that she'd found her roots.

But isn't that all the same thing? Isn't it really all just the same thing? She wasn't sure where the thought had come from, but its occurrence made her doubt her insistence that this wasn't spiritual. Maybe some people attribute this moment to God. Perhaps they believe they're feeling something ethereal. And maybe some people, as Laurel did, experience it as release and acceptance. Laurel wasn't sure what had happened to her. *Maybe I have been Saved? Not from sin or the devil... but from myself.*

* * *

Coming out of the church into the golden sunlight of the early autumn afternoon, Laurel was greeted like a hero returning home from war—or the winning Super Bowl team coming home after the victory! People rushed her from all sides, congratulating her and blessing her with love. It all made her feel both proud and utterly embarrassed at the same time.

Lottie Daws was standing near the bottom church step, waiting for Laurel with a sweet smile and a warm embrace. "I am so proud for you, Laurel. I don't know exactly what you experienced but it was beautiful to witness."

Laurel gave a friendly pat to Mrs. Daws arm and confided, "It would make no sense if I tried to explain it, but Mrs. Daws, you are responsible."

"Me?" Lottie gasped, pressing her hand to her chest. "I don't see how I could have done anything."

"You did," Laurel replied. "You just being you opened my eyes to

318

things that have been right in front of me all along. Thank you."

Nearly crying herself, Lottie whimpered, "Well, child, I don't understand how, but if I did something to help you, I am real glad. You are a fine woman, Laurel, and this community is lucky to have you."

Linc approached to take Laurel by the hand and escorted her to the tables on the side of the church. The food everyone prepared at home began lining up in a majestic style across the long connecting stone tables. Some women placed colorful tablecloths under their family's contribution, while others were fine with the concrete slab acting as the top of the buffet. From one end to the next, the food was bountiful. There were many dishes Laurel recognized, and some would be included in her book. Many more looked and tasted so delicious, she made notes and took pictures with her phone as a reminder to pay visits to the cooks to possibly fill the few remaining spots she had left.

Satisfied with the food shots taken, she quickly opened her photo app to make sure none were blurred. Once she came to the end of pics she'd just taken, her photo roll reflected the epiphany she'd experienced in church. The glaring truth of her life was that her photos were filled with breathtaking vistas and appetizing cuisine from her years of travel, but there were no people. She pushed her finger across the screen, rolling back year by year. Nothing but food and scenery she had written about.

Her eyes glanced up from her phone to look out over her friends in Scroggins. She remembered very little of those distant places or the meals she'd reviewed, but these people here in this tiny rural town, she could never forget. Laurel lifted her phone to her eye and began immortalizing the people around her that she knew and cared about. Brother Daws and his wife chatting at a table with their children. Wilson and Sheila Bevins sitting closely together at their own small table. Curtis and Althea Roberts talking with another couple that Laurel wondered might be the neighbors whose house Althea plowed into. Then there was Bud Rawlings bellowing out some sort of nonsense in his radio announcer's voice while Renzo and Bootsie sat nearby snickering as they shared a single piece of cake.

Linc and Flossie were nearly at the end of the food table when Laurel put her phone away and started loading her plate. Flossie moved on to take a seat at the long folding table Linc's father had set up for their group, while Linc waited for Laurel.

"See," he grinned, lifting his paper plate full of food. "Granny didn't make it for me this time. I'm all grown up now."

She laughed and was walking with him to their table when she spotted a little boy dressed in a beige suit running by laughing with two other small children. Her eyes followed him until she saw him swept up into the arms of someone she knew. Handing Linc her plate, Laurel asked, "Will you take this to the table for me? I'll be right there, I just see someone I'd like to meet."

Crossing the lawn, Laurel went to the boy being held in his grand-mother's arms. She tapped Brenda Rawlings from behind on the shoulder, and asked, "Is this Justin?"

"Yes, it is!" Brenda cried, grinning ear to ear. She then said to her little grandson, "Justin, this is a friend of Nanna's. Her name is Laurel."

Laurel took the happy child's tiny hand and gave it a light shake. "Justin, I am so happy to meet you. Did you know that you are going to be in a book?"

The child, naturally, held no understanding of what she'd said, but a younger woman came over, giving Laurel a warm and unexpected hug. "I am so glad to meet you, Miss Holden. I am Emily, Brenda's daughter."

Laurel spent a few minutes chatting with the Rawlings family until Bud Rawlings began howling again, rating the different foods on his plate on a scale from 1 to 5."

Making her way back to Linc, Laurel was stopped by the Daniels' sisters. She hadn't seen them at church services, but then remembered their family buried in the cemetery. "Miss Holden," Obedience called out, greeting her warmly as her two sisters stood by her smiling.

"Miss Daniels!" Laurel exclaimed, noticing they weren't at a table. "Would you three like to join us at our table? We have plenty of room."

"We are not staying through the lunch," Obedience explained. "My sisters and I only came to place flowers. But when I saw you, I wanted to make certain to tell you that I am meeting with the Department of Education tomorrow to see if we can dispel this nonsense regarding Principal Hopkins."

Laurel thanked her, grateful for whatever she could do, but also confided that Brother Daws might have put an end to it already with his sermon. The news pleased Obedience. However, Patience was practically bouncing up and down, eager to ask Laurel a question. "Is it true, Miss Laurel? I heard someone bought your book with our recipes."

Laurel nodded with a beaming smile. "It is true. A Publishing House made me an offer this past Wednesday. I've decided to accept."

"Is it a lot of money?" Patience asked. Obedience scolded her for the question, citing it was none of her business or anyone else's.

"It isn't very much," Laurel told her anyway. "But I think it is enough to help someone we all care about." She gave a sly wink to Obedience, who appeared to comprehend the inference.

Prue patted Laurel's hand and said, "Then we will all buy a copy. I'll keep my eye out for it on shelves."

It was then Laurel gave them a bit of information she hadn't shared with anyone else yet, "Don't look for it under Laurel Holden," she revealed. "I am publishing it under my real name, Laura Hogg."

The news both confused and impressed the sisters. Laurel thought she could see a flash of approval in Obedience's eyes. Offering the hint of a nod, Obedience signaled to the young writer she had earned her respect yet again. Prue asked Laurel to come visit them soon and Laurel said that she would. Obedience bid Laurel a good day and led her sisters back towards the church parking lot.

Finally, Laurel made it back to her table and sat down between Linc and Flossie. Cade's parents were several tables over, although they did not speak to their son. Cade pretended not to notice. The slight carried a mild sting, but Cade had arrived at the conclusion he was not missing out on much. They had never made him feel connected to them, even when he lived at home. It was these people at the table around him right now who made him feel connected, part of a real family. They placed no judgements on him and each of them truly cared about his well-being and his future. The thought brought an unexpected grin to his face. Glancing over at Laurel, he saw she shared the same smile. She winked at him, letting him know she was thinking the very same thing. Family is not who you are *born to*. And despite popular belief, family is not those *you choose* yourself either. Family is created by those who *choose you*.

Quite a few people stopped by the table to pay compliments to Laurel for recreating Bessie Hogue's Coconut Cake. Although, more people commented on how the chicken and dressing was the best they'd ever had. And as Delva had predicted to Laurel on the phone the night before, her daughter-in-law Maple declared once again, as she did every year, that this would be the last time she made banana nut bread because no one ate it. This was followed by the annual explanation from Owen Hopkins to his wife, that there were just too many rolls, breads, cornbread, and cakes to choose from and nothing at all was wrong with her banana nut bread. This being Laurel's first Homecoming meal, she might have felt sorry for Maple had Linc not secretly confided weeks ago how his mother has never made banana nut bread in her life, she orders it online and just puts it in her own dish.

Once Christ's Love Church members began lamenting over their swollen stomachs, and beginnings of acid reflux, the remaining food was cleared away and the platters, dishes, and cake stands returned to the trunks of cars. Everyone began wandering out across the cemetery to pay a final visit to their loved ones' graves. Janice placed an arrangement of flowers on her parents' grave before moving to Bessie's. The arrangement she laid on Bessie's headstone was a little more elaborate than that of her own parents. Laurel assumed there was a story there too, but she'd heard enough stories for a while. Maybe if the book became a hit, she'd do a sequel.

She was glad now that Janice volunteered to handle the flowers for Bessie and Ustus because Laurel would have unknowingly ordered real flowers to put on the graves. It was very evident now, looking around at the sea of artificial flowers crawling over the cemetery that no one ever put down live flowers. Janice explained how silk flowers last for months and Bessie could rest with pride knowing her grave would remain adorned until the seasons changed, and Christmas flowers replaced the autumnal arrangement.

Flossie kissed her fingers and touched them to her sister's headstone before having Cade assist her across the uneven ground to her beloved Norman. Linc excused himself to go with his family to his grandfather and great grandparents' graves, leaving Laurel and Janice alone.

Laurel linked her arm with Janice's as she looked down on her grandmother's name. The wind was kicking up a little, sweeping cooler air down from the north, ready to begin displacing the leaves which were only a week or two from changing out of their green attire for orange and gold. Laurel lifted her hand to apply a light squeeze on Janice's forearm, then out of the blue, said, "I love you, you know."

"I know," Janice replied, trying to still her quivering lip. "And—"

"I know." Laurel said.

"One door closes and a window opens," Janice sang out. "With the book nearly done, what are you planning to do next?"

Laurel leaned her head onto her friend's shoulder, replying, "Write something else, I guess. The publishing house offer includes first refusal of my next book."

"And what will you do with all that money," Janice teased.

Laughing as she guided Janice back across the cemetery towards the church, Laurel said, "All that money, I wish. But it'll be enough to get Cade into Culinary School after he graduates. And a car for him,

After that, if he wants, I know a chef in Boston who has agreed to mentor him."

"What about for you, Laurel?" Janice asked. "Planning to do anything for you?"

"I think I'll paint my house a new color. Maybe even pave the driveway."

Janice stopped mid-step, turning to face her. "You know, that is the first time I have heard you say, *my house*. You've always called it *Bessie's house* until now."

"Same thing, I guess," Laurel replied. "It is hers. And it's mine. It's home. And I think it will be from now on."

The news put a lump in Janice's throat. Laurel's decision pleased her more than she wanted to let on. Janice had prepared herself for the day Laurel might move on, though she prayed she might stay. Keeping the flow casual, Janice simply responded with, "I know Puddin, Delva, and Bootsie will be happy. They have been scouting for two more people to join the Quilting Bee just so you will keep coming. They already recruited me, whenever I am off work."

Everyone was walking back from the cemetery now, a slow solemn procession as they honored the ones they'd loved and lost. Laurel knew she would be back doing this again next year. Of course, she hoped to know a little more about cooking by then to avoid another coconut battle. She parted ways with Janice, who reminded her they were both supposed to help Puddin Corder shop for throw pillows in the morning. Laurel kissed Aunt Flossie goodbye as she helped her into Janice's car. Flossie was quick to remind Laurel of her eye doctor appointment on Tuesday which Laurel promised to drive her to. Laurel assured her she wouldn't forget. She rejoined Linc as he was saying goodbye to his parents, whereupon Laurel reminded Maple and Owen that they were expected for dinner at Laurel's house on Friday when Linc planned to smoke ribs. With their loved ones pulling away from the church, Linc, Laurel, and Cade walked towards the road where

Linc had been forced to park that morning.

In the church lot, Brenda Rawlings waved goodbye to her daughter, son-in-law, and grandson as they pulled away for home. Bud stood at his truck, holding the door open for his wife, but Brenda did not immediately get in. Something in the distance drew her attention. Shielding her eyes from the sunlight with her hand, she stared down at the roadside where Lincoln Hopkins had parked.

"Brenda?" Bud said to her as she continued watching the road. "What are you looking at? It's only Miss Laurel's little group going to their car."

Brenda felt the wide, intuitive smile tugging at her lips. Across the gravel parking lot, she saw a familiar friend. A harbinger for what was to come. The slender, starved gray cat trotted unnoticed behind Laurel. When Linc opened the passenger door for Laurel, she looked down to see the poor, emaciated thing circling around her legs. Ignoring Bud's pleas to get into the truck, Brenda stood locked onto the sight in the distance. She saw Laurel say something to Linc, then to Cade, before she kneeled to stroke the cat's tattered fur. Brenda continued watching as Laurel lifted the poor creature into her arms and got into the car, the cat snuggling against her. A dusty cloud swirled behind them as Linc pulled away from the shoulder of the road to start for home. Brenda was beaming when she stepped into the truck.

"What has you all smiles, woman?" Bud asked with a grin.

"Nothing. Nothing at all," Brenda replied. "It's just been a very nice day."

THE END

Laurel's Recipe also known as...

AUNT BOBBIE SUE'S COCONUT CAKE

(Make 3 days ahead of time serving)

Ingredients

1 cup shortening
2 cups flour
1 ¾ cups sugar
1 cup milk
1 tsp salt
5 eggs
1 tsp vanilla

1. In mixer, blend shortening and sugar
2. Add eggs one at a time, while mixing continuously
3. Add flour and milk in intervals while still mixing (adding a little flour, then a little milk, then a little flour, then more milk will keep flour from flying out of the mixer)
4. Add salt and vanilla
5. Lightly grease two round cake pans and divide mixture equally
6. Bake on 325° till done (30-45 minutes)
7. Let cake cool 10 minutes, then flip out of pan onto a flat surface to finish cooling
8. Once completely cooled, use a serrated knife to split both cakes into halves (so you have 4 total layers)

ICING

Ingredients

2 cups sugar
16 oz sour cream
12 oz frozen coconut
1 ½ cup Cool Whip

1. Combine sugar, coconut, and remaining sour cream and blend well
2. Chill mixture and reserve one cup of mixture for frosting
3. Spread large mixture (not the reserved cup) between the four cake layers and on top. Leave sides uncoated
4. Combine the reserved cup mixture with Cool Whip and blend until smooth
5. Spread on the sides and top of cake.
6. Seal cake in airtight container (like a plastic travel cake dish) and refrigerate for 3 days

ABOUT THE AUTHOR

Micah House is the author of *The Blanchard Witches* series which has won several awards since its debut, including the NYC Big Book Award, The Indie Excellence Award, and The BookFest Award. His southern style of storytelling weaves drama, humor, emotional connection to characters, and plenty of page-turning suspense. He currently resides in Birmingham, Alabama with his husband and son and their five dogs.